The soldiers paused for an instant, caught between trained instinct and the orders of their superior officer.

The instant was all Chase needed.

He grabbed the barrel of the nearest soldier's rifle, jerking it out of the startled man's grip and twisting his wrist to flip the gun over onto its back as his other hand stabbed at the trigger.

He felt the heat of the bullet through the metal barrel as the gun fired, scorching his palm. The soldier lurched backwards, the bullet ripping right through him and showering the Land Rover with blood and mashed lung tissue.

Before any of the other soldiers could react, Chase flipped the gun over again, jamming the selector switch to full auto and unleashing bursts of fire at the soldiers with the Dragunovs. They fell. If the remaining soldiers fired at him, they ran the risk of hitting their own comrades, which would deter them for a moment.

"Nina!" he shouted. She stared uncomprehendingly at him, totally unprepared for his lethal flurry of action. He reached out to grab her arm, but one of the soldiers reacted more quickly than his companions and tackled Nina to the ground. Chase couldn't shoot him without hitting her—

THE
Hunt
FOR
Atlantis

Andy McDermott

BANTAM BOOKS

A Bantam Books Mass Market Original

Copyright © 2007 by Andy McDermott

Published in the United States by Bantam Books,
an imprint of The Random House Publishing Group,
a division of Random House, Inc., New York.

BANTAM BOOKS and the rooster colophon
are registered trademarks of Random House, Inc.

Originally published in hardcover in Great Britain by Headline
Publishing Group, London, in 2007, and is published by
arrangement with Headline Publishing Group.

LIBRARY OF CONGRESS CATALOGING-IN-PUBLICATION DATA
McDermott, Andy.
The hunt for Atlantis / Andy McDermott.
p.   cm.
ISBN 978-0-553-59285-6
1. Women archaeologists—Fiction. 2. Atlantis (Legendary place)—
Fiction. 3. Geographical myths—Fiction. I. Title.
PR6113.C3749H86 2009   823'.92—dc22   2009002104

Cover illustration and design: Edward Bettison

Printed in the United States of America

www.bantamdell.com

2 4 6 8 9 7 5 3 1

For my family and friends

THE
Hunt
FOR
Atlantis

PROLOGUE
Tibet

The sun had not yet risen above the Himalayan peaks, but Henry Wilde was already awake. He had been awake, waiting for the moment when the dawn light cleared the mountains, for over two hours.

More than two hours, he mused. More like years, most of his life. What began as a boyhood curiosity had grown into an . . . he hesitated to use the word *obsession*, but there it was. An obsession that had brought him mockery and derision from the academic world; an obsession that had eaten up most of the money he had earned in his lifetime.

But, he reminded himself, it was also an obsession that had brought him together with one of the two most remarkable women he had ever known.

"How long to sunrise?" asked Laura Wilde, Henry's wife of almost twenty years, huddled next to him in her thick parka. The two had first met as undergraduates at New York's Columbia University. While they had already noticed each other—Henry was a six-foot-four ice blond and Laura had hair of such a deep shade of red it seemed almost unnatural—it wasn't until after Henry had an essay on the subject of his obsession mockingly excoriated by their professor that they spoke.

Laura's first three words caused Henry to fall in love on the spot.

They were: "I believe you."

"Any minute now," Henry said, checking his watch before putting a loving arm around her. "I just wish Nina were here to see it with us." Nina, their daughter, was the second of the two most remarkable women he had ever known.

"That's what you get when you schedule an expedition during her exams," Laura chided.

"Don't blame me, blame the Chinese government! I wanted to come next month, but they wouldn't budge, said it was this or nothing—"

"Honey?"

"Yeah?"

"I'm kidding. I didn't want to miss this opportunity either. But yes, I wish Nina were here too."

"Getting a postcard from Xulaodang doesn't really seem fair compensation, does it?" sighed Henry. "We drag her all over the world to dead end after dead end, and when we finally find a real lead, she can't come!"

"We *think* we've found a real lead," Laura corrected him.

"We'll know in a minute, won't we?" He indicated the vista before them. Three snowcapped peaks of roughly equal size rose beyond the rugged plateau on which they had made camp. At the moment they were held in shadow by the larger range to the east, but when the sun climbed above the obstruction, that would change. And if the stories they had gathered were true, it would change in spectacular style . . .

Henry stood, offering a hand to pull Laura to her feet. She blew out a cloud of steaming breath as she rose; the plateau was over ten thousand feet above sea level, and the air was both thin and cold in a way that neither of them had ever before experienced. But it also had a purity, a clarity.

Somehow, Henry knew they would find what they were searching for.

The first light of dawn reached the three peaks.

Rather, it reached *one* of them, a brilliant golden light exploding from the perfect white snow atop the central peak. Almost like a liquid, the sunlight slowly flowed down from the summit. The two mountains on either side remained in shadow, the dawn still blocked by the larger range.

"It's true . . ." Henry said quietly, awe in his voice.

Laura was somewhat less reverent. "That pretty much looks like a golden peak to me."

He gave her a smile before looking back at the spectacle before them. The mountain was almost aglow in the dawn light. "They were right. Goddamn it, they were *right*."

"That's almost depressing, in a way," said Laura. "That a bunch of Nazis over fifty years ago knew about it first, and were so close to finding it."

"But they *didn't* find it." Henry set his jaw. "*We* will."

The Golden Peak—until today nothing more than a legend, a piece of ancient folklore—was the final piece in the puzzle Henry had been assembling his whole life. Exactly what he would find there, he wasn't sure. But what he *was* sure of was that it would provide him with everything he needed to reach his final goal.

The ultimate legend.

Atlantis.

ᴠᴠ

The dazzling display of light on the Golden Peak lasted for barely a minute before the sun rose high enough to strike the two neighboring summits. By the time the expedition began to ascend the eastern slope of the peak, the sun was high overhead. Its companions now out of shadow, the mountain was indistinguishable from those around it in the harsh daylight.

There were seven people in their group, three Americans and four Tibetans. The latter group had been hired as porters and guides; while they knew the area, they had been as amazed by the folktale come true as their foreign visitors. Even by Tibetan standards the region was bleak and isolated, and Henry realized they might be the only Westerners ever to have witnessed what they had just seen.

Except, perhaps, for the people whose clues had led them here in the first place.

Henry called the group to a stop. As the others gratefully brushed snow off nearby rocks and sat down, he removed his backpack and carefully took a slim binder from one of its pockets. Laura joined him as he flicked through the pages sealed inside protective plastic sheets.

"Checking again?" she asked, teasing. "I thought you'd have them memorized by now."

"German's not one of my strongest languages," he reminded her, finding a particular page. The paper was discolored, stained by damp and time.

The secret documents of the Ahnenerbe—the German Ancestral Heritage Society, part of Hitler's SS under the direct control of Heinrich Himmler—had been found hidden behind bricks in a cellar of Wewelsberg Castle in northern Germany. Wewelsberg had been the headquarters of the SS, and the center of the Nazi obsession with mythology and the occult. At the end of the war, orders had been given to destroy the castle and the knowledge it contained. Someone had chosen to disobey those orders and conceal the documents instead.

And now the Wildes had them.

The previous year, Bernd Rust, an old friend and colleague of Henry's, had contacted him about the discovery. Most of the rediscovered SS documents had been turned over to the German government, but knowing of the Wildes' interests, Rust had—at considerable professional risk—secretly retained a few specific pages, those mentioning Atlantis. Even from a friend they hadn't come cheap, but Henry knew they were worth every penny.

While he felt a deep discomfort about using Nazi material to aid his search—to the extent that he hadn't even told his daughter about the documents' origin—he also knew that without it, he would never find Atlantis. Somehow, half a century ago, the Nazis had discovered something that had enabled them to jump almost to the end of the trail.

The Ahnenerbe had organized expeditions to Tibet during the 1930s, and even into the 1940s as the war raged in Europe. At the behest of the prominent Nazis who were members of the sinister Thule Society, Himmler among them, three expeditions had been sent to Asia. The Thule Society believed that beneath the Himalayas lay underground cities built by the legendary descendants of the Atlanteans, who shared a common ancestry with the Aryan master race. While the explorers made many discoveries about Tibetan history, they found nothing of the Atlanteans, and returned to Germany empty-handed.

But what the papers now in Henry's possession revealed was that there had been a *fourth* expedition, kept secret even from Hitler himself.

The Führer was not as inclined as his followers to believe in myths. As the war escalated, he decided pragmatically that the country's resources were better spent on the Nazi war machine than in sending expeditions halfway around the world to hunt for a legend.

But Himmler was a true believer. And the Ahnenerbe's discoveries had convinced him that legend was within his grasp.

What came as a shock to Henry was that he and Laura were on the same path . . . but half a century too late. Piecing together clues from dozens, *hundreds* of historical sources, tiny scraps of evidence gradually forming a picture like a jigsaw, the Wildes had traveled with Nina ten years earlier to a site on the coast of Morocco. To Henry's jubilation, they had found traces of an ancient settlement hidden beneath the African sands . . . only for delight to turn to despair when they realized someone had beaten them to it. Aside from a few worthless scraps, the site had been picked clean.

Now Henry knew by whom.

The Nazis had assembled the same puzzle pieces and sent an expedition to Morocco. The handful of Ahnenerbe documents he now held revealed only hints of what they had found, but on the strength of those discoveries another expedition had been mounted in South America. What they had found there, the documents didn't reveal—but they *did* reveal that the mission had led the Nazis to Tibet, to the Golden Peak.

To *here*.

"I just wish we had more information," Henry complained. "I'd love to know exactly what they found in South America."

Laura turned the pages. "We've got enough. They got us this far." She read one phrase from the decaying, blotchy paper: "'The Golden Peak, said to glow with the light of dawn between two dark mountains.' I'd say . . ." she looked up at the looming mountain, "this fits the bill."

"So far." Henry examined the text. Even though he had already read it a hundred, a thousand times, he checked it again to assure himself that he hadn't made a mistake in the translation.

He hadn't. This was the place.

"So the entrance is supposed to be at the end of the Path of the Moon . . . whatever that is." He surveyed the rising landscape through his binoculars, seeing nothing but rocks and snow. "Why do legends always have to have cryptic names? Does it seem to lead to the moon; does it follow the movements of the moon; what?"

"I think it looks like the moon," said Laura meaningfully. "Specifically, a crescent moon."

"Why do you think that?" There was still nothing even remotely moonlike in view as he panned across the face of the mountain.

"Because," she replied, placing a hand on the binoculars and gently pulling them down from his face, "I can see it right in front of me."

Henry blinked, wondering what she was talking about . . . until he saw it himself.

Ahead was a long, curving path that swung off to the left, rising up the flank of the peak before sweeping back around to the right and ending at a broad ledge some distance above. In contrast to the jumbled mix of dark rocks and patchy snow around it, the path was an almost unbroken crescent of pure white, indicating flatter, smoother ground. He couldn't believe he hadn't noticed it before.

"Laura?"

"Yes?"

"This is another one of those moments when I'm *so* glad that I married you."

"Yeah. I know." They smiled at each other, then

kissed. "So," she said when they pulled apart, "how far do you think it is?"

"A mile, maybe . . . about five hundred feet up. Fairly steep."

"If the ancient Atlanteans could get up there in sandals, I figure we can manage in hiking boots."

"So do I." Henry returned the binder to his pack, then waved to the rest of the expedition. "Okay! This is it! We're moving out!"

w

The path proved trickier to negotiate than expected. The snow camouflaged a surface strewn with loose rubble from landslides, making each step treacherous.

By the time they reached the ledge, the sun had passed over the summit of the mountain, casting the entire eastern face into shadow. Henry turned and scanned the horizon as he helped Laura up the last few feet of the path. Heavy clouds were rolling in from the north. He hadn't noticed it during the effort of the ascent, but the temperature had definitely fallen.

"Bad weather?" asked Laura, following his gaze.

"Looks like we might be in for a blizzard."

"Great. Good thing we got up here before it starts." She looked back at the ledge, which even at its narrowest was a dozen yards wide as it cut across the face of the mountain. "Shouldn't be any trouble setting up camp here."

"Get the guides to pitch the tents before the weather turns," said Henry. The path ended here; above the ledge, the rock face was steep enough to require proper climbing gear. That was no problem, as they had the necessary equipment. But if the Ahnenerbe documents were correct, they shouldn't need it . . .

Laura passed on Henry's instructions to the Tibetans before returning to him. "What are you going to do?"

"I'm going to have a look around. If there are any entrances that might potentially lead into caves, they shouldn't be too hard to find."

Laura arched an eyebrow, a flash of amusement in her intense green eyes. "Anything to get out of pitching the tents, huh?"

"Hey, that's what we're paying them for!" He turned to the man sitting alone on a rock nearby. "What about you, Jack? Coming?"

The third American member of the group peered up at them from inside the hood of his parka. "Give me a chance to get my breath back, Henry! I think I'll wait here, get some coffee once the water's boiled."

"Can't shake your caffeine habit even in Tibet, huh?" Husband and wife mockingly rolled their eyes at each other as they walked up the slope, leaving Jack on his own. "All those years he keeps telling us we're mad for searching for Atlantis, then we *finally* come up with a solid lead and suddenly he practically begs to come along . . . and when we're right on the doorstep, he decides to take a coffee break!" said Henry.

After a few minutes Henry paused, staring at the rock face. "Something?" Laura asked.

"These strata . . ." he said, pointing. Countless eons before, the immense forces causing the Himalayas to rise up where the Indian and Asian tectonic plates collided had also warped the rocks themselves, twisting the layers so they ran almost vertically instead of horizontally.

"What about them?"

"If you moved these stones," Henry said, pointing to a pile of rubble, "I think you'd have an entrance."

Laura saw a slice of absolute darkness within the folded strata. "Big enough to get into?"

"Let's find out!" He pulled at the topmost rock. Snow and loose pebbles dropped from it as he threw it aside. The dark hole beyond grew deeper. "Give me a hand."

"Oh, so you'll pay the locals to put up tents, but when it comes to moving heavy rocks, you drag in your wife . . ."

"There must have been a landslip. This is just the top of the entrance." He pulled more stones aside, Laura helping. "Use your flashlight, see if you can see how far back it goes."

Laura took off her pack and pulled out a Maglite, shining it into the hole. "I can't see the back." She paused, then shouted, "Echo!" A faint reflection of her voice came from within the dark chamber. Henry raised an eyebrow. "Heh. Sorry."

"It's big in there, anyway," he said. "Nearly as big as your mouth." Laura gently slapped the back of his head. "I think if we move this rock here, we might be able to squeeze in."

"You mean *I* might be able to squeeze in."

"Well of course! Ladies first."

"Stupid chivalry," Laura complained jokingly. They both gripped the offending rock, then braced their feet and pulled. For a moment nothing happened, then with a grinding rasp it burst free. The opening was now about three feet high and just over a foot at its widest, tapering to nothing at the top.

"Think you'll fit?" Henry asked.

Laura reached through the hole with one arm and felt around inside. "It widens out. I should be okay once I get through." She leaned closer and aimed the flashlight downwards. "You were right about the landslip. It's quite steep."

"I'll rope you up," said Henry, removing his own pack. "Any problems, I can pull you back out."

After the rope was attached to Laura's climbing harness, she tied her hair into a ponytail and inched through the opening, feet first. Once inside, she cautiously stood, feeling the loose surface shift beneath her feet.

"What do you see?" asked Henry.

"Just rocks so far." Her eyes adjusting to the gloom, Laura switched on the Maglite again. "There's a flatter floor at the bottom. Looks like . . ." She raised the light again. The beam fell on rock walls—then nothing but blackness. "There's a passageway back here, quite wide, and I've got no idea how far back it goes. A long way." Excitement rose in her voice. "I think it's man-made!"

"Can you get down?"

"I'll try." She took an experimental step, both hands raised for balance. Small pieces of debris skittered down the pile. "It's kind of loose, I might have to—"

With a crunch, a large stone broke loose beneath her right foot. Caught by surprise, she fell on her back and slid helplessly down the slope. The flashlight clattered away ahead of her.

"Laura! *Laura!*"

"I'm okay! I just slipped." She got to her feet. Her thick clothes had saved her from a bruising experience.

"Do you want me to pull you back up?"

"No, I'm fine. Might as well look around now that I'm down here." She bent to pick up the tough metal flashlight . . .

And realized she was not alone.

For a moment she froze, more in shock than in fear. Then curiosity took over, and she warily swept the beam over her surroundings.

"Honey?" she called up to Henry.

"Yeah?"

"You remember that secret Nazi expedition that went to Tibet and nobody ever heard from them again?"

"Gee, you know, I forgot all about it," he shouted back with more than a hint of sarcasm. "Why?"

Triumph filled Laura's voice. "I think I just found them."

w

There were five bodies in the cave. It quickly became clear they hadn't been killed by the rock fall that had blocked the entrance; from the almost mummified appearance of the corpses, the most likely cause of death was exposure, the cold of the Himalayas preserving and desiccating the victims. While the other expedition members investigated the rest of the cave, the Wildes turned their attention to its occupants.

"The weather must have deteriorated," mused Henry, squatting to examine the bodies in the glow of a lantern, "so they came in here for shelter . . . and never came out."

"Freezing to death, not the way I want to go," Laura grimaced.

One of the Tibetan guides, Sonam, called to them from down the passageway. "Professor Wilde! There's something here!"

Leaving the bodies, Henry and Laura went deeper into the cavern. As Laura had thought, the passage was clearly artificial, carved out of the rock. Some thirty feet ahead, the lights of the other expedition members illuminated what lay at the end.

It was a temple—or a *tomb*.

Jack was already examining what appeared to be an altar at the center of the rectangular chamber. "This isn't Tibetan," he announced as the Wildes entered. "These inscriptions . . . they're Glozel, or a variation."

"Glozel?" said Henry, surprise and delight mingling

in his voice. "I always said that was a strong contender to be the Atlantean language!"

"It's a long way from home," Laura noted.

She shone her flashlight over the walls. Carved columns ran from floor to ceiling, the style angular, almost aggressive in its clean functionality. The Nazis would be right at home, she thought. Albert Speer could have devised the architecture.

Between the columns were bas-reliefs, representations of human figures. Henry moved closer to the largest one. While the design of the relief was unfamiliar, as forcefully stylized as the rest of the chamber, he knew instantly whom it was meant to be.

"Poseidon . . ." he whispered.

Laura joined him. "My God, it *is* Poseidon." The image of the god differed from the traditional Greek interpretation, but there was no mistaking the trident held in his right hand.

"Well," said Jack, "Mr. Frost will certainly be pleased that the expedition was a success . . ."

"The hell with Frost," Laura snorted, "this is *our* discovery. All he did was help with the funding."

"Now, now," said Henry, jokingly patting her shoulder. "At least thanks to him we didn't have to choose between breaking into our daughter's college fund or selling our car!" He looked around. "Sonam, is there anything else here? Any other rooms or passages?"

"No," replied Sonam. "It's a dead end."

"Oh," said Laura, disappointed. "This is all there is? I mean, it's a hell of a find, but I was sure there'd be more . . ."

"There might still *be* more," Henry assured her. "There could be other tombs along the ledge. We'll keep looking."

He went back down the passage and returned to the

bodies, Laura and Jack following. The corpses were huddled inside antiquated cold-weather gear, empty eye sockets staring back at him from darkened, parchmentlike skin. "I wonder if Krauss is one of them?"

"He is." Laura pointed at one of the figures. "There's our expedition leader."

"How do you know?"

She moved her gloved finger towards the body, almost touching its chest. Henry brought the lantern closer to see a small metal badge attached to the material, an insignia . . .

A momentary chill, unconnected to the cold, ran through him. It was the death's-head of the Schutzstaffel—the SS. It was over half a century since the organization had been destroyed, yet it still had the power to evoke fear.

"Jürgen Krauss," he said at last, peering more closely at the dead man. There was a certain poetic irony to the fact that the leader of the Nazi expedition now resembled the skull on his SS insignia. "Never thought I'd meet you. But what brought you here?"

"Why not find out?" asked Laura. "His pack's right there; it's probably got all his notebooks inside. Take a look."

"Wait, you want *me* to do that?"

"Well, obviously! I'm not touching a dead Nazi!"

"Jack?"

Jack shook his head. "These bodies are rather more recent than I'm used to dealing with."

"Wuss," Henry chided with a grin. He reached around the corpse, trying to disturb it as little as possible as he opened its backpack.

The contents were prosaic at first: a flashlight with bubbles of corrosion from the long-decayed batteries, crumpled pieces of greaseproof paper containing the expedition's last scraps of food. But beneath these remnants, things became more interesting. Folded maps, leather-bound notebooks, sheets of paper bearing rubbings of more carved Glozel characters, a scoured sheet of copper with what looked like a map or chart scored into its surface . . . and something carefully wrapped in layers of what he was surprised to discover was dark velvet.

Laura took the copper piece. "Sand-worn . . . do you think they might have found this in Morocco?"

"It's possible." The notebooks should have been the first items Henry examined, but he was intrigued enough by the mystery object—flat, just under a foot long and surprisingly heavy—that he placed it carefully on the ground next to the lantern and peeled back the velvet.

"What's that?" asked Laura.

"No idea. I think it's metal, though." The velvet, stiffened by time and cold, reluctantly gave up its contents as Henry pulled away the last layer.

"Wow," Laura gasped. Jack's eyes widened in amazement.

Inside the velvet wrapping was a metal bar some two inches wide, one end rounded off and marked with an arrowhead stamped into the surface. Even under the cold blue light of the lantern, the object had a radiance, sparkling with a reddish-golden glow unlike anything else found in nature.

Henry, transfixed, bent down for a better look. In contrast to the piece Laura was holding, the bar showed no signs of age or weathering, seeming freshly polished. The metal wasn't gold or bronze, but . . .

Laura leaned closer as well, her breath briefly condensing on the cold surface. "Is that what I think it is?"

"Looks like it. My God. I can't believe it. The Nazis

actually found an artifact made of orichalcum, just like Plato described. A real, honest-to-God Atlantean artifact! And they had it fifty years ago!"

"You owe Nina an apology when we get home," quipped Laura. "She always thought that piece she found in Morocco was orichalcum."

"I guess I do," said Henry, carefully picking up the bar. "There's no way *this* is just off-color bronze." The underside, he noticed, was not flat—there was a circular protrusion at the squared-off end. In the same position on the top side was a small slot at a forty-five-degree angle. "I think this was part of something larger," he observed. "Like it was meant to hang from something."

"Or swing from it," Laura suggested. "Like a pendulum arm."

Henry ran a fingertip along the inscribed arrowhead. "A pointer?"

"What are those marks?" asked Jack. Running along the length of the artifact was a thin line, equally faint symbols scribed into the metal on each side. A series of tiny dots, arranged in groups of up to eight. Also visible were . . .

"More Glozel characters," said Henry. "But not quite the same as the ones in the tomb—look, some of these are more like hieroglyphics." He compared them to the ones on the rubbings. They were the same style. "Curiouser and curiouser."

Jack looked more closely. "They look a lot like Olmec, or something related. Bizarre mix . . ."

"What do they say?" asked Laura.

"No idea. It's not exactly a language I'm fluent in. Well, not yet." He coughed modestly.

"They look like they were added after it was made," Henry noted. "The inscribing's much cruder than the arrowhead." He returned the mysterious object to the velvet. "This justifies us coming here all on its own!" He jumped to his feet and let out a triumphant whoop, then hugged Laura. "We did it! We actually found proof that Atlantis wasn't just a myth!"

She kissed him. "Now all we need to do is find Atlantis itself, huh?"

"Well, one step at a time."

A shout from deeper inside the cave caught their attention. "Something down here, Professor!" called Sonam.

Leaving the artifact on the floor, Henry and Laura hurried to the Tibetan. "Look at this," Sonam said, holding up his light to the tomb wall. "I thought it was just a crack in the rock, but then I realized something." Pulling off one glove, he stuck the tip of his little finger into the vertical crack and slowly ran it up the wall. "It's exactly the same width all the way up. And there's another one just like it over there." He pointed at a spot on the wall about nine feet away.

"A door?" asked Laura.

Henry followed the path of the crack upwards, using his flashlight to pick out a barely discernible line running horizontally some eight feet above. "*Big* door. Jack's got to see this." He raised his voice. "Jack? Jack!" Nothing but echoes came back to him. "Where is he?"

Laura shook her head. "Hell of a time to take a leak. The most important archaeological find of the century and—"

"Professor Wilde!" One of the other Tibetans. "Something outside! Listen!"

The group fell silent, barely breathing. A low thudding noise became audible, rapid beats underscored by a rumbling whine.

"A helicopter?" Laura exclaimed in disbelief. "Here?"

"Come on," snapped Henry, running for the entrance. The sky outside had darkened considerably. He used the rope to pull himself up the pile of rubble, Laura behind him.

"Chinese military?" Laura asked.

"How did they know where we were? Even *we* didn't know exactly where we were going until we got to Xulaodang." Henry squeezed through the entrance and stepped out onto the broad ledge. The weather was definitely deteriorating; the wind had picked up considerably.

But that wasn't his main concern right now. He looked for the helicopter; the noise grew louder, but it was nowhere in sight.

And neither was Jack.

Laura emerged behind him. "Where is it?"

Her question was answered a moment later as the helicopter swept into view.

Not Chinese, Henry saw immediately. No red star markings. No markings *at all*, not even a tail number. Just an ominous dark gray paint scheme that immediately made him think *Special Forces*. But whose?

He didn't know enough about aircraft to recognize the type, but it was large enough to carry several people in its passenger compartment. He could see the pilots behind the cockpit glass, their heads turning from side to side as if looking for something.

Looking for *someone*.

For them.

"Get back in the cave!" he shouted to Laura. With a worried look, she disappeared into the darkness.

The helicopter moved closer. A blizzard whipped up from the ground, snow caught in its downwash. Henry backed up to the cave entrance.

One of the pilots pointed down at the ground. At *him*.

The aircraft swung around like some giant alien insect, the cockpit windows huge eyes taking a better look at him, then turned away again. A door slid open in its flank. A moment later two coils of rope fell out and whipped snakelike to the ground.

A pair of dark figures dropped from the bobbing helicopter, rappelling down.

Henry saw immediately that they were armed, automatic rifles slung over their backs.

The only weapon the expedition possessed was a simple hunting rifle, carried more to scare off wild animals than for its effectiveness. And it wasn't even with them—it had been left at the camp.

Barely a second after the first two men reached the ground, another pair began to descend the ropes. They too were armed.

Henry jumped backwards through the hole and slid down the pile of stones, hitting the cave floor hard.

"Henry!" cried Laura. "What's happening?"

"I don't think they're friendly," he said, face grim. "There's at least four men, and they've got guns."

"Oh my God! What about Jack?"

"I don't know, I didn't see him. We need to get that door open. Come on." As Laura hurried towards the tomb, Henry snatched up the artifact from the ground near the bodies, wrapping it in the protective velvet as he ran.

The four Tibetans frantically searched the tomb walls. "There's nothing here!"

"There's got to be *something*!" Henry yelled. "A release, a keyhole, anything!" He looked back. A figure was silhouetted against the cave entrance. A moment later it dropped as if swallowed by the ground, to be replaced by another. "Shit! They're in the cave!"

Laura grabbed his arm. "Henry!"

Another silhouette, and another, and *another* . . .

Five men. All armed.

They were trapped.

Red lines lanced through the darkness. Laser sights, followed by the intense beams of halogen flashlights. The dazzling lights swept back and forth, before coming to rest on the little group of people in the tomb.

Henry froze, almost blinded by the beams, unsure what to do. They had nowhere to run, and the laser spots dancing over their bodies meant they couldn't fight either—

"Professor Wilde!"

Henry was stunned. They knew him by name?

"Professor Wilde!" the voice repeated. Deep and rich, with an accent—Greek? "Remain where you are. You too, Dr. Wilde," he added to Laura.

The intruders advanced. "Who are you?" Henry demanded. "What do you want?"

The men holding the flashlights stopped, a single tall figure continuing towards the expedition members. "My name is Giovanni Qobras," said the man, enough light reflecting from the tomb walls for Henry to pick out his features. A hard, angular face with a prominent Roman nose, dark hair slicked back from his forehead almost like a skullcap. "What I want, I regret to say . . . is you."

Laura stared at him in bewilderment. "What do you mean?"

"I mean, I cannot allow you to continue your search. The risk to the world is far too great. My apologies." He lowered his head for a moment, then stepped back. "It's nothing personal."

The laser lines fixed on Henry and Laura.

Henry opened his mouth. "Wait—"

In the confines of the tomb, the noise of the automatic weapons was deafening.

Qobras stared at the six bullet-riddled bodies as he

waited for the echoes of gunfire to die away, then issued rapid orders. "Collect everything that relates to their expedition—maps, notes, everything. And do the same for those bodies back there." He pointed at the dead Nazis. "I assume that's the remains of the Krauss expedition. One historical mystery solved . . ." he added, almost to himself, as his men split up to examine the corpses.

"Giovanni!" one man yelled a minute later, crouched over Henry's body.

"What is it, Yuri?"

"You've *got* to see this."

Qobras strode over. "My God!"

"It's orichalcum, isn't it?" asked Yuri Volgan, shining his light on the object he had just unwrapped. A deep orange glow reflected on the faces of the two men.

"Yes . . . but I've never seen a complete artifact made from it before, just scraps."

"It's beautiful . . . and it must be worth a fortune. Millions of dollars, tens of millions!"

"At least." Qobras gazed at the artifact for a long moment, seeing his own eyes reflected in the metal. Then he straightened abruptly. "But it must be kept hidden." He took out a flashlight and examined the tomb walls, but saw nothing except bas-reliefs of ancient gods. Turning to the altar, he quickly examined the inscriptions. "Glozel . . . but nothing about Atlantis."

"Maybe we should search the tomb," Volgan offered, taking one long last look at the artifact before carefully wrapping it in the velvet again.

Qobras considered it. "No," he said at last. "There's nothing here, it must have been looted. I really thought the Wildes might lead us further along the trail to Atlantis itself, but it's just another dead end. We need to get out of here before the storm arrives." He turned and strode back towards the cave entrance.

Behind him, Volgan glanced over his shoulder to make sure nobody was watching, then slipped the wrapped artifact into his thick jacket.

w

Qobras stood at the edge of the ledge, waving a flare to summon the circling helicopter, then turned back to the man standing by the doomed expedition's camp. "You did the right thing."

Jack's face was hidden inside his hood. "I'm not proud of this. They were my friends—and what's going to happen to their daughter?"

"It had to be done," said Qobras. "The Brotherhood can never allow Atlantis to be found." He frowned. "Least of all by Kristian Frost. Funding intermediaries like the Wildes . . . he knows we're watching him."

"What . . . what if Frost suspects I was working for you?" Jack asked nervously.

"You'll have to convince him that there was an accident. We can fly you to ten kilometers from Xulaodang— there should be very little risk of your being seen with us. Then you can walk back to the village and contact Frost, give him the bad news: that you were the only survivor of an avalanche, a rock fall, whatever you choose." Qobras held out a hand. "The radio?"

Jack dug into his pack, returning to its owner the chunky transmitter he had used to give Qobras's team the location of the Golden Peak. "I'll have to talk to other people as well. The Chinese authorities, the U.S. embassy . . ."

"Just keep your story consistent, and your payment will be waiting for you by the time you get back to America. Should you discover that anyone else is trying to follow the path of the Wildes in the future, you'll inform me at once, of course?"

"It's what you pay me for," Jack said sullenly.

A cold smile, then Qobras looked up to watch the helicopter approaching, its navigation lights aglow against the darkening sky.

Five minutes later it departed, leaving behind nothing but bodies.

ONE
New York City
Ten Years Later

D r. Nina Wilde took a deep breath as she paused at the door, her reflection gazing pensively back at her in the darkened glass. She was dressed more formally than normal, a rarely worn dark blue trouser suit replacing her casual sweatshirts and cargo pants, shoulder-length auburn hair drawn back more severely than her usual loose ponytail. This was a crucial meeting, and even though she knew everyone involved, she still wanted to make as professional an impression as possible. Satisfied that she looked the part and hadn't accidentally smudged lipstick across her cheeks, she psyched herself up to enter the room, almost unconsciously reaching up to her neck to touch her pendant. Her good-luck charm.

She'd found the sharp-edged, curved fragment of metal, about two inches long and scoured by the abrasive sands of Morocco, twenty years before while on an expedition with her parents when she was eight. At the time, her head full of tales of Atlantis, she'd believed it to be made of orichalcum, the metal described by Plato as one of the defining features of the lost civilization. Now, looked at with a more critical adult eye, she had come to accept that her father was right, that it was nothing more than discolored bronze, a worthless scrap ignored or discarded by whoever had beaten them to the site. But it was definitely man-made—the worn markings on its curved outer edge proved that—and since it was her first genuine find, her parents had eventually, after much persuasion of the typical eight-year-old's highly repetitive kind, allowed her to keep it.

On returning to the United States, her father made it into a pendant for her. She had decided on the spur of the moment that it would bring her good luck. While that had remained unproven—her academic successes had been entirely down to her own intelligence and hard work, and certainly no lottery wins had been forthcoming—she knew one thing for sure: the one day she had not worn it, accidentally forgetting it in a mad morning rush when staying at a friend's house during her university entrance exams, was the day her parents died.

Many things about her had changed since then. But one thing that had not was that she never let a day pass without wearing the pendant.

More consciously, she squeezed it again before letting her hand fall. She needed all the luck she could get today.

Steeling herself, she opened the door.

The three professors seated behind the imposing old oak desk looked up as she entered. Professor Hogarth was a portly, affable old man, whose secure tenure and antipathy towards bureaucracy meant he'd been known to approve a funding request simply on the basis of a mildly interesting presentation. Nina hoped hers would be rather more than that.

On the other hand, even the most enthralling presentation in history, concluded with the unveiling of a live dinosaur and the cure for cancer, would do nothing to gain the support of Professor Rothschild. But since the tight-lipped, misanthropic old woman couldn't stand Nina—or any other woman under thirty—she'd already dismissed her as a lost cause.

So that was one "no" and one "maybe." But at least she could rely on the third professor.

Jonathan Philby was a family friend. He was also the man who had broken the news to her that her parents were dead.

Now everything rested on him, as he not only held the deciding vote but was also the head of the department. Win him over and she had her funding.

Fail, and . . .

She couldn't allow herself even to think that way.

"Dr. Wilde," said Philby. "Good afternoon."

"Good afternoon," she replied with a bright smile. At least Hogarth responded well to it, even if Rothschild could barely contain a scowl.

Nina sat on the isolated chair before the panel.

"Well," Philby said, "we've all had a chance to digest the outline of your proposal. It's quite . . . unusual, I must say. Not exactly an everyday suggestion for this department."

"Oh, I thought it was most interesting," said Hogarth. "Very well thought out, and quite daring too. It makes a pleasant change to see a little challenge to the usual orthodoxy."

"I'm afraid I don't share your opinion, Roger," cut in Rothschild in her clipped, sharp voice. "Ms. Wilde"—not *Dr.* Wilde, Nina realized. Miserable old bitch—"I was under the impression that your doctorate was in archaeology. Not mythology. And Atlantis is a myth, nothing more."

"As were Troy, Ubar and the Seven Pagodas of Mahabalipuram—until they were discovered," Nina shot back. Since Rothschild had obviously already made up her mind, she was going to go down fighting.

Philby nodded. "Then if you'd like to elaborate on your theory?"

"Of course." Nina connected her travel-worn Apple laptop to the room's projector. The screen sprang to life with a map covering the Mediterranean Sea and part of the Atlantic to the west.

"Atlantis," she began, "is one of the most enduring legends in history, but those legends all originate from a very small number of sources—Plato's dialogues are the best known, of course, but there are references in other ancient cultures to a great power in the Mediterranean region, most notably the stories of the Sea People who attacked and invaded the coastal areas of what are now Morocco, Algeria, Libya and Spain. But most of what we know of Atlantis comes from Plato's *Timaeus* and *Critias*."

"Both of which are undoubtedly fiction," cut in Rothschild.

"Which brings me to the first part of my theory," Nina said, having anticipated the criticism. "Undoubtedly, there are elements of all of Plato's dialogues—not just *Timaeus* and *Critias*—that are *fictionalized*, to make it easier for him to present his points, in the same way that timelines are condensed and characters combined in modern-day biopics. But Plato wasn't writing his dialogues as fiction. His other works are accepted as historical documents, so why not the two that mention Atlantis?"

"So you're saying that everything Plato wrote about Atlantis is completely true?" asked Philby.

"Not quite. I'm saying that he *thought* it was. But he was told about it by Critias, working from the writings of his grandfather Critias the Elder, who was told about

Atlantis as a child by Solon, and *he* was told about it by
Egyptian priests. So what you have is a game of Chinese
whispers—well, Hellenic whispers, I suppose"—
Hogarth chuckled at the joke—"where there's inevitably going to be distortion of the original message,
like making a copy of a copy of a copy. Now, one of the
areas where inaccuracies are most likely to have been
introduced over time is in terms of measurements. I
mean, there's an oddity about *Critias*, which contains almost all of Plato's detailed descriptions of Atlantis, that
is *so* obvious nobody ever seems to notice it."

"And what would that be?" Hogarth asked.

"That all the measurements Plato gives of Atlantis
are not only neatly rounded off, but are also in Greek
units! For example, he says that the plain on which the
Atlantean capital stood was three thousand stadia by
two thousand. First, that's one precisely proportioned
plain, and second, it's amazingly convenient that it
would match a Greek measurement so exactly—
especially considering that it came from an Egyptian
source!" Nina found it hard to temper her enthusiasm
but tried to rein it back to a more professional level.
"Even if the Atlantean civilization used something *called*
a stadium, it's unlikely it would have been the same size
as the Egyptian one—or the larger Greek one."

Rothschild pursed her lips sourly. "This is all very
interesting," she said, in a tone suggesting she thought
the exact opposite, "but how does this enable you to
find Atlantis? Since you don't know what the actual
Atlantean measurements were, and nor does anyone
else, I don't see how any of this helps."

Nina took a long, quiet breath before answering. She
knew that what she was about to say was the potential
weak spot in her theory; if the three academics staring

intently at her didn't accept her reasoning, then it was all over . . .

"It's actually key to my proposal," she said, with as much confidence as she could muster. "Simply put, if you accept Plato's measurements—with one stadium being a hundred and eighty-five meters, or just under six hundred and seven feet—then Atlantis was a very large island, at least three hundred and seventy miles long and two hundred and fifty wide. That's larger than England!" She indicated the map on the screen. "There aren't many places for something that size to hide, even underwater."

"What about Madeira?" asked Hogarth, pointing at the map. The Portuguese island was some four hundred miles off the African coast. "Could that be a location for what was left of the island after it sank?"

"I considered that at one point. But the topography doesn't support it. In fact, there's nowhere in the eastern Atlantic that the island Plato describes could be located."

Rothschild snorted triumphantly. Nina gave her as scathing a look as she dared before returning to the map. "But it's this fact that forms the basis of my theory. Plato said that Atlantis was located in the Atlantic, beyond the Pillars of Heracles—which we know today as the Straits of Gibraltar, at the entrance to the Mediterranean. He also said that, converted to modern measurements, Atlantis was almost four hundred miles long. Since there's no evidence that would reconcile both those statements, either Atlantis isn't where he said it was . . . or his measurements are wrong."

Philby nodded silently. Nina still couldn't judge his mood—but suddenly got the feeling that he had already made his decision, one way or the other. "So," he said, "where *is* Atlantis?"

It was not a question Nina had expected to be asked

quite so soon, as she'd planned to reveal the answer with a suitable dramatic flourish at the end of her presentation. "Uh, it's in the Gulf of Cádiz," she said, a little flustered as she pointed at a spot in the ocean about a hundred miles west of the Straits of Gibraltar. "I think."

"You think?" sneered Rothschild. "I hope you have more to back up that statement than mere guesswork."

"If you'll let me explain my reasoning, Professor Rothschild," said Nina with forced politeness, "I'll show you how I reached that conclusion. The central premise of my theory is that Plato was right, and that Atlantis did actually exist. What he got wrong was the measurements."

"Rather than the location?" asked Hogarth. "You're ruling out any of the modern theories that maintain Atlantis was actually Santorini, off Crete, and the supposed Atlantean civilization was really Minoan?"

"Definitely. For one thing, the ancient Greeks knew about the Minoans already. Also, the time scales don't match. The volcanic eruption that destroyed Santorini was about nine hundred years before Solon's time, but the fall of Atlantis was nine *thousand* years before."

"The 'power of ten' error by Solon has been widely accepted as a way to connect the Minoans with the Atlantis *myth*," Rothschild pointed out.

"The Egyptian symbols for one hundred and one thousand are totally different," Nina told her. "You'd have to be blind or a complete idiot to confuse them. Besides, Plato explicitly states in *Timaeus* that Atlantis was in the Atlantic, not the Mediterranean. Plato was a pretty smart guy; I'm guessing he could tell east from west. I believe that in the process of the story being passed from the Atlanteans themselves to the ancient Egyptians, then from the Egyptian priests of almost nine thousand years later to Solon, then from Solon to

Plato over several generations of Critias's family . . . the measurements got messed up."

Philby raised an eyebrow. "Messed up?"

"Okay, maybe that's not the most scientific way I could have put it, but it gets the point across. Even though the names were the same—feet, stadia and so on—the different civilizations used different units of measurement. Each time the story went from one place to another, and the numbers were rounded off, and even exaggerated to show just how incredible this lost civilization really was, the error grew. My assumption here is that whatever unit the Atlanteans used that was translated as a stadium, it was considerably smaller than the Hellenic unit."

"That's quite an assumption," said Rothschild.

"I have logical reasoning to back it up," she said. "*Critias* gives various measurements of Atlantis, but the most important ones relate to the citadel on the island at the center of the Atlantean capital's system of circular canals."

"The site of the temples of Poseidon and Cleito," noted Philby, rubbing his mustache.

"Yes. Plato said the island was five stadia in diameter. If we use the Greek system, that's slightly over half a mile wide. Now, if an Atlantean stadium is smaller, it can't be too much smaller, because *Critias* says there's a lot to fit on to that island. Poseidon's temple was the biggest, a stadium long, but there were other temples as well, palaces, bathhouses . . . That's almost as packed as Manhattan!"

"So how big—or rather, how small—did you deduce an Atlantean stadium to be?" Hogarth asked.

"The smallest I think it could be would be two thirds the size of the Greek unit," explained Nina. "About four hundred feet. That would make the citadel over a third of a mile across, which when you scale down Poseidon's temple as well leaves just about enough room to fit everything in."

Hogarth made some calculations on a piece of notepaper. "By that measurement, the island would be, let's see . . ."

Nina instantly did the mathematics in her head. "It would be two hundred and forty miles long, and over a hundred and sixty wide."

Hogarth scribbled away for a few seconds to reach the same result. "Hmm. That wouldn't just be in the Gulf of Cádiz . . . it would *be* the Gulf of Cádiz."

"But you have to take into account the probability of other errors," said Nina. "The three-thousand-by-two-thousand-stadia figure Plato gave for the island's central plain is clearly rounded up. It could have been exaggerated for effect as well, if not by Plato then certainly by the Egyptians, who were trying to impress Solon. I think you have to assume an error factor of at least fifteen percent. Maybe even twenty."

"Another assumption, Ms. Wilde?" said Rothschild, a malevolent glint in her eyes.

"Even with a twenty percent margin, the island would still be over a hundred and ninety miles long," added Hogarth.

"There's still also the possibility of confusion if the figures were converted from a different numerical base . . ." Nina could feel the situation slipping away from her. "I'm not saying that all my figures are correct. That's why I'm here—I have a theory that fits the available data, and I want . . . I would like," she corrected, "the opportunity to test that theory."

"A sonar survey of the entire Gulf of Cádiz would be a rather expensive way of testing it," Rothschild said smugly.

"But if I'm right, then I've made the greatest archaeological discovery since Troy!" said Nina.

"And if you're wrong, the department has wasted potentially millions of dollars chasing after a myth, a *fairy tale.*"

"I don't want to waste the department's resources any more than you do! I have complete documentation backing up my theory, all the historical references—I've spent two years of my life researching this. I wouldn't have brought it to you if I weren't totally sure that I was *right.*"

"Why are you doing this, Nina?" asked Philby.

The personal tone of the question took her by surprise. "What do you mean?"

"I mean," Philby said, a look of sad sympathy on his face, "are you pursuing this goal for yourself . . . or for your parents?"

Nina tried to speak, but her voice caught in her throat.

"I knew Henry and Laura very well," Philby went on, "and they could have had spectacular careers—if they hadn't been fixated on a legend. Now I've followed your career ever since you were an undergraduate, and some of your work has been quite remarkable. I believe that you have greater potential than even your father. But . . . you're in danger of going down exactly the same path that he and your mother did."

"Jonathan!" Nina cried almost involuntarily in her mixture of shock, outrage—and pain.

"I'm sorry, but I can't let you throw away everything you've accomplished on this . . . this wild goose chase. Such a costly failure would cause enormous harm to your reputation, possibly irreparable."

"I don't care about my reputation!" Nina objected.

"But we care about the reputation of this university," said Rothschild, a faint smile on her thin lips.

"Maureen," warned Philby, before looking back at

Nina. "Dr. Wilde . . . *Nina*. Your parents *died* for this. If you follow them, the same thing could happen to you. And for what? Ask yourself, truthfully—is it worth dying for a legend?"

She felt as though someone had just kicked her in the stomach, such was the horrible impact of Philby's words. Through clenched teeth she asked him, "Does this mean my proposal has been rejected?"

The three professors exchanged glances and unspoken words before turning back to her. It took Philby a moment to look Nina directly in the eye. "I'm afraid so."

"I see." She turned and disconnected her laptop from the projector, the screen going blank. Tight-lipped, she faced the panel. "Well. In that case, thank you for your time."

"Nina," said Philby. "Please, don't take this personally. Professor Rothschild is right, you know. History and mythology are two different things. Don't waste your time, your *talent*, on the wrong one."

Nina stared at him for a long moment before speaking. "Thanks for the advice, Professor Philby," she said bitterly, before turning away and exiting, closing the door with a bang.

vvv

It took ten minutes of hiding in a stall in the ladies' restroom before Nina felt ready to show her face to the world again. Her initial shock had been replaced by a stunned anger. How *dare* Philby bring her parents into it?

Since the deaths of her mother and father, Philby had been . . . not a surrogate parental figure, certainly—nobody could replace them—but a supportive presence, a mentor as she rose through academia.

And he'd rejected her. It felt like nothing less than a betrayal.

"Son of a *bitch*!" she spat, banging a fist against the cubicle wall.

"Dr. Wilde?" said a familiar voice from the next stall. Professor Rothschild.

Shit!

"Uh—no, no speak good English!" Nina gabbled, frantically flinging the door open and hurrying out of the restroom, laptop under her arm. Anger replaced by embarrassment, she soon found herself at the building's main entrance. The familiar skyline of uptown Manhattan greeted her as she emerged.

Well, now what?

She had refused to consider even the possibility of failure, never mind such a crushing defeat, and was now at a complete loss as to what to do next.

Go home, that was probably the best bet. Eat too much comfort food, get drunk, then worry about the consequences tomorrow.

She walked down the steps to the sidewalk and looked for a cab.

Then as she raised her purse to check that she had enough money, she realized she was being watched.

She looked around. The person—a man—kept his eyes on her for just a moment too long before finding something fascinating to examine across the street. He was leaning against the wall of the university building, a broad figure with very short receding hair, wearing jeans and a well-worn black leather jacket. His flat nose looked to have been broken more than once. While he wasn't much taller than Nina herself, no more than five eight, his muscular build indicated considerable strength—and there was an indefinable hint of danger in his square face that suggested he would have little hesitation in using it.

Living in New York, Nina was no stranger to threatening-looking characters, but there was something about this one that made her nervous. She looked up the street at the approaching traffic, but kept the man in the corner of her vision.

Sure enough, he was watching her again. Even though it was rush hour on a busy street, Nina couldn't help but feel a twinge of worry.

She waved an arm with considerably more vigor than necessary to flag an approaching cab down, relieved when it pulled over. As she got in and gave her destination, she looked out of the rear window. The man—she guessed he was in his midthirties, but the coarseness of his features made it hard to tell exactly— stared back, his head turning to follow her as the cab set off . . . then was blocked from sight by a bus. She let out a relieved breath.

So, a stalker, humiliation and dismal failure. She slumped in the seat. "What a crappy day."

\\\\\

Once at home in her small but cozy apartment in the East Village, Nina decided to follow at least part of her instincts and make a start on the comfort food.

Armed with a huge bag of potato chips and a tub of Ben & Jerry's, she went into the living room, glancing at the answering machine as she passed. No messages. No surprise.

She let down her hair, then huddled up on the couch under a large knitted blanket. All she needed to complete the portrait of a sad, lonely loser was a CD of sappy, depressing songs. And maybe three or four cats.

Briefly amused at the thought, she curled her legs up against her chest and opened the bag of chips. Her hand brushed against her pendant.

"Some good luck you were," she complained, holding it up. Even though the fragment of metal was heavily scuffed, it still shone with an odd reddish gleam when she held it up to the light. The markings on one side—groups of tiny apostrophe-like ticks counting up from one to eight beneath short lines inscribed along its length—stood out clearly. Not for the first time she wondered what they represented, but the answer was as unforthcoming as ever.

Nina almost decided to take off the pendant, figuring that her luck couldn't get any worse today—but then changed her mind and let it fall back to her chest. No point tempting fate.

She had just crunched the first potato chip in her mouth when the phone rang. She wasn't expecting anyone to call—who could it be?

"Y'llo," she mumbled as she answered, still chewing.

"Is this Dr. Nina Wilde?" said a man's voice.

Great. A salesman.

"Yeah, what?" She stuffed a couple more chips into her mouth, ready to hang up.

"My name's Jason Starkman, and I work for the Frost Foundation."

Nina stopped chewing.

The Frost Foundation? Philanthropic work around the world, developing medicines and vaccines, funding all kinds of scientific research . . .

Including archaeological expeditions.

She gulped down the half-chewed chips. "Um, yes, hello!"

"I was sorry to hear that the university rejected your proposal today," said Starkman. "That was very short-sighted of them."

Nina frowned. "How did you know about that?"

"The foundation has friends at the university. Dr.

Wilde, I'll get to the point. Your colleagues may not have been interested in your theory on the location of Atlantis, but we most certainly are. Kristian Frost has personally asked me to contact you and find out if you would be willing to discuss it with him this evening."

Nina's heart jumped. *Kristian Frost?* She couldn't remember his exact ranking in the list of the world's richest men, but he was definitely in the top twenty. She forced herself to stay calm. "I'd, ah, I'm sure I'd be willing to discuss it, yes. To what, um, end?"

"To the end of funding a full oceanographic survey expedition to see if your theory is correct, of course."

"Oh, well, in that case . . . yes! Yes, definitely willing to discuss it!"

"Excellent. In that case I'll arrange a car to bring you to the foundation's New York offices for a meeting and dinner. Will seven o'clock be all right?"

She glanced at the clock on her VCR. Just after five-thirty. An hour and a half to get ready. It would be a rush, but . . . "Yeah, yeah, I . . . that'll be fine, yeah!"

"In that case, I'll see you then. Oh, and if you can bring your notes, that'll be a great help. I'm sure Mr. Frost will have lots of questions."

"No problem, no problem at all," she spluttered as Starkman hung up. Putting the phone down, she sat still for a moment before kicking off the blanket and letting out a whoop of glee.

Kristian Frost! Not only one of the world's richest men, but . . . Well, normally she wasn't attracted to older guys, but from the pictures she'd seen of him, Kristian Frost could make her change her mind.

Nina lifted her pendant again, then kissed it. "I guess you're good luck after all!"

TWO

Nina paced nervously, glancing down at the darkening street each time she passed the window. She had rushed out after Starkman's call and subjected her credit card to a battering by buying a low-cut blue dress that was suitable for dinner with a billionaire. She hoped.

She could still barely believe it. Kristian Frost wanted to meet *her*! To discuss *her* theories on the location of Atlantis! She stopped pacing and mentally ran through all the points she needed to present. If she convinced Frost she was right, competing for the financial scraps the university could offer would be a thing of the past. No need to charter expensive survey ships. Frost *owned* survey ships.

She checked the window again. No sign of any car pulling up outside, but . . .

Who was that?

Her building was on the corner of a block. Across the street, someone ducked out of sight around the side of the apartments opposite.

Someone in a black leather jacket.

She watched the sidewalk intently. People walked past, but the man didn't reappear.

Just a coincidence, she told herself. New York was a big city, and a lot of men wore black leather jackets.

Something else caught her attention, a large silver car pulling up in front of her building. She looked at the clock. Just before seven.

A man got out and walked to the front door. A moment later, the entry phone buzzed.

"Hello?"

"Dr. Wilde?" came the echoing voice from the street. "It's Jason Starkman."

"I'm on my way down!" she told him, picking up the folder of printouts she'd prepared earlier. She paused to check herself in the mirror by the door—hair carefully brushed and styled, makeup elegant without being overdone, all traces of potato chips brushed away—then hurried out.

Starkman was waiting downstairs. She hadn't formed much of a mental image of him from his voice, which had revealed little beyond a hint of a Texas accent, but was impressed by what she found. Starkman was tall, well built and dressed in an expensive blue suit and pristine white shirt. He looked to be in his late thirties, and something about the skin around his eyes gave Nina the feeling that he had traveled extensively. She'd seen the same kind of sun-baked lines on other men before, including her father.

He held out a large hand. "Dr. Wilde. Good to meet you."

"Likewise." She shook it; his skin was rough.

He glanced at her pendant, which was exposed above the neck of her dress, before turning his attention to the folder under her arm. "Are those your notes?"

"Yes. Everything I need to convince Mr. Frost that I'm right, I hope!" she said, laughing nervously.

"From what we've already heard about your theory,

I doubt he'll need much convincing. Are you ready to go?"

"Of course!"

He led her to the car, which she at first took to be a Rolls-Royce before realizing that it was actually a Bentley. Just as luxurious, but more sporty—not that she knew from personal experience.

"Nice car," she commented.

"Bentley Continental Flying Spur. Mr. Frost always buys the best." He opened the rear door for her.

The interior of the Bentley was as opulent as she had imagined, the seats and trim in a soft pale cream leather. There was another suited man at the wheel. Starkman closed the door behind her, then got into the front passenger seat. He gestured, and the driver pulled away from the curb, stopping at the intersection. Nina, out of habit, checked for traffic . . . and across the street saw the man who had been watching her outside the university. He was talking on a cell phone, but his eyes were fixed on her.

She drew in a shocked breath.

"Something wrong?" asked Starkman, looking back at her.

"I . . ." The Bentley set off and turned the corner, the man dropping out of sight behind her. She considered telling Starkman about her apparent stalker, but decided against it. If he posed any threat, that was what the police were for—and besides, she barely knew Starkman any better than she did the man in the leather jacket. "Just thought I saw someone I knew."

Starkman nodded and looked away. The Bentley turned again, now heading west.

Something about that struck Nina as odd. She'd checked on the Internet to find out where the Frost Foundation's New York headquarters were—they were in east Midtown, not far from the United Nations. The easiest way to reach them from her apartment would have been to head *east*, then go straight up First Avenue . . .

She decided to wait before bringing this up. The Bentley had a satellite navigation system; it was possible there was some traffic problem farther uptown that meant a detour would be faster.

But they continued west for another block, then another . . .

"Where is it we're going again?" she asked, with feigned lightness.

"The Frost Foundation," Starkman replied.

"Isn't that on the East Side?"

In the mirror, Nina caught a glimpse of the driver's eyes. They betrayed a flash of . . . *concern*? "We're making a slight detour first."

"Where to?"

"It won't take long."

"That's . . . not really what I asked."

The two men exchanged looks. "Aw, hell," said Starkman, his Texas accent growing stronger. "I was hoping to get there first, but . . ." He turned in his seat, reaching into his jacket and pulling out—

A gun!

Nina stared at it in disbelief. "What's this?"

"What does it look like? Thought you PhDs were supposed to be smart."

"What's going on? What do you want?"

Starkman held out his other hand. "Your notes, for a start." The gun was pointing at her chest. Numbly, she handed him the folder. "Too bad you didn't bring your laptop. Guess we'll have to pick that up after."

"After what?" His silence and stony expression

brought her to a horrible realization. "Oh my God! You're going to *kill* me?"

"It's nothing personal."

"And that's supposed to make me feel better?" Desperate, she looked around frantically for any way to escape.

She tugged at the door handle. It moved, but only a little. Child locks. Even though she knew it was pointless, she threw herself across the seat and tried the other door. It too refused to open.

Trapped!

Panic rose inside her, constricting her chest. Her green eyes wide with fear, she looked back at Starkman.

His expression had changed to one of surprise, his gaze flicking away from Nina to the rear window—

Whump!

Nina was flung forward as something rammed the Bentley from behind. Starkman's breath whooshed from his mouth as he was slammed against the dashboard. He angrily shoved himself upright and aimed the gun at the rear window. Nina shrieked and dived out of the line of fire.

"It's *Chase*!" Starkman shouted. "Son of a bitch!"

"How the hell did he find us?" the driver asked.

"I don't give a shit! Ram that Limey bastard off the road and get us out of here!"

The Bentley swerved sharply. Nina slid over the smooth leather, banging her head against the door. Above her, Starkman swung the gun, tracking something outside.

Another impact!

This time it came from the side, the two-ton car lurching violently as metal crunched and twisted. Through the window Nina saw another vehicle, a large black SUV.

Starkman fired. Nina screamed and clapped her hands to her ears as the side window blew apart in a hail of glittering fragments. The SUV dropped back sharply, tires howling. Wind whipped through the broken window.

Two more shots rang out from Starkman's gun, the rear windshield shattering and spraying Nina with chunks of safety glass. Car horns hooted furiously, the sound rapidly Dopplering away behind them as the Bentley accelerated. The driver swore and swerved again to dodge something, sending Nina slithering back across the seat.

"Go right!" Starkman shouted. Nina barely had time to brace herself before the Bentley screamed into a sharp turn.

"Shit!" the driver gasped as the car hit something with a flat thud. A *person*, Nina realized with horror. Shouts and screams came from outside as somebody tumbled from the car's hood. But the driver didn't stop, instead struggling to keep the Bentley under control as he accelerated again.

Starkman fired two more shots. Nina heard the other vehicle's powerful engine revving behind them. As he took aim again, the gun was right above her.

She grabbed his wrist with both hands and pulled his arm down, sinking her teeth into the flesh of his hand as hard as she could.

He let out a roar of pain—and fired.

The flash was blinding, and the noise, just inches from her head, momentarily overpowered all her senses. The bullet slammed into the back of her seat.

Starkman pulled his hand free. Huge colored blobs danced in Nina's vision, afterimages from the gun's muzzle flame. Her hearing started to return in time to hear more gunfire.

But not from Starkman's gun.

The headrest of the driver's seat burst apart in a flurry of shredded leather and stuffing, followed a millisecond later by the driver's head. Dark red blood and gray brain matter splattered the pale lining of the roof and the front windows.

The Bentley swerved as the driver's corpse slumped to one side. Starkman yelled and grabbed the steering wheel. The vehicle straightened, throwing the still-dazed Nina back across the rear seat.

Wham!

The SUV rammed them again.

Swearing, Starkman leaned over the dead driver and grasped the door handle. The door opened. He stabbed the seat belt release and shoved the corpse out onto the road, then pulled himself over the center console and dropped into the driver's seat just as the SUV hit again, harder. The Bentley snaked from side to side before Starkman regained control, sawing at the wheel and flinging the car into a hard turn to the left as he stomped on the accelerator. The tires shrieked in protest, the heavy car wallowing.

Nina's head hit the right-hand door again as the turn flung her across the car. She pulled herself up. If Starkman was occupied with driving, then he couldn't use the gun . . .

The other vehicle, a Range Rover, drew level with them. She recognized the face at the wheel—the man in the leather jacket!

With a huge silver gun in one hand, pointing at the Bentley.

"Stay down!" he shouted.

She dropped flat onto the seat again as two booms like cannon fire came from outside. Starkman ducked and shielded his face as the windshield burst apart, the wind driving the fragments back into the car.

Holding the wheel with one hand, he twisted and fired three shots over his left shoulder. Nina heard the Range Rover's tires screech as it swerved for cover directly behind its quarry.

More horns sounded as Starkman wove the Bentley through the evening traffic, a nerve-shredding grind of metal assaulting Nina's ears as it sideswiped another car. She looked up. They were somewhere around 17th or 18th Street and rapidly approaching the western side of Manhattan, only the broad lanes of the West Side Highway ahead, and beyond that the cold waters of the Hudson River.

Starkman fumbled with his gun, barely keeping hold of the wheel. Nina realized what he was doing. The automatic's slide was locked back; he was reloading . . .

Which meant he couldn't shoot!

She sat up sharply and clawed at Starkman's face. He swiped at her, trying to use his weapon as a club. She ducked to one side and continued her attack, feeling something soft beneath the middle finger of her right hand.

His eye.

She drove her nail against it. Starkman howled, thrashing the gun violently at her.

"Stop the car!" she screamed. A glimpse of the speedometer told her that the Bentley was doing sixty and still picking up speed as it careened down the street, directly towards a knot of traffic waiting at the lights.

She screamed again, this time in panic, and pulled her hands from Starkman's face. Blood covered her fingers. He saw the danger just in time and threw the wheel to the right to miss the rearmost car by mere

inches, slamming the Bentley up onto the sidewalk. A
trash can spun into the air as they plowed into it, but
that was the least of Nina's concerns, because now they
were heading right into the path of the traffic racing
along the West Side Highway—

To her horror, Starkman sped up.

The Bentley flew off the end of the sidewalk and
smashed back down onto the road, the underside of the
car grating against the asphalt. Nina saw headlights
flash and heard the desperate shrill of locking brakes.
Cars slewed in all directions to avoid a collision, only to
be hit from behind by other drivers too close to stop in
time.

They shot across the northbound lanes, reaching the
median unharmed—only for Starkman to turn *into* the
traffic on the other side, heading uptown directly
against the southbound vehicles!

"Oh my *God*!" Nina shrieked as he flung the Bentley
between the lanes of cars and trucks. Other vehicles
flashed past on either side just inches away, their drivers
swerving frantically to dodge the maniac charging
straight at them. More horns blared ahead and behind,
an orchestra of fury and fright. "Stop the car before you
get us both *killed*!"

She struck at his eyes again—but this time he was
ready.

The gun smacked into her forehead, driving a spike
of intense pain deep into her skull. She fell back, dizzy
and sickened, as Starkman threw the Bentley hard to the
left and plowed through a metal gate onto one of the
piers jutting out into the Hudson.

Wind sliced through the shattered windows as the
Bentley accelerated along the wharf. Nina struggled upright to see warehouses flying past on one side, the rust-
streaked flanks of ships on the other.

And directly ahead, nothing but open water and the distant lights of New Jersey beyond.

She gasped, realizing what Starkman was about to do.

He looked around at her for a moment. His right eye was squeezed tightly shut, deep scratches cutting across it, blood trickling down his cheek.

Then he threw the door open and rolled out, tucking up his arms to protect himself as he fell. In a flash, he was gone, the door slamming behind him—leaving the Bentley still racing towards the end of the pier, the cruise control active and holding its speed at almost fifty miles per hour!

Nina barely had time to scream before the car ripped through the flimsy wire-mesh barrier at the wharf's end and arced down towards the dark water below.

Sudden deceleration crushed her against the back of the driver's seat. Freezing water cascaded over her, a tsunami rushing through the broken windows. Bubbles frothed past as the Bentley's heavy front end tipped downwards, pulling the car and its occupant towards the bottom of the river.

Nina tried to get out through the rear window, but the high headrests above the back seat blocked her escape. Eyes stinging, she tugged desperately at the nearest door handle, but it still wouldn't budge.

The side window . . .

The glass was smashed, and it was just large enough for her to fit. She grabbed the window frame and pulled herself through. Her shoulders cleared the door, her chest—

She was stuck!

Her dress had snagged on the metal rods supporting the driver's seat's destroyed headrest.

Nina kicked, trying to free herself. No luck. Her stupid dress was still caught fast. She kicked harder, pushing at the window frame with her arms for extra leverage. The material gave slightly, but refused to tear.

Her chest was about to explode. She wanted nothing more than to take a breath, but the only thing she would draw into her lungs was water.

She was going to drown! Professor Philby had been right: her hunt for Atlantis would get her killed—

No, there was no way she was going to let him be right!

But she couldn't do anything to stop it. She was trapped in a car that was plunging to the bottom of the Hudson, and the pounding in her head would at any moment overcome her reason and force her to take a fatal breath . . .

Someone grabbed her.

She was so surprised that the breath froze on her lips. An arm tightened around her waist, pulling. Her dress ripped, and her savior dragged her through the window, kicking forcefully upwards as the Bentley disappeared into the darkness below.

Her heart slamming desperately inside her chest, Nina breached the surface and pulled in a whooping, painful gasp, not caring about the foul taste of the water. One arm still around her, her rescuer pulled her towards shore. Her pain and panic subsiding, Nina looked to see who it was.

The man in the leather jacket grinned back at her, revealing a prominent gap between his two front teeth. "Ay up, Doc?"

"*You?*"

"Tchah! That's bloody gratitude for you!"

They reached the pier, the man guiding her to a rusted ladder. Nina wearily climbed it, dragging herself onto a concrete dock below the main level of the wharf itself. The man followed, water streaming from his jacket. "Nice dress."

"What?" Nina asked, confused, before realizing that her skirt had been torn away practically to her crotch. "Oh my God!" She clapped her hands protectively between her legs.

"Well," said the man, running a hand over his short hair, "if that's all you're worried about, you're probably okay." His accent was English, but not from a region Nina could pin down. "Which is good, 'cause we need to get out of here. Right now." He held out a hand. Nina stared at it in bewilderment for a moment, then took it. With considerable strength, he hauled her to her feet. It was only then that she realized she'd lost both her shoes.

"Who *are* you?" she demanded, as he quickly led her to a flight of steps leading up to the wharf. "What's going on?"

"My name's Chase. Eddie Chase. Don't worry, I'm not some nutter." He looked back to give her a smile that wasn't entirely reassuring. "Just mad enough to dive into a river to rescue the woman I've been hired to look after."

"Hired?"

"Yeah. I'm your bodyguard!"

They reached the top of the steps. A small group of people were waiting for them, looking amazed. A few of them applauded. "Used to be in the SAS—you know, Special Air Service. Now I'm . . . sort of a freelancer." Nina saw that his Range Rover, its front end the worse for wear, was parked on the wharf with a door open and the engine still running.

An overweight man in the uniform of a security firm jogged towards them, panting. "Hey! What the hell's going on here?"

"It's all right, mate," said Chase. "Everything's under control."

"The hell it is! A car just smashed through the gates and went off the end of the pier! I want some answers!"

Chase sighed, then reached into his jacket and pulled out his massive gun. It looked even more menacing to Nina close up, the long barrel reinforced by a slotted steel bar along its top. "Mr. Magnum here'll answer any questions," he said, waving it in the guard's general direction. The little crowd hurriedly backed away. "You got any?"

The guard fought to keep the fear off his face, with little success. "They can wait."

"Good. You might want to find the bloke who bailed out of the car before it crashed, though—he's the real bad guy. But right now I need to get this lady somewhere safe. All right?"

"Sure!" the guard agreed, backing off.

Still keeping his gun raised, Chase opened the Range Rover's passenger door for Nina, then ran to the driver's side and jumped in. He drove off down the wharf at high speed. At the end he made a tight turn, then sped along the empty sidewalk for a few hundred yards before passing the tangle of stationary cars and swerving onto the West Side Highway. "Better put the heater on, I suppose," he said, glancing at the shivering Nina as he accelerated. In the distance, the sound of sirens wailed through the night air.

She clenched her teeth. "What the hell's going on?"

"Short version? Bad guys want to kill you. Good guys want to stop them. I'm one of the good guys."

"Why do they want to kill me? What did *I* do?"

"It's not what you've done, Doc. It's what they're afraid you *might* do. That bloke in the Bentley,

Starkman? Used to be a mate of mine back in the day—
we worked together, joint ops around the world—until
he went rogue."

"He said he worked for the Frost Foundation, for
Kristian Frost," said Nina.

Chase laughed. "Well, I know for a fact that he
doesn't."

"How?"

"Because *I* work for Kristian Frost. You want to meet
him?"

THREE
Norway

C heck it out, Doc," said Chase. "Pretty nice, isn't it?"
"It certainly is," Nina agreed, gazing at the starkly beautiful landscape below.

Kristian Frost's home and corporate headquarters were both at Ravnsfjord, three miles inland of the Norwegian coast south of Bergen. The fjord that gave the area its name bisected his expansive property. On the southern side was a campus of office buildings that, while ultramodern in design, nevertheless perfectly complemented their surroundings. A road led from them to a slender arched road bridge across the fjord. Overlooking the bridge—overlooking the entire area, she realized—was another large, sleek building, its colors and curves blending into the bluff on which it stood.

"That's Frost's house," Chase told her.

"That's a *house*?" Nina gasped. "My God, it's huge! I thought it was another office building!"

"Bit bigger than your flat, eh?"

"Just a bit." The plane—a Gulfstream V business jet in Frost's corporate livery—banked to cross over the fjord. Nina spotted another cluster of ultramodern buildings farther east of the house at the base of a cliff, then on the northern side of the waterway their destination—a private airport. "All of this belongs to Kristian Frost?"

"Pretty much, yeah. He runs his whole business from here, almost never leaves. Guess he doesn't like traveling."

Nina took a last look through the porthole before sitting back. The Gulfstream was moving into its final descent. "It's a lovely place to live, that's for sure. A bit isolated, though."

"Well, when you're a billionaire, I suppose the world comes to you."

The plane landed and taxied to the small terminal building. Nina wrapped her coat more tightly around herself as she stepped down onto the concrete. "Bit nippy?" Chase asked.

"Are you kidding? I'm used to New York winters. This is nothing!" Actually, it was close to freezing even without the chill wind blowing in from the coast, but now that she'd opened her big mouth she had to endure it.

"Well, we'll be going somewhere a lot warmer soon." Nina looked at Chase for an explanation, but he just grinned. "Here's our ride."

A white Jeep Grand Cherokee pulled up next to the plane. A thick-necked man with close-cropped blond hair and muscles practically bursting the seams of his tailored dark suit, got out to greet them. "Dr. Wilde," he said, his accent German. "I am Mr. Frost's head of security here at Ravnsfjord, Josef Schenk." He extended his hand, which Nina shook. Although his grip was light, she could tell that if he chose, he could crush every bone in her hand. "Good to meet you."

"Thank you," said Nina. Chase and Schenk were eyeing each other up almost like boxers before a fight.

They had similar builds; she wondered if they also had similar—or rival—military backgrounds.

"Joe," said Chase.

"Mr. Chase," Schenk replied, before opening the Jeep's rear door. "Please, Dr. Wilde. I'll take you to Mr. Frost."

Nina got in. Chase followed her with a slightly sarcastic "Cheers," closing the door behind him. Schenk glared at him before walking around the SUV to the driver's side.

"What's that all about?" Nina asked.

"He's a company man," Chase explained while Schenk was out of earshot. "Doesn't like freelancers, thinks I'm going to rip off his boss."

"And are you?" Nina couldn't resist asking.

"I'm a professional," replied Chase, for a moment completely serious. "I always see the job through."

Schenk climbed in and they set off. Nina saw several hangars at the runway's western end. Parked outside the largest was a huge aircraft, the Frost corporate logo—the outline of a trident inside the "O" of the name—only half complete along its flank as tiny figures on cherry-picker cranes painted it. "Wow. That's a *big* plane."

"An Airbus A380 freighter," Schenk said. "The latest addition to Mr. Frost's fleet."

Nina looked back down the long runway. Steep hills rose beyond its distant eastern end. "Hope it's got good brakes! Those mountains look a bit close."

"It can only take off heading westwards. It's inconvenient, but fortunately once it's in service it will be spending more time flying around the world than here."

The Jeep left the airport and crossed the bridge. Nina expected them to turn west for the corporate buildings, but instead they headed up a zigzagging road towards the house on the bluff. Close up, its clean, elegant lines looked even more striking.

Schenk parked outside, then ushered Nina and Chase into the house. "This way."

Nina was hugely impressed by the room into which he led them. Its far wall was curved, a giant window running its full width to reveal the vista beyond, from the mountains framing the airport across the fjord to the corporate buildings below, and, in the distance, the North Sea.

And the view wasn't the only impressive thing about the room. It was almost a combination of luxurious lounge and art gallery. A Henry Moore sculpture, a Picasso painting in an alcove carefully shielded from direct sunlight, a Paul Klee . . . and several others she didn't immediately recognize, but was sure were equally valuable.

"This is an amazing house," she said, awed.

"Thank you," said a new voice, a woman's. Nina turned to see a tall and strikingly beautiful blonde entering the room, glossy hair sweeping down past her shoulders. She looked to be about Nina's age or slightly younger, the regal way she held herself countered by her high-fashion clothing—a tight white top cut off above her stomach to reveal a perfectly toned midriff, and equally tight black leather jeans with high-heeled boots. As she approached, she looked Nina up and down as if not quite sure what to make of her.

"Dr. Wilde," said Schenk, "this is Kari Frost, Mr. Frost's daughter."

"Nice to meet you," said Nina, offering her hand. Kari shook it firmly. Chase, Nina noticed with amusement, was trying not to make it too obvious that he was checking her out.

"You too, Dr. Wilde," Kari replied. "Mr. Chase. I heard your services were needed in New York?"

"Yeah, you could say that. Good job you hired me!" He shot Schenk a smug look. Schenk frowned.

"I'm glad you like the house," said Kari, turning back to Nina. "I designed it. Architecture is one of my . . . well, I would say hobbies, but that would be immodest. I have a degree in the subject." She spoke perfect English with only the slightest trace of an accent.

"It's beautiful," Nina told her.

"Thank you." Kari's name was familiar, but Nina couldn't quite recall why.

"So, your dad around?" Chase asked, hooking his thumbs into his jacket pockets.

Kari appeared slightly chilly about his informality. "No, he's in the biolab. I came to take you to him."

The memory returned to Nina. "Excuse me for asking, but . . . weren't you in the news last year, in Africa? The medical relief in Ethiopia?"

"Yes, that was me," Kari said. "I helped organize the aid effort."

"Ms. Frost does more than just help," Schenk said. "She's in charge of the Frost Foundation's medical programs around the world. I don't think there's a single country she hasn't visited in the past five years."

"That's one way to rack up the frequent-flier miles," joked Chase.

"You're working on disease eradication programs, aren't you?" Nina asked.

"Yes. The Frost Foundation does whatever it can to make the world a better place. It's a lofty goal, I admit— but it's one that I'm certain we can achieve."

"I hope you can," said Nina.

"Thank you," Kari replied. She gestured at the door. "If you'll come with me, I'll take you to my father."

w

Kari led them downstairs to a huge garage beneath the house. Nina was amazed by its contents; the space was packed with expensive sports cars and motorcycles, ranging from old classics to the very latest Italian supercars.

"My personal collection," said Kari. "My father doesn't entirely approve, but I just love the freedom and exhilaration of speed."

"Nice wheels," said Chase as he admired first a scarlet Ferrari F430 Spider convertible, then the motorbike parked next to it, a sleek machine in blue and silver.

"Suzuki GSX-R1000," Kari told him, with more than a hint of pride—the first sign of real emotion she'd shown since meeting Nina. "The fastest production bike in the world. One of my favorites. I plan to take it to Europe to race soon. That is . . . if my schedule allows. But that depends on Dr. Wilde."

"What do you mean?" asked Nina. Kari merely gave her an enigmatic look, leading them to a Mercedes limousine.

Schenk drove, taking them to the futuristic buildings east of the house that Nina had seen from the plane. As they approached, she saw the complex was actually made up of two sections: the interconnected two-story structures on the ground near the fjord, and other sections above them set into the cliff itself.

"Our biolab," explained Kari. "The underground section houses the containment area. There are samples in there which are potentially dangerous, so the whole laboratory section can be completely sealed off in case of an emergency." She pointed at a curved structure protruding from the cliff face. "That's my father's office, up there."

"Your father's office is right above the containment area?" Nina asked nervously. The idea of going into a building filled with contagious diseases and viruses made her skin crawl.

"His idea, to show his confidence in the design. Besides, he likes to keep a close eye on our progress."

They drove down a ramp into a parking garage beneath the main building, then got out and took an elevator to a lobby on the ground floor. A large horseshoe-shaped desk of black steel and marble was manned by three uniformed security guards, who nodded respectfully to Kari. Behind the desk, doors led into a high corridor with a glass roof through which Nina could see Frost's office above. The place was busy.

"How many people work here?" she asked.

"It varies," said Kari, "but usually around fifty or sixty researchers, plus the security staff."

Nina spotted another security station at the end of the corridor by the large glass and steel doors. "You, uh . . . you've got a lot of security, haven't you?"

"We need it," Kari answered matter-of-factly. "Some of the samples we work with could be used for bioterrorism if they fell into the wrong hands. And the Frost Foundation unfortunately has enemies. You've met some of them already."

"Don't worry, Doc," said Chase, "I'll keep you safe."

The sight of the trefoil biohazard logo on the door made Nina slow her approach. "Are . . . are you *sure* this is safe?"

"Absolutely," Kari assured her. "These doors are part of an airlock. They're made of ceramic aluminum oxynitride—transparent aluminum, equivalent to sixty centimeters of armor plate. Virtually unbreakable. The only way anything gets in or out of the containment section, whether it be a microbe or a person, is with our permission."

Kari spoke to the guards, and the heavy airlock doors hissed open. The group passed through, waiting for the inner doors to cycle. The containment section beyond was purely functional in design, almost brutal. The walls were tiled in white, the floors coated in nonslip rubber for ease of cleaning. Harsh fluorescent lights lit every corner with an even glare, and Nina also saw the eerie purple glow of ultraviolet sources, adding to the sterile air.

Inside, Kari led them to an elevator that took them up to Frost's office. Entering, Nina suddenly felt as though she'd been transported back to the house, the design was so similar. She could even see the house itself through the windows, perched atop its crag.

But it wasn't the view, or the architecture, or the objets d'art that caught her attention. It was the man waiting for them.

Kristian Frost was even more imposing and handsome in real life than in pictures. Well over six feet tall, and still impressively muscular despite his sixty years, in his navy blue roll-neck sweater he reminded her more of a rugged fisherman than a billionaire businessman. His hair and beard were both turning gray, but his eyes still contained a youthful energy and deep intelligence.

"Dr. Wilde," he said, taking her hand. She was a little surprised when instead of shaking it, he lowered his head to kiss it. From anyone else the gesture would have seemed somewhat silly, but coming from him it felt perfectly apt. "Welcome to Ravnsfjord."

"Mr. Frost," she began.

"Please! Call me Kristian." His English was not quite as precise as Kari's, a deep burr in his voice revealing his Scandinavian origins. "I'm very glad to meet you. And I'm also very glad that I'm *able* to meet you. Hiring Mr. Chase has paid for itself already."

"Then I guess I should thank you for, well, saving my life!"

Frost smiled broadly. "Happy to be of service."

"But . . . why would anyone *want* to kill me? What's all this about?"

"Please, take a seat and I will explain," said Frost, directing her to a long sofa. She sat, Kari joining her at the other end. "I'm afraid that your theories about Atlantis have led you to be targeted by a man called Giovanni Qobras."

"And who is Giovanni Qobras?" Nina asked.

"A madman," said Kari.

"Oh." Not just a killer, but a *mad* killer. Great.

"Qobras and his followers," Frost began, "who call themselves the Brotherhood, believe the same thing that I do—that you do. If there's one thing we all have in common, it's that we believe the legend of Atlantis is *true*. I've been convinced of it all my life, and I've put a quite substantial amount of my fortune into attempting to prove it." He walked over to the wide window. In the far distance, the sea glinted like tiny diamonds. "Unfortunately, without much success. As you know, there's very little information to work from . . . and what there is is subject to a great deal of interpretation."

"Tell me about it," said Nina. "So what about this Qobras?"

He turned to face her. "You and I want to *find* Atlantis, to bring an ancient wonder back to the world. Qobras, on the other hand . . ." His face darkened. "He wants to keep it hidden, to protect the secret for his own ends. And he's willing to resort to murder to do so. Your new theory about its location may not have convinced the committee at your university, but it certainly convinced Qobras. He believes that you're on the right track—as do I, by the way—and he wants to stop you from proving it."

"Wait," Nina said. "How do *you* know about my theory?"

"The Frost Foundation has friends in academia all around the world. They know that any new ideas about the location of Atlantis will catch my interest, so they keep me appraised. And your ideas . . ." He smiled. "I'll get right to the point. I'm willing to fully fund a survey expedition to test your theory."

Nina could barely contain her excitement. "Really?"

"Absolutely. Subject to a condition, though." He saw her expression fall, and chuckled. "Nothing bad, I promise. But the Gulf of Cádiz *is* rather large, and while I have a lot of resources, they're not infinite. I'd like you to narrow the search, pinpoint a location."

"But that's the problem," Nina told him. "There's so little information to work from, I don't know how I *can* narrow it down."

"There might be more than you think." She looked up at him, intrigued. "I'll explain later. But for now . . . are you interested?"

"Am I interested?" she gasped. "Absolutely!"

Frost walked over to her and offered his right hand. She hesitated, then shook it. "Wonderful," he said. "Dr. Wilde, together, we're going to find Atlantis."

w

The gleaming object hung in space, unaffected by gravity.

Nina stared at it in amazement. She'd never seen a free-floating hologram before, or even imagined they were possible outside the realms of science fiction or movies.

"What is it?" she asked at last, reluctantly looking away from the hologram to the other people in the darkened room.

"It's something that might help you narrow down your search," said Frost. "Or at least, that's the claim of the man who wants to sell it to me."

"Sell it?" Nina turned back to the hologram. The projection, hovering above a cylindrical pedestal in which colored lights flickered faster than her eyes could follow, was supposedly life-sized, just under a foot long and about two inches wide. It was a flat bar of metal, the bottom end rounded while the top was straight, a circular nub protruding from it. The color was almost like gold, but with an unusual reddish tint . . .

Like her pendant.

She absently fingered the metal piece hanging from her neck as she leaned closer to the hologram, moving around the pedestal to see the other side. To her disappointment, there was nothing there except a bizarre, perspective-defying inversion of its face, through which she could see Frost, Kari and Chase.

"The seller only wanted us to have a taste," said Kari. "He claims that the front of the artifact has markings that may be of use to us—but he won't let us see them until we agree to pay him."

"How much does he want?" Chase asked.

"Ten million dollars."

"Bloody hell. That's a lot for a fancy ruler."

"It might be worth even more than that," Nina said. Even though she knew there was nothing there, she couldn't help reaching out a finger for an experimental touch. The tip of her nail sank into the hologram, part of the image disappearing where her finger obstructed the laser beams generating it. "It's orichalcum, isn't it?"

"So it seems." Frost held up a small glass dish containing a little piece of metal the same color as the bar. "As well as the hologram, he also sent us a sample. He claims that he cut it from the side of the artifact." Nina saw a small nick in one side of the hologram. "I ran a metallurgical test. It's a gold-copper alloy, but with very unusual levels of carbon and sulfur, which would account for its color."

"Consistent with vulcanism?"

"Yes."

"Which would match what Plato said about orichalcum in *Critias*!" Nina's excitement rose as she realized the implications.

"Wait, what?" Chase asked. "Sorry, but when somebody says vulcanism to me, I think of Mr. Spock."

"According to Plato, orichalcum—a rare metal—was mined in Atlantis," Nina explained. "But there's no room for any unknown elements in the periodic table, which means it had to be an alloy of other metals. But you don't mine alloys, you make them—*unless* they were formed by some natural process. Volcanic activity could have caused deposits of gold and copper to fuse together into a new substance, and if there were sufficient quantities, it could have been dug out of the rock."

"The Atlanteans used orichalcum to cover the walls of their citadel," said Kari. "They considered it nearly as valuable as gold—which it is, because of the high gold content—but an object like this would be worth far more than just its weight in precious metals. If it's genuine, then it would be the first true Atlantean artifact ever discovered—proof that Atlantis exists."

Frost nodded to Schenk, who switched on the lights. The hologram faded, losing its illusion of solidity. "So where is it? Who has it?" Nina asked.

"The seller is called Yuri Volgan," began Frost. "He

used to be one of Qobras's men. Apparently he wants to leave the Brotherhood, and also wants enough money to hide from Qobras by selling this artifact. He sent the orichalcum fragment and the hologram to us via an intermediary, an Iranian called Failak Hajjar."

Nina frowned. "I've heard the name."

"I'm not surprised. He sells ancient Persian artifacts—that aren't supposed to be for sale."

"A grave robber," she said with distaste.

"He used to be, although I doubt he's gotten his own hands dirty for years. He's made himself very wealthy by selling his country's treasures to private collectors abroad. Wealthy enough that he can buy a degree of immunity from the Iranian government."

"Plus he grasses up his rivals," added Chase, "sells them out so the police'll go after them instead of him. Haven't met him personally, but I know people who've dealt with him. Not a popular bloke—but if he's selling this thing, he probably thinks it's genuine. He might be a scumbag, but he's a scumbag who's bothered about his reputation."

"He has the resources to handle the sale of this artifact, *and* to protect Volgan from Qobras," Frost said. "Which is why I'm inclined to believe that it's genuine. But I'm not going to hand over ten million dollars without some proof. And that's where you come in."

Nina blinked. "Me?"

"I want you to examine the artifact and decide if it is what Volgan claims."

"You want me to go to *Iran*?" She gulped. "Part of the Axis of Evil, hates America, *that* Iran?"

Chase laughed. "I'll be there to watch out for you. Me and a few mates. Nothing to worry about."

"You've been to Iran before?"

He looked evasive. "Not officially . . ."

"Mr. Chase and his associates will look after you," said Frost. "And Kari will be going as well, as my representative."

"But what makes you think I'll be able to tell if this artifact's real or not?" asked Nina, gesturing at the ghostly hologram.

"You are an expert in ancient languages, aren't you?" said Kari.

"I wouldn't say *expert*," she protested. "I mean, I've studied the field, I can tell my Phoenician from my Numidian, but I'm not a specialist."

"From what I've heard, you're rather better than that. Maybe even better than your mother at reading Glozel." Nina stared at Frost, surprised. "I knew your parents— I actually funded the expedition to Tibet where they . . ." He paused, looking away from her. "A great tragedy. A great loss."

"They never told me you funded them," said Nina.

"At my request. Now that you know what Qobras is capable of, you understand why I place great importance on security. Qobras will do whatever it takes to stop anyone from finding Atlantis, and he has considerable resources—and some powerful friends around the world."

"Like who?"

"It's probably safer that you don't know. But as for the artifact, if what Yuri Volgan says is true, you should be able to tell if it's authentic by reading the text. And just imagine it," Frost went on, a certain theatricality entering his voice, "you'll be able to hold in your hand an actual object from Atlantis!"

"If it's genuine."

"Which you're the most qualified person in the world to determine."

Nina considered his words. She still wasn't keen on

the idea of going to a country that was openly hostile to Westerners, and Americans in particular, but she'd been on expeditions to less-than-friendly countries before, and the potential prize in this case far exceeded the value of anything else she'd ever discovered.

Besides, as Frost had said, she wouldn't be going alone.

And if she chose not to go, what would she do instead? Return to New York, to where she had just been denied funding . . . and where she would have to constantly look over her shoulder in case Qobras's men came after her again?

"Okay," she said, "I'm in. So, when do we set off?"

Frost smiled. "Whenever you're ready."

"I like your thinking," said Nina, smiling back. "Just because Atlantis has waited for eleven thousand years doesn't mean *we* should wait."

"Then," said Kari, "let's get you started."

FOUR
Iran

Nina rubbed irritably at her arm. "This still hurts."

"You don't want to get some weird Middle Eastern disease, do you?" Chase asked, amused. "Better safe than sorry."

"I know that. It's just uncomfortable, that's all." The vaccination had been an unwelcome part of the deal, administered in the antiseptic environs of the biolab. While less painful than others she'd had in the past, it seemed to take an age for the little bead of blood to dry up.

"That was nothing! Christ, you should have seen some of the shots I got in the SAS. Needles *this* big." He held his hands eight inches apart. "And you don't want to know where they stuck 'em."

The Gulfstream had just passed over the Black Sea and Turkey on its way to Iran. It hadn't taken a direct route from Norway, instead detouring to Prague to pick up another passenger. In the plane with Nina, Chase and Kari—who sat on her own at the back of the cabin working on a laptop—was another man, whom Chase had introduced as Hugo Castille. From the way they mocked each other, it was clear they were old friends.

"Yes, Edward and I have known each other for a long

time," the long-faced, ebullient European—French, Nina thought, from his accent—confirmed when she asked. "We worked together on many special joint operations for NATO. Strictly hush-hush, as you say," he added, tapping the side of his beaky nose.

"So you were in the French army?"

Unlike on a commercial airliner, the seats on the private jet faced each other across the aisle. Castille drew himself up in his with a look of great outrage, one fist clenched against his chest. "French? Please! I am *Belgian*, madame!"

"I'm sorry! I didn't realize," Nina said in hurried apology, before it dawned on her that Chase was laughing. Castille's face cracked into a smile. "Wait, are you making fun of me?"

"Just taking the piss," said Chase with a teasing grin. "Hugo's been doing his 'Franch? 'Ow dare you!' routine for years. I mean, he comes from Belgium, it's the only gimmick he's got."

"English philistine," Castille sniffed. He took a polished red apple from a jacket pocket and examined it carefully before taking a bite.

"So, what can I expect in Iran, Mr. Chase?" Nina asked.

"Call me Eddie." His expression became businesslike. "Hopefully you shouldn't have to deal too much with the locals. Should be a straightforward job: in, meet Hajjar, decide if this thing's real, then the boss," he nodded at Kari, still occupied with her computer, "transfers the money, and out. That's if everything's legit."

"And if it's not?"

He patted his leather jacket, which was draped over the arm of his seat. The butt of his pistol was visible inside it. "Then there'll be trouble. Don't worry, though, we should be okay. I'll watch out for you, Doc."

"*We* will watch out for you," corrected Castille, mouth full of apple.

"Thanks," Nina said, keeping her concerns to herself.

Kari's laptop chimed. She regarded the screen with surprise, then her blue eyes flicked up and caught Nina's gaze for a moment before turning back to the computer. She quickly typed something, firmly tapped the return key, then closed the laptop and moved to the empty seat facing Nina.

"Something wrong?" Nina asked.

"No—just an e-mail from my father, something I wasn't expecting. Nothing to worry about, though—in fact, it's good news. But it's not important right now, so . . ." She leaned forward, smiling for the first time since Nina had met her and revealing flawless white teeth. "I thought I should apologize to you, Dr. Wilde."

"For what?"

"I haven't been the best hostess. I've been preoccupied, with my work for the foundation, with this expedition . . . I'm sorry if I've come across as cold and distant."

"There's no need to apologize," Nina assured her. "You're very busy, I'm sure you've got a lot of things all going on at once."

"Not anymore. From now on, I'm devoting all of my attention to you and this mission. I want it to be a success—and I also want to make sure that you stay safe."

"Thanks," said Nina, smiling back. Then Kari glanced at Chase.

"Mr. Chase," she said, fixing him with a disapproving look, "are you trying to look down my top?"

Nina stifled a giggle, while Castille covered his own amusement by taking a hurried bite from his apple. Chase had undeniably been caught in the act, but rather than try to deny it, he simply sat back and raised an eyebrow. "If I can do it, then so can any Iranian blokes who see you, and they're a bit funny about women in sexy clothes. We don't want to draw any more attention than we have to. I was just thinking it's probably worth you changing into something a bit more frumpy before we land."

Kari was wearing a tight white top and leather jeans similar to the ones she'd had on at Ravnsfjord. "You have a point. Fortunately, I came prepared."

"The doc here's okay, though. Just needs a coat."

Nina glared at him. "Are you saying I look *frumpy*, Mr. Chase?" She would have used the word "modest" or "practical" to describe her own outfit of jeans, sweatshirt and sturdy boots.

"You look fine," Kari grinned, standing. "If you need anything, just ask me." She went into the rear compartment.

Castille finished his apple. "Ah, England," he announced. "A country of the charming, the sophisticated, the romantic. And there's also Edward Chase."

"Ah, sod off, Hugo."

Castille flicked his apple core at him, which Chase effortlessly caught, his hand snapping up like a striking snake.

"Is he always like this?" Nina asked Castille.

"I'm afraid so."

"And the ladies love it that way," said Chase, dropping the apple core into his empty water glass. Castille tutted and rolled his eyes. Chase checked his watch, then stretched out in his seat.

"Getting comfortable?" Nina asked.

"Just making the most of it," he replied. "We'll be landing in half an hour. And I bet you the ride's not going to be nearly this smooth once we're on the ground."

W

Chase was certainly right about that, Nina thought. The Land Rover taking them to their meeting with Failak Hajjar had seen better days, and the road beneath it apparently had never seen a good day in its entire life.

The Gulfstream landed at the airport serving the Iranian city of Esfahān, in the Zagros mountains on the country's western side. Though the group had no trouble getting through customs, even when Nina presented her American passport—it turned out that the Frost Foundation had provided considerable aid following the devastating earthquake of 2003, earning the gratitude of the Iranian government—they still received plenty of suspicious looks. All of the women Nina saw as they drove out of Esfahān wore head scarves at the least, and a fair percentage were veiled. While Iran was not as strict as its Islamic neighbors like Saudi Arabia in how its women were forced to dress, overgarments that concealed the female form were mandatory, even for visitors.

Kari's preparedness had extended to having something suitable for Nina to wear, a pale brown coat that came down to her knees. Though Nina instinctively resented the presence of any system that dictated what she could or couldn't wear in public, at least she didn't have to bury herself inside a burka. However, she couldn't help feeling a twinge of jealousy at the long coat Kari had chosen for herself. While it no doubt adhered to the *letter* of Iranian law, if anything the flowing, narrow-waisted white garment made her even more striking a figure.

Although she had worn a head scarf at the airport, as soon as the Land Rover started moving Kari pulled it off. Nina did the same—once the vehicle was safely clear of the city.

Driving the Land Rover was a man whom Chase introduced as "an old mate of mine." A good decade older than either Chase or Castille, Hafez Marradejan was a stocky, dark-skinned man with a graying beard that stretched to an impressive point four inches beyond the tip of his chin. He was also a chain-smoker, to Nina's dismay—all the more so when she learned they had at least an hour's drive ahead.

"So," said Hafez—although Nina spoke a little Arabic, he opted to talk in English—"you're back in work, eh, Eddie?"

"Yep," Chase answered. He was in the front passenger seat, Nina sandwiched between Kari and Castille in the back. "Same business, new bosses." He tipped his head back in Kari's direction.

"Ah! I'd say welcome to Iran, Miss Frost, but current government? Pah! Doesn't deserve your respect." Hafez kept looking back at Kari as he spoke, making Nina wince every time he took his eyes off the worryingly busy road. "Finally get government that at least *tries* to be progressive, and then what happens? They get voted out of office at next election! Democracy, eh? No use if people are idiots!" He made a noise that was somewhere between a laugh and a hacking cough. "Still, good to see you again, Eddie."

"So you *have* been to Iran before?" Nina asked.

"No, nope, never," Chase said quickly. Castille adopted an innocent look, gazing out of the window.

Hafez laughed his coughing laugh again. "Westerners and their secrets! What happened was—"

"Absolutely nothing," cut in Chase. "NATO special forces have never run operations in Iran. Ever." He glared at Hafez, who just chuckled and drew in another lungful of smoke.

"Eh, then I must have been helping ghosts. By the

way, one of the boxes you never brought with you is in the back, like you asked."

Castille reached over the rear seats and lifted up a dirty metal container the size of a large shoe box. "Buried treasure!" he proclaimed, opening it and taking out a black automatic pistol, some ammunition clips and, to Nina's horror, a hand grenade. "Here, hold this."

Nina squeaked as he casually dropped the grenade into her hand. Castille quickly and expertly checked the gun, loaded it, then slipped it into his jacket.

Chase glanced at Nina, who was still staring, petrified, at the grenade. "Nothing to panic about," he said, taking it from her. "It won't explode unless you pull out the pin. Like this."

He pulled out the pin. Nina shrieked.

"This one's got a five-second fuse," Chase noted. "But don't worry, it can't go off unless you release the spoon here, as well." He slid the pin back into place, then took his thumb off the curved metal clip protruding from one side of the grenade. "See?" Castille and Hafez chuckled.

"That wasn't *funny*!" cried Nina.

"Gentlemen," Kari added, "I'd prefer it if you didn't terrorize the most important member of our expedition." The words were mild, but there was no mistaking the authority in her voice.

"Sorry, boss," said Chase. He handed the grenade back to Castille, who returned it to the box. "Just thought it'd be a way to pass the time."

Nina made a face. "Next time, bring an iPod!"

w

After traveling for an hour, Nina wished *she* had an iPod.

The mountains were impressive at first, but after a

while one brown peak looked much like another. The bumpy highway had been as smooth as a magic carpet ride compared to the potholed, twisting road they were now on, in places little more than a dirt track above a perilously steep slope. A lumbering diesel locomotive on the railway line below belched out fumes as it hauled a long string of grimy tanker trucks. Following the twin steel lines along the valley, she saw sidings alongside them about a mile ahead, another train stationary in one.

"How much farther is it, Hafez?" asked Chase.

"Not far," Hafez said, pointing into the valley. "Past the train yard."

"Thank God," Nina sighed. The thin seats and constant bumping of the old Land Rover were becoming a literal pain in the butt. "Why did this guy want to meet all the way out here anyway? Couldn't we just have met in the Tehran Hilton?"

"Christ, I wish," said Chase. "Nah, he's being cautious. Which means we need to be too."

"Do you expect trouble?" Kari asked.

"We're spending ten million dollars to buy an ancient artifact stolen off a maniac from a very dodgy bloke in a remote part of Iran. Don't you?"

She raised an eyebrow. "Once again, you have a point."

Ten bumpy minutes later, Hafez brought the Land Rover to a halt outside an abandoned farmhouse. The train yard was out of sight behind them around a bend in the valley; even the railway lines had disappeared into a tunnel below. A steep, dusty rise above the house was topped by scrubby trees, while on the other side of the structure the slope dipped sharply down to the valley floor. There was no other trace of human habitation in sight.

"Hugo, check around the back of the house," Chase said, sharp and businesslike again. "Hafez, stay with Dr. Wilde and Ms. Frost. Any sign of trouble, get them out of here."

"Where are you going?" Kari asked.

"To make sure the house is empty." He got out of the Land Rover and took a powerful LED flashlight from a pocket. "If I'm not out in two minutes," he told Hafez, "*that's* a sign of trouble." The Iranian nodded as the two other men jogged to the farmhouse.

It actually took less than two minutes for Chase to reappear, Castille completing his circle of the building soon after. "It's clear," Chase said, returning to the Land Rover. "Only two rooms, and nowhere for anyone to hide."

"Nobody around the back," added Castille.

"Okay then," Chase continued, "this road's the only way in or out. Anyone comes, we'll have plenty of warning."

"I don't think he's coming by road," said Castille, an odd expression of distaste on his face.

"Why?"

"Can't you hear it?"

Chase tipped his head to the side, then grinned. "Oh yeah," he said, clapping the Belgian on one shoulder. "It's the sound of your nightmares! Woo, it's coming to get you!"

"As you so elegantly say in England . . . piss off."

Nina moved to the open door to listen. "What's the matter?" She could hear it now, an unmistakable clatter echoing from the surrounding mountains.

"Hugo once had a bad experience with a helicopter," Chase said. "So now he's got a phobia about them. Chopperphobia! Every time he sees one, he reckons something's going to go wrong and kill him."

"They fly with huge whirling blades spinning at insane speeds!" Castille protested. "How can they *not* be dangerous?"

"Well, you just keep your head down back here and I'll meet him when he lands, okay?" Chase winked at him, then added in a quieter, more serious voice, "Keep an eye open." Castille nodded.

The helicopter swept over the rise above the farmhouse. The type was familiar to Nina from hundreds of movies and TV shows, and even a couple of flights as a passenger: a Bell Jet Ranger, a civilian workhorse found all around the world. It made a rapid circle of the farmhouse, then came to a hover and landed about a hundred feet from the Land Rover.

Chase waited for the rotors to slow, then walked over. Hajjar had brought company. As well as the pilot, there were three other people in the Jet Ranger. He rolled his shoulders, feeling the weight of the Wildey .45 Winchester Magnum in its holster under his jacket, ready for use in an instant. Just in case.

The helicopter's rear doors opened, two large, bearded men in dark suits and sunglasses jumping out and surveying the area before fixing their black-hole stares on Chase. He stared back, unintimidated. From the way they held themselves he could tell they were ex-military—but just regular soldiers, not special forces. Definitely nowhere near SAS level. He could handle them.

One of the men leaned closer to the helicopter and spoke in Farsi. The door opened, and Failak Hajjar emerged.

Unlike his bodyguards, Hajjar was dressed in traditional Arab robes. But like them, he was wearing sunglasses—though his were far more expensive.

Another man followed him out. He was white, with

short spiky hair, several days' growth of stubble and a distinctly wary air. Chase guessed it was Yuri Volgan.

"Are you Chase?" Hajjar called.

"Yes!"

"Where is Ms. Frost?"

"Where's the artifact?" Chase demanded. Hajjar glowered, then reached back into the Jet Ranger and took out a small black leather briefcase. Nodding, Chase backed away, heading to the Land Rover.

"In the house," said Hajjar, gesturing with the briefcase. "Out of the wind, yes?"

"What wind?" Chase muttered. Now that the rotors had stopped, there was only an intermittent breeze. He checked the area once more for signs that they weren't alone, but saw none.

He reached the Land Rover. "Well?" Kari asked.

"Looks okay, but . . ." He glanced around again, surveying the landscape. No sign of anyone—not that somebody *couldn't* be in hiding nearby. "Just be careful, okay?"

"You don't trust him?" said Nina.

"Christ, no. I'm just not sure exactly how *much* I don't trust him. Okay, Hafez, you wait out here. Any trouble, sound the horn."

"I will." Hafez reached under the dashboard and pulled out a revolver, which he placed on his lap.

Chase opened the door for Nina, Castille doing the same for Kari. "I've got to say, I'm a bit nervous about all the guns," Nina told Chase.

"What? Thought you archaeology types were always running around shooting people, like Indiana Jones."

She narrowed her eyes. "Hardly. The only shooting I do is with a camera."

"I hope it stays that way," said Kari as she headed for the farmhouse, the hem of her white coat flaring out around her as she walked. Hajjar and his companions stopped outside the door of the little building, unable to take their eyes off her. "After you," she told them, gesturing inside with her own slim steel briefcase.

The interior of the farmhouse was dark, the only light coming from a single window. Although the room's contents had mostly been cleared out when its owners abandoned it, there was still a long table made from roughly hewn wood in the center.

Castille took a large glow stick from his jacket and bent it to crack the glass inside, chemicals mixing to release a vivid orange light like a fireside glow. Such a strong reaction, Nina knew, would only be able to sustain itself for fifteen minutes at most, so presumably the entire transaction was expected to be completed before then. She didn't feel comfortable about that. It meant she would have to determine the authenticity of the artifact in a rush—and if she was wrong, the Frosts would be down ten million dollars. She could do without that kind of pressure.

So she would just have to be right.

Hajjar and his bodyguards stood at one end of the table, Chase, Kari and Castille at the other. Nina found herself facing Volgan. The Russian seemed worried, fingers jittering with nervous energy.

"Are you ready to make the money transfer?" Hajjar asked.

"Once we see the piece," Kari replied coolly. "And once Dr. Wilde has confirmed that it's genuine."

"Wilde?" Volgan asked, shocked. Nina noticed he was suddenly unwilling to look directly at her. "Related to Henry and Laura Wilde?"

"Yes, they were my parents. Why?"

Volgan didn't answer, but Hajjar impatiently interrupted before Nina could ask any more questions. "The item is genuine. Here." He placed his briefcase on the table and operated the combination locks. Nina was surprised to see that his right hand was missing, replaced by a steel hook. She couldn't help staring at it.

"You think I'm a thief, perhaps?" he asked coldly.

"Uh, no, I . . ."

Hajjar shook his head. "Westerners, always with their clichés and preconceptions," he said as he opened the locks. "I lost it in a motorbike accident. I am no thief."

"Well, not the petty kind," Chase remarked cheerily. "Or so I've heard."

Hajjar paused and glared at him. "Are you trying to insult me, Mr. Chase?"

"Nah. You'd *know* if I was insulting you."

"May we see the piece now?" prompted Kari. Hajjar gave Chase a last angry glance before clicking the catch and opening the briefcase.

Inside, resting in a bed of protective foam, was the artifact.

It *had* to be made of orichalcum, Nina knew. Nothing else would have gleamed with such a unique ruddy glow.

It had been carefully and diligently polished. There was not a mark on it, no fingerprints or smudges. The only flaw was the small nick in one side, from where Volgan had carved a sample of the metal. It was without a doubt the same piece she had seen as a hologram.

And now she could see the whole thing. On its front, directly above the protrusion on the underside, was a small angled slot. And below it were markings . . .

"Can I examine it?" she asked Hajjar, her voice almost an awed whisper.

"Of course."

Nina snapped on a pair of latex surgical gloves and carefully lifted the artifact from the briefcase. It was heavier than it looked, consistent with a high gold content. An arrowhead was inscribed into the curved end of the piece, as well as a wavering line with some sort of tiny markings on either side running up its length, but what caught her attention was the lettering parallel to it. She turned the bar to catch the light from the window.

"What are they?" Kari asked.

"They're Glozel characters, or a very close variant. At least most of them are." Nina pointed out certain symbols with the tip of her gloved forefinger. "But these are something else. A different alphabet."

"Do you know which one?"

"It looks familiar, but I can't quite place it. It's another variant, though, not a standard alphabet. Maybe a regional offshoot, or something from a slightly different time period? I'd need to check my references."

"Whatever you need, you'll have," said Kari. "But is it a genuine piece?"

Nina turned the artifact over. The underside was just as she had seen in the hologram, the metal nub protruding from the upper end. Apart from that, it was devoid of markings.

Her fingertips pressed against the curved end as she turned it over again.

Sense memory . . .

The shape reminded her of something, the curve of the metal almost instinctually familiar . . .

"Dr. Wilde?" Kari lightly touched her arm, and she flinched, realizing she had been staring at the artifact for several seconds, lost in thought. "Is it genuine?"

"Uh, it certainly looks as though it is. But you should really do a metallurgical analysis to confirm it."

"I'm afraid I didn't bring my crucible and spectrograph," Kari said with a faint smile. "It's your opinion that counts."

"Okay . . ." Nina took a breath, her throat dry. Ten million dollars was a *lot* of money, more than she would see in several lifetimes. "If it's a fake, it's a very expensive one. And an extremely well-done one—there aren't many people in the world who could write in Glozel."

"You can read it?" Chase asked.

"Parts of it." Nina tapped at certain words. "'From the north,' 'mouth,' 'river.' I'd say that this line here," she indicated the marking running down the artifact's length, "is a map or guide of some sort. Directions."

Kari beamed at her for a moment before becoming businesslike again. "That's good enough for me. Mr. Hajjar, you have a sale."

"Splendid," said Hajjar, beaming as well, although considerably more rapaciously. "The money transfer?"

Kari indicated for Nina to return the artifact to its foam tray, then closed the briefcase. Nina felt a twinge of disappointment as the gleaming metal disappeared from sight. Chase slid it over to his side of the table as Kari opened her own case.

Nina had almost expected it to be full of banknotes, but instead she saw a piece of electronic hardware the size and shape of a Palm Pilot, with a chunky telephone handset connected to it. Kari picked up the phone and folded out a thick antenna, then pressed a button and placed it to her ear.

"Transfer," she said when someone answered, then, after a few seconds, "Transfer, account number 7571-1329 to account number 6502-6809. Previously arranged, authorization code two-zero-one-tango-foxtrot. Ten million dollars U.S." She paused, listening intently as her words were repeated back to her. "Yes, confirm." She pressed her right thumb against the blank screen of the device in her briefcase, then nodded at Hajjar.

"I'll have to use my *left* thumb," he smirked, waving his hook hand at Nina.

Kari waited for confirmation of his thumbprint, then nodded to Hajjar again. The Iranian looked immensely pleased with himself, turning to Volgan. "There. Your retirement fund is about to be seven million dollars better off."

"You're taking thirty percent?" Chase asked. "Bloody hell! Thought you said you weren't a thief."

Hajjar scowled, but said nothing to him, instead turning back to Kari. "Just one thing left to do, Ms. Frost . . ."

"I know," she said with a hint of impatience, before switching her attention back to the phone. "Ready for final security check." She gave Nina a knowing glance before speaking. "'In the temple they placed statues of gold; there was the god himself standing in a chariot, the charioteer of six winged horses, and of such a size that he touched the roof of the building with his head.'"

Nina immediately recognized it as a passage from *Critias*, but couldn't imagine why Kari had quoted it. Maybe it was some sort of password—but wouldn't her thumbprint and all the other codes she'd given be enough to confirm her identity?

Whatever the reason, it worked. "Thank you," said Kari, before closing the phone's antenna. She caught Nina's puzzled look. "It's a voiceprint and stress analysis system," she explained. "The latest security measure. If my voice shows that I'm under stress, that I'm being coerced, the transfer will be canceled."

"But everything was in order," said Hajjar. "Thank you, Ms. Frost." For the briefest instant, his eyes flicked towards the ceiling. "Our business is now successfully concluded." He turned to leave—

Chase's hand flashed up, his Wildey aimed right at Hajjar's head. "Hold it!"

Hajjar froze, his bodyguards following suit as Castille whipped out his own gun and pointed it at them. "What is this?" he hissed.

"Mr. Chase?" Kari asked, concerned.

"Where's the bug?" Chase demanded. "That was a trigger phrase, you've got someone listening to us."

"I don't—"

"Tell me where the bug is, or I'll kill you." He pulled back the gun's hammer with an emphatic click.

Hajjar looked up again, breathing heavily through his clenched teeth. "On that beam."

Chase nodded to Castille, who hopped onto the table and ran his hand along a roof beam. He jumped down a few seconds later with a small black box in one hand. "Transmitter."

Nina looked between them in confusion. "What's going on?"

"It's a setup," said Chase. "He was going to wait until the money was transferred, then keep the thing for himself. Guess that proves it's genuine, anyway." He looked back at Hajjar, his gun fixed on his face. "How many men have you got out there?"

"The only man I have out there is my pilot," Hajjar snarled.

The bright red dot of a laser sight appeared on Chase's chest, followed a moment later by another, twin beams shining through the grubby window. From outside came the sound of running footsteps.

Hajjar's sneer became a mocking grin. "But my good friend Captain Mahjad of the Iranian army has about twenty soldiers with him."

Nina jumped back in fright as the door burst open. Four uniformed men rushed in, rifles raised.

"Well," said Chase, "buggeration and fuckery."

FIVE

After confiscating the group's belongings, the soldiers directed their prisoners outside at the point of their rifles, locally made copies of the German Heckler and Koch G3. Hajjar followed with the briefcase containing the artifact, a gloating smile on his pudgy face.

Chase saw Hafez kneeling with his hands behind his head by the Land Rover, all its doors wide open. Two more soldiers guarded him. Other troops surrounded the building. He immediately realized what had happened: the soldiers had been hiding at the top of the steep slope above the farmhouse, using ropes to make a fast descent.

He saw that a couple of the Iranians were carrying Russian-made Dragunov sniper rifles, equipped with laser sights as well as telescopic scopes. That explained why Hafez hadn't gotten off a warning. Being pinned under the needlelike line of a laser, with the knowledge that a high-velocity bullet could explode against the glowing red spot in an instant, encouraged a person to keep very, very still and quiet.

"I'm sorry, Eddie," said Hafez. "There were too many of them." One of the guards kicked him.

"I think we all bollocked things up this time," Chase

replied. The possibility of Hajjar enlisting military backup hadn't even occurred to him. The dealer's corruption spread much further than he'd thought.

In the distance he spotted a dull brown truck rumbling up the dirt road. It must have been parked out of sight, responding to a summons now that the soldiers' mission had been completed.

Hajjar approached an officer, hanging the briefcase from his hook as he shook hands. "Captain Mahjad! May I introduce my . . . business associates?"

Mahjad, a lanky, bearded man, grinned at the group of captives. "A pleasure. So, Failak, what do you want done with them?"

"The blond woman and the Russian, I'm going to take them with me."

Mahjad leered at Kari, who shot him an icy look in return. "I don't know about him, but I can definitely see why you'd take her."

"It's nothing like that. Although . . ." Hajjar looked thoughtful, then laughed again. "As for the others, I don't really care. Just as long as they don't come after me."

"Not a problem. The Ministry of Culture has been cracking down on foreigners trying to steal our treasures. They should get at least twenty years in prison—if they live to reach trial."

"I'll leave that up to you." Hajjar snapped his fingers at his bodyguards. "Handcuff them," he said, indicating Kari and Volgan.

"Where are you taking her?" Chase shouted. One of the soldiers slammed the butt of his rifle into his back, sending him reeling.

"To my home. Don't worry, nothing will happen to her. As long as her father cooperates."

"You're going to *ransom* me?" Kari asked, appalled.

One of the bodyguards pulled her hands behind her back, clicking a pair of handcuffs around her wrists.

"I think another ten million dollars seems fair, don't you?" said Hajjar to Chase, ignoring her. "If I had such a beautiful daughter, I'd think it was a bargain." He dropped his voice to a more menacing tone. "To make sure she *stayed* beautiful."

"You do anything to her," Chase growled, "and I'll kill you."

"Is that the best threat you can come up with?" scoffed Hajjar.

"*After* you beg me to."

Hajjar shrugged. "Better. I'll worry about it . . . in twenty years."

"Mr. Chase," said Kari as the bodyguards pulled her and Volgan away, "remember what you were hired for. Protect Dr. Wilde. *That's* your top priority."

"But—"

"Do you understand?"

Chase nodded reluctantly. "Yeah."

"Good." She turned her attention to the helicopter, then to Hajjar. "You only have five seats, and there's six of us. Or are you going to dangle from the skids by your hook?"

"You can ride on Yuri's lap," said Hajjar with a lech- erous smirk. "He deserves a last pleasure . . . before I sell him back to Qobras."

The blood drained from Volgan's face. "What? *No!* No, Failak, we had a deal!"

"And I'm sure Qobras will have a better one. Why should I settle for three million dollars when I can keep all *ten* million, and have Qobras pay me even more to get you and the artifact back?"

"*No!*" Volgan shrieked. Even though his hands were

cuffed behind his back, he threw himself against the bodyguard holding him, slamming him off balance.

The other bodyguard whirled, releasing his hold on Kari's arm—as the Russian drove a kick deep into his stomach. Volgan jumped over the bodyguard as he fell, and ran awkwardly for the farmhouse. The soldiers overcame their surprise, weapons coming up.

"Don't shoot!" cried Hajjar. Mahjad looked startled, then urgently repeated the order.

The soldiers paused for an instant, caught between trained instinct and the orders of their superior officer.

The instant was all Chase needed.

He grabbed the barrel of the nearest soldier's rifle, jerking it out of the startled man's grip and twisting his wrist to flip the gun over onto its back as his other hand stabbed at the trigger.

He felt the heat of the bullet through the metal barrel as the gun fired, scorching his palm. The soldier lurched backwards, the bullet ripping right through him and showering the Land Rover with blood and mashed lung tissue.

Before any of the other soldiers could react, Chase flipped the gun over again, jamming the selector switch to full auto and unleashing bursts of fire at the soldiers with the Dragunovs. They fell. If the remaining soldiers fired at him, they ran the risk of hitting their own comrades, which would deter them for a moment.

"Nina!" he shouted. She stared uncomprehendingly at him, totally unprepared for his lethal flurry of action. He reached out to grab her arm, but one of the soldiers reacted more quickly than his companions and tackled Nina to the ground. Chase couldn't shoot him without hitting her—

He immediately changed tactics. "Hugo!" he yelled, jerking his head at the Land Rover. Castille was already following his example, grappling with a soldier for his rifle.

Another soldier smashed his rifle onto the back of his skull. Castille collapsed.

Chase snapped his head around at the sound of a pained gasp. Hafez was trying to get to his feet, but one of the guards kicked him back down. The other was aiming at Chase with his G3—

Chase dived into the back of the Land Rover. He had just enough time to slam the door shut before the window blew apart, bullets chunking through the 4×4's aluminum skin.

"Eddie!" Nina screamed as the soldier pulled her to her feet, hauling her roughly away from the Land Rover. She struggled and kicked, but he was too strong for her to escape. Another two men pinned Castille to the ground.

The soldier kept firing, emptying his entire ammo clip into the vehicle.

For a moment, everything was silent. Then he grabbed the handle of the bullet-riddled door and yanked it open.

The Land Rover was empty. The soldier stared in confusion. Then he heard a faint noise and looked down.

In the rear footwell, the hand grenade rolled to a stop.

He opened his mouth to scream—

The scream never emerged. The grenade exploded, blasting him backwards in a storm of jagged metal.

The soldiers holding Castille were caught in the blast, as was Hafez's remaining guard. But their prisoners, flat on the ground, escaped unharmed as the deadly shrapnel shot over them.

Lying against the rear wheel on the other side of the Land Rover, Chase clamped his hands over his ears as the door above him was blown from its hinges. He watched it whirl away like a giant square Frisbee and crash down on the slope below.

Chase looked under the vehicle. The nearest soldiers were all either injured or dead, but the others were recovering from the shock of the explosion. At least ten of them, all armed.

All angry.

Kari's long white coat immediately caught his eye by the helicopter. One of Hajjar's bodyguards held her, and the Iranian captain was covering her with his pistol as he screamed orders to his men.

Nina—

The soldier who'd tackled her had his arms wrapped around her in a bear hug as he dragged her backwards.

No way he could risk a shot. And his G3 only had a few bullets left anyway.

Mind racing, he assessed the situation.

Nina was relatively safe for the moment, even as a captive, but it wouldn't take long for one of the Iranians to get the idea to use her as a hostage, forcing him to surrender. Hajjar and Captain Mahjad spoke English— and they had heard Kari order him to protect Nina above everything else . . .

Which meant that to protect her right now, he had to *abandon* her.

He grabbed the G3 and crouched in the cover of the smoking Land Rover as he backed away—then sprang up and fired his remaining bullets in a sweep. He was deliberately aiming high, not trying to hit anyone but instead forcing them to duck, confusing them as he ran, sprinting for the steep slope down to the valley floor.

Rifles crackled behind him as the solders opened fire.

The valley opened out below, the lazy curve of the railway lines vanishing into the tunnel.

A bullet hissed past his head, close enough for him to

feel its shockwave. He jumped, clearing the edge of the slope, and flew through the air to land on—

The Land Rover's door!

It skidded down the hill in a flurry of dust and gravel, Chase clinging to it like a child on a speeding sled.

He knew it wouldn't take him far—the slope was too rocky. But he didn't need it to. He just needed the extra yards it could give him before the soldiers reached the edge and fired down after him.

A boulder loomed ahead, poking out of the hillside like a bad tooth. Chase jumped again, throwing himself sideways and hitting the ground hard as the door smashed into the rock and crumpled like cardboard. He tried to use his feet to brake himself, but he was moving too fast and tumbled helplessly down the hill. Grit spat into his face, blinding him.

Gunfire from above!

Something whipped against him. Not a bullet, but plants, tough grass and scrubby bushes. That meant he was near the bottom. But how near?

He forced his eyes open against the stinging dust . . . and saw the ground drop out from under him.

With a yell that echoed all the way back to the top of the slope, Chase fell into empty space.

w

One of the soldiers winced. "Ow. That'll hurt." The foreigner had shot right over the top of the entrance to the railway tunnel and plunged out of sight onto the tracks.

"Serves the bastard right!" snarled the man next to him. Special forces or not, a drop that high onto the unforgiving steel and concrete of a railway line would break a bone or two, maybe even kill a man.

Mahjad strode over to them and looked down. The

Englishman's route down the steep slope was easy to follow, a trail of drifting dust winding down to the tunnel. "Get the ropes," he ordered. "I want three men to go down there and find him. If he's dead, take his body to the train yard. If he's alive . . ." his face twisted with a mix of anger and sadistic humor, "take his body to the train yard."

"Sir!" The soldiers saluted, three of them preparing to descend the slope.

Mahjad walked back to Hajjar. The fleeing Russian had been recaptured, and now stood under guard with the other prisoners. "This is all your fault!" Mahjad snapped, jabbing a finger into Hajjar's face. "You didn't tell me he was some sort of trained assassin!"

"I didn't know myself!" Hajjar blustered. "I thought he was just an ex-soldier she'd hired as a bodyguard!" He gestured at Kari, who glared back with chilly disdain.

"I've got four dead men and another three wounded! How am I going to explain this? *How?*"

Hajjar licked his lips nervously, sweating even in the cool breeze. "Perhaps . . . a donation of some sort to their families? And their commanding officer?"

"I'll tell you what sort of donation, Failak," snarled Mahjad. He paused for a moment. Hajjar's nervousness grew. "A *very large* one."

"I'll make the arrangements as soon as I return to my home," said Hajjar, relieved.

Mahjad regarded him coldly. "You'd better."

"You have my word. Now," he said, giving Kari another look, "I have to leave. There's some urgent business I need to take care of—and it would be best if we're not seen together at the scene of this . . . unfortunate incident."

Mahjad nodded reluctantly, and his soldiers drew

Nina, Castille and Hafez away while the others boarded the Jet Ranger. Volgan, now too scared to protest, sat in the center rear seat, one of Hajjar's bodyguards on either side, while Kari was forced onto his lap. With her hands cuffed behind her back, there was little she could do to resist as the seat belt was tightly secured around her waist, effectively tying her to Volgan.

Hajjar took the copilot's seat. "Oh, Ms. Frost," he said, reaching back to take her chin in his one hand, "no need to look like that. You won't be mistreated—you're far too valuable. As long as your father cooperates, at least."

Kari jerked out of his grasp. "You've made the worst mistake of your life, Hajjar."

He gave her a smug smile. "Now, now. There's no need to make this unpleasant. Just sit back and enjoy the ride. And if you want to help Yuri *relax* . . ." he glanced at the ashen-faced Volgan behind her, "then by all means wriggle about. I'm sure he'll appreciate it. The last pleasure of the condemned man, hmm?" The smile turned cold. "Just don't wriggle too much. It would be unfortunate if my bodyguards thought you were trying to escape and shot you." One of the men poked the muzzle of his gun into her side for emphasis.

"I'll keep that in mind," she sneered.

"Good!" Hajjar turned to his pilot. "Let's go."

ᴡᴡ

Nina watched in shock and disbelief as the helicopter took off and wheeled away. From New York academia to Iranian prisoner in the space of two days—what the hell had happened to her life?

And now Kari was being held for ransom, and as for Chase . . .

She couldn't understand much of what the soldiers

were saying, but from their unhurried pace it was clear they thought he was dead.

A large military truck arrived at the farmhouse. As the soldiers shoved her, Castille and Hafez aboard, she had to fight not to cry.

ᴠᴠ

Chase took a last deep breath and braced himself.

He had just managed to twist around as he plunged over the edge and caught a small outcrop of rock with one hand. Dangling like a puppet, it took him almost a minute to bring up his other hand and fully secure himself.

Not that it helped.

He was hanging directly above one of the railway lines. The tips of his toes were a good eighteen feet above the track, which even for an SAS man wasn't a drop to be taken lightly, and there was absolutely nothing to soften the fall. About the only way his landing could be any nastier would be if he were over a bed of spikes.

But he had no choice. Shouts and a warning rattle of stones skittering down the slope told him he was about to have company.

So—*drop!*

Even though he was ready for the impact, bending his knees and rolling, pain still ripped through his legs as if they'd been hit with an iron bar. He fell heavily, gasping in agony as the unyielding metal of the railway track smashed against his chest. Fighting through the pain, he forced himself to crawl off the line.

Damage assessment. Both legs hurt like hell, and his left ankle had taken the brunt of the impact, but nothing was broken. He knew what *that* felt like.

He sat up, grimacing at another throb of pain from

his ribs. On the plus side, it would have been a lot worse if he hadn't been wearing his tough leather jacket. After a few deep breaths, focusing himself, Chase got to his feet—

And let out a roar of fury.

It wasn't so much an expression of agony as a way to *release* it, to control it. Some of the SAS's pain management techniques were rough and ready—but they worked.

"Oh, *now* I'm pissed off," he rasped.

A noise from above attracted his attention. Not the soldiers coming after him, but Hajjar's helicopter, disappearing over a ridge. The hook-handed bastard was taking Kari away, planning to force a ransom from her father.

What to do?

Kari Frost was his employer—and he doubted her father would be very understanding if he let anything happen to her. A failure like that would probably end his career on the spot. Nobody would ever hire him again.

On the other hand, as his employer she had given him a very specific order—the reason he'd been hired in the first place.

Protect Nina Wilde.

And if the soldiers had her, they probably had Castille and Hafez as well. The truck he'd seen could only go one way, back down the road past the train yard.

The train yard . . .

If he could get there in time, he might be able to find another vehicle, a way to follow them.

And rescue them.

Gritting his teeth as pain jabbed through his ankle, Chase ran along the railway line.

SIX

"Don't worry," said Castille to Nina as the truck lurched down the dirt road, "we'll be okay."

"How?" she demanded, holding up her handcuffed wrists. "We've been arrested, Kari's been kidnapped, and Chase is *dead*!"

She was taken aback when both Castille and Hafez made amused noises. "Eddie has survived worse," Hafez told her.

"What could be worse than being shot at and then falling off a cliff?"

"Well, there was this time when we were in Guyana—" Castille began, before one of the soldiers shouted at him in Farsi, jabbing the gun into his stomach as a final punctuation. "Ai. It seems these idiots would prefer us not to talk."

"These idiots," snapped another soldier, "speak English too."

"But I bet they don't speak French," Castille smoothly continued in one of his native languages.

"I bet they don't!" Nina replied in kind. That earned her an angry shout from one of the soldiers, and Castille another jab in the gut.

The rest of the uncomfortable journey took place in

silence. Nina kept her eyes fixed on Castille, rather than on the bodies lying on the floor.

Eventually the truck came to a stop with a squeal of brakes. Nina blinked in the harsh daylight as the troops pulled her out.

They were at the train yard she'd seen earlier, four long parallel tracks running alongside the main lines and feeding back into them at each end. There was a short train on the nearest siding, three passenger cars headed by an idling diesel locomotive. A much longer freight train waited on another track. She could hear the bleating of sheep or goats coming from the wagons.

Captain Mahjad stood before his prisoners, hands on his hips. "What are you going to do to us?" Nina asked.

"Take you to trial for the murder of my men," he said. "You'll be found guilty, and put to death."

"*What!*" she shrieked. "But we didn't even do anything!"

"Don't argue," said Castille. "He's crooked, you won't be able to talk him—" A soldier savagely swung his rifle and smashed it into Castille's back, dropping him to the ground.

"You're lucky I don't just shoot you right now and say you were trying to escape," snarled Mahjad. For a moment he seemed to be considering it, but then he issued more orders. The soldiers pulled Nina and Hafez to the train's front car, another pair hauling Castille up by his arms and dragging him after them.

The car's interior was of an old-fashioned design, a narrow corridor running down one side with a row of eight-seater compartments on the other. Castille and Hafez were shoved into the rearmost compartment, four soldiers going in with them. Nina's guard started to push her in after them, but Mahjad said something to him. The guard suppressed a nasty smile, then brought her to the compartment at the far end of the corridor. It looked as though it had once been the first-class section, but those days were long gone, the seats threadbare and grubby.

"Sit down," said Mahjad, following her in. Nina thought about refusing, but before she could open her mouth he forced her down onto the seat by the window, then sat facing her. The soldier took up station outside the door, visible through its narrow window.

She thought Mahjad was going to speak, but instead he simply sat there, his unreadable gaze slowly passing over her body. She touched her hair self-consciously; the movement instantly caught his attention, eyes locking onto her face.

Nina grew horribly aware that not only was she alone in the compartment with Mahjad, but also that the soldier outside would undoubtedly turn a blind eye to anything that happened.

Or worse still . . . take part.

She shuddered. Mahjad picked up on the tiny motion, one corner of his mouth creeping upwards malevolently as the train jolted, then started to move.

\\\\

Long forced runs were nothing new to Chase. But doing one in this much pain was something else entirely.

Every fifty yards he looked back at his pursuers. By the time they reached the tunnel, he had built up a lead of about four hundred yards. But they were catching up: younger, fresher, unhurt.

He was still out of the effective range of their G3 rifles, and from what he knew about the training of the average Iranian soldier, he would be at low risk of being hit even once he entered it. But eventually they would get close enough to bring him down. Unless he reached the train yard first.

What he would do when he got there was still a mystery.

Wing it, he decided.

Waiting on the sidings were a freight train and a shorter passenger train. Parked next to the latter was a military truck.

Adrenaline pumped into his system, revitalizing him. It was the same truck he'd seen heading for the farmhouse! It must have brought the soldiers—and presumably their prisoners—back to the yard . . . which meant they were going to board the train.

Chase quickly looked back. The three Iranians were two hundred yards behind and still gaining. That wouldn't give him much time when he reached the yard to—

Shit!

The passenger train was moving! The gravelly rasp of the diesel's engine reached him, dirty exhaust fumes spewing into the mountain air.

He was too late! Considering the state of the road above, he had no chance of keeping pace with the train even if he stole the truck.

But somehow he had to find a way to rescue Nina, to say nothing of his friends.

The train was still moving slowly to negotiate the points that would put it onto the main line. One by one the cars snaked through the turn. Chase pushed himself harder, ignoring the pain. Maybe there was still a chance that he could catch up . . .

There wasn't. He had barely reached the points at one end of the yard by the time the train pulled out of the other, the locomotive's noise rising to a throaty roar as it accelerated.

Now his options were the truck . . . *or the other train*.

A lone soldier stood by the back of the truck, watching the train depart. He heard footsteps crunching over ballast behind him and looked around—taking a flying kick right in his chest. Chase followed up the move by punching the fallen man in the face.

Grabbing the soldier's gun, Chase glanced back down the track at his pursuers, then ran towards the front of the freight train.

He heard the first bullet hit one of the wooden trucks just before the crack of the gunshot reached him. Animals bleated in fear. He dropped and rolled underneath the nearest truck, emerging on the other side. He had a few moments of cover, but it wouldn't take long for the soldiers to reach the back of the train and run around it.

The locomotive was just ahead, a dirty slab of metal with a cab at each end. But there was something he had to do first . . .

He ducked into the gap between the loco and the first truck. The coupler was a standard "knuckle" type; he pulled the lever to unlock it with a heavy clunk. Now, when the engine set off, it would automatically disconnect and leave the rest of the train behind.

He looked back down the length of the train. Two of the soldiers had followed him down the left side, which meant there was only one on the right. He jumped up onto the coupler and leapt across to the other side of the truck, whipping around its corner with his gun ready. The third soldier was racing towards him.

In a single smooth movement, Chase dropped to one knee, took aim and fired. Three shots cracked from his rifle, but he scored a hit with the very first one. The soldier tumbled to the ground.

Chase ran to the front of the locomotive. A head

popped through the open door, the driver leaning out to see what was going on. He figured it out very quickly.

"Afternoon," Chase panted, pointing his gun up at the driver. "I need to borrow your train."

The shocked man raised his hands, looked around desperately, then turned and with an ululating shriek threw himself out of the other side of the cab.

"At least I asked," Chase muttered as he climbed the steps. The cramped cab was empty, the rattling chug of the engine at idle echoing from behind a narrow access door in the back wall. Through the windscreen he saw the fleeing driver running towards a signal cabin near the end of the sidings.

The largest lever on the control panel had to be the throttle. Which meant that the next largest was the brake.

He hoped.

Chase pushed the throttle lever forward experimentally. The loco lurched as the engine noise rose—but the brakes held it in place.

He released what he thought was the brake lever. There was a piercing metallic squeal, and the loco jolted. He immediately rammed the throttle forward. The big diesel engines behind him shrilled, needles on the control panel's gauges shooting into their red zones, but he ignored them and looked out of the open door.

The engine had indeed disconnected from the rest of the train, so at least he wouldn't be dragging several hundred animals along with him. The running soldiers had almost reached the front of the first wagon—

He brought the G3 around and switched it to full auto, unleashing a blaze of fire down the side of the locomotive. One of the men dropped instantly, a cloud of blood spraying from his chest. The other hurled himself onto the track in front of the stationary wagons. Chase's line of fire was blocked by the boxy engine's body.

He grunted in annoyance, then returned his attention to the controls and the track ahead. The first set of points was approaching fast.

Chase knew from playing with his dad's model railway as a kid that points were supposed to be taken at low speed. In fact, he'd been banned from the train set after his curiosity about what would happen if they *weren't* caused a Great Western express to take a flying diversion to the floor.

But he didn't have much choice—he had to catch up with Nina's train.

Chase braced himself. The whole locomotive rocked as it crashed through the points too fast, metal screaming against metal. The violent move was repeated as the six wheels of the rear truck ground over the switch as well. Then the loco straightened, but the next points were already coming up fast.

\/\/

Another howl of metal from beneath the engine set Chase's teeth on edge, but he kept pushing the throttle forward even as the sharp turn threatened to pitch him out of the driver's seat.

One more set of points and he would be on the main line, following the other train. If he forced every ounce of power out of the locomotive, it shouldn't take too long to catch up—and if he judged it right, he could match speeds and automatically couple his own engine to the back of the train, then climb out of the cab and jump aboard.

Light flashed off metal ahead: something moving.

The last set of points had changed!

Chase snapped his head around to see two frightened faces staring out of the signal cabin's window as he powered past. The driver must have told the signalman to try to stop him—and now his locomotive would end up on the track parallel to the other train.

Which meant that if another train came the other way, he would plow headlong into it!

But if they thought that would stop him, they were wrong.

With a last crash of overstressed metal, Chase's locomotive thundered through the points. He slammed the throttle forward as far as it would go. The needles jumped again, but the only one he cared about was the speedometer. Thirty kilometers per hour . . . forty . . .

The tracks ahead curved back and forth as they wove through the mountains. He couldn't see the other train yet. But it couldn't be too far ahead.

Catching up with it wasn't his biggest problem.

Getting onto it was.

\/\/

Castille and Hafez exchanged looks. Both men had long experience with soldiers, and they had been watching carefully for the telltale signs of boredom and inattentiveness that almost inevitably struck during guard duty.

The soldiers watching them were showing the signs. They outnumbered their handcuffed prisoners two to one, and were armed, so they had an innate feeling of power and superiority that could easily slip into complacency. When the two men were first shoved into the compartment, the soldiers' weapons had been raised and fixed on them.

Now, they were lowered. It would only take a moment for them to be lifted again—but a moment was all Castille and Hafez needed.

They just had to wait for the right one.

∿∿

The more Nina tried to ignore Mahjad, the more she became aware of his gaze. All she could do was turn away from him and lean closer to the window, watching the mountainous landscape roll past beyond the dirty glass.

Mahjad shifted position. Nina glanced at him—and froze in horror when she saw that he was toying with Chase's Wildey.

"My life would be easier if you and your friends *had* been shot while trying to escape," he said. "Less paperwork, fewer questions from my superiors. Maybe I should just kill you all before we arrive and save myself some work." The gun slowly came around, its thick muzzle pointing at her. She cringed in her seat. "But . . . you could persuade me to change my mind. Save your friends."

"How?" Nina asked. But she already knew the answer.

"You know how," he answered, leaning back in his seat as a gloating smirk spread across his face.

"You're sick."

The smirk intensified. "I'm not an unreasonable man," he said, looking at his watch. "I'll give you a few minutes to consider it. If you choose not to accept my offer . . ." his face twisted into a malevolent grin, "I'll kill your friends. And give *you* to my men. I'm afraid they're not . . . what's the word? As *gentlemanly* as me."

Paralyzed by the sick fear churning her stomach, Nina turned away from him again, utterly lost and alone.

∿∿

The locomotive was now doing over seventy kilometers per hour, still accelerating. Chase stared intently at the view ahead, searching for the first glimpse of the other train as he powered around a long curve.

There!

About half a mile ahead, but he was gaining.

Two minutes to catch up. Maybe less.

The gap between the tracks was around ten feet. But the distance between the sides of the two trains would be smaller, as little as five feet. An easy jump.

At least, easy when the two vehicles weren't doing close to fifty miles an hour.

Chase adjusted the throttle, hanging his rifle from it by its strap to hold down the dead-man's switch. If he eased it off just before he drew alongside, then the loco should match speeds and make his jump easier. He moved to the open door and leaned out to judge the force of the wind—

And was hit from behind, his shoulder smashing agonizingly into the metal frame as the last Iranian soldier burst from the corridor connecting the front and rear cabs. *Shit! How had he gotten on the train?*

The track bed blurred past below as the soldier tried to shove Chase out of the door. One arm numbed by the impact, the only thing he could reach for support was the handrail on the outside of the engine, which made him swing even farther out of the cab.

From where he saw the headlights of another locomotive, charging straight at them!

SEVEN

The soldier's hands clamped around Chase's throat, squeezing tight and forcing him farther over the edge of the footplate.

Chase fought for breath as the other man's thumbs dug into his windpipe. It took all his strength just to hold on to the handrail, pain burning through his other arm as it hung stiffly beneath him.

And in the corner of his eye he could see the headlights of the oncoming train growing brighter.

The Iranian loomed closer, his lips pulled back into a snarl. "Die, you American bastard!"

"American?" Chase choked out. A resurgent energy pumped through his body, and his free hand shot up, smashing into the Iranian's face like a hammer. Blood squirted from the man's mashed nose as cartilage crackled under the blow. The pressure around his neck vanished immediately as the soldier jerked back, gasping in pain.

He drove one knee into the soldier's stomach. The man groaned and rolled off him, and Chase hauled himself upright. "I'm *British*, you twat!"

A horn blared.

Through the windscreen, he saw the other locomotive barreling towards them, sparks spewing from its wheels as the driver slammed on the brakes. It was towing a long train of white tanker trucks, full of fuel or chemicals.

The driver of the oncoming train flung himself from the cab. It rushed at Chase like a cannon shell, lights blazing.

Nina's train was almost alongside him. The rear car wasn't quite level, but he was out of time—

The soldier sat up—and screamed.

Chase jumped to the other track, and just caught the guardrail on the back of the open platform. All he could do was cling to the weathered metal with his fingertips as—

The locomotives collided.

Chase's engine plowed through the other, forced upwards by the impact. The bodywork of the oncoming locomotive shattered in a blizzard of metal.

Then the chassis hit the unyielding metal block of the second loco's huge diesel engine. Chase's locomotive weighed almost a hundred tons, but against the momentum of a train weighing several thousand tons moving at almost fifty miles an hour, it was like running into an iron wall.

The locomotive flipped, its back end flying up from the tracks. For one instant, it was airborne, inverted—then it crashed down on to the other loco. Both engines disintegrated under the impact. Hundreds of gallons of diesel spewed free, igniting.

The first tanker truck, filled with highly flammable fuel oil, derailed and impaled itself on mangled metal, its contents gushing out . . .

W

"Your time is up," said Mahjad. He leaned towards Nina, his malevolent smile deepening as he reached for her leg. Repulsed, she tried to pull away, but there was nowhere to go. "So, what is your—"

Another train rushed past on the other line. Mahjad glanced at it, then looked back at Nina. He opened his mouth to speak—

An explosion shook the carriage.

ᴡᴡ

In his SAS career Chase had been on the ground uncomfortably close to the targets of NATO precision air strikes—but the earthshaking blast of a thousand-pound laser-guided bomb was a mere firework compared to the colossal explosion as the first tanker blew up. The train to which he was now desperately clinging was whisking him away from it at over fifty miles per hour, but the detonation was still deafening, and the heat as the expanding fireball chased after him was enough to singe the hairs on the backs of his hands.

There was another noise, a horrific groaning as the other tankers piled into each other just a few feet from his side. They were derailing, the concertina effect of the collision wrenching them from the track.

Another explosion! The second tanker in the train went up like the first, followed a moment later by the third.

Shit!

The entire tanker train was going to blow in a chain reaction—and the explosions were rippling down the line faster than his train was moving!

If Chase didn't find cover inside in the next ten seconds, he would be completely vaporized.

Arms straining, tendons tight as steel cables, he pulled himself up with a yell that was completely drowned out by the ear-splitting booms of more tankers exploding. Forget singed hairs, he could feel his *skin* stinging as he rolled over the top of the railing and thumped onto the wooden platform. He jumped up and tugged at the handle of the door.

Locked!

The chain of explosions raced towards him, a burning wind sweeping ahead of the expanding fireballs. Chase flattened himself against the door, nowhere to go—

Suddenly he fell, landing on his stomach inside the carriage and staring straight up at the soldier who had just opened the door.

Chase rolled away from him. Caught by surprise, the soldier gawped stupidly—then looked up to see a wall of liquid fire rushing towards the back of the train.

He didn't even have time to scream as the blaze from the last tanker burst through the door, a rectangular jet of flame fanning out and swirling around the interior. Completely engulfed in fire, the soldier let out a terrible shriek of pure agony before stumbling towards Chase, arms flailing.

Chase rolled again as the inferno roiled over him, just in time to dodge the burning fuel showering from the soldier. He jumped to his feet, ignoring the Iranian as he collapsed, writhing pitifully. Now that he was on the train, he had a job to do.

W

Mahjad was stunned by the first explosion, then positively terrified as the following string of detonations got louder and closer. Nina was forgotten as he jumped up and threw the compartment door open, bellowing orders down the corridor.

She had no idea what was going on, but it sounded almost as if the train was being bombed!

Could it be Chase somehow coming after her? She

couldn't imagine *how,* but whatever was going on had Mahjad scared.

Maybe this would give her a chance to escape.

∨∨

Castille and Hafez exchanged another look as one of their startled guards opened the door, Mahjad's screaming commands reaching them from the other end of the car. This time the look was a signal, a confirmation that both were on the same wavelength.

Get ready!

∨∨

Chase opened a heavy sliding door and found himself in the corridor of an old-style compartment car, a real Hogwarts Express job. To his relief, the compartments that he passed were empty. If they'd been full of soldiers, he would have been in real trouble—

Boots thudded on the floor as men ran into the other end of the car, the connecting door thrown open with a bang. Real trouble after all.

He whipped inside the nearest compartment, sliding the door almost shut. The running footsteps clattered past: five men. He peered through the window. A soldier stood barely two feet away, back to him.

"Psst!"

The soldier looked around with a quizzical expression, which changed to one of shock in the fraction of a second before a fist smashed into his face. Chase hauled him into the compartment, giving him another punch for good measure before taking his gun. In one swift movement he flicked the G3 to full auto and darted back out into the corridor, unleashing a blaze of fire at the other soldiers. They fell.

He ejected the spent magazine, ducked back into the

compartment to take the unconscious soldier's spare mags, then slapped one into place and moved back out, gun raised. Castille, Hafez and—most important—Nina were somewhere on this train, and he was going to find them.

www

One of their guards had already left the compartment, sent by Mahjad to find out what was happening farther down the train, and now Castille and Hafez's captors looked around in surprise at the distant but unmistakable sound of automatic weapons fire.

Castille's eyes locked onto his friend's. "*Now!*"

He jumped from his seat and twisted, his cuffed hands sweeping the gun out of the grip of the soldier on his right as he drove the heel of one boot into the face of the man sitting opposite. Teeth snapped under the impact. Simultaneously, Hafez lunged forward and kicked the man on Castille's other side, sending his gun spinning into the air.

Castille straightened and twisted his upper body again, bringing up his elbow and slamming it into the throat of the man to his right. He felt something give with a horrible wet crunch.

As he turned, Hafez brought his heel down onto the remaining soldier's kneecap with an audible crack of splitting bone. The soldier howled in pain. Hafez jumped forward and grabbed his gun, clubbing him over the back of his skull. He collapsed face first onto the floor and lay there, unmoving.

The other two soldiers were in no better state. "Nice work," Hafez said, nodding at the unconscious figures.

"You too."

"Of course I could have taken the other one as well if he'd been here."

"Of course you could, old man." Castille jokingly rolled his eyes. "Now, I just hope that one of these fools has the keys to these handcuffs . . ."

ᴠᴠᴠ

Chase ran into the second car, passing the closed door of the toilet and rounding the corner into the next corridor—only to find four more soldiers charging down it, rifles raised!

He threw himself back around the corner, managing to get off a couple of shots. A scream told him he had found a target. The wooden paneling on the corridor wall blew apart, splinters flying everywhere as a storm of bullets ripped into it.

"Jesus!" He shielded his eyes from the broken wood. The awkward length of the G3 meant he would have a hard time firing blind around the corner, while his adversaries could take cover in the compartments and use their superior firepower to hold him back until their reinforcements arrived.

Or, he realized with horror, they could just do what they were about to do and toss a grenade down the corridor!

One of the men yelled the Farsi equivalent of "Fire in the hole!," the *ching* of the safety lever springing away from the body of the grenade perfectly audible as his companions stopped firing.

It would take Chase several seconds to reach cover through the heavy connecting door, by which time the grenade would have exploded—

He didn't even try. Instead, he flipped his rifle over and grabbed it by the barrel, wielding it like a club as he whirled to see the dark green ovoid arcing at him—

And hit it with the stock of the rifle, smacking it back up the corridor like a baseball player scoring a home run!

He dived back around the corner as it exploded. Every window along the corridor burst apart, shards of flying glass adding to the lethality of the blast zone as thousands of ball bearings and fragments of the grenade's steel casing tore through the carriage.

Wind from the broken windows cleared the smoke almost immediately as Chase looked back down the passageway. He could see several dead men, or at least parts of them, but there was no sign of Mahjad—presumably he was in the front carriage with the prisoners.

Turning his rifle back around, Chase hurried towards the front of the train.

\~\~

"Grenade?" asked Hafez.

"Yes."

"Eddie?"

"Definitely." Castille unlocked the Iranian's handcuffs. "Ready?"

"Always."

"Then *go!*"

Weapons raised, the two men ducked back-to-back out of the compartment. Castille faced the rear of the train, Hafez the front.

Castille saw nothing but the wooden walls of the corridor. He said, "Clear—" when two shots cracked almost simultaneously behind him. One was from Hafez's gun; the other was farther away.

Hafez lurched backwards, stumbling into Castille as a bloody hole exploded in his left thigh. At the far end of the corridor, the soldier who had been stationed outside Nina and Mahjad's compartment ducked back into its cover as Hafez's bullet blew a chunk of wood out of the door frame.

Castille grabbed his friend with his free arm and

pulled him around the corner at the end of the corridor, lowering him carefully to the floor.

Blood gushed from the wound. Hafez clamped his left hand over it. "Agh! That bastard son of a syphilitic whore *shot* me!"

From experience, Castille knew Hafez would survive the injury—if he got first aid soon. That was assuming they got through the whole experience at all . . . "Can you still shoot?"

Hafez hefted the rifle in one hand. "I'm not dead yet—and I *refuse* to die until I've blown that little bastard's balls off! Go, help Eddie!"

Castille clapped him on the shoulder and pulled open the heavy connecting doors.

w

Chase heard movement ahead. Someone was approaching from the front of the train.

He ducked into the nearest compartment. Holding his breath, he waited until he heard footsteps, then lunged out, pointing his gun.

Castille was less than ten feet away, pointing a gun right back at him.

"Edward!"

"Hugo!" Chase let out a sigh of relief. "Typical, I go to all this bloody trouble to rescue you, and you've wasted my time!"

"You know me, I got tired of waiting for your slow—"

"Don't move!" rasped a voice from behind Chase.

Chase exchanged a look with Castille. The Belgian's eyes flicked downwards. Chase gave him the tiniest nod in return.

"Drop your g—"

Chase dropped flat as Castille fired a single shot that whipped mere inches over the top of his head. From the far end of the corridor came a choked cry, followed by the thump of a body falling to the floor. Looking around, Chase saw another soldier slumped against the bullet-riddled rear wall, a gun clattering from his lifeless hand.

"You came to rescue me, I end up rescuing *you*," said the Belgian with a sly smile.

"Aw, we'll just call it evens." Chase stood again. "Can't believe he was hiding in the bog! Where's Nina?"

Castille's face became grim. "I don't know, I haven't seen her. That captain took her into another compartment. And Hafez is hurt, he's been shot."

"Where?"

"In the leg."

"No, *where* where?"

Castille turned and gestured towards the front of the train. "Down here, come on!"

They raced into the first car. Hafez was still on the floor, covering the entrance with his gun. "Eddie!" he exclaimed painfully. "Good to see you! How did you . . ."

"You heard all those explosions?"

"Yes."

"That's how. Where's Nina?"

Hafez gestured with his rifle. "I think the compartment at the far end, but the little shit who did *this* to me," he looked at his injured leg, "is covering it. Mahjad's probably in there as well."

Chase reached into one of his pockets and took out a small steel mirror, angling it so that he could see the far end of the passageway. As he'd expected, the movement attracted a couple of shots, but in the brief moment before pulling his hand back he saw all he needed. "One guy, last compartment, crouched low." He nodded at Castille. "You up for it?"

"I'll take the far side."

"Uh-uh. You got the last bad guy for me. *I'll* take the far side." Chase prepared to jump out and take up a firing position against the outer wall of the corridor. It would give him a better shooting angle—but he would also be more exposed.

"My reverse psychology works again," said Castille. He raised his rifle. "Ready?"

Chase did the same. "Fight to the end."

"Fight to the end," Castille echoed.

Chase reached up and yanked the communication cord.

The entire train shook violently as the emergency brakes slammed on, the wheels squealing over the track. Bracing himself, Chase waited for it to come to a standstill . . .

"And, *go!*"

Castille leaned around the corner and took aim. The soldier, still recovering from the sudden deceleration, saw him and emerged from his cover to take a shot. At the same moment, Chase sprang out and slammed against the opposite wall, dividing his quarry's attention.

The rifles of both the former commandos barked at once. Before he even had a chance to fire, the soldier was dead, flung back into the compartment like a rag doll.

Chase heard Nina shriek in fright. "Come on!" he ordered, racing down the corridor. Castille followed.

The compartment door was jammed open by the soldier's body. Chase didn't stop running, instead diving forward just before he reached the door and landing in a perfect roll on the far side. A pistol shot punched a hole through the window inches behind him.

He'd glimpsed the compartment's interior as he dived past, and signaled silently with one hand to Castille as he regained his footing. One hostage, one bad guy, standing. Go in three, two, *one*—

Both men whipped around the door, rifles snapping onto their target.

Mahjad stood with Nina in front of him, left arm wrapped around her waist, his army pistol pointed awkwardly at the door. His right hand held Chase's Wildey, the muzzle pressed against her temple.

Nina was shaking. "Eddie!"

"Drop your guns!" Mahjad yelled. "I'll count to three. If you don't drop your guns by then, I'll—"

Chase and Castille exchanged lightning-fast glances.

"Three!" Chase snapped.

The two bullets hit Mahjad's forehead barely a centimeter apart. The back of his skull blew out, the light in the room instantly taking on a scarlet tinge as the window behind him was splattered with gore. His body dropped to its knees, then slumped backwards and hit the wall with a sticky thud.

"Only amateurs talk," Chase said to a nod of agreement from Castille, before turning his attention to Nina. Worryingly, she hadn't responded in any way to the shooting, simply standing there. "Dr. Wilde?" She stared blankly at him. "Nina!"

She blinked. "What?"

"Nina," he repeated, "keep your eyes on me, okay? Just keep looking at me, and take a step forward."

"Okay . . ." she replied numbly, taking the step. Emotion began to return to her face—but not fear or shock. Instead, it was almost bafflement. "Why do I have to look at you?"

"Why, what's *wrong* with looking at me?"

She took another step. "Well, er . . ."

Chase pouted. "Aw, thanks!"

"Nothing! No, there's nothing *wrong* with your face!"

She waved her hands in frantic apology. "I just wanted to know why you want me to keep looking at you."

He took hold of her hands, then quickly whisked her out of the compartment, stepping over the body of the soldier. "I just didn't want you to see the guy with half his head missing, that's all!"

She glanced down at the soldier, whose leg was sticking out into the corridor. "What, as opposed to the guy with the sucking chest wounds who just got blown away right in front of me?"

Chase shook his head. "Can't please some people . . ."

"Oh my God!" she suddenly shrieked, the full impact of what had just happened finally hitting her. "You shot him while he had a gun to my head! What if his finger had twitched or something? He could have killed me!"

Castille emerged from the compartment, handing Chase his Wildey before using the key to unlock Nina's handcuffs. "Actually, that hardly ever happens."

"Not if you get 'em in the head," Chase added. "Hit them in the body, that's a different story. Hydrostatic shock, muscle spasms . . . But a clean head shot, almost never. He wouldn't—"

Bang!

Nina shrieked.

"Ah," said Castille apologetically, looking back into the compartment to see smoke rising from the barrel of Mahjad's pistol, "he *was* a twitcher. I should have taken his other gun as well, n'est-ce pas?"

Nina glared at Chase. "I said *almost* never," he complained as he checked his gun, then slid it back into its holster beneath his jacket. "Anyway, the trigger pull on a Wildey's a lot more than that crappy little Chinese pistol he had . . . and why are we even talking about this? We need to get out of here!"

"How?" Nina demanded as she rubbed her sore

wrists. "We're still stuck in the middle of Iran! And what about Kari?"

"I'm working on that." Chase glanced down at the dead soldier. "Is he the guy who had all our stuff?"

Castille nodded, pulling a satchel from the body. "Here."

Chase quickly rummaged through it, taking out a mobile phone. "Here we go! Just hope I remembered to charge the battery."

"What are you going to do?" Nina asked.

He smiled. "I'm going to phone a friend."

EIGHT

Kari paced across the tiny room. Hajjar's home, she'd seen from the helicopter, was no mere house in the country. Perched on a crag in the Zagros mountains, it was a mixture of palace and fortress, accessible only by air or along a single winding road.

And like any self-respecting fortress, it had its own dungeons.

No dank medieval cells here, though. The building's overwrought architecture told Kari that it had been constructed some three decades earlier, bankrolled by somebody with lots of money, no taste and a domineering ego. That suggested the former shah of Iran. Some kind of retreat, a fortified Camp David with high walls and ridiculously ostentatious design.

Whatever its original purpose, it was now Hajjar's domain, and Kari got the feeling she and Yuri Volgan were far from the first occupants of the dungeons.

Volgan, in the next cell, was being little help. Hajjar's betrayal had sent him into a state of shock, and the mere mention of Qobras caused him to panic.

She turned her mind to Hajjar. He was playing an extremely dangerous game by trying to ransom her, almost certainly unaware of just *how* dangerous. Her father would move heaven and earth to get her back safely . . . but there was no way he would let the matter end there once she had been returned.

And nor would she.

She wondered how long it would be before Hajjar summoned them. Presumably he was trying to contact Qobras and her father, to make his financial demands of them both.

She had to use that time to attempt an escape.

"Excuse me," she said, walking to the cell door and addressing the guard sitting outside. "I need some help."

The guard frowned. "What?"

"I need to . . . you know." She wriggled her hips, hands still cuffed behind her back. *"Go."*

"And?"

"And, I was hoping you could take me." The guard walked to the door, running his gaze over her figure. Kari gave him a look of innocent pleading. "Please?"

The heavyset, bearded man smirked. "Let me guess. You'll ask me to open your coat for you, and then help you with those tight leather trousers, and I'll get all hot and excited because I'm a repressed Iranian man faced with a beautiful blond woman, and then you'll ask me to take off your handcuffs, and I'll do it because I'm thinking with my dick, and *then* you'll do some fancy martial arts to knock me out and escape. Is that about right?"

Kari shot him a sour glare. "You could have just said no."

The guard laughed and returned to his seat. "I don't get paid all this money to be an idiot. Nice try, though."

Annoyed, Kari turned her back on him. Now all she could think about was what to do when she needed to use the toilet for real.

With Chase and Castille carrying the wounded Hafez, his leg hurriedly bandaged, they made their escape from the train.

Nina had no idea where they were going, or what Chase planned to do when they got there. His phone conversation had been entirely in Arabic, and in his rush to get away from the train before Iranian forces arrived he hadn't been forthcoming with additional information.

The terrain was less severe than the area where they had met Hajjar, but it was still slow going, especially with an injured man. Fortunately, there was also more vegetation, and by the time Nina heard the first buzz of an approaching helicopter, they were in the cover of a wood half a mile from the railway line.

"So where *are* we going?" she asked. "Who's this friend that you called? And how's he going to find us? We're in the middle of nowhere!"

Despite his pain, Hafez managed a smile. "Eddie has many friends," he said. "All over the world."

Nina looked across at Chase. "Even in Iran, where you've supposedly never been before?"

"Hey, I'm a popular guy," he said with a shrug.

"His reputation precedes him," added Castille.

"I'm sure it does. But if I can butt into your mutual admiration society, how about letting me in on your plan?"

"Well," said Chase, "first thing is to get a lift out of here. There's a road about a mile to the south. Someone's going to pick us up."

Nina surveyed the unfamiliar landscape. "How's your friend going to find us? You don't even know where we are!"

"I just described the landmarks. Easy enough to find 'em on a map."

"Really?"

"It's not hard; basic stuff. Then . . . we go and get Ms. Frost."

"You know where she is?" Castille asked.

"Hajjar's got a little country cottage about thirty miles from here. We'll drop in and say hello."

"I've heard about it," warned Hafez. "Not an easy place to get into."

"We've gotten into worse," Castille remarked cheerily. "Like that time in the Congo—"

"Hugo," Chase said, waving a finger. Castille made an "oh, right" noise and stopped talking.

"Let me guess," said Nina. "Another country where you've never officially been?"

Chase cocked a conspiratorial eyebrow. "Something like that."

They continued through the woods. The trees eventually thinned out, revealing a dirt road ahead. "Is this it?" asked Nina.

Chase scanned the area. "Should be. We need to look out for a stream running down from . . ." He pointed up at a nearby hill. "Down from there. That's where she said she'd meet us."

"*She*, huh?" Nina asked.

"What's the matter, Doc?" Chase replied. "Jealous?"

"Oh, totally," she replied, clapping a theatrical hand to her heart. Castille and Hafez chuckled. Chase snorted and led them down the road.

After another few minutes, they saw a vehicle ahead, a battered old van. Chase directed everyone back into the cover of the trees. "Wait here," he said.

Nina watched as he slipped through the woods, moving with a lightness and agility that was almost comically at odds with his stocky build. The closer he got to the van, the lower he crouched, to the point where she practically lost sight of him. He paused ten yards from his target, then rushed over, disappearing behind it.

She realized Castille had drawn his gun, and even Hafez had armed himself with one of the rifles they'd taken from the train. "Just in case," the Belgian assured her.

No sign of movement. They waited anxiously as the seconds ticked by . . . then Chase reappeared and waved.

"It's safe," Castille said, putting away his gun.

"What if somebody's got him at gunpoint?" asked Nina.

"He would have held his thumb against his hand."

"You guys love your little tricks and codes, don't you?" she said, amused.

"It keeps us alive." He lifted Hafez, Nina helping to support him as they started towards the van.

When they reached it, Chase was talking to someone inside the cab. "Everyone," he announced, "I'd like you to meet a very good friend of mine who's going to help us get our arses out of here. This is Shala Yazid."

A young woman of about twenty-five stepped down from the van. She was extremely attractive—and also extremely pregnant.

"Oh my," said Castille, unable to hold in a smirk. "This, I was not expecting. Something you forgot to tell us about your last visit, Edward?"

"You probably remember Hugo Castille," Chase said, annoyed. "He was that very stupid Belgian with *no manners*."

Shala smiled. "Of course I remember him. Although you had a . . ." She tapped her upper lip. "A mustache?"

"Yeah, and we're all glad that's gone."

"Bonjour," said Castille, with a half-bow. "And congratulations! I take it you married since I saw you last?"

"To a wonderful man," she answered, beaming.

To Nina, Chase seemed momentarily put out, before recovering and introducing the others. "This is Hafez," he said, "who's been in better nick—"

"It is only a scratch!" Hafez insisted.

"—and the most important woman in my life right now, Dr. Nina Wilde."

Shala gave Chase a look of delight. "You are married?"

"No!" Nina gasped.

"Bloody hell, could you say that any quicker?" Chase said with mock offense before turning back to Shala. "No, I'm her bodyguard. And God, her body needs a lot of guarding."

"And you want to take her to Failak Hajjar?" asked Shala. "It will need even more."

"I don't *want* to take her to him, we only just escaped from the bugger's mates. But he's kidnapped my boss. We need to rescue her."

"It will take an hour to get there," Shala said. "Perhaps longer. I have a radio scanner in the van; there is a lot of police and military activity. Your doing?"

"Uh, yeah." Chase rubbed his neck. "I sort of . . . crashed a train. Or two."

"Oh, *Eddie!*" She batted a fist against his arm. "You are a wonderful man, and I appreciate everything you have done for my family—but do you *have* to destroy huge parts of my country every time you come here?"

"Hey, no civvies got hurt!" he protested. "Probably. I'm *pretty* sure the other driver bailed out okay . . ."

Shala shook her head in irritation, then looked at Nina. "Everything he touches is destroyed! He is ten years older than me, and he behaves like my little brother with his toys!"

"Mm-hmm," Nina replied, nodding in agreement. Her tone became mischievous. "So how do you know

Eddie? He keeps claiming that he's never been to Iran. Officially, that is."

"My family is, shall we say, no friend of the current regime," Shala answered. "So we have provided help to undercover operations carried out by . . ." she smiled at Chase and Castille, "certain gentlemen."

"Such as sabotaging the heavy water plant at Arak," said Castille, smiling back.

Chase let out a series of loud fake coughs. "*Classified!*" he hacked. Castille's smile became a sheepish grin. "Anyway," Chase said impatiently, "we need to get moving. Hugo, you and the doc put Hafez in the back of the van. Did you bring the medical kit?" Shala nodded. "Great. We'll patch him up on the move. Don't suppose you're the medical kind of doc, Doc?"

"No, and please stop calling me that."

"Whatever you say, Dr. Wilde."

"Better."

"If you two are not married . . . you should be," Shala said with a smile, stunning them both into silence as Castille and Hafez burst out laughing.

ᴡᴡ

Kari looked up as another guard, armed with an MP-5 submachine gun, arrived. "Hajjar wants them."

The bearded guard grinned at Kari through the bars. "If you're lucky, maybe Hajjar will let you go to the toilet. I'm sure *he'd* love to help you with your clothes!"

She didn't deign to respond, waiting impassively as they unlocked the door.

ᴡᴡ

Shala pulled the van over at the side of a mountain road. "There," she said, pointing.

Chase craned his neck to look. "Wow. That's not what I expected."

Nina followed his gaze. Up on the top of a steep rocky slope was a very incongruous building. "God, who designed that? Walt Disney?"

"The shah had it built," said Shala. "It was one of his summer palaces, but he only visited it a few times before the revolution. After that, the mullahs used it as a retreat, until Hajjar bought it from the government."

"It looks like a cartoon," Nina observed. The building was practically a parody of a Persian palace, its upper levels crammed with minarets and domes. "I guess the shah didn't have much taste."

"I *was* going to say I thought it looked cool," Chase remarked, "but I won't bother now." He surveyed the fortress through binoculars. "How do you get up to it?"

"From the outside, you can only get there up the access road or by helicopter," said Shala. Castille let out a muted groan at the last word.

"No cable car?" asked Chase.

"No."

"Shame. I always wanted to re-create *Where Eagles Dare*."

"The access road is guarded, I assume," Castille said.

Shala nodded. "Yes. There is a gate at the bottom, and there are television cameras along the road with another gate at the top. We have been watching Hajjar for some time; he usually has at least four men on guard. There is also an electric fence."

Chase turned the binoculars to the surrounding hills. "Don't suppose we could just blow up a power line and cut off the electricity, could we?"

"There you go again! And no, the fortress has its own generators."

"Thought it might." He lowered the binoculars, thinking. "You said from *outside* there's only those two ways in. There's something *inside*?"

"There is another way, yes." Shala looked over her shoulder. "Dr. Wilde, please can you pass me the blue rucksack?" Nina complied, pulling it from among the other bundles in the van's rear bed. Shala rifled through its contents, taking out a set of architectural blueprints. "My father obtained these before the revolution. He hoped to use them to get into the fortress and assassinate the shah, but unfortunately the revolution happened first."

Nina frowned, confused. "Wasn't the revolution *supposed* to get rid of the shah?"

"Different revolutionaries," said Chase enigmatically. "He decided to keep them in case the ayatollah stayed here, but he never did. Maybe they can help you, though." Shala tapped a fingernail on the blueprint's bottom corner. "There is a shaft up to the service basement level of the fortress. It was built for access to the sewage outflow that leads to the river."

Nina wrinkled her nose. "Ew. They just pump it right into the river?"

"Literally crapping on the people," said Chase. "But this shaft, we can get to it from the outflow pipe?"

"Yes. But there is one problem . . ."

Castille clapped a hand to his forehead. "Ah, of course there is."

"The pipe," said Shala, "it is . . . quite small. Too small for you to fit into, Eddie. And you too, Hugo, I am afraid."

"No need to apologize," Castille replied. "Crawling through a pipe full of merde? I have, as the saying goes, been there, done that . . . ruined the T-shirt."

"So, too small for me and Hugo, eh?" said Chase.

"Hafez isn't in any state for it either, and we can't exactly send you and the sprog . . ." A sly grin slowly appeared on his face. "Dr. Wilde . . ."

"Yes?" It struck Nina a moment too late exactly why he was smiling. Everyone looked expectantly back at her. "No!"

\vvv

The upper levels of Hajjar's home were as ostentatious and overblown as its exterior, Kari saw as she and Volgan were brought from the cells. The illicit trade in ancient Persian treasures had clearly been a highly profitable one, and it appeared Hajjar spent a good proportion of his profits on decorations and fittings made of gold. Unlike her own family, in this case wealth did not denote taste.

Hajjar's office was a circular room in the highest domed tower. The click of her heels on the polished marble floor echoed through the open space. Hajjar himself was seated behind a huge semicircular desk, itself marble-topped and trimmed in gold. On the wall behind him was a massive plasma screen, and Kari noticed the black shark eye of a video camera in its lower bezel.

"Ms. Frost! Yuri!" Hajjar boomed with utterly insincere heartiness. "So glad you could make it!"

"Don't waste my time, Hajjar," said Kari coldly. "Just tell me what you want."

Hajjar looked mildly offended. "Very well. I am about to have a videoconference call with your father, and I wanted you to be here so I can assure him of my . . . intent. He is a very hard man to get hold of, by the way. I was becoming impatient."

"He has a lot going on."

"Mm, I'm sure. He was almost as hard to contact as your rival, Mr. Qobras."

"You spoke to Qobras?" gulped Volgan.

"Not yet in person, but soon. After all, for something as important as this . . ." he reached out and picked up the Atlantean artifact from its bed of velvet on his desk, the gleaming reflections from its surface illuminating his face like fire, "I knew he would want to talk to me."

"Whatever Qobras is willing to pay you for the artifact, my father will pay more," said Kari.

"I'm sure he will, but I'm afraid it and Yuri come as a pair. And Qobras is apparently *very* keen to see him again."

"Please, Miss Frost," Volgan begged, "you've got to help me. Qobras will kill me!" His frenzied eyes fixed on the artifact in Hajjar's hands. "I can tell you more about the piece—I can tell you more about Qobras! I worked for him for twelve years, I know his secrets—"

Hajjar clicked his fingers, and one of the guards clubbed Volgan with his gun. His hands still cuffed behind his back, the Russian fell heavily onto the slick marble.

"Enough," said Hajjar. A soft chime from the computer on his desk drew his attention, and he smiled. "Ms. Frost, your father is calling. If you would stand in the view of the camera?" Her guard shoved her forward. "Thank you. And get him out of the way." The other guard dragged Volgan across the floor like a sack of flour.

Hajjar tapped at the computer, then swiveled his red leather chair to face the giant screen. It lit up with the image of Kristian Frost in his office at Ravnsfjord. Frost's eyes flicked to one side, looking at a screen of his own. "Kari!"

"Mr. Frost," said Hajjar before she could answer, "I'm *so* pleased that you finally contacted me. I thought the life of your daughter would be more important than your business schedule." He let out a self-satisfied chuckle.

Frost regarded him with utter contempt. "Kari, are you all right? Has this . . . *person* mistreated you?"

"I'm fine—for the moment," she told him.

"What about the artifact? And Dr. Wilde?"

"Dr. Wilde was arrested by the Iranian army and will be tried for illegal trading in antiquities," Hajjar cut in, "and probably for her complicity in the murder of several soldiers as well. As for the artifact . . . that is no longer any concern of yours."

"How much do you want, Hajjar?"

The Iranian leaned back in his chair. "Straight to business, I see. Very well. For the safe return of your daughter, I want ten million dollars, U.S."

"In addition to the ten million I already paid you for the artifact?" Frost growled.

"In the interests of efficiency, you can even transfer it to the same account," said Hajjar smugly.

"And the artifact?"

"As I said, that is no longer for sale."

"Not even for another ten million?"

There was a long pause before Hajjar answered, the dealer's greed clearly threatening to overturn his plans. "No, not even for that," he said at last, with obvious reluctance.

"Fifteen million."

Hajjar flinched. He half turned, looking back at Kari. "You value this . . . this piece of metal more than your own daughter?"

"I would have offered twenty," she told him.

On the big screen, Frost's face gave away a brief flicker of pride before turning to stone once more. "Twenty million, then."

Hajjar was lost for words, eyes darting back and forth

between the Frosts before he hurriedly swung around to face the screen. "No! No, the artifact is not for sale to you, at any price! Ten million dollars for your daughter, that is the only deal I am making. You will call me back in one hour to confirm the transfer. One hour!" He whirled around again and stabbed at the computer, terminating the call before Frost could speak.

"Hajjar," said Kari, fake admiration in her voice, "I'm impressed! Not many men could stand up to my father like that. Especially to turn down twenty million dollars."

Hajjar scuttled around the desk to her. "Twenty million!" he screeched, before clearing his throat. "Twenty million dollars!" he repeated. "For this, this *thing*?" He waved his hook hand at the artifact. "What *is* it? What is so important about this piece?"

For a moment Kari's eyes lit up with something approaching awe. "It's the key to the past . . . and the future." Then she tipped her head slightly, giving Hajjar a seductive look. "You could be a part of it, Failak. Sell us the artifact and I promise you that my father will take no action against you over this. And I . . ."

"You will what?" asked Hajjar, caught between suspicion and intrigue.

"I will *forgive* you, completely. And maybe even more than that. As I said, few men have the courage to stand up to my father." She shifted position slightly, rolling her hips and shoulders under her coat. "I was very impressed."

Intrigue won out. "Really?" He licked his lips, watching her movements intently. "Then maybe we could—"

"Sir," interrupted Kari's guard, the one who had spurned her in the cells. "Qobras will be calling soon. You need to be ready for him."

Irritation flashed across Hajjar's face. "You're right. I

do. Yes." He took a deep breath, then turned his back on Kari. "Wait with her over there until her father calls back. You," he added, clicking his fingers at the other guard, "bring Yuri over here."

"Nice try, *bitch*," Kari's guard whispered in her ear. She sighed. It had been worth a shot.

But for Hajjar to turn down twenty million dollars . . . how much was Qobras offering?

w

"I look ridiculous," Nina protested.

Leaving Hafez, who was both relieved at not having to move and frustrated at being unable to help, in the van, Shala led the rest of the group down to a small river winding along the foot of the crag. The far bank rose steeply before leveling out thirty feet above—with the electric fence surrounding the entire fortress running along the top.

Although fast flowing, the river was shallow enough for them to wade across. Shala took off her shoes and pulled up her coat as Chase and Castille helped her across, simply splashing through the cold water without even bothering to remove their boots. Nina, on the other hand, felt incredibly silly as she hurried across—in a wet suit.

"I dunno," Chase told her, helping Shala sit down, "you look pretty good to me. But then I've always had a thing for women in rubber."

"Shut up." The one-piece wet suit Shala had brought was more suited to surfing than to stealthy infiltration work: black with a hot-pink insert running from her neck down to her crotch and then up again over her back, with equally lurid strips down the legs and arms. The wet suit itself seemed fairly new, but the too-tight and grubby sneakers on her feet were another matter.

"Are you absolutely *sure* neither of you can fit into this pipe?"

"See for yourself," said Shala, pointing. A stub of rusting metal protruded from the steep bank a foot above the surface of the river, water trickling from it. Nina's hopes that she could persuade the lanky Castille to take her place were dashed when she realized how thick the metal was. The actual interior of the pipe was barely eighteen inches in diameter—too small for Castille, and she doubted Chase would even be able to get his head and one shoulder inside.

For that matter, she wasn't sure if *she* would fit.

"You'll fit," Chase said, as if reading her mind. "Might be a squeeze around your bum, but . . ."

"Hey!"

"Just kidding." He smirked, then opened the rucksack they had brought from the van. "Here's your gear. Torch, two-way radio and a headset—it's not exactly Bluetooth, but you'll be able to tell us when you've shut off the power to the fence. Gun—"

"I've never used a gun," Nina said as Chase took out a small automatic in a canvas holster with a belt wrapped around it.

"Yeah? Thought you Yanks were shooting stuff before you could walk. Turn around."

"I'm really not sure about this . . ." she said as Chase fastened the belt high around her waist, turning it so that the holster rested in the curve of her lower back.

"Just a precaution; hopefully you won't meet anyone." He clipped the walkie-talkie to the belt, then turned her around and fitted the headset, giving her a wink. "But if you do, just think Lara Croft. Bang-bang." His gaze moved to her neck, and her pendant. "Do you want me to look after that for you?"

She considered it. "No thank you. It's sort of my good-luck charm."

Chase raised an eyebrow. "Considering the day you've had, you've got a bloody funny idea about what's lucky."

"I'm still alive, aren't I?"

"Good point." Nina tucked the pendant inside the wet suit, then pulled the zipper all the way up her neck as Chase's gap-toothed grin returned. "Let's get you shafted."

Nina's trepidation turned to outright disgust as she knelt to examine the pipe. "Oh my God! It stinks!"

"What did you expect? It's a sewer!"

Her stomach churned. "I feel sick. God, I don't think I can do this . . ."

"Hey, listen," said Chase, resting a hand on her arm, "I know you can. You're an archaeologist, right? You must have dug about in muck and all kinds of horrible stuff before this, right?"

"Well, yes, but . . ."

"The pipe's not all that long. Fifty yards, tops, then it opens out into the access shaft. That's got a ladder, you can just climb right up. You can do it."

"But what if there's somebody at the top? What if—"

"Nina." He squeezed her arm. "My job's to look after you. If I thought you were going to be in danger, you wouldn't be going."

"But you still gave me a gun."

"Yeah, well . . . nothing's *totally* safe, is it?" She wasn't reassured. "Look, once you've shut down the fence, Hugo and I'll be inside in less than five minutes. Simple plan—we come in, punch Hajjar in the face, rescue Kari, done."

"Punching people in the face is pretty much your solution to everything, isn't it?" said Nina.

"Hey, if it works . . . Anyway, I'll be with you all the

way on the radio. And we've got the plans of the place—I'll tell you exactly where to go. Once you've done it, just stay out of sight and you'll be safe. Trust me."

Nina tied back her hair, then, with extreme reluctance and a look of undisguised revulsion, climbed headfirst into the filthy pipe. "I don't have much choice, do I?"

"That's . . . better than nothing," Chase said, switching on his own radio. "Here, I'll help you in. Give me a radio test." He lifted her feet and pushed her inside.

His radio crackled. "Don't you even *think* about grabbing my ass."

"Never crossed my mind," said Chase, raising an appreciative eyebrow at her wet-suit-clad buttocks as they wriggled into the pipe. He pushed her feet again, and Nina disappeared into the darkness.

The flashlight in one hand ahead of her, she crawled up the sloping pipe. It was a tight squeeze, but she was—just—able to fit. She paused for a moment to shine the light straight along the pipe. Nothing but darkness at the far end.

"I bet Lara Croft never had to crawl up somebody's toilet," she muttered, before beginning her laborious ascent.

w

Kari watched Hajjar's frustration grow as he waited for Qobras to call, his fingers drumming on his desk. It seemed he wasn't a man accustomed to waiting for anything.

"Failak," she said, "I need to use the bathroom. Please?"

"Not again," her guard complained quietly, but Hajjar waved his hand dismissively at the door. Kari stood and made a little noise of triumph at the guard. "I'm not taking off your handcuffs," he muttered as he led her from the room.

W

"How're you doing?" asked Chase, through a crackle of static.

"Oh, superfine," Nina grumbled. "Can't wait to write *this* one up for the *International Journal of Archaeology*."

A noise came through the headset that could have been muffled laughter. "You're doing great. Can you see the end?"

She directed the beam ahead. "I think . . . yes! I can see it! And I can hear something as well." She tried to pick out the noise. A kind of hissing rumble . . . like water coming down a pipe! "Oh, *shit*!"

She cringed and stifled a shriek as several gallons of cold water gushed down the pipe and splashed around her. "Oh God, *oh*! *Disgusting!*"

Chase's jovial response didn't improve her mood. "At least they remembered to flush."

W

"Feeling better?" Hajjar asked mockingly as Kari was brought back into the circular room.

"The attendant's manners leave something to be desired," she sniffed. "I hope I didn't miss Qobras."

"No, but he will call any minute. So you're just in time." He gestured, and the guard shoved her onto a lounger. Volgan looked pleadingly at her, but said nothing.

"Remember my father's offer," she said. "Whatever Qobras offers, he can—"

The computer chimed. Hajjar snapped his fingers at Kari's guard, who clapped a heavy hand on her shoulder. She stopped talking, watching as Hajjar turned to face the screen.

It was the first time she'd ever observed Qobras

"live," having previously only seen him in photographs. And those had been several years out of date. His black hair was now streaked with gray running back from his temples, his face more lined—but his eyes were as sharp as ever.

And as deadly.

"Mr. Hajjar," said Qobras. His tone made it clear that he was displeased at having to deal with the Iranian.

"Mr. Qobras," Hajjar replied, with ersatz good humor. "I am delighted to speak to you at last."

"You have something for me," Qobras stated impatiently.

"Two things, in fact! The first is this little trinket." Hajjar displayed the Atlantean artifact to the camera. "I understand this was taken from your—"

"Destroy it," Qobras interrupted. "Melt it down. I will pay you fifteen million U.S. dollars on receipt of a complete video recording of its destruction."

"Destroy it?" Hajjar was stunned. "Yes, I can do that, I have all the necessary facilities to handle precious metals, but . . ." He shook his head in disbelief. "Are you sure?"

"Melt it down. Completely. You can keep the gold and any other metals you extract, but I want it destroyed. It has caused enough trouble."

Shaken, Hajjar replaced the artifact on his desk. "Destroy it. Okay. For . . . fifteen million dollars, you said?" The oversized image of Qobras nodded.

Kari looked on, appalled. If the artifact was destroyed, then the only link to finding Atlantis would be lost forever . . .

www

With enormous relief, Nina pulled herself out of the pipe.

The chamber she found herself in was rectangular, some six feet by eight, with numerous pipes running into it from above. The floor was awash in rancid water. "I'm in," she said into the headset, turning her light onto the walls. A dirty ladder led upwards.

"Good," said Chase, voice distorted by interference. "Now go up the ladder. And whatever you do . . ."

"Yes?"

"Don't slip."

"Thanks for the advice." Water and sludge dripping off her wet suit, Nina ascended the ladder. She cautiously pushed at the metal cover at the top, and to her immense relief, it moved. She slid it aside, then climbed up. "I'm at the top."

"Okay, you should be in a room with one door."

She swept the beam around. "Yes."

"Check at the door to make sure there's nobody outside, then go left. There's another door at the end of the corridor. Go through it."

Heart suddenly pounding, Nina opened the door a crack and peered through. The stone-walled corridor outside was dimly lit and, except for a faint humming noise, silent. She looked in the other direction. A narrow flight of stairs led upwards. "It's clear," she whispered.

"Okay, go."

She kicked off the sodden sneakers so as not to leave wet footprints, then padded lightly down the corridor. "Oh. Problem."

Even through the hiss of static, she could hear the concern in Chase's voice. "What?"

"There are two doors. Which one do I go through?"

"There's only one on the plan, they must have added something. But one of them has to be the generator room. Try them both."

Both doors bore a high-voltage warning symbol, so

that didn't help. Bracing herself, Nina tried the nearest one first.

It wasn't a room full of technicians or a security station, thankfully. In fact, it looked more like the IT department at the university. She recognized one rack of equipment as a computer server—maybe Hajjar ran his own secure Internet link. Various black boxes were connected to it, as was a PC, a screensaver swirling on its monitor.

Out of curiosity—the room was small, the computer within arm's reach of the door—she moved the mouse. The screen lit up with various windows. Most of them were incomprehensible status displays, but her eyes instantly went to one in particular. It was split in two, each part showing what was apparently a videoconference call.

She didn't recognize the stern-faced man in one of them, but the other . . .

Hajjar.

"Nina?" Chase hissed. "What's going on?"

"It's a computer room—"

"Then forget it! Go into the other room, quick."

It turned out to be her intended destination. A pair of large generators occupied most of the space, thrumming away. On the wall next to them was a complicated array of fuse boxes and circuit breakers.

"Another problem," she said quietly. "All the labels are in Farsi!"

w

"I see you have Yuri there as well," said Qobras.

"Giovanni!" Volgan said desperately, staggering to his feet. His guard raised the gun as if to club him again, but Hajjar shook his head. "Please, I'm sorry! I made a mistake, I know, but I'm sorry!"

Qobras shook his head. "Yuri . . . I trusted you. I *trusted* you, and then you betrayed me—and the entire Brotherhood! And for what? For *money*?" He shook his head again. "The Brotherhood provides for the needs of its own, you know that. But you wanted *more*? That is the thinking of those we are fighting to stop!"

"Please, Giovanni!" begged Volgan. "I will never—"

"Yuri." The single word silenced Volgan instantly. "Hajjar, I have no use for him, and I am sure you do not either. I will pay you five million dollars to kill him, right now."

"Five million dollars?" gasped Hajjar. Qobras nodded.

"Giovanni!" shrieked Volgan. "No, please!"

Hajjar sat motionless for a few seconds, apparently lost in thought . . . then he opened a slim drawer set into his desk, took out a silver revolver and fired.

\vvv

Chase came back online. "Okay, I've got the wiring diagram. There should be three tall panels with a row of big switches running down them."

Nina saw them. "Yes!"

"The middle panel. Turn off the third, fourth and sixth switches."

Each heavy switch made a loud *chung!* noise as Nina moved it. "Okay, now what?"

"That's it. You're done. Find somewhere to hide and we'll see you in five minutes." The radio sent a crunch of static into her ear, then fell silent.

"Wait, Eddie—*Eddie!*"

\vvv

Kari stared in disbelief at Volgan's body. Even the guards seemed shocked by the suddenness of the killing. "My God!"

On the screen, Qobras reacted to her voice with wary surprise. "Hajjar! Who else is with you?"

Hajjar turned away from the bleeding body to face the screen. "I have a . . . rival of yours, you could say. Kari Frost."

Qobras was stunned. *"Kari Frost?* Let me see!"

w

Chase and Castille quickly scaled the slope leading up from the river. Chase tested the fence by tossing a pair of wirecutters against it. No sparks, no shorting. It was dead.

"Go!" he ordered. Castille quickly used the wirecutters to snip the bottom of the fence. Chase pulled up the loose section like a flap, creating a gap just large enough for them to fit beneath.

On the other side, they jumped to their feet and looked up at the fortress. The rocky slope led up to the twisting access road, and the main entrance of the building itself. There were no guards in sight, but from what Shala had said, they would be there somewhere.

As well as his own gun, Castille still had one of the G3 rifles taken from Mahjad's soldiers. Chase had his Wildey, and a weatherbeaten Uzi provided by Shala. He checked both guns. Ready for action.

"Okay," he said, "time to be heroes."

They set off at a run.

w

Nina decided that the server room was as good a hiding place as any. It also let her have another look at the computer.

It only took a moment to expand the window of the videoconference call the PC was relaying, and a little longer to increase the volume. Hajjar and the other man were talking about . . .

Kari!

Not only that, but now she appeared behind Hajjar, pushed into the frame by one of his men.

\\\

"What is she doing there?" Qobras demanded.

"I have some business with her father," said Hajjar. "It is not your concern."

"It is very much my concern!" Qobras almost shouted. "Kill her."

Hajjar gaped at the screen. "*What?*"

"Kill her! *Now!*"

Cold fear clenched Kari's stomach. The gun was still in Hajjar's hand. If he obeyed Qobras's order, she could be dead in moments.

"Are you *mad*?" Hajjar exclaimed. "She is worth ten million dollars to me! Her father has already agreed to pay the ransom!"

"Listen to me," said Qobras, leaning forward until his face filled the screen, "you have no idea how dangerous she is. She and her father are attempting to find what the Brotherhood has been fighting to keep hidden for centuries! If they do—"

Hajjar waved his hands. "I don't care! All I care about is the ten million dollars for returning her to her father!"

Something approaching desperation crept into Qobras's voice. "Hajjar, I will pay you *twelve* million dollars if you kill her."

"You are out of your—"

"Fifteen million! Hajjar, I will pay any price you want! But only if you kill Kari Frost, right now!"

NINE

Nina stared at the monitor, shocked. Whomever the other man was, he was serious about wanting Kari dead. And from what she had already seen of Hajjar, his greed would soon force him to cave in and accept the blood money.

And there was nothing she could do to stop it.

Unless . . .

w

"Two guards at the lower gate," said Castille as he and Chase ran up the rocky slope.

"I see 'em," Chase replied. "They'll take a couple of minutes to get up here. Sod 'em for now. What about the top?"

"They must be inside the gate. What's our best tactic? Something subtle?"

Chase raised his Uzi. "Subtle suits me."

w

Hajjar was torn, looking between the other people in the room—even Kari—as if hoping for guidance. "Fifteen million?" he said at last. "Why? Why is it so important to you that she dies?"

"Twenty million!" shouted Qobras. "Twenty million dollars to kill her, now! Don't ask questions, just—"

The screen went dark.

As did the entire room—the lights, Hajjar's computer, everything. The only illumination came from the narrow stained-glass windows.

Hajjar and his guards were caught unawares, held in bewildered surprise.

Kari moved—

w

Nina had spotted the large red switches at the bottom of the control panels when she switched off the electric fence. She didn't need fluency in Farsi or an electrician's training to work out what they did.

She pushed them all. Everything went black.

Switching on the flashlight, she hurried from the room. Somebody was certain to investigate. As she ran down the darkened corridor, she pulled her belt around to bring the holster within easy reach.

w

The main gate was a huge archway running through the thick southern wall. Chase used his steel mirror to peek around the corner.

"Two guys in a little gatehouse at the far end, left," he told Castille, "about fifteen feet. Doesn't look like they're on the ball."

Castille brought up his rifle. "Still subtle?"

Chase nodded, watching the gatehouse in the mirror. "Let's—"

The lights in the gatehouse went out, as did the CCTV monitors. The guards reacted with confusion.

"Oh bollocks!" Chase hissed. "She's turned off the

rest of the power!" The voices of the guards echoed down the passage, one of them using a walkie-talkie.

Castille made a face. "Subtle is out, then."

"Fight to the end?"

"Fight to the end."

A nod, then both men charged into the gateway, guns roaring as they blasted the gatehouse and its occupants apart.

ʍ

Kari whipped around with the effortless grace of a ballerina, pivoting on one foot as she dropped to a crouch. At the same time, her other leg lanced out and scythed into her guard's ankles from behind. He fell backwards, his head cracking against the hard marble.

She leapt up, pulling her knees high to curl herself into a ball, and bringing her cuffed wrists beneath her tucked feet.

Her heels hit the floor with a clack as she raised her hands in front of her. Somewhere outside, she heard the rattle of automatic weapons.

Chase.

In the low light, she saw Hajjar still sitting behind his desk, facing the dead plasma screen. The other guard fumbled with his MP-5.

The man at her feet had a gun, but it was still in its holster. The door was too far away.

Which left—

She vaulted onto Hajjar's desk and slid across the gleaming surface on her butt just as he turned his chair around. Her feet smashed into the Iranian's face, driving him back into the padded leather as she continued her slide right over the desk to land in his lap. The swivel chair spun around with the impact, its high back blocking both Kari and Hajjar from the guard's view for a moment.

And in that moment, Kari wrenched the revolver from Hajjar's hand.

A single shot was all she needed to hit the guard square in the forehead. He collapsed instantly, dead.

The other guard was recovering, pulling out his gun as he twisted to face her.

Kari kicked again, using Hajjar as a human spring-board to launch herself into the air. The chair and its occupant toppled over with a crash. She performed a perfect somersault as a bullet cracked against the wall behind her.

She was still upside down in midair as she pulled the trigger. The bullet exploded in the guard's chest, blood spurting out as she flopped back to the floor.

Kari landed on both feet beside the desk, coat swirling like a cape. She gave the body of her former guard a cold look. "You were right about the martial arts."

She heard a noise behind her and whirled. Hajjar had crawled from his overturned chair, flattening himself against the wall beneath the plasma screen. As he raised his hook hand to the carved skirting along the base of the wall, a twisted smile of triumph on his bloodied lips, the floor beneath him dropped away and pitched him into darkness. Before Kari could react, the trapdoor snapped back into place, only the tiniest seam in the marble giving away that it had even been there at all.

She hurried to the spot and pushed at the skirting, but although a piece of it moved under her touch, nothing happened. The trapdoor had some kind of lock or timing mechanism to prevent people pursuing its user.

The artifact!

Kari frantically searched the desk for the orichalcum piece.

It wasn't there!

She must have swept it along with her when she slid over the desk, dropping it right into Hajjar's lap. And now he had used the shah's secret escape route to make his getaway with it!

Spitting a Norwegian curse, Kari dropped the revolver into a pocket, picked up the dead bodyguard's MP-5 and hurried from the room.

w

The spiraling chute deposited Hajjar in a small room two floors below. Like the rest of the fortress the room was dark, but once his disorientation cleared, that presented him with no problems. He had prepared the room carefully with everything he might need should he have to use his emergency exit.

Not, he thought as his hand felt for the battery-powered lantern he knew was there, that he had ever actually expected to do so. Especially to escape from someone who just a few seconds earlier had been his prisoner! Qobras was right—Kari Frost was indeed more dangerous than she seemed.

He found the lantern and switched it on. The contents of the room were exactly as he'd left them. Hurriedly slinging a satchel over one shoulder, he dropped the orichalcum bar into it before choosing a weapon.

Hajjar's disability limited him to relatively small and light guns, but that didn't mean he was limited in terms of firepower. The gun he selected was an Ingram M11, scarcely bigger than an ordinary pistol but able to spew bullets at the frightening rate of sixteen hundred rounds per minute. This particular gun had a special modification ordered personally by its owner: the magazine, protruding from the bottom of the handgrip, ended in a drum, more than doubling its capacity. With only one hand, reloading was a task Hajjar preferred to delay.

There was one other weapon he chose. He unscrewed the steel hook from the metal cup covering the stump of his right wrist . . . and replaced it with a vicious, eight-inch serrated blade.

His pilot had standing orders in case of an emergency—get to the helipad and start the chopper. Hajjar had many enemies, and was under no illusions that the fortress was impregnable. Running from the danger and letting his men handle it was his preferred option.

But if he happened to run into any of his enemies along the way, he wanted to be prepared.

vv

Nina went up the stairs and found herself in another corridor, this one lavishly decorated by someone with an apparent fetish for red velvet. Tall windows at each end let in enough light for her to switch off the flashlight. Through the nearest window she could see the surrounding mountains; the other one overlooked the courtyard at the center of the fortress.

From where she could hear gunfire. Chase and Castille were making their entrance.

She also heard running footsteps from around a corner coming towards her—probably somebody heading for the generator room to restore power. She ducked through the closest door. The brief glimpse she caught before closing it and plunging the room into darkness told her it was a library, the walls lined with bookcases of reference texts and historical tomes. Hajjar obviously liked to be as well informed as possible about the artifacts he traded.

Hands shaking, she pulled the gun from its holster,

pointing it at the door as she backed away. The footsteps came closer.

If the door opened, would she have the necessary willpower to pull the trigger?

She didn't need to find out. They faded, clattering down the steps into the basement.

With a sigh of relief, Nina turned on the flashlight again. A library would be a good place to hide out. It was unlikely that any of Hajjar's people would feel the need to check a historical reference in the middle of a crisis. She just needed to wait for Chase to contact her again . . .

Suddenly Nina froze, puzzled. The room seemed a lot brighter, as though her flashlight had magically doubled in power.

Filled with dread, she turned.

Hajjar stood barely three feet from her, having just emerged from a room hidden behind a moving bookcase, a lantern hanging from a strap over one shoulder. He seemed almost as surprised as she was—but not so surprised that he didn't think to point his sinister-looking gun at her.

"Dr. Wilde," he said, running his gaze up and down her body before raising the blade attached to his right wrist to her throat. "Good to see you again."

w

The courtyard was a long rectangle with the main gate at the center of the southern wall. Off to each side were large raised marble stands containing ornamental plants, three in each row. Chase and Castille took cover behind one of them as they got their bearings.

"The way down to the cells should be through that door," said Chase, pointing ahead.

"She might not be in there," Castille replied. "We should split up, so one of us can check the upper floors."

"What about his men?"

"He's a criminal, not a warlord! It's not as though he has a private army."

The door Chase had indicated burst open, five men armed with MP-5s rushing into the courtyard.

"On the other hand..." Chase grimaced as he opened up with his Uzi. Castille popped up and let rip with the G3 over the top of the plants. Two of Hajjar's men fell immediately, blood splattering the walls behind them. The remaining three split up, two sprinting across the courtyard for the cover of the planter diagonally opposite Chase and Castille, the third diving behind the one ahead of them.

Chase hunted for an escape route. Besides the main gate, the nearest exit from the courtyard was through a set of arched French windows in the west wall, but reaching them would require a sprint of almost forty feet—with no cover. "Shit! If they pin us here for too long, those guys from the bottom gate'll catch up from behind!"

"What about—" Castille began, just as the flowers above him blew apart in showers of petals. "Excusez-moi!" he yelled at the gunmen in complaint. "What about those windows?"

Chase followed his line of sight—ten feet away in the south wall were two windows, at roughly chest height. But they were each less than two feet wide. "Bit small, aren't they?" He counted the shots from Hajjar's men, already sensing a pattern. Pop up, fire a three-round burst, duck back while his mate repeated the process...

He paused for a second, then leaned around the side of his cover. Right on cue, one of the men across the courtyard jumped up to aim at them—only to reel back and drop out of sight as a single bullet from Chase's Uzi blew a hole in his face. "One down! If we can nail another one, we can cover each other until we reach those doors."

More innocent flowers were blasted into potpourri. Castille flapped a hand as fragments of petals rained around his face, their scent at bizarre odds with the acrid tang of burnt gunpowder. "It's a good thing they don't have grenades."

"Yeah, and too bad we don't either! We could—" Chase stopped as he heard a warning shout. "Oh, you had to bloody tempt fate, didn't you? *Grenade!*"

Both men fired at the windows as they sprang up and ran towards them. Behind, a grenade arced down from the other end of the courtyard, landing with a thump of soft soil in the planter.

The glass shattered as Chase stitched a line of bullets up it, diving headlong at the narrow opening. Beside him, Castille did the same. They let go of their guns just before hitting the shower of glass, protecting their faces with their arms as the exploding grenade blew out a huge chunk of marble from the side of the planter and hurled soil and vegetation over thirty feet in the air. A lethal hail of metal flew after the two ex-soldiers, but by then Chase and Castille were already through the windows. What little glass remained in the windows flew after them like razor-edged confetti as they hit the floor.

Chase shook off the fragments of glass. The room was a gallery of some kind, lined with statues. His ears were ringing, but besides the jolt of the hard landing on his elbows and knees and a stinging cut on the back of his head, he didn't feel any new pain. "Are you okay?"

Castille winced. "I've been better!" He held up his left arm; his sleeve had been slashed open and a long jagged cut ran down his forearm, splinters of blood-slicked glass protruding from it.

"Can you fight?"

"Always!" He picked up the G3. Chase looked for the Uzi. It wasn't there—it must have hit the window frame and landed outside.

He drew his Wildey, pressing his back against the wall next to the smashed window. Castille did the same on the other side. The two guards were running for the French windows, intending to enter the building and cut them off.

A shot from the Wildey blew the lower jaw off one man. He crashed to the ground, limbs thrashing. Castille fired twice, plugging the second man in the chest. He fell into the French windows, slamming head-first through the glass.

"Come on," Chase snapped. They needed to find Kari—and Nina—fast.

As they left the gallery, the lights pulsed, then came back on.

w

Kari was certain Hajjar would try to flee the fortress. If her rescuers were attacking from the main gate, he would head for the helipad, a platform recessed into the northern side of the building.

She mentally connected the routes she'd taken from the helipad to the cells, then the cells to Hajjar's office. Down another floor, then right . . .

w

After restoring power, one of Hajjar's men hurried back up the stairs—to find his boss waiting for him with an unexpected guest. Apparently today was "beautiful Western women" day at the fortress.

Though he couldn't help noticing that this one, a

ponytailed redhead rather than the taller ice-blonde he'd seen earlier, *really* needed a shower.

"Bring her," Hajjar ordered. The bodyguard grabbed her shoulder, pushing her along as he stuck his MP-5 into her back.

"Where's Kari?" demanded Nina. "What did you do to her?"

Hajjar glared back at her as he jogged along, smears of blood around his mouth and nose. "What did *I* do to *her*? It's what *she* did to *me* you should ask about! If I had known she was so dangerous, I would have tied her legs!"

Nina was intrigued, but didn't have the chance to inquire further as they reached a kink in the corridor. A large window looked out over the mountains—and the helicopter on its pad below. Its rotors were turning, picking up speed.

Hajjar gave the bodyguard orders in Farsi, the man stepping back to hide around the corner where the passageway kinked. Then he turned to Nina. "You, stay here! Wait for your friends!"

"What, so he can shoot them? Screw you!"

He jabbed his blade-hand up against her chin, the point cutting her. She gasped. "When they get here, you will wave to them, make it seem everything is all right. If you say a word, try to give them any warning, he will kill you. Do you understand?"

"Perfectly," she said, glancing at the bodyguard's machine gun. Hajjar nodded, then turned away. "Hajjar! Where's the artifact?"

He patted his satchel. "It is a shame to destroy something of such historic value . . . but the fifteen million dollars Qobras is paying me to do so is a lot of money."

"Plus the ten million Kristian Frost paid you as well," Nina said with disgust.

Hajjar shrugged. "What can I say? Today was a good day for business." He frowned at the sound of gunfire echoing through the marble-floored corridors. "A bad day for my home, though. It seems I will be spending some of the money on redecorating. But better that than on my own funeral! Good-bye, Dr. Wilde!" He scurried away.

The bodyguard gestured with his gun, directing Nina to stand in the center of the corridor. Anyone approaching from the other end would see her . . . but not her captor, tucked out of sight.

\\/

"Do you hear something?" asked Castille as he and Chase hurried through the fortress.

"Chopper," Chase confirmed. The distant but rising whine of the Jet Ranger's turbine engine was unmistakable.

"Merde! I *knew* we were going to have to deal with that thing, I just *knew* it!"

"Down there," said Chase, pointing. They turned a corner.

\\/

Kari heard running footsteps as she approached the T-junction leading to the helipad. She raised the MP-5—

Chase and Castille rushed around the corner, both of them with *their* guns aimed right at *her*!

"Christ," said Chase, face cracking into a smile as he lowered his Wildey, "what is it with people not needing me to rescue them today?"

Kari smiled back. "Perhaps I should ask for a refund."

"Let's not go that far," Castille said.

"Where's Nina?"

"Hiding, if she did what I told her," Chase replied. "Are you okay? Where's Hajjar?"

"I'm fine—but Hajjar has the artifact!"

Castille made a face. "Let me guess, he's in his helicopter."

"Yes! Come on!"

They ran up the corridor, Chase leading the way. "Go left at the next junction, then follow it around!" Kari told him.

"How many men does he have with him?"

"I don't know—I shot the two guarding me."

Chase gave her a quizzical glance. "You killed them?"

"Yes." She returned the look. "What's wrong?"

"Nothing! I'm just not used to having clients do the job for me!"

They followed the corridor—then stopped when they saw a familiar figure ahead. "Nina!" Kari called.

"I told her to stay hidden," Chase complained. "Doc! Are you okay?"

w

Pressed against the wall, the bodyguard gestured with his gun: *wave them to you*. Nina raised her hand.

w

Kari began to run down the corridor—only to be stopped in her tracks as Chase seized her arm. "Wait!" he ordered, pulling her back.

Nina was waving . . . *with her thumb tucked against her hand*.

Chase and Castille's warning signal.

Chase ran, heading for the kink in the corridor. Just before he reached it, he threw himself into a twisting dive, raising his gun.

The bodyguard leapt out, aiming his MP-5—only to

find that his target was on the floor, pointing a huge gun up at him!

Chase fired three shots.

The impact of the Magnum bullets blew the bodyguard backwards, the gun dropping from his hands. He smashed through the window, falling fifteen feet to land in a broken heap on the helipad. The noise of the Jet Ranger rushed into the fortress.

"Are you all right?" Chase asked.

"I'm fine, I'm fine!" Nina cried.

Kari rushed up to her and, to Nina's surprise, hugged her. "Thank God you're safe!" She pulled back a little, nose wrinkling. "What's that smell?"

"That's *his* fault," Nina said, scowling at Chase, who looked away innocently. The wind from the helicopter cut through her relief. "Hajjar! He's got the artifact!"

"Shit!" Chase ran to the broken window. The aircraft rose from the pad. "Maybe I can shoot out the engine, force him to land—"

"No time," said Kari. Letting go of Nina, she hefted her MP-5 and strode to the window, unleashing a stream of fire at the helicopter's cockpit on full auto.

The window of the pilot's door shattered under the onslaught. Inside the cockpit, the helicopter's windscreen was showered with a vivid red. The pilot thrashed in his seat, the Jet Ranger going into a spin as he released the controls.

The chopper's tail swerved towards the window, its vertical rotor like a giant circular saw.

"Down!" screamed Chase, grabbing Kari with one hand and Nina with the other as he hurled himself away from the window.

Castille was almost transfixed by the sight of the helicopter bearing down on him, snapping out of it and diving back down the corridor just as the rotor carved into the stone surround of the window and disinte-grated. A foot-long piece of blade shot free and buried itself in the wall barely three inches above his head.

With its tail rotor gone, the helicopter swung around violently. Hajjar screamed and grabbed the duplicate controls in front of him, but even if the tail had been in-tact, he didn't have enough hands to operate them.

The main rotor blades smashed into a million frag-ments as they hit unforgiving concrete and stone. The aircraft rolled onto its side and plunged downwards to hit the helipad with a colossal bang, its skids collapsing.

Chase had landed on top of Nina, trying to shield her with his own body. "Are you okay?"

"I think I'm dead," moaned Nina.

"You're okay. But God, you need a shower!" She hit him. "Ms. Frost? Are you all right?"

Kari jumped to her feet. "The artifact! We've got to get it!" She ran to the helipad stairs.

"It's still dangerous!" Chase yelled, but too late. "Buggeration!"

"Mon dieu!" shrieked Castille, staring in dismay at the piece of rotor embedded in the wall. "Helicopters! Always it's fucking *helicopters*! I knew it!"

"You're still alive, Hugo, so stop complaining! Come on!" Chase got up. Nina was about to do the same, but he shook his head. "It's too dangerous. Wait here." He set off after Kari, Castille following.

The helicopter hadn't caught fire, to his relief, but there was a strong stench of fuel—and the engine was still running, the broken stubs of the rotor blades whirling around above the wrecked fuselage. The air-craft's body was tilted at almost a forty-five-degree an-gle, its nose crushed like an eggshell. Kari was already at the wreck, ducking under the spinning blades to reach the door.

"Ms. Frost, wait!" Chase shouted again as he hurried down the stairs to the pad. "Kari! It's not safe!"

"We have to get the artifact!" she answered, fumbling with the handle. Inside she could see Hajjar slumped in his seat, blood running from a cut on his forehead. The catch clicked, and she pulled the door open—

Hajjar burst into life, swinging his right hand at her and slicing right through the sleeve of her coat. She screamed as blood spattered the pure white material. Instinctively she clutched at the wound with her other hand.

In that moment Hajjar leapt from the cockpit and knocked her onto her back, pinning her to the ground as he pressed the tip of the serrated blade against her throat. The modified M11 was in his other hand.

"Drop your guns or she dies!" he yelled. "*Now!*"

Chase realized that even a head shot would be no use in this situation—if Hajjar fell, he would drive the blade through Kari's neck with the weight of his own body. With no choice, he dropped the Wildey. Castille did the same with his rifle. They kicked the fallen guns away.

"Good," said Hajjar. Still holding his knife-hand against Kari, he rose to a crouch and brought his gun around to cover Chase and Castille. "Her I still want alive. You? Not so—"

Blam!

A bullet smacked into the fuselage, punching a hole through the thin sheet metal. Everyone looked up to see Nina standing in the broken window, aiming the dead bodyguard's MP-5 down at the helicopter.

"Let her go, Hajjar!" she yelled.

"Nina, don't shoot him!" Chase warned. "If he falls, he'll cut her throat!"

"Let her *go!*"

"You have never used a gun before, have you?"

Hajjar called mockingly. "I can tell just from the way you are holding it! Do you really think you can hit me before I kill her?"

"I wasn't aiming at you!" she answered.

Castille raised an eyebrow. "I hope you weren't aiming at Ms. Frost!"

Hajjar's voice was still filled with derision. "Then what?"

"I was aiming at the *gas tank*. Which is now on fire."

All heads turned back to the crashed aircraft. Dirty black smoke rose from the engine cowling, whipped up by the spinning rotor.

Momentarily frightened by the new danger, Hajjar flinched, the pressure of the blade easing—

Giving Kari the chance to snatch up her left hand and force the weapon away from her neck.

She felt one of the serrations tear her skin, but it was just a scratch. The instant the cold metal was clear of her throat, she swept up her right hand to deliver a karate blow to Hajjar's jaw. Her awkward position didn't provide much leverage, but the heel of her palm still struck hard enough to drive his lower jaw against his upper with a sharp crack of snapping teeth. Spitting blood, he let out a gurgling scream and staggered backwards. Kari rolled away, and Chase leapt over her to tackle Hajjar.

"Get the thing!" he shouted at Kari as he struggled with the Iranian, grabbing his wrists. Hajjar was stronger than he looked, muscle beneath the fat. And he had a lethal weapon in each hand, while all Chase had were his two fists.

Kari scrambled to her feet, keeping her head low to avoid the rotor blades. She moved to the open cockpit door.

"No! Kari! It's in his bag!" Nina yelled.

Chase looked down. Hajjar had a satchel over one shoulder—

The brief distraction was enough to give Hajjar an opportunity. Driven by pain and fury, he twisted his left wrist and squeezed the trigger of the Ingram. Flames exploded from the barrel of the evil little machine pistol, the fire close enough to burn Chase's cheek and neck as the bullets seared past. Castille, running to help his partner, abruptly changed course and pulled Kari away as the shots raked along the helicopter's side.

Hajjar brought his gun around for a lethal shot.

Two fists, *and one head*—

Chase pounded a crunching head butt straight into the Iranian's face, crushing his nose flat in a rosette of blood. "Stitch that!"

More smoke belched from the chopper, the crackle of flames rising even above the howl of the engine.

Still gripping Hajjar's wrists, Chase pulled his dazed opponent upright. "Hajjar!" he yelled. *"Hands up!"* He lifted Hajjar's arms into the air—

Hajjar realized what was about to happen, but too late.

His good hand and the Ingram it was clutching disintegrated in a shower of gore and shattered steel as Chase thrust them into the spinning rotor blades. His knife-hand fared no better, the eight-inch blade snapping like a lollipop stick before the whirling rotor took another two inches off the stump of his wrist.

Hajjar stared in horrified disbelief at the blood gushing from the ends of his arms. Then he looked down as the Englishman swung him around—

Chase's huge fist delivered a pile-driver blow square in the middle of his flattened, bloodied face. Hajjar staggered back, falling into the cockpit as Chase snagged the strap of his satchel, pulling it from him.

The impact rocked the helicopter, which creaked ominously as its weight shifted.

Chase turned and ran, seeing Castille already racing away for the cover of the stairs with Kari right beside him.

The first lick of flames escaped the battered fuselage, curling around the top of the engine casing as the helicopter toppled completely onto its side. What was left of the rotor blades plowed into the concrete and shattered, torque grinding the chopper's nose into the helipad. Fuel spilled from the ruptured tanks, raining down on to the burning engine—

Hajjar screamed, but the sound was completely obliterated as the helicopter exploded.

Castille and Kari threw themselves into the arched doorway at the bottom of the stairs. Chase, some yards behind them, could only dive for the ground.

Burning debris rained down, but the fuselage had contained most of the blast. The largest pieces landed well short of him. That didn't stop a few smaller chunks of mangled metal striking his back and legs. He yelled in pain.

"Edward!" Castille shouted, running back to him.

"Shit!" Chase said, standing painfully and clutching his leg. "Feels like I got kicked by a fucking horse!"

Nina ran down the stairs to Kari. "Are you okay?"

"Yes, I'm fine!" she said, eyes wide with gratitude. Both women hurried over to Chase. "Did you get the artifact?"

"Are you all right?" Nina asked at the same time. They exchanged smiles, then hurried over to him.

"You see? Helicopters!" said Castille, waving a hand at the burning wreckage. "Twice in five minutes one has almost killed me! Vehicles of the Devil!"

"Hugo? Shut it," Chase told him wearily, limping to pick up his Wildey.

"The artifact?" Kari asked.

He handed her the satchel. "Here. Hope it's worth it."

"It is," she said, opening the bag and carefully lifting out the metal bar. The nearby flames reflecting from its surface gave it even more of a glow. "This is it," she said, passing it reverently to Nina. "This is the path to Atlantis."

Nina took it, examining the symbols scribed into the metal. At once familiar, yet *different*, mysterious. Then she looked back at Kari. "Not wanting to put a downer on things, but before we go looking for Atlantis, we *are* still stuck in Iran."

"I wouldn't say we're *completely* stuck," said Chase. "I saw something that might be handy . . ."

w

Hajjar's other men were either dead, or had decided that survival outweighed loyalty to their late employer and run away. The group encountered no further resistance as Chase led them to the main courtyard.

In the northeastern corner was a set of large doors. He swung them open.

"Hajjar's taxi service," he proclaimed, sweeping an arm at the rows of expensive vehicles parked within. "Not quite as good as your collection, boss, but it'll do. So, what do you want?"

"I don't think we'll get very far in a Ferrari," Castille noted of the yellow F355 near the doors, "not on the local roads. And it may be a little . . . high profile."

"A Hummer isn't exactly hard to spot either," added Kari, examining a bright green H3 disdainfully.

"You got any preferences, Doc?" Chase asked Nina.

"*Please* stop calling me that. And I just want whatever gets us out of here as quickly as possible."

"Well in that case," he said, eyes lighting on a particular vehicle, "might as well do it in style. Maybe Hajjar wasn't so bad after all . . ."

∿

A few minutes later, a silver Range Rover charged down the twisting road from the fortress, then with the throaty roar of a V-8 engine headed away into the mountains.

TEN
France

Iran was a long way behind her. And thank God for that, thought Nina, as she gazed out from the hotel balcony over Paris. From the penthouse suite, she had a clear view across the city. Landmarks like Notre-Dame and, farther away, the Eiffel Tower stood out in their floodlit glory against the clear night sky as if placed there for her personal pleasure.

But sightseeing would have to wait. She had work to do first. And she didn't seem to be getting anywhere.

Someone knocked on the door. "Come in," she called, turning away from the balcony. Kari entered.

"Are you ready, Nina?" she asked.

"I don't know . . ." Nina shot an aggrieved look at the Atlantean artifact, which was surrounded by her notes beneath an illuminated magnifying lens. "I've done as much as I can, but it's not enough. I still can't translate some of the symbols. Why, is your father waiting for me?"

Kari nodded, then smiled. "But don't worry. You're one of the few people in the world he's willing to wait upon."

"Well, I'm honored, but it doesn't make me any less nervous."

"There's no reason to be nervous. You're already closer to finding Atlantis than anyone since the ancient Athenians."

"Yeah, and look what I've been through—what *we've* been through—to get there! I still don't think I've got that horrible stink out of my hair."

"Come on," Kari said reassuringly, "let's tell my father what you've found out."

Nina picked up the artifact and Kari led her into the adjoining room, a lounge at the center of the suite. Chase lurked near the door, his jacket off and his Wildey's shoulder holster in plain sight. Castille was absent; Nina suspected he was guarding the corridor outside. "Hi, Doc," Chase said cheerfully. He nodded at the top-of-the-line laptop sitting on a table. "Hope you've got your makeup on, you're going to be on camera."

"Oh, we're videoconferencing?"

"My father likes to talk face to face, even when he can't do so literally," said Kari. "Come on, sit down. Do you want anything?"

"No thanks." Although she wouldn't have minded a drink to settle her nerves.

Nina sat in front of the laptop, Kari joining her and tapping a key on the computer. The screen came to life, revealing Kristian Frost in his office. "Dr. Wilde! I'm glad to see you again!"

"I'm glad to be seen!" Nina told him. "It was a bit more . . . well, *violent* than I expected."

"So I heard. Were there any problems getting out of Iran?"

"Nothing serious," said Kari. "Mr. Chase's local contacts got us back to Esfahān, and the foundation's influence with the government let us clear the country unchecked."

"And Hajjar?"

"Dead."

Frost nodded. "Good. A shame about the ten million dollars, but it's a small price to pay." His face became eager. "So, Dr. Wilde. Please tell me what you have found."

Nina cleared her throat. "Well, I'm afraid it's not a direct route to Atlantis, unfortunately. But it's definitely a map of some kind." She held up the metal bar, turning it to the laptop's camera. "The line running down its length represents a river—the Glozel word is unmistakable. And there are other markings, which I've been able to partially translate." She checked her notes. "'Begin from north mouth of' the something 'river. Seven, south, west. Follow course to city of,' um, something. 'There to find . . .' I'm afraid that's all I've got so far. But these markings to each side, I think they show the number of tributaries you have to pass to reach the destination. Four on the left, seven on the right, and so on."

Frost was intrigued. "I take it the words you can't translate are not Glozel."

"No. They're actually more like hieroglyphics than letters, part of a different linguistic system. The frustrating thing is that they seem familiar, but I can't place them. They could be a regional variation . . ."

"Interesting. Kari, can you take pictures of the markings and send them to me, please? I want a closer look."

"Of course, Far," Kari answered, using the Norwegian term for father. She took the artifact from Nina and started a program to photograph it with the laptop's camera.

Chase came over as she worked. "So who are these Glozelians, Doc? I did GCSE history, but I've never heard of them."

Nina laughed. "You wouldn't have, because they don't exist."

He looked puzzled. "Eh?"

"Glozel is—at least at the moment—the oldest known written language," she explained, "a sort of ancestor to several others, including Vinca-Tordos and Byblos." Chase's expression didn't change. "Which I guess you've never heard of either!"

"I said I *did* GCSE history. I didn't say I *passed* it."

"It's named after the town where it was discovered. Here in France, actually."

Kari finished taking pictures and put the artifact down, addressing Chase as she sent the files to her father. "The Glozel Tablets were found in a cave beneath farmland in 1924 by a man called Émile Fradin. Because they indicated an earlier origin than any language known at the time, they were dismissed as fakes—but when they were tested with new dating techniques fifty years later, it turned out that they really *did* date back to at least 10,000 BC."

Chase whistled. "Bloody hell. That's *really* old."

"There was a civilization using a complex written language in Europe several millennia before even the ancient Greeks," said Nina, "and that civilization was widespread enough to influence the languages of the Phoenicians, the Greeks, the Hebrews . . . even the Romans and Persians."

"And that civilization . . ." Chase gazed at the artifact, the golden reflected light illuminating his features from below. "You think it was Atlantis?"

"She does," said Kari. "And so do I."

"In that case? I do too." He smiled at Nina. "So how do we find out which river to check?"

"That's the problem," Nina told him reluctantly. "I don't know. This figure on the main inscription," she pointed out the little group of seven dots, "seems to be some unit of distance. The words following it mean 'south' and 'west.'"

Chase examined the artifact more closely. "So it could mean seven miles southwest of somewhere, or seven south and then go west . . ."

"Exactly. The problem is, we don't know what units are being used, or even what they relate to—their 'zero point.'"

"Atlantis, I'd guess." Nina looked at him, impressed. "Hey, I've been known to use my brain from time to time."

"Dr. Wilde," said Frost over the videolink, catching everybody's attention, "I've just looked at the markings. I didn't expect that my knowledge would be any greater than yours, and I was right. I don't recognize them either. But," he went on, catching Nina's glum expression, "I will arrange for an expert in ancient languages to view the artifact."

Nina's face fell further. "Oh. So you don't need me anymore, or . . ."

Kari laughed. "Don't be ridiculous, Nina! You're the most important person on the entire mission! In fact, without you there wouldn't even *be* a mission."

"Kari is absolutely right, Dr. Wilde," said Frost reassuringly. "You're irreplaceable."

"Our expert can decipher the remaining characters when he gets to Paris," Frost said. "Then, once we know which river to search, we can prepare for a full expedition."

"Wouldn't it be easier just to e-mail this guy some pictures?" Nina asked.

"After your last experience, I don't want anybody to see the artifact except under conditions we can totally control. The fewer people who know about it, the better."

"Good point."

Frost gave her a broad smile. "There's no need to feel

downhearted, Dr. Wilde. You've done excellent work! I think we're now closer to finding Atlantis than ever before. Congratulations!"

The praise boosted Nina's spirits immediately. "Thank you!"

"Since there's nothing more you can do for the moment, I suggest you take a break and enjoy Paris. Kari can show you around. I'll speak to you again soon. Good-bye." The screen went black.

Kari checked her watch. "It's a bit late to show you around town now, unfortunately. We should probably go to bed."

"Oh, aye?" said Chase, waggling his eyebrows suggestively. Kari glared at him again. "Sorry, boss," he said, without a hint of genuine contrition behind his smirk.

"Have you ever been to Paris before, Nina?" Kari asked.

"Yes, but only briefly. I was with my parents; they were going to an archaeological conference. And I was only nine, so I didn't really appreciate it."

Kari smiled. "In that case, tomorrow we'll do something that you *can* appreciate."

∧∧∧

That something turned out to be art, cuisine . . . and shopping.

They spent the morning at the Louvre, Chase acting as Nina and Kari's escort while Castille guarded the Atlantean artifact at the hotel, before moving on to Paris's consumerist heart.

"Uh, I don't think so," said Nina, pausing at the entrance to Christian Lacroix's store on the rue du Faubourg St-Honoré. "My credit card'll spontaneously combust if I even *look* at the prices. I'm more of a T. J. Maxx kind of girl."

"Thank God," Chase exclaimed with a mocking smile. "Nothing more boring than standing about watching women try on clothes. Unless they're bikinis." Nina made a face at him, which only served to widen his grin.

"Don't worry about it," said Kari. "From now on, you have unlimited credit. The Frost Foundation will pay for anything you need. Or want, for that matter."

"Seriously?" Nina asked.

Kari nodded. "Absolutely. Well, within reason. If you want to buy a Lamborghini, you should probably ask first! But you can get anything you want. Treat yourself."

"Thank you," said Nina, feeling oddly uncomfortable about receiving such largesse. It wasn't something she was used to. She decided to restrain herself, whatever Kari might buy.

An hour later, she was staggered to realize that she'd spent almost a thousand euros. Definitely not T. J. Maxx prices. And that was barely a quarter of Kari's total bill.

"Better be careful, Doc," said Chase. "You get into the habit of spending that much, you'll be in trouble when you get back to New York and blow your rent money on shoes!"

"I don't think so," Kari countered. "When we find Atlantis, money will be the last thing you need to worry about. We'll take care of you."

"Really? Thank you," said Nina.

Kari smiled at her. "We always look after our own."

Nina wanted to ask exactly what she meant by that, but Kari was already hailing a taxi.

WW

Their next destination was a restaurant called L'Opéra. The place was busy with well-heeled Parisians enjoying the traditionally lengthy French lunch.

Nina didn't think there were any tables available, but

she soon discovered that for daughters of billionaire philanthropists, tables very quickly *became* available. "I despise crowds," Kari sighed, after speaking to the maître d' in perfect French and getting a flurry of activity from the staff in response. "It always reminds me that there are just too many people on the planet. The resources we have aren't sustainable for a population of close to seven billion."

Nina nodded. "Too bad there's not much you can do about it."

"We'll see. The Frost Foundation is doing what it can."

While they waited for the maître d' to return, Chase examined a menu and grimaced. "I'm more of a fish and chips kind of bloke," he objected. "Think I'll sit this one out and grab a burger later."

"First you complain that the *Mona Lisa*'s 'a bit small and grubby,' and now this? You're such a philistine, Eddie," Nina said, amused. "You're not just going to sit there and get drunk, are you?"

"Not while I'm on the clock. Besides, I can keep a better eye on the entrance from the bar," Chase told her. "Make sure nobody tries to ruin your dinner."

"You, ah . . . you think there might be trouble?"

Chase gave her a smile that was simultaneously reassuring and ominous. "There'll only be trouble if anyone tries anything. You two enjoy your nosh, I'll watch out for you." With a final survey of the other patrons, he headed for the bar, perching on a stool where he could observe the restaurant.

Their table now prepared, a waiter led Nina and Kari to it. Nina glanced over towards Chase once they were seated. "Do you think we really might be in danger?" she asked Kari.

"It's always a possibility," she replied. "Qobras and his people will almost certainly have found out by now that we escaped from Iran. Which is why we need to work as quickly as possible—the longer it takes, the greater the risk of him finding us."

"And trying to kill us again?"

"We're not going to allow that to happen," Kari said firmly. Her expression softened. "Nina, I never thanked you properly."

"For what?"

"You saved my life! In Hajjar's fortress, when you shot at the helicopter. That was a very clever and incredibly brave thing to do."

Nina blushed. "Ah, actually . . . I was terrified that if I shot the chopper, it would instantly blow up!"

Kari laughed again. "That only happens in movies! No, you were very brave, and I am incredibly grateful that you were." She gently squeezed Nina's hand. "If there is anything you ever need—*anything*—just ask me."

A little overwhelmed, Nina had no idea what to say. "Thank you," she eventually managed.

Kari held her hand for a moment longer before releasing it. "Anything for you."

"So, er, do Eddie and Hugo get the same deal?" she asked, blushing again with the attention.

Kari's smile became more jokey. "Not exactly. After all, they're being *paid* to look after us!"

"From what Eddie said, it sounds like you don't need anyone to look after you. Did you *really* escape from Hajjar on your own?"

"You helped me again! When you turned off the power," she added on seeing Nina's confusion. "It distracted them for a second, and I . . . Well, I've done a little self-defense training. And another reason I'm glad you cut the power when you did was because I think Hajjar was about to accept Qobras's offer and shoot me."

"That was Qobras?" Nina remembered the face of the man she'd seen on the videoconference split screen.

"You saw him?"

"Yes, there was a computer room in the basement; I saw him on a monitor."

Kari looked solemn. "So now you know who we're up against. And how ruthless he is. He offered Hajjar five million dollars to kill the Russian, Yuri, there on the spot. He's an extremely dangerous man, a psychopath . . . and he will do anything to stop us from finding Atlantis. I won't underestimate him again. But for now, we're safe. We have the artifact, and more important, we have you. We'll find Atlantis, I know it. Now," she asked, "are you ready to order?"

vw

By the time they returned to the hotel later that afternoon, Nina was exhausted. How much of it was just tiredness caused by touring Paris, and how much was a delayed reaction to her experiences in Iran, she didn't know. All she did know was that before Frost's expert in ancient languages arrived, she needed a nap.

Even lying on the huge, comfortable bed, however, Nina's rest was uneasy. Part of her mind was still trying to process all the frightening and violent events she'd witnessed—been part of—since Starkman's phone call. Her academic life in New York seemed almost like another world.

And even in her half-sleep, she couldn't escape from the mysterious artifact, her mind still focused on the puzzle within her dreams. There was something about the piece, the strange feeling of memory she had experienced when holding it in the farmhouse.

Something familiar.

Something *here*.

Nina jolted to full wakefulness, knowing what it was, and how she knew it. She was curled up, knees tucked almost to her chest, one hand resting on the base of her neck.

Holding her pendant.

That was the sense memory she'd felt.

She leapt from the bed and raced to her desk. She snatched the artifact from under the magnifier and with her other hand hurriedly pulled the loop of the pendant over her head, holding the two pieces next to each other.

That was the connection! She'd had it all the time, and never even realized.

The telephone rang, startling her. Still clutching both pieces of metal, she clumsily picked up the receiver. "Yeah! Hello?"

"Nina?" It was Kari. "Are you all right?"

"Yeah, yeah, I'm fine! I just woke up." She was about to tell Kari what she had just discovered, but the Norwegian spoke first.

"I just wanted to tell you that the expert is here, so when you're ready, could you bring the artifact?"

Nina caught a glimpse of herself in a mirror. Her hair was standing up on one side where she'd slept on it. "Uh, can you give me five minutes?"

w

"That was *seven* minutes," whispered Chase as Nina entered the lounge.

"Oh shut up," she whispered back, looking around the room. Kari was sitting expectantly in an armchair, Castille leaned against the door to the corridor, eating an orange, and on a couch, sipping a cup of coffee, was . . .

"Hello, Nina," said Philby, standing up.

"What are *you* doing here, Jonathan?" Nina blurted,

thinking—hoping—this was a joke. Of all the people in the world Kristian Frost could have called upon to help analyze the artifact, he had chosen *Professor Jonathan Philby*?

"I think that's the reason," said Philby, looking down at the object Nina was carrying, wrapped in its cloth. "I got a call yesterday morning from none other than Kristian Frost, who told me that you'd helped find a most remarkable item but were having difficulty translating what was written on it. He asked if I would be willing to help you out. It was rather short notice, but . . ." He glanced at Kari. "Your father does have a way of making offers that can't be refused!"

"Horse's head in your bed?" asked Chase.

Philby looked at him uncomprehendingly. "No, a rather generous donation to the university. And, well, a flight in a private jet! Not something I've had the pleasure of before."

"So, Jonathan," said Nina, looking at him askance, "since when did you become the world's greatest expert on ancient languages?"

"Really, Nina," said Philby, "not wanting to blow my own trumpet, but I would have hoped you'd read my recent papers for the *IJA*. I think it's fair to say that I'm one of the top five authorities in the world on the subject, and certainly the top man in the West. Although I'm sure Ribbsley at Cambridge would disagree!" He chortled at his joke, stopping when he realized that the absence of undergraduates in the room meant nobody else was laughing with him. "Well then," he continued, "shall we have a look at what you've found?"

Nina carefully placed the artifact on the table as Kari adjusted a lamp to illuminate it. Philby's eyes widened. "Oh, now that's . . . that's remarkable." He looked up at Kari. "May I hold it?"

"Please do."

Philby picked up the artifact, weighing it in his hands. "Heavy, but not pure gold, the color's wrong . . . a gold-bronze—no, more like a gold and copper mix?"

"The word you're looking for," said Nina pointedly, "is orichalcum."

"Let's not jump to conclusions. Has a metallurgical analysis been done yet?"

"Not of the entire piece," said Kari, "but a small sample has been tested, yes."

"And?"

"And I believe Dr. Wilde is correct."

Nina gave Philby a self-satisfied nod.

"I see." Philby clearly had more to say, but kept it to himself. He turned the artifact over. "Small circular protrusion on the underside, and on the top surface . . . ah!" He shot Nina a smug smile. "Nina, I'm disappointed! Surely you can translate this!"

"I've translated *most* of it," Nina snapped. "It's a map, directions up a river to a city. I couldn't identify the other characters, but they're definitely not Glozel."

"Well of course they're not," said Philby. "But really! How could you not recognize Olmec inscriptions?"

She looked more closely. "What? Those aren't Olmec."

"Not *classical* Olmec, but the family resemblances are unmistakable. Don't you see?" He indicated certain characters. "Some of the symbols have been inverted or restyled, but they definitely—"

"Oh my God!" Nina exclaimed. "How the hell didn't I *see* it?"

Kari peered at the artifact. "Then they *are* Olmec?"

"God, yes! I mean, like Professor Philby said, not the classical form of the symbology, but definitely a variant. Older?" She looked at Philby for affirmation.

He nodded. "Almost certainly. They're less refined, and maybe with an influence from the Glozel in certain places. Very strange." He leaned back. "Glozel alphabetical influences in proto-Olmec hieroglyphics? That ought to ruffle a few feathers . . ."

"Who or what is an Olmec?" Chase asked.

"An early South American civilization," Nina told him. "They were at their height around 1150 BC, mostly on the southern coast of the Gulf of Mexico, but their influence went a lot farther inland."

Chase shrugged. "Oh, *those* Olmecs."

"Professor," said Kari, "what does the rest of the inscription say? I assume you can translate the Olmec symbols."

"I can certainly make an attempt. It may not be entirely accurate; as I said, the characters aren't quite the same as the traditional forms, but . . . Well, let's see, shall we?" He adjusted his glasses and leaned forward, Nina doing the same from the other side of the table.

"That first symbol, could it be—an alligator?"

"An alligator or a crocodile," Philby mused.

Castille perked up. "The crocodile river? That could describe a few places that Edward and I have visited. There was one time in Sierra Leone—"

"The next word is a combination of symbols," said Philby, ignoring him. "God . . . and water?"

"Or ocean," Nina offered. "Hey! The god of the ocean! Poseidon!" She and Kari both said the name at the same moment.

"Begin from the north mouth of the crocodile river," Philby went on.

"Seven, south, west. The river *at* seven, south, west, presumably," said Nina. "Follow course to the city of Poseidon. There to find . . . to find what?" She tried to make sense of the remaining symbols. "Damn it. I'm not exactly fluent in Olmec."

"Let me see . . ." said Philby, running a fingertip above the artifact. "This first symbol looks like the one for 'home,' but with these extra marks. It's almost like 'descendant'—no, 'successor,' but that doesn't really fit."

"Yes it does," Nina realized. "Successor home—*new* home. There to find the new home of . . . of this symbol."

"Hmm." Philby leaned so close that his breath clouded on the artifact's surface. "Now this one I really don't recognize. It could be a representation of a personal name, or maybe a tribe . . ."

"Atlanteans." Everyone turned to Kari. "The new home of the Atlanteans. That's what it says."

Philby pursed his lips. "Now, Ms. Frost, that could be wishful thinking. There are many other possibilities, which a detailed study of the ancient writings found in that region could clarify."

"No," said Nina, picking up the artifact. "She's right. It *has* to be the Atlanteans. There's nothing else it could be. The Atlanteans built a new home for themselves following the sinking of the island, somewhere in South America—and this piece is the map that'll take us right to it. All we need is to identify the river. If we can work out what the numbers represent—"

"*Or* we could just do a pub quiz," cut in Chase, grinning. "Seriously, Doc! South America! Big river full of crocodiles! What's the first answer that comes into your head?"

"The . . . Amazon?" she answered, unsure if Chase was, as he put it, "taking the piss" again.

"Bingo! Come on, look how many notches directing you left and right there are on this map of yours, and each of them has a number next to it. If that's how many tributaries you go past, that's a bloody big river. And if there's a lost city out there, it has to be in the Brazilian rain forest. If it was anywhere else, somebody would have found it already." He looked over his shoulder towards Nina's room. "You had an atlas in there, didn't you? Hold on a minute."

Chase jogged through the connecting door, returning with the large atlas, which he opened. "Here. There's the northern mouth at Bailique, and if you go upstream you pass four tributaries on the left, seven on the right . . ." He laboriously tracked the route westward against the markings scribed into the orichalcum bar. "Eight on the left, and that brings you to the first big junction at Santarém." The marking under his finger was more deeply indented than the others.

"Where it says to go right," Nina said.

"So it's working so far, then." They followed the directions farther upriver until their course finally branched off the Amazon itself, onto a tributary over a thousand miles inland. The thin blue line on the page of the atlas continued westward for another hundred miles before stopping. There were still several more direction markings left to follow on the artifact.

"We need a better map," said Kari. "Satellite imagery too."

"But at least we know the general area," Nina said excitedly. "Somewhere along the Tefé river. Right in the middle of the rain forest!"

"A proto-Olmec civilization, that far inland?" wondered Philby. "That doesn't fit with any of the current theories about their origins and population distribution."

"Nor does Atlantis, but things seem to be holding up so far," said Nina, slightly caustically.

Philby huffed. "And how exactly would the Atlanteans be able to sail from the Gulf of Cádiz, according to your theory, all the way across the Atlantic? Even if we accept that the Sea People of ancient legend were in fact the Atlanteans, a journey of a few hundred miles in a trireme is rather different from a journey of several thousand. Especially when they had no way to navigate!"

"Actually," Nina said, "they *did* have a way to navigate."

"What do you mean?" Kari asked.

"I just realized it before you called me." Nina picked up the artifact. "There was something about this that felt familiar, but I couldn't work out what until now. Look." She held the piece by the circular protrusion, letting it swing gently from her fingers like a pendulum. "It's meant to hang down, like this. And then . . ." She held her pendant beneath the curved end of the artifact. "They match up exactly. My pendant has a few numbers marked on it, and if you extend it along the same curve and also continue the sequence of numbers . . . Well, with a sighting system of some kind, like a mirror that fits in the little slot, then you've got a way to measure the angle of inclination of an object relative to the horizon!"

"An object like a star?" asked Kari, caught up in Nina's rising excitement. "Or the sun?"

"Exactly! It's a *sextant*! The Atlanteans had a navigational instrument in 10,000 BC that wasn't reinvented until the sixteenth century!"

"Imagine the military advantage that would give them over any other nation of the time . . ." Kari said thoughtfully.

Chase looked doubtful. "It's not exactly like they had GPS."

"Well no, because to work out longitude you need a very accurate chronometer, and it's a stretch to think the Atlanteans were *that* advanced," Nina said. "But a sextant lets you calculate *latitude*, how far north or south you are, with reasonable accuracy by using the sun or a star as a guide, as long as you adjust your calculations for the time of year. Which every ancient civilization with knowledge of astronomy was able to do." She held up the two orichalcum pieces and pretended to take a sighting on Chase's forehead, swinging her pendant back and forth as if it were part of a larger arc centered on the bar's pivot. "Without something like this, the only way to navigate at sea is to either follow the coastline looking for landmarks, or use dead reckoning—just head in a particular direction and hope you don't go off course."

"But being able to calculate latitude makes longer voyages possible," added Kari.

"Yeah. In fact . . ." Nina showed Chase the markings on the bar again. "The number here, seven, then south and west—the seven could be a latitude using whatever scale the Atlanteans worked in, and the compass directions . . ." The thought that had been taking form in her mind finally solidified. "It's telling the user how to get to the river on the map from Atlantis! Go south to what they called latitude seven, then turn west. As long as you're at the right latitude, then all you need to do is keep going west and you'll eventually reach your destination. Since we know where their latitude seven *is,* that means . . ."

Kari completed her thought. "That means, if we can determine exactly how many degrees are in an Atlantean unit of latitude, we can backtrack and work out the exact location of Atlantis!"

"Okay, so," said Chase, "all we need to do to find Atlantis is mount an expedition into the middle of the Amazon jungle, find a lost city and see if it's got any old maps still knocking around?"

Nina nodded. "More or less."

"Yeah, I'm up for that," he said with a mock casual shrug.

Philby stood up. "Ms. Frost?"

"Yes?"

"This may be completely out of line, but . . . if your initial surveys show that there may indeed be a lost city somewhere along the Tefé, would it be possible for me to accompany your expedition?"

"Wait, Jonathan, let me get this straight," said Nina, scenting victory. "Are you saying that now you *do* believe I was right all along and that Atlantis really existed?"

"Actually," Philby sniffed, "I was thinking more about the importance of discovering evidence of a pre-Olmec civilization and the chance to study its language firsthand. It would be an incredible find. Any connection to Atlantis would be . . . well, a bonus."

Kari was slightly thrown by Philby's request. "I'll check with my father, Professor, but . . . Are you sure that would be practical? We will be going deep into the jungle—and what about your commitments to the university?"

"I think I can arrange the time off—I *am* the head of the department, after all!" Philby laughed. "Besides, if Dr. Wilde can take off at a moment's notice on an expedition around the world . . ." He gave Nina a pointed look. "It's been several years since I went properly out into the field, but I've been to worse places than the jungle, believe me."

"Then as I said, I'll check with my father. But for now . . ." They shook hands. "Welcome aboard, Professor."

"Thank you," Philby replied.

Nina put her pendant back around her neck and placed the artifact on the map of Brazil. She gazed at the blank swath of green surrounding the Tefé river, trying to imagine what she would find there. "So," she whispered, "that's where you went . . ."

ELEVEN
Brazil

W elcome to the jungle!" Chase sang as he exited the plane.

Despite having traveled all around the world, Nina always found arriving in the tropics an unwelcome shock. While she didn't mind a hot environment per se, it was far easier to adjust to the dry heat of a desert than it was to emerge from an air-conditioned aircraft cabin into the sticky, humid heat of a tropical jungle.

And it was hard to get much deeper into a tropical jungle. Tefé was in the heart of the Amazon basin, the temperature over eighty degrees Fahrenheit and the humidity sticking her clothes to her skin.

But they would be going farther still into the rain forest. Examination of maps, satellite photos and aerial surveys of the region had narrowed down the possible location of the lost city to an area roughly eight miles in diameter, over a hundred miles upriver from Tefé. The nearest permanent settlement was more than thirty miles from the target area, and even that was just a small village. Nina had seen the aerial photographs; they showed nothing but a solid carpet of verdant green, the only thing breaking the monotony being the snakelike twists of rivers.

That same unbroken canopy of jungle had dictated the group's mode of transport. A helicopter could have reached the area from Tefé in less than ninety minutes—and Kristian Frost had indeed arranged for one to be standing by in case of any emergency requiring a rapid evacuation—but it would have found nowhere to land. People and equipment would need to be winched into the jungle, and Chase, overseeing the logistics of the operation, had decided it was too risky—much to Castille's relief.

Instead, they would be traveling upriver by boat.

But, Nina thought, it was one hell of a boat.

The expedition would actually be using *two* boats, but the *Nereid* was undoubtedly the most important. A Sunseeker Predator 108 motor yacht, the sleek vessel was painted in shades of charcoal gray and silver, the Frost logo prominent on the hull. Nina was astounded to learn that it had been flown to Brazil from Europe in the three days of intense preparation for the expedition, carried to the city of Manaus in the belly of a massive Antonov An-225 transport aircraft and then piloted the three hundred miles upriver to meet its passengers at Tefé. The resources that Kristian Frost was prepared to put behind the search for Atlantis—behind *her*—staggered her.

Despite its size—from the very tip of its sharply pointed bow to the stern, the *Nereid* was over a hundred feet long—it was expected to take the expedition quickly and comfortably to within as little as ten miles of their destination, despite the twists and constrictions of the river. The Predator's shallow draft of less than four feet, and a set of bow and stern maneuvering thrusters enabling it to turn in its own length, meant it could navigate the larger waterways with relative ease.

For those parts of the river the *Nereid* couldn't negotiate . . . that was where the second boat came in. The
Nereid's tender, hanging from a crane at the stern, was a
fifteen-foot inflatable Zodiac dinghy. It was the antithe-
sis of its luxurious mother craft, but if everything went
to plan it would only be needed for the very last leg of
the trip.

The need for a boat the size of the *Nereid* had come
about because the expedition had grown. In addition to
Philby, the original team of Nina, Kari, Chase and
Castille had been joined by four other people. Two of
them comprised the *Nereid*'s crew: the bearded, rotund
Captain Augustine Perez and his "first mate"—the title
was used jokingly—Julio Tanega, who smiled fre-
quently and broadly to reveal not one, but two gold
teeth.

The third new member was Agnaldo di Salvo, a
broad, powerfully built Brazilian in his fifties with the
air of a man who was surprised by little and frightened
by nothing. Kari had introduced him as their guide to
the area, but di Salvo, when Nina asked, called himself
an "Indian tracker." She felt a little too intimidated to
ask further about the exact difference between the two.
To her surprise, Chase and Castille seemed to know him
quite well.

Accompanying di Salvo, and not with his total ap-
proval, was another American, a tall, reed-thin graduate
student from San Francisco called Hamilton Pendry. He
was an environmentalist studying the effects of commercial exploitation of the rain forests on their indige-
nous population—and was also the nephew of a
Democratic congressman, who had persuaded the
Brazilian government to let him accompany one of their
experts into the jungle. Di Salvo, it seemed, had drawn
the short straw. Since the Frosts had specifically re-

quested that di Salvo accompany the expedition, they were now saddled with Hamilton as well, though the exact nature of the mission had been kept from him. Just as well, Nina thought; the long-haired young man seemed genuine in his enthusiasm for the cause of the native Indians and preserving their environment, but God! *Shut up about it for five minutes!*

Chase had hoped there would be another person joining them, but the reason for her being unable to do so became clear the moment Nina saw her. His friend Maria Chascarillo, when she met them at the dock, turned out to be every bit as beautiful as Shala . . . and also every bit as pregnant.

"I swear this is just a coincidence!" Chase told the amused Nina and Castille over Maria's shoulder as they hugged.

"Sure, we believe you," said Nina. "Don't we, Hugo?"

"Oh, of course," Castille replied, munching on a banana.

While Chase was disappointed that Maria wouldn't be joining the expedition, he was anything but when he opened one of the crates she'd delivered to the dock. Nina couldn't see the contents, but could guess easily enough. "Guns?" she asked, once Maria had left.

"And some other toys," he replied cheerfully. "We got caught short in Iran—I'm not going to let that happen again. Besides, from what Agnaldo said about the locals, we might need something to warn them off."

"What *did* he say about them?"

"Well, he's never met them personally—he's only heard stories. Because people who *do* meet them . . . they tend not to come back home to tell anybody about it."

"What?" Nina shook her head. "No, that sounds like total Indiana Jones stuff. The whole 'lost tribes of the jungle' thing doesn't work anymore. We're in the twenty-first century."

"*You* may be," said di Salvo from where he had seemingly materialized right behind her. For such a big man he had an uncanny ability to move without being noticed. "But they are not. You think it sounds like a story, but every year dozens of people—loggers, prospectors, even tourists—are murdered by Indian tribes deep in the jungle. It makes my job harder." He narrowed his eyes and surveyed the dockside, where various people were watching with suspicion. Hardly surprising, Nina realized; compared to the rundown little boats that called the docks home, the gleaming, futuristic form of the *Nereid* was like a visiting UFO. "These people hate the native Indians, because tribal lands are protected by law—so their livelihoods can be destroyed overnight if a new tribe is found. And it doesn't help if the Indians are believed to be killing intruders with impunity. So they hate me as well, because it's my job to find the Indians."

"It's an outrage!" squawked Hamilton. Unlike di Salvo, Nina heard him coming, his sandals slapping along the deck. "There shouldn't even be any need to confirm the existence of a tribe before an area becomes protected. This entire *region* should be protected! Logging, mining, ranching, it's all destroying the rain forest! They're just burning down thousands of acres every single day to make room for cattle ranches! It's like cutting out your own lungs to sell them for a few dollars so you can buy a burger!"

Chase shot a quick sidelong grin at Nina before adopting a completely straight face. "Yeah, that burning thing's terrible, isn't it? A total waste."

"I know!" Hamilton waved his arms, friendship bracelets flapping. "It's just . . . unbelievable!"

"I mean," Chase went on, "just one mahogany tree could make *dozens* of toilet seats. I've got one in my place at home. You ever sat on a mahogany bog seat? It's *the* most comfortable place to plonk your arse while you read the paper. Lovely and warm."

Hamilton stared at him open-mouthed. "That's . . . that's outrageous!" he finally managed to stutter. "That's the kind of uncaring dominator culture blindness that, that, that . . ." He trailed off and glared at Chase before turning and stalking away. Nina, who normally took a proenvironmental viewpoint, couldn't help smiling, while di Salvo roared with laughter.

"Eddie," he said, "you've done in five minutes what I couldn't in five days—you got the boy to shut up! You are truly a man of many talents."

"Well . . . yeah, I am." Chase tugged the lapels of his jacket immodestly.

"That was mean," said Nina, still smiling.

"Aw, come on! He might as well have a big target on his chest and a sign saying 'please take the piss.'"

Kari emerged from the main cabin onto the aft deck. "Is everything ready?" she asked. "Captain Perez wants to know when we'll be casting off."

"All our gear's aboard," Chase said. "Just got to load Nina's trunk full of new clothes from Paris."

"It's only a *suitcase*, and it's already in my cabin," Nina said, pouting playfully at him.

Kari glanced down at the dock, satisfying herself that everything had been brought aboard. "If we're ready, then there's no reason to wait. The sooner we start, the sooner we'll be there. I'll get Julio to untie us." She headed back into the cabin.

"A trip up the Amazon," said Chase, going to the other side of the boat and looking out across the wide river. "Haven't done that for a while."

"Well, up the Tefé, technically," Nina corrected. The town of Tefé was built on the bank of the river from which it took its name just before it joined the Amazon proper, at the eastern end of a broad lake over thirty miles long.

"All right, Dr. Smart-Arse. Either way, so long as I don't have to wrestle any bloody crocodiles this time, I'll be happy." He picked up one of the crates and followed Kari inside the boat.

Nina chuckled. "Yeah, right. Wrestling with crocodiles? As if!"

"You're right," said Castille as he picked up the second crate and started after Chase. "They were caimans."

"Caimans?" Nina said. "But aren't they basically the same . . . hey!" She chased after Castille.

W

The *Nereid* reached the southwestern end of the lake in just over an hour, giving its engines a workout without really taxing them before dropping to a speed more suitable for navigating the river feeding the great body of water. From here, the Tefé became a constant series of long undulating curves, never flowing in a straight line for more than a few hundred yards at a time. In places the river was over two hundred feet wide, while in others the banks were less than a quarter of that distance apart. With a slim twenty-foot beam the *Nereid* was in no danger of getting stuck, but the trees along the sides of the river were sometimes so large and overhanging that they formed a tunnel of foliage above the boat.

Dusk came, and Nina wandered onto the foredeck to watch the sun set through the trees. At the equator, day became night with an almost startling swiftness. She found Kari already there, leaning over the railing at the *Nereid*'s prow. "Hi."

"Hi!" said Kari, pleased to see her. "Where have you been? I've hardly seen you since we set off."

"I was going over the satellite photos again."

"Did you find anything?"

Nina shook her head, sitting on one of the loungers built into the deck. "If there's anything there, it's completely hidden by the tree canopy. We'd need a radar survey of the ground to see through it. I don't suppose your dad could whistle one up?"

"He did suggest it, actually. But it would have taken longer to get a satellite into the proper orbit than it would for us to go and look for ourselves, so . . ." She sat down next to Nina, indicating the passing jungle. "Have you seen this? I mean, really looked at it? It's extraordinary. So much variety, so many unique kinds of life. And all people want to do is cut it down and grub it up so they can *consume* it."

"I know. Hamilton might be kind of annoying, but he does have a point." Nina leaned back, staring up at the twilight sky. "I was thinking about what you said in Paris, about there being too many people in the world. It's true, isn't it? All of them fighting over the same resources, all of them believing they have a greater right to exist than anyone else." She sighed. "Shame there's not a lot we can do."

Kari gave her a half-smile. "Who knows? Maybe in the future we'll be able to change things for the better."

"I don't know. Human nature being what it is, it's hard to see how. And I don't think I'm really the world-changing type."

"You will be," Kari assured her, putting a hand on her arm. "When you discover Atlantis," she clarified at

Nina's confused look. "*That* will change the world. Not many people get to rewrite human history at a stroke."

"It's not just me! You're as big a part of this as I am. More so. I wouldn't even be here without you. It's you and your father's resources that made this possible."

Kari shook her head. "No, no. Money is worthless without a purpose. My father and I, we *believe* in the goals we are using our money to achieve. And so do you. I think . . ." She paused, considering her words. "I think we have a lot in common."

"Well, apart from the billions of dollars . . ."

"I don't know—I think discovering Atlantis will be worth quite a lot!"

The throbbing note of the engines dropped to idle. The *Nereid*'s steady progress upriver slowed, the relentless churning of water under the bow falling to a gentle slap of waves against the hull. "Why are we stopping?" Nina asked. "Is something wrong?"

"On the contrary," said Kari. "Navigating a river like this in the dark, especially in a boat this big, can be risky. Captain Perez is being safe." At that, there was a loud rattle from below the deck, followed by a splash as the anchor plunged into the water. "And also, I think dinner is ready. You're in for a treat. Julio is an outstanding cook."

⋎⋎

Kari wasn't kidding, Nina decided. She'd expected the provisions for the journey to be on the level of sandwiches and canned beans, but Julio had somehow managed to use the *Nereid*'s little galley to whip up a meal of fresh vegetable soup, roast pork au gratin in a port sauce and even a dessert of freshly made chocolate mousse. The whole meal was, if anything, better than anything she had eaten at the extremely expensive restaurants in Paris.

Now, feeling completely sated and a little buzzed from the wine, she wandered onto the rear deck—as much to escape the increasingly politicized debate going on between Hamilton, di Salvo and Philby as to get some fresh air. The boat's lights provided just enough illumination for her to pick out individual trees on the Tefé's banks, but the silhouette of the jungle canopy above was easy to make out against the brilliance of the night sky.

She sipped her wine and looked up at the stars. Whatever discomforts there might be from being out in the field, far from civilization, being able to appreciate the full beauty and majesty of the heavens was—

"Bloody hell, I'm stuffed," said Chase, clomping up behind her. Castille followed, nibbling a guava. "What're you up to, Doc? Come out here to let one off in private?"

"*No*," she said. "I wanted to look at the stars."

Chase looked up. "Oh, yeah. Pretty good."

"Is that all you've got to say?" Nina tutted. "You're in the middle of the Amazon jungle, with the most incredible sky overhead, and the best you can come up with is 'pretty good'?"

"What do you expect?" said Castille. "He is English, he thinks poetry"—he exaggeratedly pronounced it *poe-ee-tree*—"is a *kind* of tree, something you chop down to make toilet seats!" Nina laughed.

"*Actually,* I said it was pretty good because I've seen better," Chase told her, for once seeming a little offended himself. "In Algeria. Out in the desert in the Grand Erg. Not a single light for fifty miles, and the air was so clear I could see every single star in the sky. Even went out from the camp and lay on a rock for half an hour just staring up at it all. Amazing."

"Really?" Chase had never struck Nina as the type for stargazing.

"When were you in Algeria?" Castille asked suspiciously.

"Four years back. You know, when I had words with that gun-runner. Fekkesh, or whatever his name was."

"Ah! So *that's* what happened to him. Did they ever find his—"

"So you see, Doc," Chase interrupted quickly, "I can appreciate a good sky as much as anyone. I've been all over the world—I know natural beauty when I see it."

He was looking directly at Nina as he spoke. She turned to face the river, hoping he wouldn't notice her cheeks flushing. "Sorry. I didn't mean to imply that you were some sort of, well . . ."

"Crude, rude, bad-mannered yob from Yorkshire?"

"I never said yob!"

Chase chuckled. "Here, check this out." He reached around her to a box on the side of the deck, pressing against her as he took a flashlight from it. "Hugo, give me that."

"Hoy!" Castille protested as the guava was snatched from his hand. Chase tossed the half-eaten fruit out into the river, where it landed with a soft splash. More splashes suddenly echoed from the darkness.

"Watch this," Chase told Nina, leaning close to her again as he shone the flashlight out across the dark water. As if from nowhere, dozens of pairs of yellow lights glinted back at them like gemstones from the surface of the river.

"What are they?" Nina asked, just as one of the pairs of lights blinked. She gasped, instinctively backing against Chase.

"Crocs," he said. "Or maybe caimans, I can never re-member the difference." He lifted his other hand to point at them, holding Nina between the solid muscle of his arms. Her breath caught for a moment. "See how they're swimming along really slow just below the sur-face, pretending they're not actually moving? I've seen these buggers close up. They're *really* patient. They'll wait as long as it takes for something to get into range, and then . . ."

Seeing all the eyes watching her so coldly made Nina very nervous. "Are we safe?"

"As long as they don't figure out how to climb the ladder from the boat deck, yeah. But there's probably loads more on the other side as well. Just thought I'd show you in case you were planning any midnight skinny-dipping."

"Hardly," she huffed, stepping away from him.

Chase slowly panned the beam of the flashlight around the rear of the boat, more sinister eyes reflecting it back at the observers. "Even without this lot, I wouldn't recommend swimming anyway. There's prob-ably piranhas too—*and* that nasty little bastard that swims up your pisshole if you take a leak in the water."

"I was hardly planning to do *that*."

"Nah, you're too classy, I suppose." Chase switched off the flashlight, then let out a very loud fart. "Ah, that's better. Been waiting to do that since the main course."

"God!" said Nina, both disgusted and—she had to admit—amused.

"Better make sure I didn't follow through!" He handed the flashlight to Nina, then padded back into the main cabin.

She blew out her cheeks. "God, what is *wrong* with him?"

"It's just his way," Castille assured her, leaning on the railing.

"Well, I wish it wasn't. Why does he have to be so . . . *gross*?"

To her surprise, Castille almost sighed. "It's a defense mechanism, I'm afraid. He tries not to get too close to his clients. Especially when they are . . . well . . ." He nodded at her. "Attractive women. But he wasn't always like that. When I first met him, when he was in the SAS, he was always . . . what's the word?"

"Polite?"

"*Chivalrous*, that's it."

"So what happened?" Nina asked.

Castille looked pained. "It's not really for me to say."

"Well you started it! What happened?"

"Ai, I shouldn't have said anything . . . Promise me you won't tell him I told you?" Nina nodded. "He . . . he once fell in love with a woman he was supposed to protect."

"What happened?" She already thought she knew. "Did she . . . die?"

Castille snorted. "Of course not! Edward is not so incompetent. No, he married her."

"He was *married*?" *That* wasn't a possibility she had imagined.

"Yes. But . . . it did not last long. They were very different people, and she did not treat him well. And then she, ah . . ." He glanced at the cabin door, lowering his voice. "She had an affair. With . . . Jason Starkman."

"*What!*" Nina exclaimed. "You mean the same guy that tried to . . ."

Castille nodded. "We used to work together in joint operations for NATO. Jason was a friend—maybe even Edward's best friend, at the time. Then Jason disappears to join with Qobras for whatever mad reason, and *then*

Edward learns the truth . . . It was not a good time. He thought he had been betrayed by everyone he trusted."

"Except you."

"Ah, if Edward did not trust me, who would keep him out of trouble?" The moment had passed; it was obvious to Nina that Castille was not about to return to the subject.

She looked out over the river again, this time with the knowledge that she was being watched herself. The idea gave her a chill. Finishing her wine, she hurried back into the safety of the cabin.

TWELVE

The *Nereid* raised its anchor shortly after dawn, resuming its snaking voyage upriver. But the boat's passage was so smooth that Nina didn't wake up. It wasn't until the scent of breakfast permeated her luxurious cabin that she stirred.

After washing and getting dressed, she made her way up to the bridge. Kari was there with Chase and Perez, studying a picture on her laptop. Julio smoothly guided the craft through the river's sweeping turns.

"Morning, sunshine," said Chase.

"Hiya. What's up?"

"We've been sent the latest aerial photos of the search zone," Kari said, turning the laptop to face Nina. The curves and twists of the river on the screen were even more pronounced, like a child's doodle. In places, the Tefé even looped back on itself, creating circular islands surrounded by a natural moat. "There are four areas that are the most likely sites for the city, based on the terrain."

Nina examined the image. The vivid green of the jungle canopy was more broken in the new, higher-resolution photo, revealing tantalizing hints of the shadowed world beneath. She zoomed in on one of the four marked sections until it pixelated. A gray smudge lurked in a gap between the trees. "Could that . . . could that be a ruin under there?"

"Could be," said Chase. "Or it could just be a rock. This kind of jungle, you could hide an aircraft carrier under it and not be sure what you were looking at from the air. Only way to be sure is to get boots in the mud."

Kari brought up a map on the screen. "Captain Perez now thinks we should be able to get the *Nereid* to within three miles of the search zone before the river becomes too narrow to navigate."

"That's a lot closer than we thought," said Nina, examining the map. "How long will it take to get there?"

Perez looked at the controls. "We're doing twelve knots at the moment, but I doubt we'll be able to hold that for much longer. In about another fifteen kilometers we'll be heading up a tributary with much tighter bends, and we'll have to slow down. But we made good time yesterday, so . . . If the river's with us, it could be as little as four hours."

"Well before nightfall, then," said Nina. "So what's the plan when we get there?"

"That's up to you," Kari said.

"Me?"

"It's your expedition."

Nina shook her head. "No, Kari, it's definitely yours! I'm just, I dunno, an adviser."

Kari grinned. "Then advise me! What should we do when we arrive? Do we wait on the boat until tomorrow so we can have a full day's exploration—"

Chase clapped his hands. "Sounds good to me! Julio's cooking again, right?"

"Or do we take the Zodiac and start the search for the city as soon as we arrive?"

All eyes were upon Nina. "Er . . . we . . . take the Zodiac?" she finally decided.

"Aw, bollocks," Chase complained, not meaning it.

"Good," said Kari. "In that case, we'd better get prepared. I don't want to waste any time." She closed her laptop and left the bridge.

"You bloody workaholic," Chase said to Nina after she had gone. "We could have had another nice night on the boat if you weren't in such a rush to find this place! You know, it's been there for ten thousand years, it'll still be there tomorrow."

"Oh, admit it," she replied. "You're just as curious about finding it as I am!"

"Okay, maybe I am. But," he said, his tone becoming more serious, "You've got to promise me something."

"What?"

"If we find this place—and I think we will; you obviously know what you're doing . . ."

"Thanks."

"Then I want you to promise me that you'll keep calm, okay?"

"What do you mean?"

"I mean, I don't want you to get all excited, go running off—and then fall down a pit, or set off a giant boulder that goes rolling after you, or something."

"You've been watching too many movies," Nina teased. "As you said, it's been there for ten thousand years. Even if the place was crawling with booby traps, which is *highly* unlikely, the mechanisms wouldn't be working after all this time. Any moving parts would have seized up or rotted away by now."

"You know what I mean," said Chase, slightly exasperated. "I just don't want you to get hurt, okay?"

"Okay, okay. If we see any spear traps, I'll *stay out of the light*."

"Promise?"

"Promise."

"Good." Chase grinned. "By the way, that was officially the worst Harrison Ford impression in the world. Ever."

"Oh, I'd like to hear you do any better," said Nina. "With your Cockney accent."

"*Cockney!*" Chase pulled a face of exaggerated outrage. "Bollocks to that! I'm not a Cockney, I'm a *Yorkshireman*! Ought to throw you in the bloody river for that. Hmm . . ." He looked at her calculatingly.

"Oh no you don't," said Nina, backing away.

"Time for a swim, Doc!"

She shrieked and fled, Chase pursuing her with a maniacal laugh.

w

With a last throaty rumble, the *Nereid*'s engines fell silent. "This is as far as we can go," said Perez.

According to the GPS, they were just under three miles from the search zone; slightly closer than Perez's prediction, but his instincts about the navigability of the river were correct. Not only were the serpentine twists of the narrowing tributary too tight for the lengthy Predator to negotiate, but the sluggish water was increasingly clogged with debris. Despite Perez's best efforts to avoid them, several fallen trees floating in the water had banged alarmingly against the hull.

Nina looked through the bridge window at the jungle. It appeared much the same as it had during the rest of the voyage . . . but now that the banks were so much closer, it seemed to loom higher. More menacing, almost alien.

"We've got just over five hours until sunset," said Chase. "Enough time to let us get the lie of the land.

Hell, maybe we'll be lucky and walk right into this place."

"That'd be nice," Nina said. She had spent most of the day inside the air-conditioned cabin, finding the atmosphere outside more humid and stifling than ever.

"Is the Zodiac ready, Mr. Chase?" asked Kari.

"All set. Just add water."

Everyone returned to their cabins to collect their packs and equipment. Nina decided to carry as little as possible, sticking to basics like water, food and insect repellent on the grounds that between them Chase, Castille and di Salvo would have all the survival gear the team could need. But she paused before picking up her pack, staring at the Atlantean sextant arm on the desk. She touched the pendant around her neck, thinking for a moment.

"What the hell," she decided, picking up the metal bar and wrapping it in its cloth.

Kari tapped on the half-open door. "Can I come in?"

"Hi! Of course."

"You're bringing it with us?" asked Kari as Nina put the artifact in her pack. "I thought you were going to leave it in the safe."

"I was, but . . ." Nina shrugged uncertainly. "I don't know, I just thought it might be useful. If we get lucky and find something, maybe I can compare any text with it, be sure we're in the right place."

"I think we are. I know we are."

A piercing whistle cut through the air. "Oi! Doc! You ready?" Chase called from outside. "Shift your arse!"

"Coming!" Sharing an amused roll of the eyes with Kari, Nina hoisted the pack over her shoulder and left the cabin. Chase was waiting for them.

"Don't you ever get hot in that thing?" Nina asked, prodding the sleeve of his leather jacket.

"Hey, if it's good enough for Indiana Jones . . . Anyway, I only sweat when I'm hassled."

"And how often do you get hassled?"

"Since I met you, a lot more!"

The Zodiac was loaded, Perez and Julio lowering it into the river. The water was thick with algae and dead leaves, the boat making more of a turgid splat than a splash. Chase poked at the surface with a stick, sweeping rotting vegetation aside to check the color of the water.

"Top tip of the day," he told the rest of the party, "don't go in the water. And definitely don't drink it either."

"But surely the water should be perfectly fine," declared Hamilton, who had donned a rather vivid red shirt in contrast to the earth tones worn by everyone else. "It's fresh rainwater, with no man-made pollutants!"

"Well, stick a straw in the river and suck away if you want. But *you* can clean out the bog afterwards."

Hamilton looked confused. "Bog? Are we going into a swamp?" Chase sighed and shook his head.

They boarded the Zodiac, Chase sitting at the rounded bow while Castille worked the outboard motor. Nina and Kari sat facing each other on the boat's fat inflated sides behind Chase. Di Salvo, Hamilton and finally Philby clambered aboard behind them. There were no seats, but those packs containing camping gear—Chase had decided to prepare for any eventualities—served as substitutes.

There was one pack that nobody wanted to sit on, however. Although it was closed, it was obvious from its angular bulges that it contained guns.

"Okay," said Chase once everybody was settled, "all aboard the Skylark!" He waved to Julio, who untied the ropes. Castille started the outboard, which rasped and burbled into life. He guided the Zodiac carefully around the flank of its parent craft, then revved the engine and started the boat on its journey upriver.

w

"Christ," muttered Chase. "*Apocalypse Now* time." They were now inside the search area, looking for somewhere to make landfall—but being hampered by a dense mist. Even though the banks were barely twenty feet apart, the roiling fog was sometimes thick enough to obscure the trees.

The temperature had dropped noticeably. Nina had thought she would be glad of the relief from the oppressive, muggy heat, but instead found herself feeling uneasy. Even the constant shrieking and whooping of birds and animals had died away.

Di Salvo and Chase apparently felt the same, both men watching the banks intently, something about their postures suggesting that they were poised for action.

"What is it?" she asked Chase as the boat rounded another turn.

"I think we might have company." No trace of his usual levity; he was all business.

"Eddie," said di Salvo quietly, pointing off to the left. Nina followed Chase's gaze, but saw nothing.

"Yeah, I see it," Chase replied.

All Nina could see were trees. "What?"

Chase pointed. "Footprint in the mud." She still couldn't make it out even with his help.

"This is excellent," Hamilton said, talking in his normal overloud voice and earning annoyed glares from Chase and di Salvo. "This is everything I hoped for! We'll be the first people to meet this tribe, won't we, Agnaldo?"

"Other people have met them before," di Salvo said

in a low, ominous tone. "They just didn't come back to tell anyone."

"Hugo," Chase hissed, making a throat-cutting gesture. Castille immediately switched off the outboard.

"What is it?" Nina whispered. In reply, Chase pointed ahead.

Something emerged from the mist as the Zodiac drifted forward. Objects seemingly floating above the water . . . until the fog thinned enough to reveal that they were tied to bamboo poles.

Not tied to them. *Impaled* on them.

Nina cringed when she realized what the objects were. Corpses. The skeletal remains of people, most of the flesh long since rotted away and consumed by wildlife. All that remained were bones, shreds of clothing . . .

The blunt nose of the boat bumped gently against the first bamboo pole. Chase gestured to di Salvo, who tossed him an oar before picking one up for himself. "How long's it been there, do you reckon?"

Di Salvo stared up at the body. "A long time. Years. The last time anyone was reported missing in this area was about seven years ago."

"Looks like we found him." Chase used the oar to push the boat sideways, then started rowing, easing it past the first poles. More of the awful markers came into view ahead.

"Amazing," said Hamilton, watching the first corpse go by with an expression that blended awe with disgust. "A genuine lost tribe, completely isolated from civilization."

Nina's own expression was nothing but disgust. "I get the feeling they want to keep it that way. This is obviously a warning—*keep the hell out*."

"We just need to show them that we're no threat,"

Hamilton breathed. "Think of all the anthropological data we can learn from them."

"This is why I prefer archaeology," Nina muttered. "All my finds are dead, they can't stick you on a pole— Oh my God!" She jumped to her feet, rocking the boat, and tugged insistently at Chase's jacket. "Eddie, Eddie! Stop the boat! Stop!"

Chase snatched his Wildey from its holster before realizing that Nina was excited, not scared. "Jesus, give me a heart attack, why don't you?" he complained as he used the oar to stop the boat. "What is it?"

"That body . . ."

"What about it?"

She pointed up at one of the corpses. Even less of it remained than the first one they had encountered, the jawbone and one arm missing, all the connecting tissue eaten away. Its clothing was similarly rotted—but even through the accumulated filth and mold of decades, a glint of metal was still visible.

An insignia.

Just the sight of it made Nina shiver. It should have been incongruous, its impact diluted by time . . . but it still had the power to chill. An icon of evil.

The death's-head insignia of the Schutzstaffel. Hitler's SS.

"What the bloody hell's that doing here?" Chase wondered aloud. "Nazis? *Here?*"

"It must have been one of the Ahnenerbe expeditions," said Nina. "The Ahnenerbe was the archaeological arm of the SS," she added, in response to Chase's puzzled look. "The Nazis sent teams all over the world hunting for artifacts connected to Atlantean mythology—they believed that the Aryan race was descended from the ancient rulers of the world, all part of their "master race" crap. But their expeditions were focused on Asia, not South America . . ."

"Something brought them here," said Kari. She gestured at Nina's pack, and the sextant arm within. "Maybe the same thing as us."

"No, that doesn't make sense," Philby said, frowning in thought. "At the time of the Nazis, the Glozel Tablets were considered fakes, they'd been discredited. They wouldn't have been able to translate the inscriptions. It must have been something else, something we haven't seen . . ."

Kari examined the neighboring bodies, more curious than repulsed. "From the state of these other corpses, they seem to have died at the same time. But there's only four of them? That seems small for an expedition. The Ahnenerbe would send *dozens* of men on such a mission."

"Maybe this lot didn't run fast enough," said Chase, with gallows humor. "So what're we going to do? Whoever's out there, they don't want us around."

"We have to go on," Kari said, determined. "We haven't come all this way just to be frightened off by a tribe of savages and their . . . *scarecrows.*"

"Ah, ah, you see?" said Hamilton, waving an admonishing finger at her. "You're betraying your dominator culture prejudices there with your choice of words. These people have been living in perfect harmony with their environment for thousands of years—isn't it possible that by comparison, *we're* the real savages?"

Kari looked as irritated as Nina had ever seen her. "Oh, shut *up*, you stupid little man." Di Salvo barely contained a laugh at Hamilton's affronted gawp. "Mr. Chase, can you see anywhere we can get ashore?"

Chase peered into the drifting mist. "Hard to tell . . . there might be something on the right bank." He started rowing again, di Salvo joining in to propel the boat away from the grisly warning signs.

There was indeed a gap in the dense vegetation along the bank, and a few minutes later the Zodiac was tied up. Once everyone was on solid ground, the equipment was unloaded—and weapons handed out, to Nina's discomfort and Hamilton's outrage.

"You're seriously proposing that we make first contact with these people at gunpoint?" he shrilled as Chase passed compact automatic rifles to Castille and di Salvo.

"From the state of those bodies, I'd say they were met at *spear*point, so yeah," Chase replied. There was another rifle in the pack: after a moment's consideration, he took it out and offered it to Kari. "Do you know how . . ."

She took it from him. "Colt Commando M4A15.56-millimeter assault rifle, magazine load thirty rounds, maximum effective range three hundred and sixty meters." Keeping her eyes fixed on his, she ejected the magazine, pushed down on the exposed bullet with her thumb to check that it was fully loaded, reinserted it and chambered the first round, never once looking down at the weapon.

Chase was impressed. "Okay, I'm adding that to my list of things I want in a woman . . ."

"You don't want me anymore? I'm heartbroken," Nina told him.

"Heh. Okay, we've got . . ." he checked his watch, "three and a half hours to sunset, so no matter what happens, whatever we find, we're back here at the boat in three. Until we find out more about our pole-up-the-jacksie friends out there, we're not going to be doing any camping. Me and Agnaldo, we'll take point, Hugo'll watch our arses. Everyone else, keep between us—stay close, but don't bunch up too tight. Nina, you stick with Ms. Frost. It's funny, but I'm starting to think she could have a decent second career as a bodyguard."

Kari smiled and adopted a military pose, making Nina giggle. "All right! Let's go find this lost city!"

"What lost city?" asked Hamilton, as everyone followed Chase and di Salvo. "Wait, is there something I haven't been told?"

w

It took them close to an hour to reach the first of the four potential sites for the city, and another twenty minutes of exploration before it became obvious there was nothing there. What on the aerial photos had seemed like hints of former civilization were, on the ground, revealed as nothing more than exposed rocks, fallen trees and tricks of the light.

"Oh well, can't expect to hit it on the first try," Chase reassured Nina as he took a compass reading and checked his map. Beneath the trees, getting line of sight on a GPS satellite was problematic at best. "Still got three more to go."

"How far away's the next site?" she asked.

Chase pointed. "Mile or so that way. If we shift, we might have time to check out the third site before we go back to the boat. Or we could just head back now. I bet Julio's got something nice in the oven for us . . ."

Nina smiled. "Tempting, but no."

"Tchah. Okay," he said, raising his voice, "everyone, we're moving out!"

The group reassembled and set off behind di Salvo and Chase. Di Salvo slung his rifle over one shoulder and wielded a machete. After about ten minutes, the undergrowth thinned out noticeably. Occasionally he swung the blade to hack at some obstructing branch, but most of the time the route was clear, the party able to move at a faster pace than before.

"Yeah, I thought this seemed a bit too good to be natural," Chase said to him.

"What do you mean?" Nina asked. She and Kari were following ten feet behind, heeding his warning not to bunch up.

"We're on a path. That's why we don't need to cut through much." He indicated the thicker vegetation off to each side.

Nina looked around warily for any signs of movement. "So we might run into the Indians coming the other way?"

"Christ, I hope not. I don't want to miss my dinner!"

They kept moving through the jungle, ducking under low branches. The mist was still drifting between the trees, reducing visibility to at most fifty feet even when the view wasn't blocked by vegetation. Suddenly di Salvo stopped, holding up a warning hand for everyone else to do the same. "Footprint," he said, crouching.

Chase squatted next to him. "How old?"

"Less than a day. Definitely an Indian."

"How can you tell?" Nina asked. She could just about make out the faint outline of a bare foot in the dirt and fallen leaves.

"The toes are splayed, from walking barefoot all the time." Di Salvo stood and squinted through the mist. "Even if we don't find your lost city, this is still a previously uncontacted tribe. Another reason for the loggers and farmers to hate my guts."

"No, this is incredible!" said Hamilton, pushing past Nina and Kari. "We really will be the first people to make contact with this tribe! Once we establish peaceful communication, there's so much we'll be able to learn from them—"

A spearhead burst through the front of Hamilton's chest, his bright red shirt darkening with blood.

Nina screamed. Hamilton's eyes widened in shock as he sagged to his knees. Then he keeled over, the wooden shaft of the spear protruding over four feet out of his back.

Chase and Castille whipped up their rifles and aimed in the direction from which the spear had come. Kari grabbed Nina and pushed her to the ground as she lifted her own gun.

An arrow hit di Salvo in his right arm, the carved obsidian head slicing deep into his bicep. He dropped his machete, yelling in agony as he stumbled back and fell over Hamilton's body.

At the same moment, something whirled through the air and cracked against Chase's head—then wrapped around it.

A bola.

Chase staggered and dropped to the ground, clutching at the weighted cords digging into his flesh.

Behind her, Nina heard Castille let out a choking gasp. Another bola had caught him around the neck, squeezing his throat with the grip of a maniac.

Philby threw himself flat on the ground next to Kari and Nina. Another spear flew overhead, passing barely a foot above them.

Kari desperately looked for a target—but saw nothing except trees and mist.

Fleeting glimpses of shapes darted between the towering trunks. She brought the gun around, tracking one of the ghostly figures—

Crack!

Something hit her on the back of her head. Not a bola, not even a spear. The crudest of all weapons, just a rock—but thrown with great precision and force. It wasn't enough to knock her out, but it dropped her to the muddy ground, stunned and disoriented.

The rifle fell from her hands. Nina stared at it for a moment, frozen by fear. Then she reached for it.

But too late.

Where a second before there had been nothing but jungle, now there were people, springing into view as if they had been spat out of the ground.

Dark hair, dark skin, faces fierce behind their primitive but deadly weapons.

All of them aimed at her.

THIRTEEN

Nina hardly dared breathe.

The Indians closed in, treading silently over the moist earth. Ahead, Chase groaned. She could still hear Castille choking.

The nearest Indian was now barely ten feet away, a black-tipped spear held unwaveringly in his hand, poised to strike.

Nina glanced at Kari's gun . . . then looked away. Instead, she very slowly slipped her pack off her back, opening the top flap.

"What are you *doing*?" hissed Philby. "Get the gun! They're going to *kill* us!"

She ignored him, her eyes fixed on the man with the spear. Six feet away now. Another couple of steps and he would be able to impale her without the spear even leaving his hand.

Her fingers touched soft cloth wrapped around heavy metal. Still not taking her eyes off the Indian, she slipped the sextant arm out of the pack, letting the cloth fall away. Bowing her head in an unmistakable gesture of submission, she held up the orichalcum bar, offering it to him.

Silence.

She raised her eyes slightly, seeing the man's feet now barely a yard away. Splayed toes, the analytical part of her mind noted pointlessly. If he was going to kill her, it would be within the next few seconds . . .

Instead, he excitedly shouted something, the language completely foreign. One of the other Indians replied, sounding puzzled. Languages varied, but emotional tones were a human constant anywhere in the world.

He snatched the bar from Nina's hands. She flinched as the spear tip entered her field of vision, inches away. The Indians closed in and she was pulled roughly to her feet. At least twelve men now stood in a ragged circle around her. The other members of the group were likewise hauled upright. Kari gasped in pain, her eyes still unfocused, and di Salvo let out a strangled growl of agony as the Indians grabbed his injured arm.

They knew what guns were, Nina realized. Clearly they'd had enough contact with the outside world to recognize modern weapons. The rifles were quickly whisked away, and Chase and Castille were deprived of their sidearms before the bola cords around their heads were unwound.

"Nina! Kari!" Chase called. "Are you okay?" An Indian held the tip of an obsidian knife to his neck. Chase glowered at him, but fell silent.

"Kari's hurt," Nina said.

"No, I'm okay," Kari told her woozily. "What happened?"

"I gave them the artifact."

That brought Kari's eyes back into focus, staring in disbelief at Nina. "What?"

"I think it saved our lives. Look."

Kari followed her nod, seeing one of the Indians holding the sextant arm up to the light, examining it almost with reverence. The others looked on with similar astonishment, occasionally glancing suspiciously at their captives as they exchanged questions.

"Agnaldo," Nina whispered. "Can you understand them?"

"Some of it," di Salvo grunted, face tight with pain. "They know what it is, but . . . I don't think any of them have ever seen it before."

"Can you talk to them?"

"I can try."

"Tell them . . . tell them we're bringing it back to them," Nina said. "Tell them we've brought it back to— to the city of the water god."

Through his pain, di Salvo managed an incredulous look. "That might be hard to translate."

"Just do it!" she ordered.

Both Kari and Chase gave her glances of mixed surprise and admiration as di Salvo followed her order and began talking haltingly. The Indians listened, still suspicious—and confused whenever the Brazilian lost something in translation—but they apparently got the message. The man holding the artifact said something back to di Salvo.

"What'd he say?" Nina asked.

"I think they're going to take us to their village. Something about the tribal elders . . . I couldn't make it all out."

"They're not going to kill us?" said Philby. "Oh thank God!"

"Yeah," Nina told him grimly. "Too bad about Hamilton." Philby's face fell.

"I wouldn't start celebrating just yet, Prof," added Chase. "If these tribal elders don't like us, we're going to end up as the new 'keep out' signs on the river."

w

After tying their prisoners' hands behind their backs, the Indians led them deeper into the jungle.

"Can't believe we got ambushed like that," Chase said almost apologetically to Nina and Kari. "No way that would have happened if I'd still been in the SAS. God, I must be going daft."

"It wasn't your fault," Nina tried to reassure him. "This is where these people *live*. They know the terrain. And they're obviously big on keeping out visitors."

"That's not the point! The SAS has *never* been successfully ambushed on jungle patrol."

"*None* of us saw them, Edward," said Castille, his voice still raspy from being choked.

"Yeah, but . . ."

"Eddie," said Nina, "we're still alive, that's the main thing. If you'd started shooting, more of us might be dead. Maybe even *all* of us."

"The day's not over yet," he reminded her.

The trail began to rise, a low hill cautiously peeking above the great flat expanse of the Amazon basin. Nina noticed more signs of human presence, other paths joining the one they were traveling, converging on one location.

The hill became steeper, the path zigzagging towards the top and the trees thinning out.

"My God," Nina gasped as they reached the summit.

The hill was not tall, but it was high enough to give a spectacular view of what lay below. Greenery dominated the landscape, a branch of the river winding through it, but between the gaps in the trees she could make out the ruins of ancient buildings, the tumbledown remains of what must at one time have been an expansive settlement.

There was one building that was not in ruins, though. And she couldn't take her eyes off it.

From the air it would be mostly shielded by the overhanging jungle, little more than a broken shadow. But from this angle Nina could see it clearly, a brooding, menacing structure. And huge, around sixty feet high, four hundred feet long and about half as wide.

No, she thought. It's *exactly* half as wide.

She remembered a line from *Critias*: "Here was Poseidon's own temple, which was a stadium in length and half a stadium in width, and of a proportionate height, having a strange barbaric appearance." The dark stone structure before her certainly fitted the bill, the ancient Greeks considering "barbaric" just about anything that wasn't Greek. If anything, to Nina it seemed more like an Incan or Mayan structure, large blocks of carved stone carefully slotted together with almost unnatural precision. Jagged spires rose from its corners, foliage entangled around them, further camouflaging its shape. The lower parts of the walls were stepped like a ziggurat, but the curve of the roof resembled something more modern, like an aircraft hangar.

She was looking at the Temple of Poseidon, god of the sea.

Or rather a replica of it, a copy. The original, according to Plato, had been sheathed in precious metals, whereas this was just raw stone, covered in moss and vines. It was also smaller, well short of the length of a Greek stadium, 607 feet.

Unless she had been right all along—and an Atlantean stadium *was* smaller than a Greek one. Which would make a profound difference to the search for the island's location . . .

Nina didn't have a chance to think any further on the subject, the Indians driving them down the slope. She could now see that while the city was in ruins, it hadn't been abandoned. At the nearest end of the temple was a village of wood and stone huts. She counted fifteen of the circular structures. Either the tribe was spread out in more than one location, or their numbers were very small. It didn't seem likely that there could be many more than a hundred people.

The group was led into the village, the face of the temple looming over everything. Other Indians— young and old men, women, children—emerged from the huts to watch them pass, suspicion clear in their dark eyes. Near the base of the temple wall was a hut larger than any of the others.

"They're calling for the elders," said di Salvo, listening to the Indians' excited chatter. The animal skin covering the hut door was pulled aside, and three men emerged. Ancient, faces wrinkled beneath headbands adorned with feathers, but still strong and vital.

"Amazing," Kari whispered, more to herself than to Nina. "The genetics . . . With a population this small and this isolated, inbreeding would normally have caused clear genetic abnormalities by now. But there's no sign of it in any of these people. A superior genome . . . I'd love to get a DNA sample for the foundation to analyze."

"Let's convince them not to stick us on spikes before we ask if we can drain their blood, eh?" said Chase.

The Indians prodded the group into a ragged line before the elders, who regarded them with cold scorn as they listened to the leader of the hunting party. Their expressions changed as the hunter produced the Atlantean artifact. Awe . . . mixed with anger.

One of the elders asked a sharp question, the hunter pointing at Nina. The elder advanced on her, scowling as he examined her face closely. She tried not to show the fear racing through her body. After an agonizing moment, he made a slightly dismissive sound and turned his attention to Kari. His stern expression became more like fascination as he stared into her blue eyes, then reached up to touch her blond hair. She raised an eyebrow, but submitted.

Then he turned back to Nina, asking something. She glanced helplessly at di Salvo.

"He's asking about the artifact," di Salvo told her. "I think he wants to know where you found it."

"You *think*?" Nina said, her voice rising a couple of octaves. "If I say the wrong thing, he might *kill* me!"

"Just tell him what you know! I'll do the best I can to translate. The dialect's similar to those of tribes from much farther north."

"Similar's not the same as identical!" Nina pointed out. The elder was still watching her coldly. "Okay, okay! Tell him we took it from a thief in another land, that we followed the map on it to return it to its people."

Di Salvo began the translation. "You sure it's from here?" Chase asked quietly.

"It *has* to be. They know what it is."

The elder spoke again, di Salvo listening intently before translating. "He says it was stolen by white men in the time of his great-grandfather. They punished some of the white men, but the others escaped."

"The Nazi expedition," said Kari. "It must be."

Chase grimaced. "Sharp stick up the arse—now *that's* punishment."

Di Salvo looked confused. "Now he's asking about . . . I don't understand it. He wants to know if Ms. Frost is one of . . . the old ones?"

Kari and Nina exchanged glances. "Ask him what he means," said Nina.

"The old ones who built the temple," di Salvo translated. "He says they had hair like . . . white gold."

"Tell them that's why we came here," Kari said, authority returning to her voice. "To find out."

"You sure that's a good idea?" Chase muttered. "If
they think you're lying, you'll be the first one on the
pole!"

The elder spoke again, his two companions joining in
with additional declarations. Di Salvo struggled to keep
up. "They're saying that the artifact—they call it the
'pointing finger'—must be returned to its home in the
temple. They want you to do it, Ms. Frost."

"Me?" Kari chewed her lip.

"He says that putting it back will prove if you're
really one of the old ones—no, a *child* of the old ones."

"And what happens if she's not?" Nina asked.

Chase made an aggrieved noise, tipping his head to
indicate the sharp weapons still aimed at them. "Come
on, Doc. Keep up."

"Oh . . ."

Di Salvo continued. "They want you to go into the
temple and face . . . three challenges. The Challenge of
Strength, the Challenge of Skill and the Challenge of . . .
of Mind, I think."

Nina gave him a frozen grin. "Again! Thinking not
the same as *knowing*!"

"If you beat the challenges, you will have proved
yourself worthy to enter the temple. If you lose . . ." Di
Salvo pursed his lips. "What Eddie just said. For all
of us."

Chase winced. "Anyone else just pucker?"

Kari took a deep breath. "Tell them I accept the
challenge."

"You do *what*?" Nina yelped.

"Really?" asked di Salvo, shocked.

"Yes. But tell them that I want my friends to come with me." She indicated Chase and Nina.

"Oh, *bollocks*," said Chase as di Salvo relayed her request.

"Are you *insane*?" Nina hissed.

"You'll be safer in there than out here," Kari said. "At least we have a chance inside the temple. And I can't read their language—I suspect I'm going to need someone who *can*, and I don't think Professor Philby is quite up to the challenges."

For a moment, offense almost overcame fear on Philby's face. "Well actually, I think that—"

The elder interrupted him, one of the hunters giving him a warning jab in the back. Di Salvo continued to translate. "He says yes," he said, surprised. "The challenges are for two people. Because you're a woman, he'll let you have more help."

Kari nodded. "Hmm. I never thought I'd say this, but thank God for sexism."

"You have until nightfall. If you haven't returned by then, the others will be . . ." di Salvo paled, "put to death. And so will you, if you emerge."

Castille looked up at the sky. "Sunset is only an hour away. Maybe even less."

"In that case," said Kari, giving the elder an imperious look, "we'd better get started, hadn't we? Tell him to cut us free so we can go. And ask him what we can take with us." She looked over at the team's packs, which had been dumped in a pile nearby.

"Explosives, ropes, a crowbar or two . . ." Chase suggested quietly.

The hunters untied their wrists. "He says all you can take in with you are your clothes, and torches," di Salvo told them. "That's all you'll need if you're worthy of the challenge."

"I think this is a bad idea," Nina told Kari, rubbing her stiff arms.

"Then help me make the best of it," Kari replied.

"How are you staying so damn *calm*?"

"I'm not. I'm absolutely terrified. But I'm not going to show it in front of these people. And nor should you." Kari took Nina by the shoulders. "I *know* you can do this, Nina. Trust me."

Despite her growing fear, Nina felt oddly buoyed by Kari's faith. "Okay, I do. But if we get killed—"

"We won't."

Nina let out a nervous laugh. "Promise?"

Kari nodded. "Promise."

"Sunset's in fifty-eight minutes," said Chase, checking his watch. "So if you're done with all the female bonding chick flick stuff, you need to be thinking more *Tomb Raider*-y." One of the tribesmen emerged from a hut, carrying several long sticks with their ends dipped in what looked like tar. "Torches, eh? I think we can do better than that." Raising both hands, Chase looked questioningly at the rucksacks, very slowly sidling towards them. All around him, bowstrings creaked as the hunters took aim. "Okay, just me being harmless, see, big friendly smile . . ."

Sweating, and not just from the heat, he reached the rucksacks. Acutely aware that one wrong move would bring about a rapid and extremely painful death, he gently slid an LED torch out of his pack. "See? Not a gun. Just a torch. Which is in your rules, right? Agnaldo, remind 'em that it's in their rules?" He switched on the torch and shone it first at himself to show what it did, then at the hunters around him. Some of them jumped back in surprise, blinking at the bright light—but to his intense relief, none of them released their arrows. One of the men stepped forward and waved his hand back and forth over the lens, amazed that it gave off no heat. He said something to the elders, who considered it before giving di Salvo a reply.

"They'll let you use it," di Salvo told Chase.

"Good. Now, about those explosives . . ."

"We're running out of time," Kari said. She strode forward to the elders and held out one hand. Slightly taken aback, he placed the metal bar in her palm. "Okay. Nina, Mr. Chase, let's go."

"See you soon," said Castille as the trio was guided to the entrance. "Please?"

w

The dark passageway was under six feet high. Nina and Chase could fit in it easily, but the top of Kari's head barely cleared the ceiling, forcing her to duck under clumps of overhanging moss and creepers. The temperature and humidity dropped rapidly as they progressed.

Nina saw something on one wall as Chase swept his flashlight back and forth. "Eddie, hold it. Give me some light here."

The beam revealed a long line of symbols carved into the stone. Familiar symbols.

"It's the same language as on the artifact," Nina confirmed. "It reads like . . . I think it's an account of the building of the temple." She leaned closer. Among the Glozel and Olmec characters was something new: groups of lines and chevrons. "I think they're *numbers*. Could be dates, or maybe—"

"Nina, I'm sorry, but we don't have time," Kari reminded her. "They'll have to wait until we get back." Disappointed, Nina followed her and Chase down the passage.

About thirty feet in, they reached a left turn. Chase

flicked the flashlight beam suspiciously around the walls and ceiling.

"Mr. Chase, what's wrong?" Kari asked.

"I don't know about you, but I'm getting a bad vibe from this whole 'three challenges' thing," he said. "I just want to check that we're not going to walk into any traps."

"Eddie," Nina sighed, "I already told you that even if there were any, they would have stopped working centuries ago."

"Yeah?" Chase directed the beam back towards the entrance. "What if our feathered friends out there've been fixing them? Wouldn't be much of a challenge otherwise, would it?"

"Oh." Nina's stomach clenched with the realization that he could well be right. "Then . . . let's be careful."

The passage seemed safe, so they set off again. Another turn soon presented itself.

"Challenge of Strength, you reckon?" Chase asked as they paused at the entrance to a small chamber.

It was only slightly wider than the passageway, about eight feet to a side. Against the right wall was a rectangular stone block running across the chamber at roughly knee height, like a bench. At its foot was another passage, little more than four feet wide. Above the head of the bench, disappearing through a slot in the wall, was a thick branch bound tightly in vines, a smaller branch attached to its end to form a T shape. Apart from that, the chamber was empty.

Chase held up a hand for the two women to stay back as he cautiously advanced. He shone the light down the narrow passage.

"What do you see?" Kari asked.

"Little obstacle course. The passage's about twenty feet long, but there's poles coming down from the ceiling, so you have to twist between 'em." He made a face. "Poles with spikes on. Guess they're not for dancing."

"What about the wooden thing?" Nina asked, indicating the bench.

"That? There's stuff like that at my gym!" Chase nodded for them to come in, then straddled the bench, lying on his back under the bar. "I guess you lift it as if you're doing a bench press, and if you're strong enough, it opens an exit." He realized there was an indentation in the ceiling directly above matching the size and shape of the bench, but couldn't see any reason for it.

Kari took the flashlight, aiming it down the confined passage. It seemed to be a dead end—but there was something on the far wall, a square hole. "Or one person has to hold the weight up while the other goes down there and triggers the release. The elder said two people were needed to perform the challenges."

"So why not just go down to the other end before anyone lifts the weight?" Nina suggested.

"'Cause that'd be way too easy." Chase reached up and experimentally raised the bar. It moved easily for a couple of inches before encountering resistance. "So what do we do? Do I lift this and see what happens, or . . ."

Kari peered down the passage again. "We have to go down here anyway, so it might be a good idea to get to the other end first . . . What do you think, Nina?"

"Me?" Nina nervously regarded the two-inch barbs protruding from the maze of metal poles. There was enough room between them for even Chase to fit, but they would all find it tricky to avoid the spikes. She looked up, to see that each pole disappeared into a hole in the ceiling about five inches across. Oddly, the holes in the floor fitted them far more precisely. "I have absolutely no idea."

"Fifty-three minutes, Doc," said Chase, holding up his watch arm.

Hating being put on the spot, Nina looked to the end of the passage. The recess in the wall was big enough to reach inside; maybe it contained a lever to open a door. "Okay, well then . . . we'll go to the other end. Once we get there, you lift the bar and we'll see what happens."

"Right. And Nina?"

"Yes?"

"Don't get scratched. You neither, boss. Tetanus shots are a right pain."

"We'll try," said Nina, almost smiling.

Kari went first, turning sideways and effortlessly slinking between the poles. Nina followed her more awkwardly. Without exchanging words, they fell into a routine: Kari lit the way and advanced a few steps, then switched the light to her other hand so that Nina could see as she followed.

"Keep talking," Chase said. "Let me know how far you've got."

"There's about four meters to go," Kari called out as she stepped forward. "I still don't see an exit, but I think the recess—"

Clunk.

Something shifted under her foot.

"What was that?" Nina gulped. Dust trickled down through the gaps between the blocks. "Oh crap."

"Move!" Kari shouted, grabbing Nina's wrist and pulling her down the passage between the spiked poles as the entire ceiling started to descend with a horrific grinding sound, the individual blocks lowering in unison.

Even in the dim light, Chase saw the ceiling drop towards him too—as a door slammed shut, sealing the entrance. Now he realized the purpose of the indentation above the stone bench—it allowed the entire ceiling to descend all the way to the floor, leaving nowhere for anybody to hide—

No way to escape being crushed!

FOURTEEN

"Oh my *God!*" Nina screamed as Kari pulled her between the poles.

A protruding barb slashed through Nina's sleeve. She cried out, instinctively pulling away from the source of pain—and slamming into another one, driving a spike into her left shoulder.

Behind them, Chase desperately pushed up the bar, not knowing what else he could do. It was heavy, but not so heavy that he couldn't support it, like bench-pressing two hundred pounds.

The ceiling slowed, but didn't stop.

"I'm holding it!" he yelled. "Keep moving!"

Nina squealed in agony as Kari's attempt to pull her onwards twisted the spike inside her flesh. Kari immediately let go and tried to turn back to help her—but the lowered ceiling forced her into a semicrouch, making it harder to maneuver.

"Keep going!" Nina shouted, pointing at the end of the passage. Tears streamed down her face.

"I'm not leaving you!" Kari grabbed her hand. "Come on! You can do it!"

Holding in an anguished wail, Nina pulled free. Blood spurted down her shirt. "Oh *God!*"

"Come on!" Kari guided her through the poles. They were halfway down the passage, ten feet to go—but there were still more of the spiked obstacles to negotiate.

The ceiling kept descending, dust and grit cascading from the blocks. It was now almost at Nina's head height, Kari hunched over ahead of her.

Chase held up the bar, his arms extended to their limits. At least he could support the weight almost indefinitely . . .

Another *clunk,* the sound of something large and heavy moving behind the slot in the wall. A mechanism—

Bang!

The pressure on Chase's arms suddenly increased.

"Jesus!" he gasped, caught by surprise. An extra fifty pounds, at least, had been dropped onto the weight he was already supporting. His elbows bent . . . and the ceiling began to move faster.

"Shit!" Muscles straining, he forced his arms straight again.

The descending stones slowed—slightly. The passage was only five feet high now, and still shrinking.

"Keep going!" Kari cried. Only eight feet to go, seven, but each step she took became smaller as she fought to keep her balance in her unnatural position.

Chase heard the mechanism rattle again. Teeth clenched, he gasped, "Watch out!" just as—*bang!*—another weight fell, even heavier than the last. He roared as he forced his arms to stay locked under the extra strain. He was now supporting well over three hundred pounds, and the impact alone when the new weight dropped had almost slammed the bar out of his grip.

One more like that, and the challenge would be over. The ceiling jolted sharply downwards before slowing again. It hit Kari, making her stumble and fall against one of the poles. A jagged barb stabbed deep into her left bicep. She choked back a scream, trying to pull herself free of the spike, but the ceiling pressed relentlessly down on to her, driving the barb deeper into her arm.

"Nina!" she groaned through the pain. "I'm stuck! You'll have to get to the end!"

Nina looked down the passage. Only six feet to go— but Kari was blocking the easiest route between the poles. "I can't make it!"

"Yes you can! You *have* to! Nina, *go*!" Kari released her hand.

Sweat streaming down his face, Chase heard the mechanism again. Another weight was about to drop. "I can't hold it!"

Nina moved.

Bent over, head scraping along the shuddering ceiling, she squashed herself as hard as she could against one wall and squeezed through the first gap. A barb ripped her shirt, but she was through.

Four feet.

Chase braced himself for the impact of the next stone, knowing he wouldn't be able to hold it.

Nina twisted between the next two poles, but the ceiling was now too low for her to walk upright. She dropped to a crawl, another spike slicing one thigh.

The cold stone blocks pressed against Kari's face and shoulders, forcing the spike deeper into her arm.

Two feet—

Clunk!

"Shit . . ." grunted Chase, every muscle tensing.

Nina saw the dark hole set in the far wall start to disappear behind the last ceiling block.

The pain in her arm became unbearable. Kari screamed.

As did Chase, his straining arms finally giving way under the pounding sledgehammer impact of the final weight.

The ceiling shot downwards.

Nina lunged for the hole as the last block dropped like a guillotine blade.

Her hand closed around something: a wooden handle. She pulled it.

Nothing happened—

Thunk.

With an echoing crunch of stone, the ceiling stopped.

Chase opened his eyes. In the distant light, he saw that the wooden bar was now resting an inch above his neck—and barely the length of a finger above that was the cold stone that had been about to crush him.

Kari held perfectly still. Any movement just made the pain in her arm worse. She tried to see what had happened to Nina.

Nina's right arm was inside the hole in the wall. *Trapped* inside. The ceiling had dropped so low that she couldn't pull it back out. Another inch, and it would have first crushed the bone, then sheared off her arm above the elbow.

With another monstrous grinding of stone and a flurry of dust, the ceiling started to ascend.

Chase glanced to his side. The door blocking the entrance opened again.

Nina snatched her arm out of the hole and looked back. Kari's face, lit spookily from below by the flashlight, was full of pain—but also an almost disbelieving relief. Nina picked her way back through the poles to help her. With a moan, Kari lifted herself off the spike. Blood gushed through the hole in her sleeve.

"Oh God," Nina said, pressing her hand against the wound. "Eddie! *Eddie!* Kari's hurt, she needs help!"

"She's not the only one," Chase gasped as he slid out from beneath the bar, then rolled off the stone bench. He pushed himself to his feet, aching arms barely cooperating. "I need some light."

Nina took the light and directed it down the passage so Chase could make his way through the poles. By the time he was halfway through, the ceiling had returned to its original position and the awful noise had stopped.

There was another *clunk,* this time from the dead end of the passage.

Nina whipped the flashlight around to see an opening appear, one of the stone blocks in the wall pivoting backwards to reveal darkness beyond.

"Nina . . ." said Kari, looking at the blood on her shoulder.

"Forget about me, you're hurt worse than I am. *Eddie!*"

Barely fitting between the poles, the barbs plucking at his leather jacket, Chase reached them. "What happened? Let me see."

Nina held up the light. "One of these spikes got her."

"Jesus," Chase muttered, carefully peeling back the wet material for a better look. "That's deep—and the first aid kit's outside in the village."

"Forget that," said Kari, struggling upright. "We don't have time, we've got to keep moving. How long have we got?"

Chase raised his arm to look at his watch, letting out a strained grunt. "Are you okay?" Nina asked.

"Feels like some bugger dropped a car on me. We've got . . . forty-nine minutes."

"And two challenges to go," Nina said ruefully.

"We can do them," said Kari, no doubt in her voice. "Come on."

vw

Once through the opening, Chase insisted that they stop so he could treat the women's wounds. By ripping off Kari's torn sleeve he was able to tie it around her arm to slow the bleeding. The injury to Nina's shoulder was less deep, so he wadded up one of *her* sleeves and used it as a makeshift bandage.

"That's the best I can do for now," he said apologetically. "You'll both need stitches when we get back out. And shots too. Don't want some nasty little bastard insect infecting you with anything."

Nina shuddered. "God. I can't believe how close that was."

"Still got two more to go," Chase reminded her.

"Yeah, thanks for the reassurance. And you're sweating."

"I think this officially counts as hassle."

"We've beaten the Challenge of Strength," said Kari, cautiously flexing her arm and wincing a little. "So we've still got the Challenge of Skill, and of Mind."

"I was going to say that I hope they're easier than the last one," Chase said, "but . . . I'm not getting that feeling."

"Nor am I," said Kari. "But I know we can do it. How much time?"

"Forty-six minutes."

"Okay, then. Let's see what the Challenge of Skill involves."

They walked cautiously down the new passage, which turned several times before the sound of their footsteps was joined by something else. Chase directed the light ahead. The corridor opened out into a larger chamber. "Water," he said.

"*Inside* the temple?" Nina asked.

"You said it's the temple of the sea god . . ." They increased their pace. "Definitely running water. Maybe that little river we saw by the village goes through the temple as well."

His theory was proven correct moments later as the narrow passage widened out. The trio found themselves on a platform along the long edge of a giant rectangular pool of brackish green water. The ceiling above the platform was at the same claustrophobic height as the passageway, but the chamber over the pool was far taller.

Chase directed the light at the water, rippling reflections crawling over the chamber's walls. The pool, at least a hundred feet long, was about twenty-five feet across. Spanning it was what Nina at first thought was a rope until she realized it was actually a narrow wooden beam, little more than an inch wide, supported along its length by poles emerging from the pool. The beam was two feet below the level of the platform—and only six inches above the sluggishly flowing surface of the water.

"Okay, now what?" Chase wondered.

Kari pointed across the channel. "What's that?"

The flashlight revealed a glinting golden dagger, resting point-down inside a shallow recess directly above the opposite end of the beam. About ten feet above that was a ledge running along the far wall, but there didn't appear to be any way up to it. "Well, that's the Challenge of Skill," said Nina, moving to the edge of the platform and crouching for a closer look at the wooden beam. "You have to balance on this thing and walk across to get the dagger."

Chase found something else of interest, at one end of the pool against the stone wall. "And then that comes down so the others can get across." On the far side was a narrow drawbridge, held up by ropes. He traced an arc from its upper end with his forefinger, all the way down to the edge of the platform on which they stood.

Nina looked more closely at the pool. At each end of the chamber she could just about make out the arched top of what she assumed was an aqueduct, channels for the water to flow through. "Why not just swim across?" she wondered aloud. "I don't know how deep it is, but—"

The dull green surface of the water suddenly exploded into life. A set of gaping jaws burst out of it, lunging at Nina—

Kari seized her by her collar and yanked her backwards as the caiman's mouth snapped shut where she had been a moment earlier. The twelve-foot predator thrashed and clawed at the side of the pool, trying to pursue its quarry, but was defeated by the vertical stone wall. Unable to gain traction, it dropped back into the water with an evil hiss.

Nina was too shocked to speak. "Are you okay?" Kari asked as Chase let out a considerably louder shout of "Jesus!"

Her voice returned. "Oh my *God*!"

"*That's* why you can't swim across," Chase said. "Wouldn't surprise me if there's piranhas in there too."

"How did that thing get *in* here?" Nina yelled, her whole body shaking. "We're in a five-thousand-year-old fucking *temple*!"

Chase warily examined the pool, watching the ripples subside. "Same way the traps still work—those bastards outside."

"Nina, it's okay, it's okay," said Kari, trying to comfort her. "Mr. Chase, can you see anything else?"

Keeping his feet a cautious distance from the edge, Chase leaned out over the pool, shining the light up at the ceiling. "There's something up here, over the beam, but I can't see what it is. Like a recess in the wall."

"Can you reach it?"

"No, it's too high . . . Oh, I get it. To get a proper look, you've got to cross the pool to where the dagger is."

Kari let out a long breath. "Okay. Then I suppose I'm going to have to go and get it."

"You?" Nina objected. "But you're hurt!"

"You sure?" Chase asked. "I mean, it's a narrow beam, but I could probably make it . . ."

In reply, Kari effortlessly cartwheeled into a handstand, holding herself on just her uninjured right arm before flipping back elegantly onto her feet.

"Okay," said Chase, nodding. "So *you* go and get the dagger . . ."

Nina looked at the pool, worried. "Kari, are you sure? If one of those things sees you . . ."

"We don't have a choice," Kari said, going to the end of the beam. "How much time have we got?"

"Forty-one minutes," Chase told her.

"Then I'd better hurry." She stepped down carefully from the platform onto the wooden beam. It creaked, flexing slightly. Chase held up the flashlight to illuminate her path. Composing herself, Kari slowly stretched out her arms for balance, holding in a little moan as pain jabbed through her injured arm. "Okay. Here I go."

She took a first step. The beam creaked again, more loudly. To everyone's alarm it also wobbled, the supporting poles swaying in the water, causing ripples.

Other ripples appeared in the pool, near the aqueduct at the downstream end of the chamber. The sinister eyes of a caiman broke the surface, the rest of its long body barely visible beneath the algae-filled water. "Kari . . ." Nina warned.

"I see it," she said, returning her full attention to the

beam as she advanced, step by careful step. She was at a point halfway between two of the support poles, and the beam was sagging alarmingly, only a couple of inches above the water.

The caiman moved, its tail undulating sinuously from side to side as it drifted towards her.

Kari ignored it, concentrating solely on keeping her balance. The next support pole was now almost beneath her. That stopped the beam from sagging—but the whole affair was still wobbling. It took all her effort to keep upright.

A soft splash made Nina look around to see a second caiman surface at the other end of the chamber. It was even larger than the first, and seemed unconcerned about remaining unseen, floating on the surface like a log.

A log with *teeth*. It lazily opened its mouth, letting out a malevolent hiss.

Kari increased her pace. She was now halfway across, the beam drooping again under her weight. Every step made it sway a little more.

She could see the dagger clearly now. Its tip rested in a little metal cup that seemed to be connected to something behind the shallow recess. Another booby trap?

There was also a *very* narrow ledge just above the end of the beam, so thin she hadn't been able to spot it until now. It was under a meter across and barely a centimeter deep, just enough to provide a toehold. It had obviously been placed there deliberately by the temple's builders, but for now their reasoning remained unclear, and Kari had the distinct feeling she wouldn't like the answer when it revealed itself—

The beam wobbled.

Her attention had been diverted by the mysterious ledge, just for a moment—but a moment was all it took for her to lose her balance. She tried desperately to straighten up, but her weight had already shifted too far over. In a second, she would fall into the pool, into the jaws of the waiting caimans—

She threw herself forward, grabbing the beam with both hands as she landed on her stomach. The narrow wood slammed against her like a truncheon blow. She clamped her knees around the shuddering walkway, trying to stop herself from rolling into the pool.

"*Kari!*" Nina screamed.

Chase pulled off his jacket, ready to jump in after her. "Shit, she's not going to make it!"

The caimans, attracted by the noise, closed in.

"Stay back!" Kari shouted. Her knees were still in the water, but she managed to hook both her boots around the beam to drive herself forward.

The long head of the nearest caiman came fully out of the water, opening to expose its jagged teeth—

"Oi!" Chase roared, dropping onto the end of the beam and stamping one foot hard into the water, creating a huge splash. "Over 'ere! Hey!"

The larger of the two caimans changed direction with a flick of its tail, heading for him. The first, still gliding rapidly towards Kari, turned its head towards the noise—and took the heel of her boot against the side of its skull with a *crack* that echoed around the chamber.

The caiman released a sharp bark of air, thrashing its tail and dropping back into the water. Frantically, Kari hauled herself along the beam, looking back over her shoulder at the great reptile. It was circling in a sinister line through the water, arcing back around for her.

Chase kicked up another splash before leaping back onto the ledge as the caiman erupted from the water, its giant mouth agape. Powerful claws raked the stone wall as its heavy body thudded against the beam.

Kari was nearly jolted into the water by the impact.

She clung to the beam with all her strength, the caiman crashing into it again and again in its attempt to pursue Chase, before it finally admitted defeat and dropped back into the pool.

The other caiman was still heading back at her, slimy water streaming from its mouth as it broke the surface. This time it had learned its lesson and was aiming for her upper body, out of range of her legs. Straining, she dragged herself forward again.

Her fingers touched cold stone, and she clawed for the tiny ledge, gaining just enough purchase to pull herself up from the beam and plant one foot upon it, thrusting herself upright.

The caiman lunged—

With a yell, Kari snatched the dagger from its resting place and plunged it down between the caiman's malevolent yellow eyes, stabbing deep into its brain.

The reptile crashed onto the beam, then slid lifelessly back into the pool as she pulled the dagger out with a spurt of blood.

And where the blood blossomed in the dark water, it suddenly frothed, churned from below by dozens of fins.

Chase had been right.

Piranhas!

Kari flattened herself against the wall. One foot was on the beam, which juddered as the caiman's body ground against it. The very tip of her other heel was on the little ledge. She waited until the beam stopped shaking, then looked around to see the result of removing the dagger. Something had definitely clicked when she'd grabbed it . . .

Two things happened at once.

From somewhere above Chase and Nina came a loud *clang* of metal. She caught a flicker of movement inside the opening Chase had seen, but it was too dark to make out the cause.

But she had no time to think about it, because the beam had started moving, retracting into the wall behind her. The supporting poles moved with it, slicing V-shaped ripples into the water—the whole thing was mounted on some sort of framework at the bottom of the pool, and now it was disappearing with alarming speed into the cold stone at her back.

"Eddie, do something, stop it!" Nina wailed, helpless as she watched the beam slide away from the side of the platform.

"*How?*" he demanded, looking for something, *anything* he could do to stop its relentless retreat. There was nothing.

Close to panic, Kari hopped her foot along the beam, only to have it forced back against the wall within moments. At the speed the beam was moving, she had a minute—less—before it completely disappeared and she was plunged into the pool with the remaining caiman . . . and the piranhas tearing at the flesh of its dead companion.

She still had the dagger in one hand, for all the good it would do her.

The dagger . . .

There must be something more, she realized. She had to *do* something with the dagger, not simply retrieve it.

"Throw me the flashlight!" she shouted.

"She'll fall in!" Nina protested as Chase pulled back his arm.

"She'll fall in anyway in a minute!" he shot back. "Kari! Ready?"

"Yes!"

He flung the flashlight. The brilliant light arced across the chamber like a falling star. Kari reached up with her wounded arm, and the light landed in her hand with a slap. Swaying to keep her balance, she brought it up, aiming the beam at the recess high above the other side of the pool. It was revealed as an alcove, a cube three feet to a side. Metal gleamed within, copper or gold, a foot-wide circular object like a shield standing up inside it.

Not a shield; a *target*.

There was only a meter of the beam still exposed, just seconds before it disappeared completely.

Kari turned and stepped onto it with both feet, snapping back her right arm to throw the dagger. The blade flashed through the torch beam—

It struck the target with a bang, dead center. The metal disc toppled backwards, disappearing from sight.

The beam stopped moving. With a creak of wood and straining ropes, the narrow drawbridge at the far end of the chamber fell, hitting the platform opposite with a *whump*.

Kari looked down. There was just enough of the beam still protruding from the wall for her to fit both her feet, if she turned them sideways.

She put her free hand against the wall for support, feeling very vulnerable. "*Now* what am I supposed to do?" she asked aloud.

As if in answer, there was a noise above her. A length of knotted rope, a chunk of wood weighing down its end, dropped from the ledge running along the wall.

Chase and Nina were already making their way to the bridge. "We'll meet you on the other side!" Chase called as Kari gripped the rope and pulled on it, checking that it wasn't about to break—or that it wasn't booby-trapped itself. It seemed firm. Favoring her right arm, she climbed onto the ledge. It was only a foot across, but compared to what she'd just been standing on, it seemed as wide as a motorway.

Nina and Chase were waiting for her at the end of the drawbridge as she dropped down. "That was a hell of a throw," said Chase as Kari slumped against the wall, exhausted. "How big was the target?" She held her hands a foot apart as Nina checked her makeshift bandage. "Bloody hell, I don't think *I* could've made that. They weren't kidding when they said it was a challenge of skill."

"We've still got one more challenge to go," Nina said.

"The Challenge of Mind? That sounds like your cup of tea, Doc. You up for it?"

She smiled nervously. "Do I have a choice?"

"How long have we got?" Kari asked Chase, voice tired.

"We've got . . . thirty-six minutes." They all looked down the passage leading deeper into the temple. Even though it was no different from the others they had traversed, it somehow seemed more forbidding.

"Okay, then," said Nina, standing straight with a defiance she definitely didn't feel. "I hope my mind's up to the challenge."

FIFTEEN

Wary of traps, they made their way down the passage.

Something was troubling Nina, but she wasn't quite sure what. It wasn't just the adrenal aftershock of having narrowly escaped death. There was something else, a feeling, a *certainty* that she was overlooking some vital fact.

There was no time to think about it, though. Another chamber opened up ahead.

"Hold it," said Chase, stopping at the entrance. He shone the light into the space beyond. "Smaller than the last one."

Compared to the expansive pool chamber, this one was miniscule, only about fifteen feet across. As Chase moved the circle of light around, Nina saw that the walls were covered with markings—the same language as on the Atlantean sextant arm, and the entrance of the temple itself.

"Looks safe," he announced, "but don't quote me on that. Just be careful." He stepped into the room, pausing as if expecting some hidden trap to be triggered, then signaled for Nina and Kari to follow. "Okay. So, Challenge of Mind. Go for it, Doc."

"Right . . ." she said, taking the flashlight so she could examine the inscriptions on the walls. "Oh God! This could take days to translate!"

"We've only got thirty-three minutes to sunset. Think fast."

"Nina, over here." Kari had gone to the wall opposite the entrance. A stone block, unmarked by text, appeared to be a door, and next to it was what looked almost like . . .

"It's a scale," said Nina. "A weighing scale." She aimed the beam beneath it. A trough was carved out of the stone, and inside it were a hundred or so lead balls, each the size of a cherry. "I guess we have to put the right number of balls into the scale. But how do we work out how many to use?" There was a lever by the scale's copper pan; she reached for it, but Kari stopped her.

"I have a feeling that we only get one attempt," she said, pointing up at the ceiling. Suspended above them was a large metal grid of foot-long spikes, ready to impale everyone in the room when it fell. Nina hurriedly pulled her hand away from the lever.

She flicked the light across the walls until she spotted large symbols carved over the closed door. They were arranged in three rows, one above the other, with groups of six different symbols in the uppermost one, five in the remaining two. Nina immediately recognized the first symbol. Groups of little marks like apostrophes . . .

"They're numbers," she announced. "It's some kind of mathematical puzzle. Working out the answer tells you how many balls to put into the pan."

"Is that all?" Chase sounded almost disappointed. "Christ, even I could do that. Let's see . . . the top one, there's three of those little dots, five upside-down Vs, seven bent-over Ls, two sideways arrows with a line under them, four backwards Ns and one backwards N with a line next to it. That's 357,241. Doddle."

"And you'd be wrong," said Nina, managing a smile. "The numerical order is reversed from ours—the first symbol, the little dot, is actually the smallest number; each one of them is one unit. So the first number's actually 142,753. It's the same symbol from the river map on the sextant arm, and I know I'm right about it being a one, because otherwise we would never have found this place."

"All right, smarty." Chase grinned. "So the other numbers are . . . 87,527 and 34,164. So, what, we subtract them? That makes, uh . . ."

"Twenty-one thousand and sixty-two," Nina and Kari said together, almost immediately.

Chase whistled, impressed. "Okay, so we don't need a calculator. But there's no way there's twenty-one thousand balls in that trough."

"What if it's a combination of operators?" Kari suggested. "Subtract the second number from the first, then divide by the third?"

"Too complicated," Nina said, staring at the numbers. "There's no symbol suggesting that you need to perform different operations. Besides . . ." She frowned, working it out. "The result would be a fraction, and I don't think putting one-point-six-two balls into the scale is likely to be the right answer."

Chase winced. "Bloody hell. It hurts just *thinking* about doing that in my head."

"The first number plus the third divided by the second is two-point-oh-two," Kari suggested. "I doubt they would have calculated results down to one fiftieth accuracy. They may have rounded it to two . . ."

"It's still too complicated!" Nina cried. "And it's too *arbitrary*. The first plus the third divided by the second?

It's like setting a crossword puzzle but missing all the down clues!" She pointed the light back at the other walls. "The clue must be somewhere else, in the other text. I just have to find it."

"Tick-tock, Doc," said Chase, pointing at his watch. "Twenty-nine minutes."

Nina knelt at one of the walls, scanning the light over the symbols. After a minute, she blew out her breath in frustration. "All of this is about the building of the city and the history of the people afterwards. I don't see anything that relates to the puzzle at all."

"There's nothing about the people before they came here from Atlantis?" Kari asked.

"Not that I can see." Nina hurried across the chamber to look at the text on the opposite wall. "This is more of the same. It's almost like a ledger, a record of the tribe year by year. How many children were born, how many animals they had . . . There must be a couple of centuries of data here. But none of it has anything to do with the challenge!" She jerked an angry thumb at the symbols over the door.

"I just thought of something," Chase said. "This thing's a challenge of the *mind*, right? Well, what if it's some sort of lateral thinking puzzle?"

"What do you mean?" asked Kari.

"This is obviously a door, right?" Chase stepped up to it. "We didn't even think about just opening it."

"Give it a try!" Nina told him.

Chase reached out and pushed the door. It remained completely still. He tried one side, then the other. Nothing happened. Just to be thorough, he also attempted to lift it, then pull it outwards from the wall. Still nothing.

"Bollocks!" he exclaimed, stepping back. "I really thought that might work."

"So did somebody else," Nina said, joining him. "Look! I just realized, the door's not quite the same color as the rest of the chamber. It's been carved from different rock. And there are marks on the stones around it—chisel marks, and crowbars. But none on the door itself. This is a newer door; the Indians have replaced it! Somebody didn't want to solve the puzzle, so they just smashed the door open."

"The Nazis?" Kari wondered.

"Sounds like their kind of approach," said Chase. "They must have been able to persuade the Indians to let them bring more than just a flashlight inside."

Kari nodded. "Probably at gunpoint."

"Right. Problem is, we don't have any crowbars. So we've got to do it the hard way."

Nina hurried back to the carvings on the side wall. "I think we still can. These numbers, there's something odd about them. Look." She ran her finger along the lines of symbols. "You see? They're arranged in groups of *eight*, at most. Never nine or ten. Eight here, eight here, eight here . . ."

"You think they could have been working in base eight?" asked Kari.

"It's possible. They wouldn't be the only ancient civilization to use it."

"What've you found? What's all this eight stuff?" Chase asked.

"I think we've been projecting our own biases onto the people who built this temple," Nina said, excitement glinting in her eyes. "We assumed they were using base ten math, like we do." She caught Chase's questioning look. "Our numerical system is based around multiples of ten. Tens, hundreds, thousands . . ."

"Because we've got ten fingers, right. I *did* pass my GCSE maths," he said. "Well, just about."

"It's a very common system," Nina went on. "The ancient Greeks used it, the Romans, the Egyptians . . . It's common because it's literally right there in front of you." She held up her fingers to demonstrate. "But it's not the *only* system. The Sumerians used base sixty."

"Sixty?" hooted Chase. "Who the hell would use that?"

Kari smiled. "You would. Every time you look at your watch. It's the basis of our entire timekeeping system."

"Oh, right." Chase nodded sheepishly.

"There've been plenty of other bases used by ancient civilizations," Nina continued. "The Mayans used base twenty, Bronze Age Europeans used base eight . . ." She snapped her head around to look at the symbols again. "Base eight! That's it, it must be!"

"Why would anyone use eight?" Chase asked. In response, Kari held up her hands, fingers splayed—but with her thumbs tucked against her palms. "Oh, I get it—they used their thumbs to count on their fingers, but didn't actually *count* the thumbs?"

"That's the theory," said Nina, searching through the inscriptions. "So instead of going one, ten, one hundred, the numbers actually go one, eight, sixty-four . . ." She rushed back to the door. "So the first column is single units, the second multiples of eight, then sixty-four, five hundred and twelve, four thousand and ninety-six and . . ."

"Thirty-two thousand, seven hundred and sixty-eight," Kari finished.

"Right. So the number would be, let's see . . . three single units, plus five units of eight, forty, plus sixty-four times seven . . ."

Chase made a pained noise. "I'll let you two work all that out."

Kari came up with the answer first. "Fifty thousand, six hundred and sixty-seven."

"Okay," said Nina. "You do the second number, I'll do the third." Another burst of mental arithmetic produced the answers: 36,695 and 14,452. "All right! So the first minus the second minus the third is . . ."

They both thought hard about it, Chase watching intently—only to see both their faces fall at almost the same moment. "What? What's the answer?"

"It's *minus* four hundred and eighty," Nina told him despondently. "It can't be base eight."

"What about base nine?" asked Kari. "If decimal gives too large a result, and octal too small . . ."

"The answer would still be in the thousands. Shit!" Nina gave Chase a questioning look.

"Twenty-four minutes."

"Damn it! We're running out of time!" She angrily kicked the door. "What the hell are we missing?"

Chase crouched and rummaged through the lead balls, hoping there would be some hidden clue in the trough. There wasn't. "What if we just take a best guess and put that many balls in the pan? There's a *chance* we might get lucky."

Nina touched her pendant. "That would need the biggest piece of luck in the world."

"It's all we've got. We can't just give up—even if we go back through all the other challenges, the Indians'll kill us as soon as we get outside. And Hugo and Agnaldo and the Prof."

"If we get it wrong, we'll be killed anyway," Kari reminded him, pointing at the spikes suspended overhead.

"Maybe there's some way we can pull the lever from outside the room . . ."

But Nina was no longer listening. Something else Chase had said was now foremost in her mind.

Back through all the other challenges . . .

That was what had been troubling her, gnawing at her mind. And now that she knew what it was . . .

"There's another way through!" she burst out. "There *has* to be! The tribespeople maintain the temple, and the traps—they must, they need to be reset. And repaired." She indicated the stone door. "But there's no way the temple's builders would have forced the very people who were supposed to be protecting it to go through the challenges every time they needed to go inside—one little mistake, and they're dead! So there *has* to be some way for them to get through safely without running the gauntlet every time."

"A back door?" asked Chase.

"Yes, like a service access, or even just some way to open the exit of each challenge without actually having to complete it." Nina turned the light back to the chamber walls. "Maybe there's a switch, or a loose block, some way to open the door."

They hurriedly searched the walls of the chamber, fingertips brushing over the cold stone to feel for anything out of place. After a minute, Chase raised his voice. "Here!"

Nina and Kari joined him in one corner of the room. At floor level, right where the two walls met, was a small vertical slot. It wasn't much of an opening—but compared to the precise joins of the other blocks, it was clearly a deliberate feature rather than poor workmanship. "What's inside?" Kari asked.

"No idea—it's too small to get my hand into. Nina, you've got nice dainty little fingers—have a root around."

"And I'd like them to *stay* nice," Nina complained,

but she knelt by the slot anyway. "Oh God. I just hope there's not some finger-chopping thing or a scorpion inside . . ."

She warily slipped her fingers between the blocks. A little more . . . more . . .

Her fingertip touched something. She flinched, afraid it was a hair-trigger that would drop the spikes onto them. But the trio remained unimpaled.

For now.

"What is it?" asked Kari.

"There's something metal in here."

"A switch?"

"I don't know . . . hold on." Nina tried to slide her fingers around the obstruction. "It could be."

Chase leaned closer. "Can you pull it?"

"Let me," said Kari. "Nina, you should wait in the passageway. Just in case something goes wrong."

"If it doesn't work, then we're going to be dead soon anyway," Nina said. "You two get out of the chamber. Go on!" she added, before either of them could object. She took several deep breaths as they backed through the entrance to the chamber. "Okay. Here goes . . ."

She wrapped her fingers around the metal, paused for a moment to wonder what the hell she was doing, and pulled it.

Clink.

The hanging framework of spikes remained still.

Another, louder clink of metal came from the stone door. Nina exhaled loudly. "I think it worked . . ."

"Get out of the room," Chase ordered, waving Kari to stay back as he walked to the door. Nina gratefully obeyed. He braced himself, then pushed. The door swung open, heavy stone rasping over the floor. Another dark passage lay beyond.

"You did it!" Kari cried.

"Nice work," said Chase. "But we really need to shift—we've only got twenty-one minutes left."

"We'd better get a move on then." Nina patted Chase's arm as she passed him. "And you were right about the lateral thinking."

"We make a pretty good team, don't we?" he said. "You've got the brains, I've got the brawn, and Kari's got . . ."

"The beauty?" suggested Nina. Kari smiled.

"I was going to say agility, but yours works too." He took the light from Nina. "Okay. So we beat the three challenges. Now what?"

"Now we put the artifact back where it belongs, then get the hell out of here," Nina said, advancing down the passage.

ᴡᴡ

Castille glanced nervously to the west. The sun had long since dropped behind the high canopy of trees, but pinpoints of bright light still made it through the dense foliage.

It was very close to the horizon, though. And the sky overhead was rapidly turning a deeper blue as dusk crept in . . .

He looked back at the temple entrance. The square of darkness was devoid of any movement, as it had been from the moment the glow of Chase's flashlight had disappeared about forty minutes earlier.

"Hurry up, Edward," he said to himself.

"Wh-what if they're dead?" Philby asked, sweat covering his panicked face. The three prisoners were on their knees outside the elders' hut, several hunters encircling them.

"They'll make it," Castille said, wishing he felt as confident as he sounded.

An unexpected harsh crackle cut through the mutterings of the Indians and the chatter of birds. It was coming from the abandoned packs.

"Survey team, do you read me? This is Perez. Do you read me? Over."

The Indians reacted with predictable shock, jumping into defensive positions and aiming their weapons out past the perimeter of the village as if expecting an attack.

"Survey team, come in, come in, over."

"If we can answer him, he can call in the helicopter," di Salvo said under his breath. "With some support."

"And guns!" Philby added, almost hopeful.

"*If* we can persuade them to hand us the radio," said Castille. The Indians had now worked out where the sound was coming from, and were cautiously investigating the packs, prodding them with their spears.

"Survey team, I don't know if you can hear me . . ." One of the tribesmen jabbed Castille's pack, momentarily muffling the transmission. *". . . got company. I can hear at least one chopper, maybe two, approaching my position. They're not ours, I say again, they are not our helicopters. Please respond."*

"Military?" Castille asked, concerned.

"I would have been told if they were planning any jungle operations," replied di Salvo.

"Merde." Castille had a horrible idea who might be in the helicopters. "Agnaldo, try to get them to bring us the radio. We need to—"

One of the Indians pulled out the walkie-talkie. Perez's voice was now clearer. *"Survey team, I see one of the choppers! It's—Jesus!"*

A piercing screech of static blasted from the speaker, the Indian dropping the radio in fright. Philby looked between Castille and di Salvo in confusion. "What just happened? What was that?"

Castille gave him a grim look, twisting to look in the direction of the river. A few seconds later, a sound like a distant clap of thunder reached them. "That was the *Nereid* exploding," he said.

"*What?*"

"It's Qobras. He's found us."

w

Chase checked his watch. "We've only got eighteen minutes left."

"Then we need to keep moving," said Kari. She took out the sextant arm. "Find where this needs to go."

"Maybe we could just leave it here and *pretend* we put it back," Nina said, not entirely joking.

"I think they might check," replied Chase sarcastically.

"Well, it was a thought . . . *Oh.*"

They had reached the end of the passage.

Chase lifted the flashlight. Even its bright beam was almost lost in the huge room beyond.

"The Temple of Poseidon," Nina whispered.

Chase stared in awe. "Bloody hell."

By Nina's estimate, the great chamber was two hundred feet long, half the length of the entire building, and nearly as wide. The vaulted stone ceiling, wreathed with gold and silver, rose like a cathedral roof, supported along its length by buttresses at the sides of the vast room. In each alcovelike space between the buttresses was a statue, glinting with the unmistakable color of gold. There were dozens of them, ranks of unimaginable riches.

But they were nothing compared to what had seized the attention of the three explorers. At the far end of the chamber, stretching to the very highest point of the ceiling nearly sixty feet above, was another statue.

Poseidon.

"My God," said Nina as she walked towards it, any concerns about traps completely banished from her mind. "It's just as Plato described it . . ."

"'There was the god himself standing in a chariot, the charioteer of six winged horses, and of such a size that he touched the roof of the building with his head,'" recited Kari alongside her.

"You'd get a few quid for that on eBay," Chase remarked.

"Those must be the hundred Nereids," said Kari, ignoring him and pointing at a circle of much smaller statues around Poseidon's chariot.

"Doesn't look like a hundred to me," Chase said as they headed for the giant statue.

"I bet there's sixty-four of them," said Nina. "In base eight, that would be the number as important as a hundred in base ten. Plato was using a word translated from a different numerical system, but the actual number it represented was different—"

"I count seventy-three," interrupted Kari.

"*What?* Seventy-three?" Nina snapped incredulously. "What the hell kind of system would use *seventy-three* as an important number?"

"Nina? Seriously? We don't care," said Chase. "We're here—now let's do what we've got to do before we all get killed, okay?"

"Okay," Nina pouted. "But it still doesn't make any sense . . ."

Behind the massive statue was an opening leading to a flight of stairs. They ascended to find another chamber, smaller than the main temple, but even more elaborate—and extravagant. Although it was lower, the ceiling was vaulted to match the temple outside. But where that had been made from stone, this was something else.

"Ivory," said Kari as Chase directed the torch upwards. She frowned. "According to Plato, the roof of the *entire* temple was meant to be lined with ivory . . ."

"This isn't the Temple of Poseidon," said Nina. "It's a *replica*, a copy. The Atlanteans tried to re-create the citadel of Atlantis in their new home. I guess ivory was harder to come by here, so they made do with what they had . . . *Whoa*." She came to an abrupt stop. "Eddie, give me the flashlight." She snatched it from his hand. "We've found what we came for."

She aimed the beam at the chamber's rear wall. A warm reflected glow filled the room. Orichalcum.

The entire wall was coated with the metal, thin sheets inscribed with line upon line of ancient text. Nina quickly saw that it was another variation on the language, older, but no less advanced.

But that wasn't what transfixed her attention. She played the torch over the large illustration dominating the wall, following the distorted but very familiar lines . . .

"Is that a *map*?" Chase said in disbelief.

"It's the Atlantic," Nina whispered. "And beyond."

Although inaccurate in detail, the shapes of the continents were impossible to mistake. The eastern coasts of North and South America on the left, Europe and Africa on the right. And past Africa, the map continued around into the Indian Ocean, tracing the shape of India itself and even parts of Asia. Lighter lines connected various points, apparently charting courses between ports and marking routes to settlements inland.

Most of the lines converged on something in the eastern Atlantic, the shape of an island found on no modern map . . .

"Jesus." For a moment, Nina felt as though her heart had stopped. "We've found it. Atlantis. Right where I said it was."

"My God," said Kari, stepping forward for a closer look. "You found it! Nina, you found it!"

"*We* found it," Nina replied, sharing her delight. "We did it, we found Atlantis!" For a moment she almost whooped with glee—until the reality of the situation returned to her. "Eddie, how long have we got left to get back?"

"Fourteen minutes. The only bit that'll be tricky will be getting back through those poles with the spikes— we can do it in eight, if we shift." Chase moved away from the map, spotting something in the rear corner of the chamber.

"So we've only got six minutes left to explore? Shit. *Shit!*" Nina banged her clenched fists against her thighs in utter frustration. "I need more *time!*"

Kari held out the orichalcum artifact. "Let's find where this goes. If we can get back to the village in time, we might be able to convince them to let us back into the temple if we promise we won't take anything. All we need are photographs . . ."

"It's not *enough*," Nina moaned, feeling everything she'd worked for slipping away. She knew there was no chance of the Indians allowing them inside the temple again—assuming they weren't killed just to keep its mere existence secret.

"Hey." At first Chase thought he'd found another exit, a chute leading downwards from the chamber. But a quick glance told him it was blocked, clogged by rough chunks of rock. That the debris was far from the exacting standards of the rest of the temple didn't escape him, but then he saw something more interesting nearby. "Over here."

Nina and Kari hurried over to find an altar, a high slab of polished black stone. On it rested several objects, all made of orichalcum.

"That must be the other part of the sextant," said Kari, pointing at a flat pie-slice-shaped piece inscribed with Atlantean numerals. Nina quickly took off her pendant and held it against the bottom of the sextant. The curvature was an exact match.

"God, I had part of one like it all along," she said, putting the pendant back around her neck. "Give me the arm."

"How come the Nazis got away with that piece, but not the rest of them?" Chase asked.

"Maybe the men carrying the others were the ones we saw on the river." Nina quickly placed the nub on the arm's underside into the corresponding hole at the top of the triangle, swinging it around so the arrowhead scribed into its surface lined up with the mark above each number. "It works," she said, with a mixture of vindication, and sadness that she wouldn't be able to show anyone else her discovery. "Whatever they used as mirrors are missing, but you can see the slots where they'd fit. God, they really *could* calculate their latitude, over ten thousand years ago . . ."

"Okay, the thing's home, let's go," said Chase.

Nina waved her hands. "Wait, wait!"

"Nina, they're going to *kill* Hugo and the others, and us too if we don't move our arses!"

"One minute, just one more minute! *Please!*"

"Let her," said Kari firmly. Chase reluctantly acquiesced, but pointedly held up his watch hand.

"The map," Nina said, almost gabbling in her haste to get the words out. "Look, the destinations at the end of the trade routes, or whatever they are, they've got numbers and compass directions marked next to them. The mouth of the Amazon, here," she pointed at it, "it says seven, south and west, just like it does on the sextant arm." She moved across the map to the distorted representation of Africa, indicating the continent's southern tip. "But look at this! The Cape of Good Hope's marked as well—it shows its latitude relative to Atlantis!"

Chase shook his wrist, waving the watch at her. "Point, Nina! Get to it!"

"Don't you see? We already know how far south the mouth of the Amazon is relative to Atlantis, seven units of latitude, and now we know how far south they said the Cape is as well—so since we know their positions relative to each other in modern measurements, we can use the difference to find out exactly how big an Atlantean unit of latitude is, and then work back north from the Amazon to find Atlantis itself! We can *do* it! Now that I understand their system, we don't even need the artifact any more—all we need is time to make the calculations!"

"We're *out* of time, Nina," said Chase, his tone making it clear that there would be no further discussion. "We've got to get out of here. Now!" He took the light from her. "You too, Kari! Let's go!"

They ran out of the chamber, passing the colossal statue of Poseidon. Nina strained to listen over the sound of their footsteps echoing through the huge room. "What's that noise? I can hear something!"

Chase could hear it too, a low-frequency rumble, growing louder with every second. "Shit, sounds like a chop—"

The entire temple shook as an explosion blasted a hole in the roof.

SIXTEEN

*D*own!" screamed Chase, throwing himself on top of Nina as shattered stone rained around them. Much larger blocks tumbled to the temple floor below the gaping hole, smashing deafeningly apart on impact.

A fierce wind blew through the gap, whipping the clouds of dust into a swirling vortex. Chase rolled clear of Nina and squinted up at the sunset sky, which was almost immediately obscured by something.

Something *big*.

The roar of the helicopter's engines and the machine-gun thudding of its rotor blades were so intense that he could *feel* them. A Russian-built Mi-26 Halo, the biggest helicopter in the world, designed to carry large loads over long distances.

Large loads—or large numbers of troops.

The chopper moved into a hover directly above the hole. The fuselage doors were open, and at any moment ropes would drop from them so men could rappel into the temple . . .

"Come on!" he yelled, his voice barely audible over the Halo's thunder. He helped the women up. "Get to the tunnel! Now!"

"What the hell's going on?" shrieked Nina.

"It's the Brotherhood! Get into the tunnel! Run!" He grabbed the still-bewildered Nina's arm and pulled her after him, Kari sprinting alongside.

Six black lines snaked from the Halo. They fluttered in the downdraft before tightening as men dressed in black combat gear and body armor expertly descended each one, brilliant beams of light lancing out from their chests. Chase saw enough in his brief backwards glance to know they were professionals, ex-military.

And each man was armed with a Heckler and Koch UMP-40 submachine gun, and probably other weapons as well.

They reached the passage, Chase leading the way with the flashlight in his outstretched hand. The noise of the chopper was still audible even as they negotiated the twists and turns and ran through the door into the chamber housing the Challenge of Mind.

"How could they have found us?" Kari demanded.

"I don't know," said Chase as they entered the next tunnel. "Maybe they put a tracker on the boat."

Nina was breathless, unused to the pace. "What do they want?"

"The same thing as us," Kari told her. "Only they want to destroy it, to make sure nobody can use the information to find Atlantis."

"And destroy us, too," added Chase.

"Oh my God!" Nina gasped. "What about Jonathan, and Hugo?"

"Just got to hope they went straight for the temple and bypassed the village," Chase said grimly.

They reached the last stretch of passage before the drawbridge over the pool. Running footsteps echoed up the tunnel behind them.

"Get to the exit," said Chase, handing Kari the light

as they ran over the bridge, which flexed under their weight. "Wait for me."

"What are you going to do?" Nina asked.

"Try to stop them from catching up. Go on!" He stopped at the end of the bridge, letting Nina and Kari past. Then he grabbed the endmost plank and strained to lift it from the ledge before pushing it sideways with all his strength. The bridge warped along its length, creaking and groaning.

With a pained grunt, Chase shoved it down into the pool. The wood tried to bend back to its original shape when he let go, jamming the bridge against the vertical side. He kicked at it, driving the end into the water with a splash. The remaining caiman surfaced nearby, taking a sudden interest.

"Okay, go!" he shouted, running for the exit. Kari led the way, Nina hesitating as she waited for Chase to catch up.

"Their weight'll put the end into the water," Chase said as they hurried down the passage. "Then we'll see if that croc's still hungry."

"Thought it was a caiman," Nina panted.

"Whatever! Okay, here's the poles. Kari, you go first, then Nina."

Even without the incentive of the descending ceiling, they still picked their way between the spiked poles faster than Nina would have liked, the barbs plucking at their clothes. Finally they cleared them, emerging in the confined chamber housing the Challenge of Strength. Chase retook the lead.

"Okay," he said as they ran, "the second we get out, I want the two of you to run like hell into the jungle. Get away from the temple, then find cover and stay in it."

"What about you?" Nina asked. "And the others?"

"I'll get 'em. I'm just hoping that the Indians are

pissed off about Qobras blowing up their temple and went after the helicopter. If we're lucky, there'll hardly be any guards left."

"And if we're not?" said Kari.

"Then I guess we're fucked!" They came around the last corner, a square of fading daylight ahead. "You ready?"

"No," Nina moaned.

"You can do it, Nina. Kari, look after her. I'll catch up as soon as I can."

"I will," Kari promised. They were almost at the entrance.

"Okay, get ready . . . *go!*"

They raced into the open—

And stopped. There was nowhere to go.

Waiting for them were ten more men in black combat gear, weapons at the ready, standing in a semicircle around the temple's entrance. The bodies of four Indians lay among the huts; of the rest of the tribe, there was no sign. Castille, di Salvo and Philby were still prisoners, on their knees in a line in front of . . .

"Hello, Eddie," said Jason Starkman.

He didn't look the same as when Nina had met him in New York. The suit was gone, replaced by a military outfit—body armor, equipment webbing holding ammo and a sheathed knife, what looked like a grappling hook slung over his back. A black patch covered his right eye. The sickening memory of her finger digging into something wet made her shiver.

"Arr, matey!" said Chase with a nasty smile as he raised his hands. "Going for the pirate look, are you?"

Starkman regarded him coldly. "I see your sense of humor's as lousy as ever."

"Don't you mean you *half* see?"

Starkman's face tightened for a moment before he

turned his attention to Nina. "Dr. Wilde! I'm *so* glad to meet you again."

Chase and Kari both moved protectively in front of her. "Leave her alone," Kari snapped.

Starkman raised an eyebrow. "Kari Frost. Never thought I'd meet you in person. Hajjar should have taken Giovanni up on his offer, it would have saved us all a lot of trouble." He gestured with his gun, his men advancing. Overhead, the helicopter circled—followed by a *second* Halo, the downdraft from the two enormous aircraft setting the trees thrashing as if caught in a hurricane.

"What happened to the Indians?" Nina demanded.

"Most of them ran off," said Starkman. He looked over at the corpses. "The smart ones, anyway. Some of them actually thought they could take us on."

The other men started to search Chase, Kari and Nina. "What do you intend to do with us, Starkman?" asked Kari, her eyes narrowed. "Kill us?"

"Yup." The casual way in which he said it turned Nina's blood to ice. "But first, I want to find out what's in that temple." He turned away as he took a radio from his belt, giving Nina a better look at the piece of hardware on his back. It was a grappling hook, as she'd thought, but it was protruding from what looked like a fat-barreled shotgun. Most of his other team members were similarly equipped. "Eagle Leader to entry team, come in."

"What is it with you Yanks and eagles?" Chase taunted. "I had you pegged as more of a budgie."

Starkman clicked his fingers. One of his men, a mountain of muscle almost a foot taller than Chase, balled his fists together and clubbed the Englishman at the base of his neck. Chase dropped to his knees.

"Eddie!" Nina gasped.

Starkman looked surprised. "On a first-name basis with the clients, Eddie? Or . . . is she something more? You should be careful about that, you know what happens."

"You shut your fucking mouth," Chase growled. Starkman smirked, and seemed about to say something else when his radio crackled.

"Entry team to Eagle Leader," said the man on the other end. "We're in the temple, and we've located the stolen artifact. It's in a smaller chamber behind a statue. Jason, this place is incredible!"

"I'm sure it is," Starkman said dismissively. "What else have you found, Günter?"

"You won't believe this, but there's a map here, an actual map! It's scribed onto a huge orichalcum sheet on one wall. It shows the location of Atlantis!"

Starkman became a lot less dismissive. "How accurate is it?"

"The continents are quite distorted, but recognizable. And there's something else, Jason. The map . . . it shows the positions of landmarks relative to Atlantis. We can use them to work out Atlantis's exact position!" The man's voice became more excited. "The northern mouth of the Amazon is marked as being at latitude seven south, just as it said on the artifact Yuri stole, and the Cape of Good Hope is at . . . there are six dots and an inverted V. We know from our archives that this symbol first appears after eight single units, so it must represent nine. Nine plus six equals latitude fifteen."

"The Cape's at thirty-four degrees south," Starkman informed him. "The top of the Amazon delta's at about one degree north."

"A difference of thirty-five degrees, then, with fifteen minus seven, eight Atlantean units of longitude between them. So one unit is thirty-five divided by eight . . ." The

radio fell silent for a few seconds as he made the calcula-
tion. "It's 4.375 degrees!"

"So what latitude is Atlantis at?" Starkman asked.

"Let me check on the laptop . . . 4.375 multiplied by
seven is 30.625 degrees, and add one degree to account
for the position of the delta . . . Atlantis is located somewhere between thirty-one and thirty-two degrees
north!"

Starkman gave Nina a mocking look. "That's quite a
way south of the Gulf of Cádiz. Guess we didn't need to
worry about your theory after all."

Nina said nothing. The map in the temple had clearly
placed Atlantis *within* the Gulf of Cádiz. The shapes of
the continents had been inaccurate, but surely the
Atlanteans couldn't have been *that* far out?

Günter spoke again. "Even allowing for errors—the
Atlantean system is not as precise as ours—a sonar
sweep of the area should only take a few days."

"And then we can make sure nobody ever finds
Atlantis," said Starkman with rising excitement. "Good
work, Günter. Plant the thermite charges and prep for
evac. Melt the place down."

"You're going to *destroy* it?" Kari cried, appalled.

Starkman fixed her with a cold stare. "We'll do whatever we have to do to stop people like you and your father from finding Atlantis."

"The greatest archaeological find in history, and all
you care about is destroying it so your insane boss can
keep the knowledge for himself?" said Nina, her fear
overcome by her utter disgust. "You make me *sick*."

Starkman snorted in disbelief. "Jesus. You really
don't have a clue what's going on, do you?"

"Why don't you enlighten me?" she sneered.

"You think your friend Kari here and her dad are
looking for Atlantis as a *hobby*?" said Starkman. "You

know how much money they've spent? Tens of millions of dollars, maybe *hundreds*! Even for a billionaire, that's one hell of a hobby!"

"We're doing it for a good reason," said Kari. "Unlike Qobras."

"I know what your reasons are. That's why *I* joined up with Giovanni." He looked questioningly at Nina, then back to Kari. "But does *she* know? Did you even bother to tell her why you're so desperate to find Atlantis?"

"As long as they don't want to destroy it, that's good enough for me," Nina told him. Kari gave her an admiring look.

"You might have changed your mind," Starkman said as his radio squawked again. "Not that you'll get the chance now."

"Eagle Leader, we've got everything we need. Setting the charges," said Günter.

"Roger that." Starkman looked up. The two Halos were still following their slow circle, about two hundred feet above the ground. He switched radio channels. "Chopper two, this is Eagle Leader. Move into pickup position."

"Roger," replied the pilot. One of the helicopters wheeled lazily about to head for the temple. More ropes dropped from its side.

"Well, I guess this is the end," said Starkman, looking back at his prisoners. "Sorry about this, Eddie, but I've got my orders."

"You can take your fake sympathy and shove it up your arse, you two-faced twat," Chase snarled. "I should've let those al-Qaeda wankers kill you in Afghanistan."

"The world'll be glad you didn't. Good-bye, Eddie."

Starkman gestured to his men, who forced Nina and Kari down onto their knees next to Chase.

Nina felt the cold, hard barrel of a gun touch the back of her head. She closed her eyes . . .

And heard a hissing noise.

Thok!

The man behind her let out a wet, bubbling gasp before crashing to the ground. Nina opened her eyes to see spears and arrows flying overhead. One of the men behind Philby took an arrow to his leg. He grimaced, then reached to pull it out . . . only for his eyes to bulge wide. Fingers spasming, struggling to breathe, he collapsed.

Poisoned!

Starkman whirled—and was hit in the chest by another arrow. But it struck only his Kevlar body armor, not flesh. "Open fire!" he shouted, taking cover by the nearest hut as he raised his UMP-40 and unleashed it into the surrounding trees.

The men covering Nina and Kari jumped back, following Starkman's lead and firing into the jungle. Kari grabbed Nina's arm. "Go!"

She hauled Nina with her as she ran. A commando behind her turned to shoot them, but a bola whirred from the jungle, two of its weighted strands yanking his gun away from its targets. The fist-sized stone on the third strand smashed into his face, knocking out teeth.

∿

Chase saw his chance as the huge man behind him moved, and thrust his elbow savagely backwards to catch him in the groin.

He missed. The man grunted in pain, but had taken the impact on the bulging muscles of his upper thigh. Chase looked up to see him staring back, anger twisting his face. The mercenary's gun came around—

Chase flung himself backwards at the man's knees, trying to knock him off his feet. The man staggered, then fell—landing on top of him, his knees slamming onto Chase's chest. Wheezing, Chase grabbed at his adversary's UMP-40—

A fist smashed into his face. Chase heard a sharp crack as his nose broke. He was almost surprised at the lack of pain, but he knew from experience that it would come soon enough.

The fist drew back for another strike. Chase released the gun and snapped his hands up to block it as it descended. He squeezed, trying to crush the man's fingers . . .

w

Kari and Nina ran towards Castille and the other prisoners. "Get into the hut!" Kari shouted as a spear sliced through the air just behind them.

"No, we've got to help them!" Nina answered. One of the dead Indians lay on the ground in her path. She snatched up his knife. "Come on!"

w

Starkman fired off more rounds into the trees as he shrieked into his walkie-talkie. "Chopper one! I need suppressing fire on the treeline! *Now!*"

One of the men near the captives was hit from behind by a spear, the razor-sharp obsidian blade penetrating deep into his skull. Still firing wildly, he fell against the wall of a hut, breaking the wood.

w

The big man pulled his hand free of Chase's grip with a roar, then drove his knees down with piledriver force onto his ribcage. Chase tried to yell, but there was no air left in his lungs.

\\/\\/

Their guards distracted, Castille and di Salvo were already on their feet as Nina and Kari reached them. Nina grabbed Philby and hacked at the twine binding his hands as Kari tugged at Castille's knots.

"Our guns!" said Castille, indicating their piled-up belongings nearby.

Another of Starkman's men fell, a poisoned arrow in his neck.

A raging wind tore through the village as the Halo hovered overhead. Spent shell casings clattered down like hail as a six-barreled rotary cannon mounted inside the cabin door opened up, spraying fire into the wildly waving trees.

Philby was free. "Kari!" Nina shouted, throwing her the knife. Kari snapped it out of the air and hacked at di Salvo's bonds as Castille dived for the rifles. "Get into the hut, get down!" She all but threw Philby into the flimsy structure as an arrow pierced the wood.

One of the Brotherhood's team threw himself back against another hut to avoid an arrow, and in doing so realized that his prisoners were now free.

The Halo turned in place, raking the trees with Minigun fire. The downdraft from its main rotor was so strong that the huts were blown apart, debris scattering in all directions.

\\/\\/

The huge soldier bent down and clamped his hands around Chase's neck, thumbs pressing hard against his carotid artery.

The pulsing roar of blood in Chase's ears drowned

out even the noise of the helicopter. He could see it almost directly overhead, the rotors a blur behind the sadistic grin of the man strangling him. He raised his arms to strike at the man's face, but he was too big, his arms longer, and Chase's clawing fingers fell short.

Blackness swirled at the edges of his sight, his head pounding.

He couldn't reach the face of the man crushing his chest—but he could reach his body . . .

\\\\

The barrage of primitive but effective weapons from the jungle stopped abruptly as the firestorm from the helicopter carved through the attacking Indians. Horrific screams echoed from the trees.

Castille grabbed one of the team's Colt rifles and brought it around, only to see one of Starkman's men already aiming at him with a UMP.

The man pulled the trigger—just as di Salvo hurled himself bodily in front of Castille. The three-round burst hit di Salvo in his hip and thigh, blood spurting from the wounds as he crashed screaming to the ground.

Castille fired back. With his target wearing body armor, he aimed for the head. All three of his shots landed on target. The man's skull blew apart in a gruesome shower.

Another of Starkman's men heard the shots and turned to confront his new adversary—

A boot heel smashed into his face.

Even as the man reeled, Kari spun around and delivered another crushing kick into his groin. He crashed through a hut wall.

Kari picked up his gun, paused for a fraction of a second to make a decision—then shot him in the head.

w

Chase felt consciousness, *life*, slipping away. The commando loomed over him like a demon, the whirling blades of the helicopter a dark halo behind his head.

With the last of his strength, his right hand finally reached the object for which he'd been grasping: the grappling gun on the man's back.

He pulled the trigger.

The grapple flew out with a loud thump of compressed gas, rocketing almost vertically upwards with a nylon-coated steel cable trailing behind it . . . into the Halo's rotors.

The carbon-fiber grapple itself was smashed to pieces by the blades—but the cable was almost instantly drawn into the spinning rotor head, tangling around it.

And winding up.

The commando's eyes widened in shock as he realized what was about to happen—then he was yanked off the ground so hard that several of his ribs snapped. Flying skywards as if launched by a catapult, the cable dragging him inexorably into the rotors, he burst on impact, gory shredded scraps raining back down onto the village.

The helicopter lurched, out of control. The cable around the rotor shaft was jamming the pitch controls, and now the blades themselves were damaged . . .

"*Cover!*" shouted Chase.

w

Kari looked around. Starkman was sprinting for the side of the temple. Overhead, the huge helicopter began to spin, the roar of its engines joined by the shriek of wounded machinery. There was only one of Starkman's men now still standing, close to Chase.

She and Castille fired simultaneously, taking the man down.

The Halo continued spinning. A man fell from the cabin door, screaming all the way to earth, where he landed headfirst on the elders' hut, breaking his neck. Control completely gone, the helicopter rolled towards the temple, losing height.

The pilot of the other Halo saw it coming and frantically jammed his throttle to full power, pulling up on his collective control to increase altitude. The men being winched out through the hole in the temple roof were smashed against the jagged edges and plummeted back to the stone floor beneath.

Smoke pouring from its engines, the spinning Halo hit the temple roof. The curved stone structure, already weakened by the hole blasted in it, collapsed under the impact. The aircraft fell through the ceiling and into the temple itself. Its rotors were dashed to pieces as they hit the unbending stone, huge shards thrown hundreds of feet into the air before arcing back down.

All power lost, the massive aircraft plunged almost vertically to crash at the base of the statue of Poseidon, where it exploded.

A fireball swept through the temple, flames consuming the remaining men. The enormous statue of the god rocked, then fell forward to crush the blazing wreckage, its golden skin already melting in the intense heat.

A heat that reached the thermite charges in the altar room.

They detonated, the temperature inside the chamber flashing in an instant to over two thousand degrees. The gold and orichalcum artifacts within didn't merely melt—they *vaporized*, obliterated completely by the searing wave of fire.

∧∧∧

Castille turned at the sound of the explosion—and reflexively threw himself backwards as a jagged piece of rotor blade over a meter long stabbed into the ground between his legs like a javelin. "Merde!" he screeched. *"Helicopters!"*

∧∧∧

The rest of the temple roof gave way, thousands of tons of stone cascading down to bury everything within. A shockwave tore through the other tunnels and chambers, a huge cloud of dust and debris exploding from the temple entrance like an express train. Chase barely threw himself clear as it swept past.

The ancient replica of the Atlantean Temple of Poseidon, hidden in the jungle for thousands of years, was destroyed forever, along with all the secrets it contained.

∧∧∧

Nina peered from the hut, shielding her eyes as the dust cloud swept past. "Jesus!"

∧∧∧

Chase used the temple wall to pull himself up. He wiped blood from his face with the back of his hand. His broken nose was starting to hurt. Through the dust, he saw Kari and Castille running towards him. "Where's Starkman?" he gasped.

"That way!" Castille pointed. Starkman was now out of sight around the corner of the ruined structure.

"Nina?"

"In one of the huts," Kari told him.

"Give me your gun."

Kari handed him the Colt. "What are you doing?" Castille asked.

"I'm not letting that bastard get away! Kari, look after Nina. Where's Agnaldo?"

"He's been shot."

"Then help him! Go, both of you!" Chase broke into a pained run after Starkman.

\/\/

Starkman jumped onto the stepped base of the temple and ran along it, shouting into his walkie-talkie. "Chopper two! This is Eagle Leader, I need pickup *now!*" The surviving Halo was hovering cautiously over the jungle a few hundred yards away.

\/\/

Chase rounded the corner of the temple, hunting for Starkman.

There!

"No you bloody don't," he growled, climbing up onto the first tier after him.

\/\/

Kari ran back to the remains of the hut where she'd seen Nina take cover with Philby. She flung back the animal skin covering the door. "Are you okay?" she asked.

"We're fine!" Nina said.

"Speak for yourself," Philby muttered.

Nina ignored him. "What about the others? Where's Eddie?"

"Di Salvo's been shot," Kari replied. "Hugo's giving him first aid. Chase has gone after Starkman."

"What? Come on, we've got to help him!" Running out, Nina saw Chase ascending the side of the temple and headed after him.

"It's too dangerous!" Kari protested, but to no avail. "Nina! Damn it!" She hurried back to the team's equipment, picking up another rifle and Chase's Wildey, then ran after Nina.

w

The remaining Halo moved in, warily skirting the plume of thick black smoke rising from the collapsed end of the temple. As it descended, the trailing ropes dragged through the surrounding foliage.

Starkman slowed to a jog, yelling into his radio: "Come on, faster! Get me out of here!" He waved his arms furiously to summon the chopper closer—

The dark stones around him splintered and cracked under bullet hits.

"*Jason!*" roared Chase, still shooting.

Starkman flung himself on the next tier up and fired back, UMP blazing. Chase ducked as bullets smacked into the stone above his head, showering him with dust and fragments. He crawled several feet before popping up again to let fly with another burst.

w

Nina heard gunfire and ducked into cover on the lowest tier of the temple's side, peering cautiously ahead. Chase was exchanging fire with Starkman, several feet higher and close to the devastated far end of the temple. The helicopter was closing on him, ropes trailing beneath it.

w

Chase fired another burst—and his gun clicked on the last shot.

Empty!

Starkman could count shots as well as he could. He

would know he was dry. Scrabbling forward another few feet, Chase popped his head up, then immediately ducked back. As he'd expected, his brief appearance attracted gunfire, more stone chips spitting onto him. Starkman wasn't worried about running out of bullets.

The wind from the descending helicopter whipped at his clothes. At low altitude, a Halo could easily blow a man off his feet.

Which would make aiming *very* difficult.

Chase threw himself onto the next tier, immediately rolling against the wall as more bullets raked the ancient stones. He could just barely hear Starkman shouting into his radio: "Lean out and shoot him!"

Shit!

He looked at the helicopter. A man poked his head through the open cabin door, staring down at him. Then he ducked back—only to reappear a moment later with a gun in his hands.

Not another submachine gun, but an M82 sniper rifle, which could put a hole through a man's skull from eight hundred yards away—and Chase was barely fifteen yards beneath the chopper!

w

"Nina!" Kari caught up with her, the rifle in her hands.

"In the helicopter, they're going to shoot him!" Nina cried, pointing.

Kari instantly took in the scene. The massive helicopter had drifted into position above Starkman so that he could grab one of the hanging ropes and be winched aboard—and a man was leaning out of the cabin, the sniper rifle in his hands aimed directly at Chase—

She lifted the gun and emptied the entire magazine into the helicopter's fuselage.

The sniper staggered, then fell out, his rifle dropping

just ahead of him. Starkman jumped out of the way as they plunged towards him. The gun's barrel hit the unyielding stone of the temple—and its erstwhile owner landed headfirst on top of it, the stock punching right through his collarbone and burying the weapon deep inside his chest. The body flopped grotesquely down the side of the temple, still impaled on the weapon.

Starkman recovered and seized one of the ropes with his right hand as he shouldered his gun, yelling into his radio for the pilot to ascend.

"Eddie!" yelled Kari over the rising din of the engines. Somehow he heard her, and looked around. *"Here!"* She threw his Wildey.

Chase caught the gun neatly in one hand as he jumped to his feet, then spun and pointed it at the helicopter as Starkman swung overhead. The Halo was already rising fast, its nose dipping as it prepared to power away over the rain forest.

Chase aimed for the pilot and fired twice. Both shots punched through the Halo's underbelly near the nose, but the downdraft threw off his aim. The aircraft was unaffected.

Starkman climbed hand over hand, quickly rising as his rope was reeled in.

Another rope flicked past, a black nylon snake gyrating in the blasting wind. Chase jumped after it and grabbed hold.

"Oh my God! No, you idiot, *no!*" Nina shrieked helplessly after him as he was whisked off the side of the temple.

Holding on to the rope with his left hand, Chase raised the Wildey in his right and pointed it up at Starkman's ascending figure. He still had several feet to go before reaching the relative safety of the cabin. "Get you right up your *arse*, you bastard—"

The Wildey barked twice. Spinning and twisting on the end of the rope, Chase had no idea where the first shot landed—but the second one cratered the fuselage above Starkman, showering him with flecks of paint.

Starkman looked down and saw Chase dangling below. For a moment Chase thought he was trying to unshoulder his UMP to shoot back down at him . . .

Until he realized he was unsheathing his combat knife.

Chase suddenly became very aware of his position. He was hanging by one hand from a rope beneath a helicopter, already at least seventy feet in the air and rising as the Halo moved out over the jungle.

His gaze met Starkman's one good eye. Starkman grinned—and sliced through Chase's rope, severing it with a single brutal slash.

"Oh, *fuck*!" Chase just had time to gasp before he plummeted towards the endless jungle canopy below.

SEVENTEEN

The rope was still in his left hand. In the split second before he hit the uppermost leaves, Chase let go of his gun and snatched for the black nylon line with his right.

Branches pummeled him as he plunged through them, each one thicker and more inflexible than the last. One slammed against his shoulder, and Chase flung the rope at it.

Suddenly he was clear and falling again, nothing between him and the ground—

The line snapped taut.

He clamped his hands around the rope, screaming as friction seared his skin. He was slowing, *slowing* . . .

The severed end of the rope shot through his grip, and was gone. He was free-falling, the canopy of foliage rushing away—

Impact.

Blackness.

vv

A distant voice, echoing down a pipe, saying something familiar . . .

Saying his name.

"Eddie?" A woman's voice, getting closer. "*Eddie!*"

Chase's eyes snapped open. He could make out scattered spots of the dusk sky through the jungle canopy, one larger hole directly above him.

It took several seconds for a thought to congeal into words. "I just *fell* through there!" he gasped, trying to sit up.

And immediately regretting it. Every muscle in his body ached as though he'd been beaten. He flopped back down again with an anguished moan.

"Eddie!"

"Nina?" He squinted as a face appeared above him, looking down anxiously. "My God, you look beautiful . . ."

"Well, at least he can still see," said another voice. Kari came into view behind Nina, peering at him before turning her head upwards to the trees. Leaves drifted down around them like green snow. "That must be over twenty meters high . . ."

"My God!" said Nina, leaning closer. "I can hardly believe he survived!"

"Takes more than that to kill me off, Doc," he said, forcing a painful grin. Even his face muscles hurt.

She stared at him for a moment, a mix of emotions flooding across her face, before suddenly flailing at his chest with her hands. "You *moron*! You absolute, utter, complete *idiot*! What the hell were you thinking? Why did you do that? What's *wrong* with you?"

"Ow, ow! It's a long list . . ." Chase cautiously lifted his head. Pain rolled in from all over his body, but none of it seemed to be the sharp stab—or the numbed shock—of a broken bone.

Well, except for his nose.

To Nina and Kari's amazement, he began to laugh, a wheezing cackle of pure relief at being alive. "Oh

Christ. That really, *really* hurt. And I didn't even get the bastard!" His face contorted as he slowly sat up, Nina kneeling to help him. "What happened? How long was I out?"

"Not long," said Kari. "The helicopter's gone, it flew off northeast."

"You might have a concussion," Nina warned him. "Keep still."

Chase saw something that instantly dismissed the pain from his mind. "I think that's the least of our worries," he said, very slowly.

Nina followed his gaze. And froze.

They were surrounded by Indians.

w

Supporting Chase between them, Nina and Kari were taken back to the village.

Though they weren't openly aggressive—yet—Nina could tell the Indians were angry. Hardly surprising, considering that many of them had been killed, their homes were wrecked and the temple they and their ancestors had protected for thousands of years was now a smoking ruin. She was amazed that any of the explorers were still alive.

Her surprise grew as they reached the village. A fire had been lit, and di Salvo was lying next to it, still alive and conscious. His bloodstained clothes had been cut open and bandages applied to the bullet wounds. Next to him, Castille, with Philby's help, was giving first aid to one of the Indians. "Edward!" he called as the party approached. "Mon dieu! You're still alive!"

"Just about," Chase croaked. "What's with the MASH?"

"We have some new friends. Well, perhaps *friends* is

not quite the word. Nonbelligerents may be better."
Castille nodded at the Indians.

"What happened?" asked Nina as she and Kari set
Chase down. The Indians escorting them backed away,
watching warily.

"When they saw us fighting Jason and his men, it
seems they had a change of mind about us. What's the
saying? 'The enemy of my enemy is my friend'? Naive,
perhaps, but it saved us."

Nina looked at the Indians. Some of them were going
through the items taken from the bodies of Starkman's
men, arranging them in piles and apparently taking a
tally by making marks on pieces of parchmentlike bark.
The bullets held a particular fascination; two of the
women were clicking them out of the spare magazines
with their thumbs, holding the shiny casings up to the
firelight. "Is it really a good idea to let them play with
bullets like that?"

"Better than letting them play with loaded guns,"
Chase grunted. "How's Agnaldo?"

Castille glanced at his patient. "I had to give him a
shot, but he can still translate for us. Edward, we need
to call for help. I'm sure the boat's been destroyed, and
that Captain Perez and Julio are dead." Kari looked dis-
mayed.

"Oh no," Nina said softly. "Wait, if the *Nereid*'s been
destroyed, how are we going to call for help?"

Chase managed an approximation of a smile. "Same
way we'd order a pizza. We'll ring for it. There's a satphone in one of the packs."

"That's all well and good," Philby snapped, voice
tight with frustration, "but am I the only person concerned that a literally priceless archaeological find has
just been *blown up*? This is worse than the Taliban!"

"You didn't even see the interior, Jonathan," said

Nina sadly. "It was incredible. A replica of the Temple of Poseidon, exactly as Plato described it. And there was even a map showing the location of Atlantis . . ."

She trailed off. *The map.* There was something about it . . .

"Unfortunately, your gun-toting friends are already on their way there," said Philby. She ignored him, thinking hard about what she'd seen inside the temple.

"Nina? What is it?" Kari asked.

"The map . . . Atlantis was *definitely* in the Gulf of Cádiz," Nina insisted. "Starkman's guy was *wrong*, he had to be. The Atlanteans were able to navigate across whole oceans—there's no way their map could have been off by hundreds of miles with the position of their *home*! There's something we've missed, something about the Atlantean . . . system . . ." She looked back at the women counting bullets. It was the *way* they were counting that caught her attention, opening up an unexpected line of thought.

She moved to crouch by di Salvo. "Agnaldo? Can you hear me?"

His face was drenched in sweat, but he was still responsive despite the painkiller. "Yes, I can. What is it?"

"I need you to translate for me."

"I'll do my best . . . What do you want to say?"

"First I need to know if it's okay for me to go to those women, look at what they're writing." Di Salvo haltingly asked the two surviving elders, and nodded to Nina after getting a reply. Hands raised, she carefully approached the women. They reacted with surprise and a little fear, but it didn't take long for her to persuade one of them to let her examine their pale sheet of bark.

Her guess was correct: it was a tally. She held it up to the firelight, trying to get a better look at the smudgy symbols, then spotted a chemical glow stick among the equipment. She bent it, releasing a vivid blue light. The Indian women jumped away, before slowly returning, fascinated. Other members of the tribe moved to stand around her, entranced by the sight. Nina gave them a reassuring smile, then returned her attention to the numbers.

Kari joined her. "What is it?"

"Remember how I thought the Atlantean numerical system used base eight?" Nina began, running a fingertip down one of the columns, careful not to smear the charcoal markings. "But that didn't work for the Challenge of Mind, right? And the statues of the Nereids in the temple—according to Plato, there should have been one hundred, but you counted seventy-three?"

Kari nodded. "Have you found out why?"

"I'm not sure . . ." Nina looked down at the bullets on the ground. There was a pile of empty magazines next to them. She held one up. "Eddie! How many bullets does one of these hold?"

"UMP? Thirty rounds."

"So there's over a hundred bullets here, good . . ." She picked up one of the bullets. "Okay, let's see . . ."

Kneeling, she moved closer to the nearest Indian woman, giving her what she hoped was a friendly, non-threatening look. The woman reacted with suspicion, but didn't back away as Nina picked up a piece of charcoal and a blank scrap of bark. On it, she made a small mark—the symbol for a single unit. Then she held up the bullet, pointing to the mark and raising her eyebrows questioningly. "One, yes? One?"

The woman stared at her oddly for a moment, before suddenly smiling, saying something. "She says yes," di Salvo told her.

"Great! Okay . . ." Nina reached back and picked up

a handful of bullets, dropping them next to her knees, then lined up two of them below the parchment before making a second mark next to the first. "Two?"

The woman nodded again. Nina added another six bullets to the line, then made more marks. Eight little ticks in a line . . .

Another nod. Nina smiled, then took a ninth bullet, placed it by the first row, then added another tick to the line. "Nine?"

The woman shook her head. Nina wiped away the nine marks, then instead drew an inverted V and pointed back at the bullets. "Nine?"

A second shake of the head, this time accompanied by a somewhat exasperated expression and what sounded like a mocking comment to the other Indians. A few of them chuckled, as did di Salvo. "What did she say?" Nina asked.

"That she can't believe you don't even know how to count," he replied, amused even through his weariness.

The woman took the charcoal from her hand and added a single mark to the left of the symbol, then pointed at the nine bullets. "So *that's* nine?" Nina said thoughtfully.

"What have you found?" asked Kari.

"Starkman's guy thought the circumflex symbol on its own represented nine," said Nina, mind racing. "But it doesn't—I started to realize it when I saw *how* they count. They don't use their fingers—they use the *gaps* between them. Watch." She moved one of the bullets away from the others, then tapped a finger between the thumb and forefinger of her other hand. "One." The Indian woman stared at her, not sure what she was doing. Nina put a second bullet by the first, and tapped the skin between her thumb and forefinger again, then that between her forefinger and middle finger. "One, two?"

The woman nodded, smiling again. She held up both her hands, quickly using the little finger of each to count off the gaps between the fingers of the other until she reached eight.

Nina realized the significance of the shape her hands formed, the tips of her little fingers touching after she stopped counting. "The circumflex—it represents eight 'full' gaps. So nine is represented by one circumflex plus one, which means that . . ." She pointed at the tally, where a single dot was followed by a pair of circumflexes. "That's seventeen—one plus eight plus eight. But look, they don't represent sixteen with two circumflexes, but with eight single units plus one circumflex. It's like they're *filling up* the gaps between their fingers, and each time they're full, the next number is however many full hands of eight they have, *plus* one."

"It's not a linear progression," Kari said, understanding.

"No wonder we couldn't work out the puzzle in the temple—we were using the wrong system! It's like a weird hybrid of notational and positional systems!"

"English, Doc," groaned Chase.

"Okay, okay . . . In our system, you add a new column every time you multiply by ten, right? Tens, hundreds, thousands—it's a regular progression. But in their system, which also seems to be the Atlantean system, the new symbols that we saw in the puzzle room aren't introduced along the same regular progression— instead, they fill in the gaps . . ." she held up her open fingers, "so to speak. If they were using standard base eight, the next symbol, the circumflex, the little hat—"

"Yeah, I know what a circumflex is, Doc," Chase said testily.

"Sorry. It would represent eight in a normal base eight system. But it doesn't—it stands for eight, but doesn't appear until you get to *eight plus one*. And the symbol after that, the leaning 'L'—in base eight that would be sixty-four. But because this is a cumulative rather than linear progression, where you don't advance until you've filled up each of the gaps between your fingers—"

"It comes in after eight groups of eight, *plus* eight," Kari continued, excitedly pointing out the relevant group of symbols on the tally.

"Right! And the first time it's used is at eight groups of eight, plus eight . . . and then plus one. Or—"

"Seventy-three!" they both cried simultaneously.

"Like the number of statues?" Chase asked, frowning as though he now had a new pain inside his head to add to all his other aches.

"Yes! Of course! *That's* why Plato said there were a hundred! It was a misinterpretation of the Atlantean numerical system over the centuries. In their system, it's the equivalent of one hundred, when the third digit comes in—but it's not decimal *or* base eight. It's a completely unique system."

"But Qobras won't know that," Kari pointed out. "Which means that when he converts the latitudinal figures from the map into modern figures, they won't be accurate."

Nina brought the map into her mind's eye. "No, they'll be way off! They thought that the circumflex on its own was nine, and a circumflex plus a tick was ten. But a circumflex plus a tick really equals *nine*. Their figures are wrong—they're one off! They thought the Cape of Good Hope was at latitude fifteen south—it's not, it's at latitude *fourteen*! So they should have divided the thirty-five degrees difference by *seven* Atlantean units, not eight, which means one Atlantean unit is *five* degrees. Atlantis is seven units north of the Amazon, and seven times five is—"

Chase laughed. "Even I can manage that! Thirty-five degrees north."

"Plus one degree to account for the Amazon delta's latitude above the equator," Kari added. "So Atlantis is at thirty-six degrees north—which *is* in the Gulf of Cádiz! You were right!"

"They're hundreds of miles off course!" Nina exclaimed, unable to hold in her excitement. "We can find it first; we can still beat them!"

Castille finished treating the wounded Indian. "All that is well and good, but I have a suggestion—before we start congratulating ourselves, can we at least get out of the jungle?"

"The satphone's in my rucksack, Hugo," said Chase, sounding tired. "Chuck it over and I'll call the cavalry."

"Ai, merveilleux," Castille complained as he found the pack. "Another helicopter."

Nina looked up at the circle of Indians still watching her. "What are we going to do about the tribe? Never mind the temple, their *homes* have been trashed because of us. They're going to need help."

"I can take care of that," said di Salvo. "As a representative of the Brazilian government, I can say that the tribe has been officially located and contacted, eh? That means they are now protected."

"Not quite the contact we were hoping for," Nina observed. "They killed Hamilton, remember?"

"At least they didn't kill us too," Chase reminded her as Castille handed him the satellite phone.

"I can make sure they get whatever they need," Kari said. "The Frost Foundation has some influence with the Brazilian government; we've provided aid in the past. We can make sure they survive. After all, they're quite possibly the only direct descendants of the Atlanteans. A DNA analysis could be fascinating . . ." She stared into the darkness at the temple.

Di Salvo explained the situation as best he could to the Indians. Some of them, particularly the elders, looked extremely unhappy. "They're worried that if more outsiders come, they'll try to raid the temple," he told Kari.

"Raid it of *what*?" Chase asked sarcastically, looking up from his phone call. "Helicopter parts? There's nothing left to steal!"

"No, they're right," said Nina. "Even if a large part of it's destroyed, there's still a lot of gold in there."

"I can arrange for security," Kari said. "The Foundation has reliable people who aren't motivated by money—they can protect the tribe while they provide aid. And I think it's best if the knowledge of exactly what the temple contains remains our secret, don't you?"

"*I* didn't see any gold," commented Chase with exaggerated innocence as he finished the call. "All I saw were crushy things and crocs with big teeth and a puzzle we couldn't work out the answer to."

"Oh, it was forty, by the way," Nina told him casually, leaving him open-mouthed. "Forty lead pellets. Now that I understand the numerical system, it was easy."

"You're joking, right?" he asked. Nina just gave him a knowing smile in reply. "Okay . . . Anyway, they're sending the chopper for us. It'll be a couple of hours, though—even with a GPS fix, they still have to find us in the dark."

"Will Agnaldo be all right for that long?" Nina asked Castille. "Don't we need to get him to a hospital?"

"Don't worry about me," di Salvo told her sleepily. "It's not the first time I've been shot."

"He's stable," Castille said. "I'll do what I can to help the other Indians while we're waiting."

Kari went to Chase and took the phone. "I'll call my father and let him know what's happened so that he can make all the arrangements with the Brazilians. And then . . ." she came back to Nina, squatting next to her, "we need to get *you* to a map. We may have lost the information in this temple, but we can still get to Atlantis before Qobras. The hunt is still on."

EIGHTEEN
Gibraltar

Chase examined the chart covering the table in the hotel suite, running his finger along the line marking thirty-six degrees north. "That's a lot of sea to cover."

"Fortunately, we don't have to," said Kari. "One of my father's survey aircraft is already doing a high-resolution synthetic aperture radar survey of that region of the Gulf seabed. If there's anything buried beneath the sediment, it will show up—even up to twenty meters deep."

Chase raised an eyebrow. "And if it's over twenty meters deep?"

"Then, as you like to say, we're fucked." Nina smiled; it was the first time she'd heard Kari swear, and it sounded incongruous coming from her. "Has there been any more word on Qobras?"

"Oh yeah," Chase said. "I've got a friend in Morocco; she's been keeping an eye on things."

"She's not pregnant as well, is she?" Nina couldn't resist asking.

"Funny you should say that . . . She says Qobras's people set sail from Casablanca yesterday. He's got a survey ship—not as flashy as yours, Kari, but it had a submersible aboard. You were right, Nina—he's looking in the wrong place. If he holds course, he'll be over two hundred miles southwest of us."

"We'll just have to hope that he stays there," said Kari. "I'm still very concerned that his people managed to track us so quickly in Brazil."

"The *Nereid* would've attracted a lot of attention," Chase mused, "but yeah, I don't like it that Starkman came right to us. Could be there was a tracker on the boat, but we'll never know now." The burnt-out wreck of the *Nereid* had been found capsized in the river, hit by an antitank missile fired from one of the helicopters. "So we need to keep the knowledge of where we're going to as few people as we can. How many crew are there on your ship?"

"Twenty-four," said Kari, "but they're all loyal to my father."

"You absolutely, one hundred percent *sure* about that?" Kari's lack of an immediate reply gave Chase his answer. "I'd keep exactly where we'll be going to just the captain and the navigator until we actually arrive, if I were you. And even then . . ."

"We'll just have to wait and see what the radar survey shows," said Kari, seeming pensive. "Thank you, Mr. Chase."

"If you need me for anything, I'll be next door," he said, before walking out.

"See you," said Nina, looking back at the map. At its largest, the Gulf of Cádiz's northern and southern coasts were about three hundred miles apart. Smaller than Atlantis as described by Plato—but the ancient philosopher's figures had already been proven wrong once before, thrown off by the conversion from the odd Atlantean numerical system into decimal. The actual size would be, at most, roughly two thirds of what Plato had said—and that was assuming that an Atlantean stadium was the same size as a Greek one, which now seemed unlikely. If the temple in the jungle were an exact replica of the original, then one Atlantean stadium—the length of the Temple of Poseidon—was only four hundred feet long, considerably smaller than its Hellenic counterpart.

The combined reductions in scale brought the size of Atlantis down to approximately 125 miles in length, and under a hundred wide. Which would easily fit within the Gulf—and more important, could be located on the relative shallows of the continental shelf before the seabed plunged away to the abyssal depths of the Atlantic itself. The Brotherhood's search would be well off target.

The Brotherhood . . . She stared silently at the map.

"What's on your mind?" Kari asked.

"I was thinking about the Brotherhood. About Qobras." She looked up at Kari. "Who *is* this guy? Why is he so desperate to stop us from finding Atlantis?" A memory creased her brow, something Starkman had said. "Or rather, why's he so desperate to stop you and your father from finding it?"

"I . . ." Kari's expression became conflicted.

"What? Kari, what is it?"

Kari gestured at a nearby sofa. "Nina, there's something I want to tell you."

Unsettled, Nina sat, Kari next to her. "What's wrong?"

"Nothing's *wrong*, it's just . . . There's something else that my father and I are looking for as well as Atlantis itself."

"Something *else*?" Nina said. "What else could there be?"

"This might sound strange, but . . . finding Atlantis is only the *beginning* of what we're doing. You know that the Frost Foundation has been involved in medical aid programs all around the world?" Nina nodded. "We've also been taking genetic samples from as many different peoples as we could. Blood tests."

Nina's hand went to the little mark on her arm where she had been vaccinated before leaving for Iran, what seemed like years before.

"Yes, you too," Kari said. "*Please* don't make any judgments before I've told you everything! Everything we've done has been for a very good reason."

"You tested my DNA?" asked Nina, shocked. "Without telling me?"

"We *had* to keep it a secret. *Please*, let me explain! Please?"

"Go on," Nina told her, tight-lipped.

"What my father and I discovered—more my father; he had already found the first evidence while I was still a child—was that there is a particular genetic marker that is only present in approximately one person in every hundred. It's rare—but it's also widespread. We found it all over the world. We think . . ." Kari paused, as if reluctant to reveal a long-held secret. "We believe this genetic marker can be traced all the way back to the Atlanteans. In other words, those people who have that particular sequence of genes within their DNA—"

"They're the *descendants* of the Atlanteans?"

Kari nodded. "Precisely. Atlantis may have fallen, but its *people* had an empire that wouldn't be equaled for another nine thousand years. They became a diaspora, spreading throughout their former lands—and beyond. We found concentrations as far afield as Namibia, Tibet, Peru . . . and Norway."

"Norway?"

"Yes." Kari took Nina by the hands. "Nina, the Atlanteans were never lost. They were here among us all along. They *are* us. My father and I, we have the marker in our DNA." She looked straight into Nina's eyes. "And so do you."

"*Me?* But . . ."

"You're one of *us*, Nina. You're a descendant of the Atlanteans. *That's* what we're trying to find. Not just ancient ruins—but *people*, who are alive today."

Nina's head swam. She wanted to pull her hands away from Kari, but couldn't. As confused and overwhelmed as she felt, the analytical, scientific part of her mind demanded to know more. "How?"

"We think that finding Atlantis will help us retrace the expansion of the diaspora. We've already seen how the Atlanteans tried to reproduce their civilization in Brazil—we believe there are other locations where they did the same. The map in the temple showed how far they had explored, all the way to Asia. We want to find those places, follow their paths. Maybe even—"

"Find their descendants?"

"The Indians wanted to know if I was one of the 'old ones.' There's obviously some racial memory there, stories passed down through the generations."

"So I guess at least we know the Atlanteans were blonds," said Nina, managing a brief half-smile. Kari smiled back. "So where does Qobras fit into this?"

Kari's face turned grim. "From what we've been able to find out, he considers the Atlantean descendants a threat."

"Are they?"

"You tell me. You *are* one."

Nina didn't have an answer to that. "So what's his problem with them—with *us*?" she asked instead. "Does *he* know about the DNA marker?"

"Almost certainly. About a year ago, we learned he had a mole working in our genetic research institute, though my father thinks he's been spying on us for much longer. It's obvious now that Qobras will go to any lengths to stop us from finding Atlantis—and the closer we get, the more desperate he'll become."

Nina sucked in her cheeks nervously. "I'm kind of starting to wish I'd gotten into UFOs or Bigfoot rather than Atlantis."

"I'm glad you didn't." Kari squeezed her hands reassuringly. "Without you, we would never have come this far. And now that we know what the stakes are, we'll do everything we can to keep you safe."

Nina looked back at the chart. "Glad to hear it. Although that does assume that we even manage to *find* Atlantis."

"If there's anything down there, the SAR survey will find it."

"But how are we going to get to it? God knows how deep the sediment will be. And it's not as if we can just dig it up. Excavations are hard enough even in shallow water, never mind at several hundred feet."

Kari flashed her a knowing grin. "You haven't seen our subs yet. They're quite impressive."

"Subs? Plural?"

"Starkman was right when he said that the search for Atlantis was more than a mere hobby for my father. More than his businesses, even the work of the foundation, it's the most important thing in his life."

"More so than you?"

"It's just as important to me too." Nina was about to say that that wasn't what she meant, but before she could, Kari released her hands. "It will be a while before the first results from the radar survey come in, so . . ." She gestured at the windows. The hotel looked out across Gibraltar's harbor, the Rock itself looming beyond. "Shall we do something?"

Nina shook her head. "I . . . I don't know, Kari. I'm feeling a bit overwhelmed by all this."

"Oh. Okay . . ." Kari sounded disappointed. "If you change your mind . . ."

"Thanks."

Kari reluctantly left the room. Nina stayed, staring at the chart.

Not for the first time, she wondered: *What the hell have I gotten myself into?*

ᴡᴡ

It took another day before the aerial survey yielded any results, and Nina was suffering slightly from cabin fever. Chase made it clear that she was not going to be left unaccompanied outside the hotel; while she enjoyed Chase and Castille's company, even with Chase's ribbing, their mere presence hammered home the threat she was facing. Kari tried to get her to go out, but Nina was still in a turmoil over her revelation. She suspected Kari was hurt by her rejection, but she needed time to think, alone.

That time came to an end, and Nina was no nearer untangling her feelings than before. But now she had something else to occupy her mind.

"There," said Kristian Frost over the videolink. A second LCD monitor had been attached to the laptop, displaying a duplicate of the large radar survey printout being examined by the expedition members. On the screen, a cursor drew a red circle around a particular section.

Nina's breath caught in excitement as she looked more closely at the area Frost had marked. The image on the printout was in shades of gray, variations in tone corresponding to different reflections of the radar signal as it penetrated the water—and the seabed beneath.

Dominating the printout was a series of concentric circles, narrowing the closer they got to the center. And at the center itself . . .

"What's the scale?" she asked. "How big is it?"

"One millimeter is five meters," said Kari, handing her a ruler. Nina laid it down to measure the circular area at the center.

"One hundred and twenty-five millimeters in diameter, more or less . . . that's six hundred and twenty-five meters. Just over two thousand feet. And the proportions of the rings as you move outwards . . ." She looked up at Kari, her reservations completely blown away in her excitement. "They match what Plato wrote. The only difference is the size, but . . ."

She moved the ruler to the object at the center of the innermost circle, a rectangle made up almost entirely of solid whites and blacks rather than the shades of gray of the rest of the picture. "Four hundred feet long and two hundred wide," she announced, quickly converting from metric to imperial measurements. "Exactly the same size as the temple in Brazil!"

"There's no chance those circles could be some natural formation?" Philby asked. "A collapsed volcano, or a meteor crater?"

"It's too regular," said Nina. "It's man-made, it *has* to be. How deep is it?"

Frost had the answer. "The seabed is two hundred and forty meters below the surface, with approximately . . ." He glanced off to one side, checking something on another screen, "five meters of sediment."

"Eight hundred feet," Nina said for Chase's benefit, as he made a pained face trying to do the conversion in his head.

"Kind of deep," he said, before turning to Kari. "Good job you've got subs, that's close to the limits for scuba gear. We could only stay underwater for a few minutes at that depth."

"Actually, we have some new diving gear that should help with that," she replied. "I'll show you when we're on the ship."

"How are we going to deal with the sediment?" asked Nina.

Kari smiled. "I told you, wait until you see our submersibles. We built something quite special. This will be our first chance to use them for real."

Philby leaned closer to examine the printout. "Am I right in thinking that the lighter something is on the picture, the stronger the radar return?"

"Not quite—the white areas are more like shadows, blank areas where the radar was blocked. The black objects are particularly strong reflections," Kari explained.

"Which means there must be a lot of solid objects down there." Philby pointed east of the center. "Look at this, for example. To me, that looks almost like an aerial photograph of ruins. Everything's jumbled, as though the walls have collapsed, but it still has a fairly regular outline."

"It's Atlantis," said Nina. "It *must* be. It matches Plato's description too closely for it to be anything else. The three rings of water around the citadel, the canal heading southwards . . ." She tapped a finger on the dark rectangle. "And this—it's the Temple of Poseidon, the original. There's nothing else it can be!"

"How did it end up so deep?" wondered Chase. "Eight hundred feet's a long way down."

"A major tectonic shift or the collapse of a subsurface volcanic caldera could easily cause part of the continental shelf to subside over a very short period. It'd cause massive tsunamis as well, which would account for the cataclysmic sinking of the island that Plato described—

and over time, it would continue to settle and sink deeper. Also, global sea levels have risen since the end of the last ice age, about ten thousand years ago—*after* the sinking of Atlantis. Combine the two events and you have something that nobody would ever find—unless they knew exactly where to look."

"Which you did." Kari beamed at her. "My God, Nina, you did it! You found something that people thought was just a legend!"

"Yeah, they did, didn't they?" said Nina, with a pointed glance at Philby.

"Yes, yes," he harrumphed, "obviously I was mistaken." He extended a hand. "Congratulations, Dr. Wilde."

"Thank you, Professor," she replied, shaking it. After a moment, he leaned forward and put an arm around her.

"Well done, Nina," he said. "Outstanding work." She smiled, filled with pride.

"Well, I don't want to interrupt this archaeological orgy," cut in Chase, "but we still actually have to *get* to the place. Eight hundred feet of water, remember?"

"I can take care of that," said Frost. "I'll tell the captain of the *Evenor* to set sail as soon as possible. He has already made all the preparations—you can catch up by helicopter tomorrow." He smiled. "Once again, Dr. Wilde, congratulations are in order. You've made another incredible discovery. I just wish I could be there to see it for myself."

"So do I, Far," said Kari.

"The next time we speak . . ." Frost smiled again, more broadly, "you will have discovered Atlantis. I am certain of it. Good-bye . . . and good luck." The screen went dark.

"I second that," said Kari. "Congratulations, Nina!"

She went to the minibar, taking out a bottle of Bollinger champagne. "We should celebrate!"

"Out of the minibar?" laughed Chase. "Christ, that'll probably cost you more than you've spent on the whole expedition!"

"I think it's worth it. Here, Nina." She handed over the bottle. "You deserve the honors."

"And you haven't just won a Grand Prix, so don't shake it up!" Chase added. "Don't want to waste any booze."

Nina tore away the foil and unwound the wire cap as Castille handed out glasses. She twisted the cork. "Oh, I always hate this bit. I'm scared that I'm going to take somebody's eye out."

"Like Jason Starkman's?" said Chase with a cruel smirk.

"That's not funny—aah!" The cork popped free, Chase swooping in to catch the overflowing froth. "Thanks."

"No problem. Go on, fill it right up. It's yours."

"Trying to get me drunk?"

"Yeah, I bet you're a right raver when you're pissed! Here." He took the bottle from her and handed her the full glass in return, pouring drinks for everyone else.

"To Nina," said Kari, raising her glass. Everyone else echoed the toast.

Nina paused. "Thank you . . . but I think we should remember the people who got hurt, or . . . or didn't make it this far with us. Hafez, Agnaldo, Julio, Hamilton, Captain Perez . . ."

The others solemnly repeated the names before sipping their drinks. "That was very thoughtful," said Philby.

"It just seemed appropriate. I hope whatever we find is worth it . . ."

"It will be," Kari assured her. "It will be."

NINETEEN

The Gulf of Cádiz

"There she is!" said Kari, pointing ahead through the helicopter's windscreen.

The deep blue of the Gulf of Cádiz stretched out before them, sunlight glinting off its surface. They were ninety miles from the Portuguese coast, a hundred from Gibraltar, and their destination was itself in motion, making a steady twelve knots into the Atlantic. The RV *Evenor* stood out against the endless blue as a slice of gleaming white, a 260-foot oceanographic survey vessel representing the state of the art in undersea exploration. As with all his other concerns, Kristian Frost had not cut any corners.

"Ah, finally!" said Castille. The Belgian had been extremely nervous throughout the flight, to the amusement of the other passengers. "I can't wait to get my feet back on solid ground." He considered this. "Solid deck. Rocking deck. Ah, so long as it's not a helicopter, I don't care!"

"You got any idea how hard it is to land a helicopter on a moving ship?" Chase asked mischievously. Castille gave him a sour look, then took a green apple from a pocket and crunched deeply into it.

"That won't be a problem, sir," the pilot assured him

as the Bell 407 began its descent. "I've done this a hundred times."

"It's number hundred and *one* I'm worried about," Castille muttered through a mouthful of apple. Even Philby joined in the jovial mockery that followed.

Nina looked over Kari's shoulder as they approached the *Evenor*. The research vessel had an ultramodern and, to her admittedly inexperienced eyes, somewhat odd design. The hull was normal enough, but the superstructure seemed almost top-heavy, a tall, tapered block squeezed into the midsection of the ship with a radar mast towering above it.

The reason for the unusual design became obvious as they got closer. At the stern, protruding out above the propellers on a fantail, was a helicopter pad, while most of the deck area at the bow was devoted to heavy cranes and winches to support the *Evenor*'s two submersibles. The people had to fit in the space between their machines.

"Only a year old," Kari said as they approached. "Three thousand two hundred metric tons, with five officers, nineteen crew and able to support up to thirty scientists for two months. My father's pride and joy."

"After you, I hope," said Nina.

"Mmm . . . sometimes I wonder," joked Kari.

As the pilot had promised, the landing was performed quickly and safely. Castille practically leapt from the cabin as crewmen secured the aircraft to the deck. "Safe at last!" he proclaimed.

"Just don't throw up your hands in joy," Nina told him, indicating the still-spinning rotor blades above him. "Remember what happened to Hajjar!"

"Least you'll be safe from choppers down there," said Chase, looking overboard. The sea was calm, the gentle waves the perfect disguise for what lay beneath.

Kari led the group into the superstructure and up to the pilot house on level four, where they were met by the *Evenor*'s commander, Captain Leo Matthews, a tall Canadian in a spotless white uniform. Once the introductions were made, he updated them on the situation. "We'll reach the target area in about three hours. Are you sure you want to send both subs down on the first descent, ma'am?" he asked Kari. "It might be better just to send the *Atragon* to inspect the seabed first."

Kari shook her head. "I'm afraid time is a factor. Qobras already has a ship at sea—it's looking in the wrong place, but he must know by now that we've set sail. Sooner or later he's going to investigate, and I suspect it will be sooner."

"Are you worried about an attack?"

"Wouldn't be the first one," Chase pointed out.

Matthews smiled. "Well, the *Evenor* might not be a warship, but . . . let's just say we can look after ourselves." He turned to Kari. "Your father sent some, ah, special equipment. We'll be ready for any trouble, ma'am."

"Thank you, Captain."

Matthews ordered one of his crew to show the team to their staterooms. Despite offering it to Nina, on the grounds that she deserved the title, Kari had the chief scientist's stateroom below the pilothouse, while Nina took a cabin next to Chase a deck beneath.

"Excellent," he cackled, popping his head around Nina's door. "Got a room to myself. No sharing with Hugo on *this* boat."

"Does he snore?"

"He does much, *much* worse than that." To Nina's relief, he didn't elaborate. "It's not as posh as the *Nereid*, but it should be a lot harder to blow up."

"Please, don't even joke about that."

"I wasn't joking." Chase came fully into the room. "Like Kari said, Qobras has *got* to know we're out here. I know she thinks the crew's loyal, but wave enough money around and anybody can be bought."

"You think Qobras has a spy aboard?" Nina sat on the bed, worried.

"I'd put money on it. For that matter . . ." He trailed off.

"What?"

He sat next to her, lowering his voice. "Back in Brazil, Starkman found us way too fast. Those choppers couldn't have just shadowed us as we went upriver, we were moving too slow. They would have run out of fuel. Which meant when they set off, they already knew where we were. Either there was a homing device on the boat, which is possible . . . or somebody aboard told them our position."

Despite the warmth of the cabin, Nina shivered. "Who?"

"Couldn't have been that idiot tree-hugger; nobody told him why we were really going there. Not to speak ill of the dead, but Captain Perez and Julio are on my list."

"But they were killed when the *Nereid* was blown up. You saw the bodies."

"Could be that Starkman killed them so there wouldn't be any loose ends. So they're still a possibility. On the other hand, I'm *fairly* sure Kari's not trying to sell out her own dad . . ." He grinned at the understatement. "And you, well. Beyond reproach."

Nina smiled. "I'm glad you think so."

"Problem is, that doesn't leave many suspects. There's Agnaldo, the Prof . . . and, well, me and Hugo."

"It can't have been Jonathan," Nina said immediately. "I've known him for years. He wouldn't do anything to hurt me."

"Okay then," said Chase, raising an eyebrow, "I trust Agnaldo, and hell, I trust Hugo with my *life*. Which leaves . . . aw, buggeration and fuckery. It was me all along, wasn't it? Bollocks."

Nina giggled. "I think we can rule you out."

"Hope so. I'd hate to have to beat the shit out of myself." He smiled again, then shook his head wearily. "I dunno. Anybody on the *Nereid* could have had a satphone hidden in their personal kit—I only checked through the stuff we took aboard in Tefé. And as for *this* boat . . ." He sighed. "All we can do is just keep an eye out, look for anything funny."

"What are you going to do if you find someone?" asked Nina.

Chase stood. "Make the bastard walk the plank." She could tell he wasn't joking.

vvv

Nina spent a while familiarizing herself with the layout of the *Evenor*, eventually making her way to the foredeck to check out the two submersibles. Kari was already there, talking to a pair of young men whose scruffy shorts and garish unbuttoned Hawaiian shirts went far beyond "beach casual" into actual "beach bum" territory.

"Nina," said Kari, "these are our submersible pilots. And designers, in fact."

"Jim Baillard," said the taller of the two men, like Matthews a Canadian, only with a considerably more languid turn of speech. Nina shook his hand, his wristband of little seashells rattling. "So you think you found Atlantis, eh? Awesome."

"You want it dug up? We'll get it done," said the

shorter, more tubby of the pair, a deeply tanned Australian with bleached spiky hair. "Matt Trulli. If it's underwater, we can dry it off for you."

"Nice to meet you," said Nina. She looked at the submersibles. "So these are your subs? They don't look like I expected." They resembled earthmovers or other industrial machinery more than submarines.

"You thought they'd have the big bubble on the front, right?" Trulli said enthusiastically. "Jesus, you don't want that! One crack, and splatto! Well, maybe you want one if all you're doing is taking snapshots of weird fish or poncing about on the *Titanic*, but these beauts, we built them to *work*. Tough as hell."

"The last thing you want to do with a pressure hull is make a big hole in it," added Baillard, continuing his partner's train of thought as smoothly as if they were the same person. He pointed at the large white and orange metal sphere at the front of the smaller sub, the name *Atragon* painted on it in an elegant script. "Keep it in one piece and it's a lot stronger—and you can go much deeper."

"How do you see out?" Nina could see a porthole in the sphere's side, but it was only a few inches across.

"We use a LIDAR virtual imaging system instead of a viewing bubble—like radar, but using blue-green lasers. The U.S. Navy designed them as a communications system, to contact their missile subs. They work on a wavelength that isn't blocked by seawater."

"Two lasers," Trulli jumped in, "one for each eye. Proper stereoscopics! The lasers sweep in front of the sub twenty times a second, and any light that gets reflected back, we see on the big screen inside the pod in 3-D. No need to suck your batteries dry with a load of spotlights that do squat more than twenty feet away. We can see for a mile!"

"And because we have a much wider field of view than we would through a bubble, we can work a lot faster with the arms," Baillard said, reaching up and patting one of the imposing steel manipulators. "It's a revolutionary design."

"You said it!" Trulli high-fived his partner. "*Too* revolutionary. Nobody else even wanted to risk giving us development money. Kari's dad, though? Bam! Soon as he saw what we had in mind, we were in business."

"And now, not only do you get to prove your design," said Kari, "but you get to do so as part of the greatest archaeological discovery of all time."

"Like I said," nodded Baillard, "awesome."

"Too right," agreed Trulli. Nina smiled as they high-fived each other again.

"So what do they do?" she asked. "I mean, I guess the *Atragon*'s like a regular sub, but that one?" She indicated the larger submersible, a bright yellow behemoth with what looked almost like the mouth of a giant vacuum cleaner beneath its crew sphere. A broad pipe led back from the nozzle into the main body of the vessel; at its rear a second pipe, a flexible concertina arrangement that looked as though it could extend for some length, ran into a second compartment that Nina realized could be detached from the submersible's spine. Yet another length of extending pipe hung down from the module's stern almost like a tail. The words "Big Jobs!" were spray-painted, graffiti-style, on the side of the sphere.

"That?" said Trulli proudly. "*That* is the *Sharkdozer*. You know, like a bulldozer, only 'cause there's no bulls underwater, we named it after a shark instead?"

Nina grinned. "I think I get the idea."

"It's a self-contained underwater excavator," Baillard told her, pointing at its two heavy-duty arms. Rather than the claws on the smaller sub, these ended in buckets like those of an earthmover. "The arms move larger rock deposits, and the vacuum pump," he indicated the maw of the pipe beneath the sphere, "removes silt and sediment—"

"And because the main pump module's detachable," Trulli cut in, pointing at the "trailer" section of the vessel, "we can park it away from the site so all the crap we clear doesn't hang around and wipe out visibility."

Nina was impressed. "How quickly will it be able to clear the silt over the site?"

"Five meters?" said Baillard. "No time at all; at least enough to see that there's something underneath it."

"Actually dredging out enough to see what it *is*, though . . ." Trulli shrugged. "Depends how big a hole you want to dig. It's, what, two hundred feet wide? If it's nothing but silt covering it, we could suck one end clear in a couple of hours."

"Then if there's anything there, we can either use the *Atragon*'s manipulator arms to pick it up, or send in *Mighty Jack*."

"Who?" Nina asked.

Baillard pointed out a small cage attached to the *Atragon*, inside which was a bright blue boxy object that turned out to be a tiny vessel in its own right. "*Mighty Jack*'s our ROV, Remotely Operated Vehicle. He's a robot, basically, a Cameron Systems BB-101. He's connected to the *Atragon* by a fiber-optic cable, and we've fitted him with a stereoscopic camera so I can operate him right from the pod. Even got his own little arm as well."

Nina smiled at Baillard's anthropomorphization of the robot. "And this'll be the first time you've used them?"

"We've tested them, but yeah, this is the first full-on

real operation," said Trulli. "Can't wait to see what we find!"

"Nor can I." Kari looked at the horizon ahead. "We should be in position in about two hours. How soon will you be ready to launch?"

"We can do all the prelaunch prep in transit. Everything else . . . about an hour," Baillard said.

"We've got repeater monitors already set up in the main lab," Trulli told Nina. "You'll be able to see everything we see, as we see it—in 3-D, as well! Pretty smart, eh?"

"Sounds great." Nina felt a thrill of anticipation, a sense of impending discovery—but also of stress and tension. If there turned out to be nothing down there . . .

Kari picked up on her unease. "Are you okay?"

"I just haven't got my sea legs yet," Nina fibbed. "I think I'll go and lie down for a while. You'll let me know when we arrive?"

Kari adopted a deadpan expression. "No, I thought I'd let you miss the moment when we discover Atlantis."

"Don't *you* start," Nina chided as Kari cracked a smile. "I can't cope with having *two* sarcastic friends!"

∿

Nina returned to her cabin and lay on her bed for a while, trying not to think about the enormous amount of money and labor the Frosts were putting behind her deductions. When she eventually realized this was a fruitless hope, the thought of "sarcastic friends" prompted her to get up and knock on Chase's door. On being invited in, she was mildly surprised to see him on his bed reading a book—and more surprised when she saw the cover.

"Plato's dialogues?" she asked.

"Yeah," said Chase, sitting up. "Don't look so

shocked! I read. Thrillers mostly, but . . . Anyway, I thought that seeing as you've been going on about them so much, I ought to actually read the things. You know, the bloke doesn't spend all that much time actually *talking* about Atlantis."

Nina sat next to him. "No, not really."

"I mean, in *Timaeus* there's, what, three paragraphs on Atlantis? All the rest of it's like some stoned student talking bollocks about the meaning of the universe."

Nina laughed. "That's not the *usual* academic description . . . but yes, you're right."

"And the other one, *Critias*, he doesn't even start talking about Atlantis for about five pages. And when he does . . . it's interesting." There was a thoughtful tone to his words that caught Nina's attention.

"In what way?"

"I don't just mean about the description of the place, and how spot-on he was about the temple. I mean about the *people*, the rulers. It doesn't really add up."

"What do you mean?"

"I mean, in the notes here, some scholars think that *Critias* was Plato's blueprint of a perfect society, right? But it's not. You read what he *actually* says, and the Atlanteans are a pretty nasty lot. They're conquerors who invade other countries and enslave their people, they're a completely militarized society, the kings have absolute power of life and death over the citizens with no democracy . . ." Chase leafed through the pages. "And then you get to the end, just before the bit that he never finished. 'The human nature got the upper hand. They then, being unable to bear their fortune, behaved unseemly, and to him who had an eye to see grew visibly debased.' So Zeus calls up all the gods to punish them. Glug glug. Doesn't sound like they were that great to me. In fact, seems like the world was better off without them."

"I'm impressed," said Nina. "That was quite a good analysis."

"I was crap at maths and history—but I did all right at English." He put the book down, shifting closer to her. "Not wanting to sound funny or anything, but reading this did kind of make me wonder why you're so keen to find these people."

Nina felt oddly uncomfortable, almost as if she were being accused of something. Had Kari told Chase about the Atlantean DNA markers? It seemed unlikely. She shook off the feeling, replying, "It's something I've been fascinated by my entire life. So were my parents, actually. I went all around the world with them trying to find anything that might reveal where Atlantis was." She pulled her pendant out from beneath her T-shirt, holding it up to the light from the porthole. "The irony is, I had something all along and never realized it."

"Did your parents ever find anything else?"

She let the pendant drop back against her chest. "That's . . . I don't know, I really don't. They *thought* they did, but I never saw what it was. The year they, uh, died . . ." Her voice caught.

"I'm sorry, I didn't mean to . . ." Chase began.

She shook her head. "It's okay. I just don't often talk about it. They were on an expedition in Tibet while I was taking my university entrance exams . . ."

"Tibet?" asked Chase. "That's a hell of a long way from the Atlantic."

"It's been connected to the Atlantis legend for a long time. The Nazis sent several expeditions there, even during the war."

"Nazis again, eh?" mused Chase. "The bastards get around. So they found the temple in Brazil and nicked the sextant piece from it—but they must have found something else as well, something that made them go to Tibet."

"There could have been something on the map or in the inscriptions—there were definitely signs that the Atlanteans had visited Asia. I didn't have enough time to check."

"Why did your parents go there?"

"Again, I don't know. They found *something*, but they didn't tell me what it was." She frowned. "Which was weird in itself, because normally I was a part of everything."

"Maybe they didn't want to distract you from your exams."

"Maybe." Nina's frown didn't go away. "But the last thing I ever heard from them was by postcard, believe it or not. From Tibet. I still have it, actually."

"What did it say?"

"Not much, just that they were about to set off from a Himalayan village called Xulaodang. They were expecting to be gone for a week, but . . . ."

Chase put a sympathetic hand on her shoulder. "Hey. We don't have to talk about this if you don't want to."

"No, it's okay. It's funny, though. I hadn't even considered the Nazi connection until now. And my father *did* go to Germany the year before . . . Maybe that's what they had, something from the Ahnenerbe expeditions. Something that led them to Tibet. But why wouldn't they tell me?"

"'Cause they didn't want you to know they were using something from the Nazis?" Chase suggested.

"I suppose." She sat up with a sad sigh. "Not that it mattered. They were caught in an avalanche somewhere south of Xulaodang, and almost the entire expedition was killed. The bodies were never found, so whatever they had with them was lost."

Chase raised an eyebrow. "*Almost* everyone? Who survived?"

"Jonathan."

"Jonathan? What, you mean Philby? The Prof?"

"Yes, of course. I thought you knew. He was on the expedition with them. That's why we're so close—even though I'm sure there wasn't anything he could have done, he said he felt responsible for not being able to save them. He's been looking out for me ever since."

Chase leaned back on the bed. "Philby, huh?"

"What?"

He looked away. "Nothing. Just never knew that was how you knew each other."

"He worked with my parents for years, they were friends."

"Hmm." Something seemed to be on Chase's mind, but before she could ask him about it, she heard knocking from outside. Not on Chase's door, but from her own cabin. "In here!"

Kari cautiously leaned through the door. "I'm not interrupting anything, am I?"

Chase snorted mockingly. "I wish!"

"I wanted to let you know that we're almost at the coordinates. Captain Matthews is going to use the ship's thrusters to hold position rather than drop anchor—we don't want to risk damaging anything down there—and then we're going to lower the subs. I thought you might want to watch."

"Wouldn't miss it," said Nina, standing up. "Eddie, are you coming?"

"Give me a couple of minutes," said Chase. "You'll be on the sub deck, right?"

\\/\\/

The design of the *Evenor* meant there were few places where anyone could stand outside the superstructure without being in plain sight of the fore or aft decks. But after considerable exploration, Jonathan Philby found a short gangway on the second level that was open to the sea on one side.

He looked around nervously. Forward, he could see the extremities of the crane lifting the larger of the two submersibles into position. For his GPS receiver to work, its antenna needed to have unobstructed line of sight to at least half the sky—but leaning over the side of the ship to get coverage put him at risk of being seen.

There was no choice. He *had* to make the call.

The compact satellite phone had been a constant companion ever since he had informed Qobras that the Frosts had contacted him. Simply removing it from concealment inside his belongings sent him into a state of anxiety; if any of his companions saw it, even Nina, suspicions would immediately be raised, and it would all be over. Finding an opportunity in Gibraltar to give the *Evenor*'s approximate destination had been relatively stress-free, but trying to pass on the *Nereid*'s final position in Brazil without being discovered had almost given him a panic attack.

This was little better. The doors at each end of the gangway had no windows. At any moment, somebody could walk through them. He waited anxiously for the connection to be made . . .

"Yes?" said a voice. Starkman.

"It's Philby. I don't have much time. We're almost at our destination—here are my current coordinates." He relayed the figures from his GPS unit. "The *Evenor*'s final position will be a few miles west of there."

"The *Evenor*'s final position will be eight hundred feet *down* from there," said Starkman. "We're already on our way. Good work, Jack. You'll be rewarded."

"The only reward I want is to get *out* of this." Philby wiped sweat from his brow. "It'll all be over, right?"

"Oh yes." Starkman's voice was firm. "The hunt for Atlantis ends here."

ʷ

The two submersibles were lowered into the ocean, one on each side of the *Evenor*. Their pilots were already inside; the "cowboys," crewmen in wetsuits standing on top of the vessels, checked that their systems were in order and the communications umbilicals properly connected before releasing them from the cranes. Once free, the submersibles dropped without ceremony beneath the waves. The cowboys were picked up by a Zodiac, which returned them to a dock at the fantail.

With only eight hundred feet of water to penetrate, the descent took less than ten minutes. Nina had pride of place in the lab before the various monitor screens, Kari sitting next to her. Philby, Chase and Castille watched over their shoulders, as did a handful of the *Evenor*'s crew.

Nina found the whole experience disorienting. Each of the two large screens in front of her displayed exactly what the pilots were seeing inside their pressure spheres, using an autostereoscopic LCD display that gave a 3-D image without needing special glasses. For most of the descent the illusion of depth was barely apparent, but every so often a fish would pass in front of the submersibles' scanning lasers and leap out of the screen in a flash of ghostly night-vision green.

"Seven-fifty feet," said Trulli over the communications link. "We're in the pipe, five by five. Slowing descent."

"*Evenor*, please confirm bearing to target," Baillard said.

"*Atragon*, turn to two-zero-zero degrees," Kari said into her headset. "You're less than three hundred meters away. *Sharkdozer*, hold position until contact is confirmed."

"We should be able to see it by now," Trulli complained. The seabed swung into sharp dimensional relief in front of Nina as he turned his vessel, dropping the nose slightly to point the lasers downwards. The resolution was high enough for her to pick out crabs scuttling over the rippled sediment.

She turned her attention to the view from Baillard's submersible, which was now advancing at walking pace, hanging about twenty feet above the seabed. A smaller screen showed the spotlit view from a standard video camera, but the LIDAR image extended much farther.

The sea floor rose ahead.

"*Evenor*, I have something here," Baillard reported. "Getting a very strong sonar return . . . it's not silt. Something solid coming up, and it's *big*. Could be a shipwreck . . ."

"It's no shipwreck," Nina whispered as the object came into view on the 3-D screen. She recognized the shape instantly. It was the same as the replica of the Temple of Poseidon in the Brazilian jungle.

And unlike that now ruined structure, this one was intact.

"Bloody hell," muttered Chase, leaning closer over her shoulder.

"Jesus. *Evenor*, do you see this?" asked Baillard.

"We see it," Kari confirmed, handing Nina a headset. "Nina, you're in charge."

"Me? But I don't know anything about submarines!"

"You don't have to. Just tell him what you want to look at, and he'll do it."

"Okay . . ." Nina said nervously, suddenly terrified at the idea of accidentally causing the submersible to crash. She donned the headset, fiddling with the microphone. "Jim, this is Nina. Can you hear me?"

"Loud and clear," replied the Canadian. "I'm about a hundred and fifty meters away. Can you see it clearly?"

"Oh yes." The lower parts of the temple walls were buried beneath a sloping mound of sediment, but the top of its curved roof rose a good thirty feet above the ocean floor. Reflected laser light shone back brightly in places where the sheath of precious metals over the stone had remained intact even through the deluge. "I can't believe it's still standing."

Philby leaned closer, apparently having trouble with the stereoscopic effect and dealing with it by simply closing one eye. "The design must have been incredibly precise, so all the blocks would support their own weight. When the island sank, it held together even when everything else collapsed. Amazing!"

"What's the current like?" Kari asked.

Trulli gave a reading. "I'm getting about half a knot of drift, heading northeast."

"No wonder it's not completely buried," said Baillard. "If that's the prevailing current, then it'll sweep a lot of the sediment towards the Spanish coast."

"Is there anything else above the surface?" Nina asked.

The 3-D image jolted disconcertingly; the *Atragon* hadn't changed course, but the laser scanners had been redirected to look off to one side. "I can see a few bumps where there might be things under the surface, but nothing actually standing out. How tall is this thing?"

"If it's the size we think it is, it should be about sixty feet tall. Eighteen meters."

"If that's the case, then it's maybe half exposed. There's a lot of silt piled up around it." The image shifted back to the temple.

"*Sharkdozer*, move in closer," Kari ordered. "Head to the north end, keep clear of the *Atragon*."

"Gotcha," said Trulli. The second 3-D display showed his advance.

"Jim?" Nina asked. "Can you circle the building, please? I want to see what it looks like from the other side."

Baillard complied. The maneuver took a couple of minutes, revealing a view much the same as their first sight of the temple. Its curved back, partly buried by sediment, reminded Nina of a turtle's shell.

"Hey, *Evenor*," said Trulli excitedly, "the north end here, the sediment's lower. It must have been cleared away by the current. I can see more of the wall."

Nina quickly switched her attention to the *Sharkdozer*'s screen. There was a smooth, almost bowl-like depression at the northern end of the temple, as though some-one had used a giant scoop to clear the silt away. "Can you get in closer?"

"No worries. Hold on a tick."

It took rather longer than the promised tick, but a few minutes later Trulli brought the hefty submersible to a hover a short distance from the temple wall. "I'm going to take a sonar reading," he announced. "Hang on."

One of the monitors flashed up a jagged graph. Nina couldn't make head nor tail of it, but to the submersible pilot it was as clear as a photograph. "There's some-thing under the sediment—or rather, there's something *not* under the sediment. Could be a hole in the wall."

"Room to get *Mighty Jack* through?" asked Baillard.

"Maybe. *Evenor*, do I have permission to clear the sediment?"

Kari looked at Nina, who nodded in excitement. There was a way into the temple! "Go ahead, *Sharkdozer*."

The operation that followed was frustratingly slow. Nina forced herself not to rap her nails on the desktop as Trulli moved his sub away from the temple. He carefully lowered the pump module to the surface about a hundred meters off to the northeast, extending its "tail" in the direction of the current, then returned to the temple. The *Atragon*'s LIDAR display showed the connecting tube stretching between the pump module and its mother ship as the *Sharkdozer* returned to position, taking up station above the base of the northern wall. The whole process took over twenty minutes.

"Ready to go, *Evenor*," Trulli said at last. "Just give the word."

"Go for it!" Nina cried, to everyone's amusement.

The pump started.

Like the world's largest vacuum cleaner, the *Sharkdozer* began to suck the accumulated silt into its gaping maw. The pressure difference created by the pump wasn't huge, but it was more than enough to draw the layers of sediment into the pipe and through the detached module to spew out of the waste pipe one hundred meters away. The prevailing current gently swept the expanding cloud of suspended particles away from the temple. The value of a technique that had initially struck Nina as overcomplicated now became clear; simply digging up the silt would have wiped out visibility within seconds.

Another ten minutes passed with agonizing slowness, the *Atragon* providing a ringside view as the *Sharkdozer* slid from side to side over the foot of the wall, on each pass clearing away another layer. Then . . .

"I think I've got something here!" exclaimed the Australian. He directed his video camera at the spot. Drifting silt clouded the image, but not enough to stop Nina's heart from thumping at the sight. "Looks like a way in."

On the screen, a passageway disappeared into darkness. It was hard to judge scale, but if the temple had been constructed the same way as its counterpart in Brazil, the opening was roughly four feet across.

"I'll use the secondary vac to dredge it out," said Trulli. "Give me a few minutes." One of the *Sharkdozer's* arms extended, but instead of using the large bucket at the end to clear the obstruction, a narrow metal pipe extended from beneath it, probing the opening and sucking away the deposits inside.

Chase leaned over Nina's shoulder to examine the 3-D display, his cheek almost touching hers. "You know . . . if this temple has the same layout as the one in Brazil, that passage might lead right into the altar room. There was a shaft at the back, but it had been filled in with rocks."

Nina gave him an accusing glance. "There was? Why didn't you tell me?"

"I didn't have time! You know, with the whole imminent death thing."

"A priest hole," said Kari thoughtfully. "A secret exit."

Trulli worked for several more minutes before retracting the arm. "I've cleared out as much as I can. Jimbo, warm up *Mighty Jack!*"

While Trulli backed the *Sharkdozer* away, Baillard brought his own submersible closer, parking it at the edge of the expanded depression around the north wall. Once in position, he announced, "*Evenor,* I'm releasing the ROV . . . now."

All eyes went to the *Atragon*'s 3-D display, which switched from the ghostly monochrome of the LIDAR system to a full-color video image as *Mighty Jack* left its cage and headed for the temple. The little robot didn't have the laser imaging system of its parent vessel, but it still had stereoscopic cameras. As it entered the opening, the tight confines of the passage beyond gave a vertiginous sensation of speed. "God, it's like attacking the Death Star," Chase observed.

Mighty Jack proceeded down the passage. There were still clumps of sediment along its floor, but Trulli had cleared enough for the ROV to pass. The tension in the control room rose as the robot advanced, to find . . .

A blank wall.

"No!" Nina gasped, disappointed. "It's a dead end!"

The ROV turned left, then right, its spotlights finding nothing but solid stone. "What do you want me to do?" asked Baillard.

Nina was about to tell him to bring the robot back out when Chase interrupted, leaning close to speak into her headset's mike. "Jim, this is Eddie. Can that thing go straight up?"

"Yes, sure. But—"

"Do it."

After a moment of hesitation, the ROV rose cautiously towards the ceiling . . .

And kept going.

"Whoa!" said Baillard, rotating *Mighty Jack* to examine the side walls as the robot ascended. "How did you know that was there?"

"Just a hunch," said Chase, grinning at Nina. "Watch out, though. There might be traps on the way up."

She gently swatted him away from her headset. "Eddie, somehow I doubt there's been anybody maintaining *this* temple for the past eleven thousand years."

"I dunno, those mermaids are tricky bitches . . ."

Nina smiled, then turned her attention back to the screen. Baillard angled the camera upwards as much as he could, the shaft taking on perspective.

"I see something," he announced. A dark line on the wall of the shaft came up fast, a shimmering distortion . . .

The image suddenly rolled, tipping back to the horizontal. One of the stone walls filled the screen. "Jim!" Nina called. "What happened? Did you hit something?"

"Just a second . . ." The robot slowly turned, the image still shaking queasily. Nothing was visible except the walls. "Okay. I guess that's as far as *Mighty Jack* can go."

"What do you mean?" Kari demanded. "Is it stuck on something? Have we lost the ROV?"

Baillard almost laughed. "Not at all. It's just that . . . well, *Mighty Jack*'s only designed for use in the water. So you'll need some other way to explore from this point on."

"Why?" asked Nina.

"Because we've run out of water. *Mighty Jack*'s floating on the surface. There's *air* inside that temple."

TWENTY

The submersibles returned to the surface. The *Sharkdozer* was recovered and winched back aboard the *Evenor*, but the *Atragon* remained in the water, a cable attached so it could recharge its batteries.

A second dive was being prepared. And this time, the exploration of the temple would not be left to robots.

"I wish I could go with you," Nina said. Kari, Chase and Castille were in the final stages of suiting up for their descent.

"Bet you wish you'd brought your swimming certificate, don't you?" Chase joked as a crewman assisted him with his helmet.

The three divers were wearing newly designed "deep suits"—a kind of hybrid of traditional scuba systems and the armorlike, almost robotic hard suits employed for deep, long-duration dives. The divers' limbs were enclosed in the same neoprene rubber used in regular dry suits, but their heads and bodies were contained in a rigid unit connected to ring seals around the thighs and upper arms.

At a depth of eight hundred feet, close to the limits of scuba diving, the pressure on a diver's body was over twenty-five atmospheres, requiring air to be supplied at an equal pressure to enable his lungs to expand against the crushing force surrounding them. But breathing such highly pressurized gas came with a price: the compressed gas that entered the bloodstream expanded as the diver ascended and the pressure around him reduced. Nitrogen bubbles swelled inside the blood vessels, causing excruciating pain, tissue damage and even death . . .

Decompression sickness. *The bends*.

The deep suits were a way to avoid this. By keeping the body within a shell able to withstand the external pressure, the divers breathed air at just one atmosphere, while keeping their arms and legs free to move with far greater maneuverability underwater than in any heavy, clumsy hard suit. It was a compromise—it was impossible to turn or bend at the waist, and the fact that their limbs were exposed to the pressure of the deep still placed limits on how long they could remain submerged—but it hugely reduced the risk of the bends.

"You'll still be able to watch us on the video feed," Kari promised.

"It's not the same thing. This sort of discovery really should be hands-on."

"Don't worry," Castille said. "We'll bring you back a golden Nereid."

"God, no! Leave everything exactly as you find it, please! And on that subject . . ." She turned to Chase. "Do you really *have* to take explosives with you?"

"If the passage is blocked higher up, we might need to clear it. Don't worry, I'm not going to blow the whole place up! I know what I'm doing."

"I hope so." She rapped his helmet. "What's it like in there?"

"Cramped. Good thing I'm not claustrophobic."

"Lucky you," sighed Castille. He looked down at the

yellow shell covering his body. "I feel as though I'm trapped inside a giant bar of soap."

"Or a corset," added Kari, putting a hand on the waist of her own suit. While Chase and Castille's units were of a generic design, size adjustments made by moving the seals on their limbs, hers was custom made to fit her precisely, still managing to show off her feminine shape beneath the steel and polycarbonate. "This must be how Victorian women felt!"

"Yeah, as they fell off the *Titanic*," joked Chase.

"That was Edwardian, not Victorian," Nina corrected him.

"Bloody historians ruin all my jokes . . ." He looked at his companions as the crewmen closed the last clips on their suits. "Okay . . . Are we ready?"

"Absolutely," Kari said enthusiastically.

"Ready to go into danger again?" said Castille, rather less so. "Well, if I must . . ."

"Come on, Hugo, you love it," grinned Chase. "And at least you don't have to worry about helicopters down there."

"Ah, but what is a submersible but an *underwater* helicopter?"

Chase banged a hand on Castille's helmet. "Yeah, yeah. Now stop moaning and get your Belgian arse in the water!"

w

With the three divers holding on to its steel bumper cage, the *Atragon* disappeared into the ocean.

Nina watched it go before hurrying to the control room. Chase's suit had a video camera mounted on the right shoulder, transmitting to the *Atragon* along a fiber-optic link, the submersible in turn sending the image to the ship via its umbilical. "Hey, Kari, I can see you," she said, putting on a headset. The figure on the screen waved its free hand.

"Divers, can you check coms?" asked Trulli from the next monitor station. "Eddie?"

"Loud and clear," said Chase. His voice was distorted, but no more so than if he'd been talking on a telephone.

"Kari?"

Her response was more garbled, heavily marred by static. "I can hear you, but there's a lot of interference."

"Same for me," Castille's voice crackled.

"What's the range of those transmitters?" Philby asked. Chase's communications systems were hardwired to the submersible, but to avoid the risk of entangling cables, Kari and Castille were using an underwater radio link, making him a human relay station.

"At most, maybe fifteen meters," Trulli told him. "Depends on the salinity of the water. If it's real salty, the signal attenuation could be so much that it'll only travel two or three meters. That close, you're better off just shouting."

"You guys?" Nina said into the mike. "Make sure you stay close together, huh?" Kari gave her a thumbs-up.

The descent was slower than the first, but Captain Matthews had moved the *Evenor* directly over the site of the temple to reduce the transit time on the sea floor. Before long, the structure appeared on the LIDAR display.

"Okay, divers?" said Baillard. "I'm going to set down where I did before, at the edge of the excavation."

Nina watched the view from Chase's camera. The *Atragon* had fewer spotlights than a conventional submersible, so the temple was little more than an oppressive shade against the near black of the sea. A small flurry of sand swirled up under the thrusters as the sub came to rest with a gentle bump.

"*Evenor*," Baillard announced, "we are down and safe. Divers? Good luck."

w

Chase let go of the tubular bumper and dropped to the seabed. Kari and Castille followed. "Okay, we're here. Radio check."

"I hear you," said Kari.

"Radio check okay," Castille confirmed. Then, more casually: "I have an itch right in the middle of my back. I think I'll head back to the ship to scratch it."

"What, and miss the fun of going through a narrow stone passage where you don't know what's at the top?" Chase took a few experimental steps, his flippered feet kicking up more silt. Even with the neutral buoyancy the deep suit provided, its inflexible body meant the best he could manage was an unflattering waddle. Its broad, flat chest also caused a surprising amount of resistance from the water when he tried to move forward. "Sod it, walking's going to take forever. Let's try the thrusters."

He kicked himself off the seabed, tilting into a horizontal position. Castille and Kari followed suit. Once they were with him, Chase reached up with his left hand to take hold of a control stick protruding from the suit's chest on a flexible stalk.

"Okay, stay close," he ordered. "If we have any trouble, or anyone has com problems, get straight back to the sub and wait for the others. Let's go."

He pushed his thumb down on the sprung wheel set into the end of the stick. The controls for the thrusters built into the suit's casing were simple: three speed settings to go forward, one for reverse, and releasing the wheel would automatically stop the motors. He started off at the lowest speed, using his feet to adjust his pitch. Once satisfied that he had full control, he increased speed to the second setting. The fiber-optic cable linking him to the submersible spooled out behind him like a line of spider silk.

Castille matched his speed. "This is very easy!" he said, voice distorted even over the short distance. "All those years I wasted using my legs to swim . . ."

"Just don't crack your head straight into the wall," Chase cautioned cheerfully. "Kari, you okay?"

She swept past him, effortlessly rolling in a lazy corkscrew motion. "Who do you think helped design these suits? I have other passions besides archaeology and architecture!"

"I do like a passionate boss," joked Chase. The temple was approaching quickly, taking on color in their suit lights. "Okay, slow down."

"Eddie, I can't see anything except the seabed," Nina complained over the radio. "How close are you to the temple?"

Chase let go of the controller and brought himself upright, aiming the camera on his shoulder at the building ahead. "About so close. You seeing that?"

"Oh, definitely," she replied, awed.

The trio touched down less than ten feet from where the sloping wall rose from the piled sediment. Ragged sheets of orichalcum glinted under their spotlights. Fish darted over the temple's surface, oblivious to the ancient power it represented.

"Which way to the entrance?" Chase asked.

"About six meters to your left," Baillard said.

The group headed for it, Chase and Kari using powerful flashlights as well as their suit lights. Chase glanced back at the *Atragon*. Although he could see its spotlights clearly, as well as the unearthly pulse of its scanning lasers, the sub itself was barely visible in the deep gloom.

"There!" said Kari. Her light shone on the opening.

Chase crouched as best he could, directing his own light inside. It wasn't as far as he'd expected to the vertical shaft; the fish-eye effect of the ROV's camera had exaggerated the distance. "Okay, I'll go first. Hugo, hook me up." Castille connected a tether from a reel on his equipment belt to a clip on the lower back of Chase's suit. "If there isn't enough room to get around the bend in the shaft, pull me out."

Castille yanked on the tether to make sure it was properly connected, then moved to the far side of the entrance so it wouldn't become tangled in the communications line. "If you ate more fruit and less steak, you wouldn't be worrying about getting stuck."

"You know where you can shove your fruit . . . Okay, here I go."

Kari and Castille helped him to a horizontal position, guiding him into the opening. Flashlight in his extended right hand, Chase took the controls with his left and started the thrusters on low power. The stone walls crept past. Under normal circumstances a four-foot-wide passage would have been easy to negotiate even underwater, but the unbending bulk of the deep suit made him more cautious.

It wasn't long before he reached the end of the passage. He rolled onto his back to look up the shaft. It stretched away into blackness. "I'm at the shaft. *Shaft!* Can you dig it?" Nina groaned. "Going to try to head up."

The corner was tight, his helmet scraping against the wall, but he levered himself upright without too much difficulty. "I'm through!" he announced, relieved. "Let's see what's up here."

He activated the thrusters again, the ducted propellers whirring quietly as he rose. The shaft was at least thirty feet high, the walls sheer. Looking up, he saw the dark square where *Mighty Jack* had come to a stop—where air had been trapped by the rising water. It was only three feet above him now, two, one . . .

He broke the surface, water streaming down his faceplate. Shining the light, he saw he was about six feet short of the top of the shaft, a black void above him.

No problem. He clipped the flashlight back onto his equipment belt and brought up one of his other items—a gas-powered grappling gun. Bobbing awkwardly like a giant cork in the confines of the shaft, he aimed it over the top of the south wall, then fired.

The thump of gas echoed through the shaft as the grapnel shot upwards. A few seconds later, he heard it clank against stone. He worked the controls to wind in the cable. After a tense wait, the grapnel caught on something. He pulled it a couple of times to check it was secure, then attached the gun's strap to his suit and pulled himself up, the motor whining in protest at the weight.

The top was just a few feet above him now, opening out into . . .

w

"Look at that!" Nina gasped. She watched the video feed intently, barely blinking. The view from Chase's camera revealed the altar chamber, in dimensions an exact match for the one in Brazil.

In magnificence, however, it was something else entirely.

Even in the grainy, low-resolution video, she could clearly make out the red gleam of orichalcum, flashes of gold and silver, cat's-eye sparkles from gemstones set into the walls . . .

"My God," breathed Philby, "it's incredible. The entire chamber must be lined with precious metals!"

"It's not just decorative," said Nina. She fiddled with her headset. "Eddie? Talk to me. What can you see?"

"I see . . . that if I had some tin snips and a crowbar, I could retire on this lot."

"Very funny. Can you get closer to one of the walls?"

"Christ, let me get onto my feet first . . ." The video image jerked as Chase pulled himself out of the shaft and detached the cable gun, his breath rasping into his microphone. "Okay. Well, I was right about the shaft, it's in the same place as the blocked one in Brazil. They must have used the same plans. The walls are . . . God, they've used the stuff like wallpaper. There's sheet after sheet of orichalcum, and it's all inscribed."

"Let me see, let me see!" said Nina, bouncing in her chair in excitement.

Chase moved closer, his flashlight beam sliding over one section of wall. Nina immediately recognized the script: Glozel, though with none of the hieroglyphic symbols from the Brazilian temple.

Philby stroked his mustache as he peered at the screen. "Interesting. Maybe they assimilated the language of the Indians . . . The temple in Brazil would have taken years, even generations to build. That would be enough time for the two systems to intermix . . ."

"Eddie, give me a look at the whole chamber, please. Slowly."

Chase stepped away from the wall and slowly turned in place, panning his camera around the room.

"Stop, stop!" Nina shouted, seeing something. "Back to the right a little bit . . . there! Go over there!"

"Now I know how *Mighty Jack* feels," he complained

amiably as he waddled across the room. "What've you seen? There's nothing there."

"Exactly!" The section of wall before Chase was sheathed in orichalcum like the rest of the chamber, but it was blank, the inscribed text stopping abruptly halfway down. "The whole chamber, it's a record of Atlantis—but that's where it ends! Which means whatever's written there is the final record of the Atlanteans! Get closer, let me read it!" She hurriedly checked that the video feed was being recorded.

"*Or* you could let me unhook this rope from my arse and fix it to something so Hugo and Kari can climb up here as well," said Chase. "You remember Kari? Attractive blonde, tall, *has a camera*?"

"Well, yeah, that might work too," she replied, slightly deflated but still desperate to get the first look at what was written on the wall.

The first look. Nobody had set eyes on the text for over eleven thousand years . . .

She waited impatiently as Chase set things up. Finally he announced that Kari was on her way. "Okay, while we're waiting, can you *please* go back to the final record?"

"You're so domineering. I like that in a woman . . . sometimes," he quipped, directing the camera at the text.

Nina looked across at Trulli. "Matt, is there any way to get a freeze-frame from the video?"

"Sure. The recorder's digital, got a terabyte of storage—it'll keep on recording. What screen do you want it on?"

"My big one."

"It won't be in 3-D."

"I can live with that." A few seconds later, the screen came to life with a frozen still of the last section of text.

The image was fuzzy, the colors smeared, but it was clear enough for her to make out the letters. She stared at it, deep in thought.

One of the crew hurried into the control room. "Captain Matthews? There's a ship approaching."

"What?" Matthews snapped. "How far?"

"About five miles. It was on a course for Lisbon when we first saw it on radar, but it turned towards us a couple of minutes ago."

"Speed?"

"At least twelve knots, sir."

"Is it Qobras?" The name caught Nina's attention. She looked around at Matthews, worried.

"Very possibly. The ship fits the description of the one that set out from Casablanca."

"Damn it!" Matthews rubbed his chin, thinking. "All right. Let everyone know that we have company, and to be ready. If it gets to within two miles, or they launch boats, break out the weapons. I'll be on the bridge."

"Yes, sir." The crewman left, Matthews following.

"Eddie, did you hear any of that?" Nina asked. "They think Qobras is on his way!"

"What? Shit!" On one of the smaller monitors, Nina saw him helping Kari out of the shaft. "What do you want to do?"

"Record as much as you can, as fast as you can. As soon as I hear anything else, I'll let you know. His ship's still five miles away—Captain Matthews's going to keep us updated."

"Only five miles? There's no way we'll be able to get back to the surface and recover the sub before he gets here!"

"The submersible's expendable, we can abandon it if we need to," said Kari, ignoring the yelp of "*What?*" from Baillard. Out of the water, her transmission was much clearer. "We can build another, but the information in here is priceless. Video as much of it as you can— we can process it later if we need to enhance anything. I'll take pictures."

"Hugo, did you get that?" Chase asked.

The reply was barely audible, masked by static. "Most of it. What do you want me to do?"

"No point you coming in here now. Stay at the entrance in case we need any help."

"Roger, mon ami. Don't wait too long."

Nina watched as Chase returned to the inscription-covered walls, then looked back at the still image on her main screen, trying to decipher its secrets.

W

Unseen by anybody aboard the *Evenor,* a head broke the surface of the ocean beneath the research vessel's fantail. Then another, and another . . .

Thirty feet below the gentle waves, more divers released their Manta tow sleds, fast, streamlined three-man vehicles. The abandoned minisubs dropped slowly away into the darkness as their passengers headed silently for the *Evenor*'s boat dock. The ship was using its thrusters to hold position; the propellers were still.

The first man reached the ladder and carefully ascended, peering over the edge of the deck. One of the *Evenor*'s crew was about twenty feet away on the helipad, his back to him. Nobody else was in sight.

The frogman ducked back down, unslinging his weapon—a Heckler and Koch MP-7—and popped the red rubber seal from the end of the fat silencer with his thumb in one easy move. That done, he crept silently back to the top of the ladder and took aim.

There was almost no noise save the sharp metallic clack as the bolt cycled, the spent casing of the single

4.6-millimeter bullet caught in a mesh bag attached to the compact weapon before it could hit the deck. Even as the crewman fell, the frogman was already scrambling up onto the deck. He raced for cover against a bulkhead, listening for sounds of alarm. Nothing reached him but the slap of waves and the plaintive cries of gulls circling above.

Other men quickly boarded the *Evenor*, spreading out. The first man removed his mask, revealing a black patch over one eye.

Jason Starkman.

"Take the ship," he ordered.

w

Chase continued around the altar room, scanning the texts on the walls. The video camera on his shoulder was fixed in one position, and his inability to bend inside the suit made it a cumbersome process.

He reached the stairs. If the structure was like the one in Brazil, they would lead to the vast main chamber. He directed his flashlight down them. Water reflected the beam back at him, shimmering patterns rolling over the walls and ceiling.

"Good thing we didn't take off our helmets," he said, crossing the top of the stairway to check the wall on the other side. "If the water pressure outside's at twenty-five ATA, then the air in here and in the temple will be as well."

"You mean the temple itself isn't flooded?" asked Kari.

"Only partly. The floor in here's higher than the temple, but the ceiling's at about the same height. There must be air trapped in there as well."

Her voice filled with frustration. "If only we had time

to investigate! It's astounding that the temple survived the deluge."

"Guess they really built 'em to last back then. How are you doing?"

Another flash from her camera. "About half finished."

vvv

Castille stood by the entrance, watching the slight shifts of the fiber-optic cable as Chase moved around inside. Of all the times for Qobras to show up! Chase was undoubtedly right: somebody had given their location away to the opposition. But who?

At only a meter from the stone wall, the lights of his deep suit overpowered the stronger but more diffuse spotlights on the *Atragon*. So he didn't notice as the glow slowly became brighter, the lights on Baillard's submersible joined by another source . . .

vvv

Up in the *Evenor*'s pilothouse, Matthews observed the approaching ship through a pair of powerful binoculars. It was now three miles away, and still heading for them.

Definitely a deep-sea survey ship, a submersible crane on its foredeck, which meant it was almost certainly the one Qobras had chartered. Somehow he had found out about the true location of Nina Wilde's discovery and directed it here at full speed. And in another few minutes it would reach the two-mile mark, at which point he would have no choice but to consider it a threat.

No sign of any boats being launched, however, even though a group of men in a Zodiac could reach the stationary *Evenor* much sooner than the ship itself. It looked as though they meant to close right in.

In which case, they were in for a surprise. The weapons Kristian Frost had provided—a P-90 submachine gun for each member of the crew, plus a pair of heavy machine guns and a number of rocket-propelled grenades and launchers—would be more than enough to drive off anyone who tried to take his ship.

No boats . . .

No boats being launched—for that matter, no boats even *ready* to be launched.

And if that was the crane for a submersible . . . where the hell was the sub itself?

Matthews realized with shock the significance of that fact, but too late to act upon it as the door of the pilothouse burst open.

w

In the control sphere of the *Atragon*, Baillard drummed a tune on one of the control panels with his fingertips. On the 3-D screen, he could see Castille standing with his back to him, observing the entrance to the sunken temple.

That was one disadvantage of the LIDAR system, he mused. The lack of color made it very dull to look at when nothing was happening. He glanced up at the monitor showing the feed from the submersible's main video camera. The view wasn't much better in color, the building obscured by too much light-sapping water for any real detail to be visible . . .

What the hell?

Something had just moved in the corner of his vision, outside the small porthole.

A fish? No, there was something *different* about the view . . .

It hit like ice.

The lighting had changed!

He hadn't moved the exterior spotlights, and the sub was stationary . . .

"Evenor!" he yelled into the radio. *"Evenor,* there's another sub—"

A loud crackle in his headphones, then silence. All the indicator LEDs on the communications console flicked from green to red.

"Evenor! Do you copy? What's happening?"

The answer came a moment later. Something hit the top of the hull with a dull *clonk.* A long object snaked down in front of the LIDAR turret.

The umbilical. Neatly severed.

And now more light flooded through the porthole as his unseen attacker closed in.

"Shit!" He grabbed the controls, bringing the motors to life and blasting the *Atragon* off the seabed in an explosive cloud of silt. "Hugo! I'm under attack! Get out of there!"

Something plowed into his vessel, slamming him sideways against the steel wall.

w

A harsh buzz in Chase's ear made him wince. His suit relay passed it on to Kari, who gasped in surprise. "What was that?"

w

All the *Evenor*'s underwater feeds went blank simultaneously, some of the screens turning black, others bright blue with a "No Signal" warning.

"What was that?" Nina asked.

"That, Dr. Wilde," said a new voice from behind her, "was the end of your expedition."

Nina whirled. *"You!"*

Starkman stared coldly down at her, flanked by two

of his wet-suited men. All three had their guns raised, covering the occupants of the room. "If you'd like to join the rest of the crew on the aft deck?"

W

Castille spun at the garbled shout in his headphones, to see a *second* sub bearing down on the *Atragon*!

Baillard's vessel had just started to rise from the seabed as the intruder, a smaller conventional submersible with a thick steel cage around its bubble cockpit, rammed into its side. The *Atragon* was driven back down, almost disappearing inside a roiling cloud of silt.

"Merde!" he gasped, before recovering his composure. "Edward! Edward, can you hear me? Kari!"

There was no answer. The radio relay on the submersible was down, cutting him off from the other divers.

The attacker rose from the cloud and made a sharp turn, thrusters swiveling and pumping out swirling toroids of bubbles in their wake. Its spotlights picked out white and orange metal within the billowing sediment.

Castille thought it was going to ram the *Atragon* again, but instead it extended its manipulator arm. Something was clutched between the pincers, a blocky package that it placed almost delicately against the side of the command sphere . . .

W

Baillard knew something bad was about to happen as he saw the shadow of the other sub's outstretched manipulator arm move across the porthole. A second later, something rasped against the pressure sphere.

The LIDAR was down—aside from the tiny portholes, he was blind. Pressing a palm against the deep cut on his temple and trying not to hyperventilate in fear, he worked the thruster controls.

Nothing happened. While he and Trulli had designed their subs to be sturdy, they hadn't been intended to resist a deliberate attack, and the electrical control board was flashing multiple warning lights.

He quickly considered his options. He could either reset the affected circuits and try to restore thruster power—or just shut off the electromagnets holding the heavy steel ballast plates to the sub's belly, an emergency system that would put him back on the surface in under three minutes.

Doing so would mean abandoning the three divers. But he couldn't help them if he couldn't see, and the other sub was still out there, its spotlights driving a menacing beam through the porthole as it moved around.

He made his decision, and pulled the red-painted lever beside his seat.

w

Castille watched in horror as the *Atragon* released its ballast slabs, which dropped like bombs onto the sea floor, kicking up another huge rolling wave of sediment. The dull boom of their impact was strong enough for him to feel through the water.

Freed of the weight, the submersible shot upwards, spotlights flickering. The fiber-optic line whipped upwards with it, snaking like a cracking whip.

"No!" he yelled helplessly.

As if hearing his shout, the enemy sub swiveled to face him, its banks of spotlights regarding him like glowing compound eyes. The manipulator arm reached back, expertly collecting something attached to a pannier on the steel sideframe before extending again.

Another package, larger than the first.

Castille knew instinctively what it was.

A bomb!

\vv/

Baillard fought to restore power as the *Atragon* rose. Nothing he did seemed to improve matters—

He froze at an unexpected sound. The sub was creaking and groaning as it ascended, but those noises were so familiar that they barely registered. This was something else.

A rhythmic noise, mechanical, coming from the side of the sphere. Where the other sub's arm had ground against it.

A *ticking* . . .

Baillard didn't even have time to realize the full terror of the situation before the shaped charge exploded, ripping a foot-wide hole in the steel pressure sphere. A spear of water hit him with the force of a train, killing him instantly.

\vv/

Even through his helmet and the thick stone walls of the temple, Chase heard the low rumble. "Shit!"

"What was that noise?" Kari asked.

"An explosion."

"Are you sure?"

"Oh yeah," he said. "Either someone dropped a thousand-pound bomb on the *Evenor*—or the sub just blew up." He looked down at his suit. "Which means— oh shit, *shit*! Cut my coms line, quick!"

"But we'll be cut off!"

"We're *already* cut off! Do it!"

Kari put down the camera and clumsily hurried to

him, taking her diver's knife from her belt. The fiber-optic cable attached to the back of Chase's suit was sheathed in protective plastic. She grabbed it and sawed away with the knife.

"Come on, come *on*!" Chase yelled.

"I'm *trying*!" The line finally sheared in two, a blue pinpoint of light shining from the stub still attached to Chase's suit. A moment later, the rest of the cable was snatched from her gloved hand. It shot across the chamber before disappearing over the edge of the shaft. "What the hell just happened?"

"If the sub blew up, the ballast would've been dropped automatically when it lost power. That means the thing's on its way to the surface like a fucking rocket—and it would have tried to take me with it." He turned to face her. "Thanks. Sorry I shouted."

"No need to apologize, given the circumstances!" She looked at the shaft. "If the sub's been destroyed, what are we going to do?"

"Get the fuck out of here, for starters." He moved back over to the shaft. "Hugo? Can you hear me? Hugo? Shit!"

"I'm still getting you on the radio," said Kari.

"Yeah, but you're standing five feet away in air, and he's got to receive it through Christ knows how many feet of stone and water. Hugo!"

w

Castille grabbed the control stick and pushed his suit's thrusters to full power, shooting upwards in a spray of bubbles as the submersible swooped down at him. It was close enough for him to see the word *Zeus* painted on the control sphere and the pilot lying on his belly inside, face magnified and distorted into a leer by the glass bubble.

The manipulator arm swung at him, but he rolled, using his fins to change direction and duck under it. He looked back, but the pilot was keeping hold of the explosive package, determined to deliver it before dealing with him.

There was only one possible target.

The entrance to the temple.

"Edward!" he screamed, knowing there was no chance of being heard. "Get out of there! *Get out!*"

The sub's thrusters spewed out bubbles, the whirling propellers reversing to bring the vessel to a stop at the base of the wall. The arm extended, reaching smoothly into the narrow passageway before retracting again.

The gleaming steel claw was now empty.

Castille put his thumb on the thruster control. If he could get in there fast enough, he might be able to pull the explosives clear.

The submersible pilot wasn't going to give him the chance. The arm rising above its hull like a scorpion's tail, the vessel swung around again, hunting for him.

Spotlights dazzled him. Another burst of froth from the sub's propellers, driving it forwards.

Straight for him.

"Very well . . ." he whispered. He released the control stick, reaching for his equipment belt.

The submersible accelerated, its arm descending and stretching out ahead of it like a lance.

Castille waited, holding still.

And he whipped up his grappling gun and fired it straight at the cockpit bubble.

The pointed steel tip of the grapnel hit the glass—and stopped dead, penetrating barely more than a centimeter before the force of the water sweeping over the submersible tore it free. It clattered away beneath the sub, trailing its cable behind it.

Castille had already dropped the gun and powered up his thrusters again, twisting to climb over to one side of the onrushing sub. The pilot, startled by the impact, couldn't react quickly enough to catch him with the outstretched arm.

But he was fast enough to pull the sub around in a sweeping turn, ready to pursue.

Castille knew his suit didn't have the power to outrun the sub. He just hoped he wouldn't have to.

In the cockpit, the pilot grinned savagely as he saw the bright yellow shell of Castille's deep suit pinned in his spotlights. He brought the throttle to full power, preparing to ram him, an underwater hit-and-run . . .

The tiny mark left by the grapnel suddenly grew. And *kept* growing, crazed tendrils sweeping outwards across the bubble with an awful, tooth-grinding screech of cracking glass. The immense pressure of the ocean bore down against the new flaw in the surface, expanding it—

With a *bang* as loud as artillery fire, the submersible's cockpit imploded. Huge shards of three-inch-thick glass hit the pilot at the speed of sound, reducing him to a red haze that bloomed through the churning air bubbles like a huge and gory flower. The sub nose-dived into the seabed, plowing up a huge swath of sand.

Castille turned around. There might still be time for him to reach the explosives . . .

There wasn't.

A shockwave burst from the end of the passage. Castille was slammed away by the deafening blast as if hit by a car, tumbling out of control, all vision obliterated by the enormous cloud of silt.

But he didn't need to see to know that the thunderous vibrations hitting him through the water after the blast were caused by massive stone blocks collapsing into the tunnel, sealing it forever.

w

Inside the altar chamber, Chase was about to lower Kari into the shaft when a surge of water erupted beneath them, knocking them both onto their backs as it blasted into the chamber like a geyser. Chunks of debris rained down, hammer-blow impacts against their suits.

"Oh my God!" Kari screamed. For the first time since Chase had known her, she was on the verge of panic. "What was that, what happened?"

"Kari. Kari!" He held her arms, trying to calm her. "We're okay, we're all right! Let me check your suit."

They helped each other to their feet, examining the casing of the deep suits. Both had sustained some dents, but nothing that seemed to compromise their integrity. Not, Chase realized, that it mattered.

"What happened?" Kari asked again.

Chase looked at the shaft. "They blew up the passage. We're sealed in."

w

Starkman's men had forced the passengers and crew of the *Evenor* to assemble on the helipad. A quick head count told Nina that eight of the crew were dead.

The other ship moved alongside, crewmen throwing ropes across to tie the two vessels together. Bumpers hanging over the side of the decks creaked and squealed as they rubbed against each other in the swell.

A tall man climbed aboard the *Evenor*, accompanied by two armed guards. He strode across the aft deck, signaling the men to bring Nina to him. Captain Matthews protested, but the guns waved in his face quickly silenced him.

Nina already knew whom she was facing. She had seen the hard, angular features before.

"Dr. Wilde," he said. "We meet at last. My name is Giovanni Qobras."

TWENTY-ONE

"I know who you are," Nina said, trying not to let her fear show. "What do you want?"

"What do I want?" The question provoked the tiniest flicker of amusement on Qobras's stern face. "I want what everybody wants, Dr. Wilde. I want peace and security for the world. And thanks to you, I can now bring that about." His intense gaze flicked over to Philby. "And thanks to you too, Jack. It's been some time since we last met. Ten years, wasn't it?"

"I was rather hoping I'd never have to meet you again," said Philby, voice quavering.

Nina rounded on him. "You *know* him, Jonathan?"

"Jack—*Jonathan*, rather, I suppose it's more dignified for a professor—has helped me keep anyone from finding Atlantis before," said Qobras. He gestured to one of his men, who led Philby from the group of prisoners. "And now . . . Well." He waved a hand at the empty ocean. "Atlantis will be lost forever, because it will be *destroyed*."

"*Why?*" demanded Nina. "What secret could there possibly be that it's worth destroying the most important archaeological find *ever*? And the lives of all the people you've killed?"

"If you knew, you wouldn't need to ask that question," Qobras replied. "You would be *helping* me. But I see your mind has been poisoned by the Frosts, like your parents. A shame. You could have accomplished so much if you hadn't chosen the wrong path."

"Wait, what about my parents?" But Qobras turned away as Starkman emerged from the superstructure.

"I've trashed the hard drive with the recordings from the dive, Giovanni," Starkman announced. "All we have to do now is destroy the temple itself and there'll be nothing left."

"Excellent," said Qobras. He was about to say something else when somebody urgently called his name. One of his men jumped between the two ships and ran to the helipad.

"Sir!" the man gasped, looking concerned. "Something's gone wrong down below!"

"What happened?" Qobras asked.

"The *Zeus* destroyed the Frost submersible"—Trulli shoved forward, shouting and swearing at Qobras, until two of the guards pushed him back at gunpoint—"and detonated one of the demolition charges. But . . . our hydrophones heard an implosion."

"Could it have been the Frost sub?"

"No, sir. That was already heading back to the surface, while this was on the seabed. One of the divers must have destroyed it."

Qobras turned to Philby for an explanation. "Kari—I mean, Ms. Frost—and Chase were inside the temple," the professor said, almost stuttering in his nervousness. "It must have been Castille."

"Go, Hugo!" Nina said, with no joy. Starkman fixed her with a nasty look from his good eye.

The furrows on Qobras's brow deepened. "We

needed the *Zeus* to plant the explosives! How long will it take to get a replacement here?"

"At least five days, sir."

"Too long. Frost can get more people and equipment here before then. And this time, they'll be prepared for us."

"What about their other sub?" Starkman asked, gesturing towards the *Evenor*'s bow, and the *Sharkdozer*.

"Only I know how to pilot it," Trulli said defiantly. "And if you bastards think I'm going to help you after you killed my mate, you can fuck right off."

Starkman looked annoyed and raised his gun, but Qobras shook his head. "Have the remaining demolition charges from our ship brought aboard this one," he said after a few seconds of thought. "Set two thirds of them below the waterline forward, and the remainder aft."

"What are you going to do?" Nina asked.

"Since I can no longer destroy the temple with explosives," said Qobras, turning back to her, "I need some other method. Three thousand tons of steel dropped directly onto it should be an effective alternative."

Ignoring the armed men around him, Captain Matthews stepped forward. "Qobras! What about my crew? What are you going to do with us?"

Qobras eyed him dismissively. "I believe there's a maritime tradition that the captain should go down with his ship. In this case, that will apply to his crew as well." He glanced back at Nina. "And his passengers."

"You son of a bitch," Matthews spat.

"You're going to *drown* us?" Nina said, horrified.

Qobras shook his head. "No, no. I'm not a cruel man, or some crazed sadist, whatever your friends the Frosts may have said about me. When the ship sinks, you will already be dead."

vv

Chase checked his air supply. The deep suits were designed for long durations underwater, but they still had
a limit. He had around another hour's supply.

One hour. After that, he and Kari would become permanent residents in the ancient temple . . .

Kari had had the same thought. "There *must* be another way out," she said, pointing down the stairs. "The
water couldn't have filled the main chamber through
the secret passage, otherwise this room would be
flooded as well."

"Doesn't mean we'll be able to get through it," Chase
reminded her as he descended the steps.

"We still have to try."

"I know, I was just preparing for the worst. It's a
British thing. How many of those big glow sticks do you
have? We'll need as much light as we can get."

Kari checked the pouch on her belt. "Six."

"Same here. Okay, let's take a look."

They waded into the frigid water.

vv

Castille swam back to the site of the entrance. The cloud
of silt kicked up by the explosion was still hanging
there, and he knew from past experience that such
murky water could take hours to clear.

Undaunted, he entered the cloud anyway. It was like an
extremely thick brown fog, even the beam of his flashlight
almost completely obscured by the drifting sediment.

He didn't need to see to know that the passage had
been sealed, however. Chunks of shattered stone lay on
the seabed beneath his feet. Locating the line Chase had
led into the tunnel, he tugged it experimentally. It didn't
give at all.

Using the suit's thrusters to return to clearer water, he checked his air supply and considered his options. An hour left. He could easily return to the surface . . .

But the mere fact that they had been attacked suggested that the situation topside was dire. Qobras's ship would have reached the *Evenor* by now. Apart from his knife he was unarmed, and on the surface, trapped inside the bulky deep suit, he would be almost useless in a fight.

Which meant that all he could do now was find some way to help Chase and Kari escape from the temple.

If they had survived.

ᴡᴡ

The atmosphere on the helipad was tense. A few of the crew were close to tears, or panic. Others muttered fast prayers. Qobras's men circled them, raising their MP-7s . . .

"Wait," said Nina, masking her terror with as much determination as she could muster.

"For what?" Qobras asked.

"I'll make you a deal. Let the crew use the lifeboats before you sink the ship, and . . ." She took a deep breath. "And I'll give myself up to you."

Starkman snorted dismissively as Qobras let out a brief, humorless laugh. "I already *have* you, Dr. Wilde! There's nothing you can offer me—I have what I want. I know the location of Atlantis, and now I'm going to destroy it!"

"There's something you *don't* know, though," Nina said with a thin smile. "The location of the *third* Temple of Poseidon."

Qobras's expression changed to one of wary surprise. "There is no third temple, Dr. Wilde. There is the one in Brazil, which has been destroyed, and the one below us, which will soon join it. The trail of the Atlanteans ends here."

"Uh-uh." Nina shook her head. "There's a third one. And sooner or later, somebody's going to find it. You think that just smashing the temple's going to eliminate all the clues? People *know* where Atlantis is now. Word's going to get out, and people will come looking. There's a whole *city* down there, not just the temple. Sooner or later, someone'll put the pieces together and be able to follow the trail. The secret you've been trying to hide's going to be found, and there won't be anything you can do about it. Unless . . ."

"Unless what?" There was menace in Qobras's tone, but he was also intrigued.

"Unless I tell you where it is. So you can destroy it personally."

"This is bullshit," Starkman cut in. "She doesn't know anything, she's just trying to buy time and save herself."

"Mr. Qobras, tell Patch here to shut the hell up," Nina said, defiant despite her fear. Starkman bristled, but said nothing. "There *is* a third temple, a third citadel. Before the deluge, the Atlanteans were preparing to establish *two* new colonies. One expedition went west, to Brazil, the other . . . Well, I know where they went. And I'll tell you. *If* you let the crew live."

Starkman pressed his gun against Matthews's head. "Or we could just execute them one by one until you tell us."

"Seeing as you were going to kill us all anyway, that's not really much of a deal," Nina retorted.

Qobras rounded on Philby. "Is she telling the truth?"

"She, ah, could be," Philby said, flustered. "The final inscriptions inside the temple *did* seem to indicate that the Atlanteans were planning to resettle in more than one location—but I didn't have time to translate enough of it to be sure." He regarded Nina suspiciously. "And I don't see how she could have either."

"I'm a quick study, *Jack*," Nina sneered.

"Can you translate the rest?" Qobras asked.

Philby shook his head and sighed. "Not anymore."

"Ha!" Nina made a face at Starkman. "Betcha wish you hadn't smashed the hard drive now, huh?" She turned to Qobras. "So, what's it going to be? I made you an offer, and it still stands. Let the crew live and I'll take you to the last outpost of Atlantis."

"You'll *take* us?" said Starkman. "What, you want to turn this into a working vacation now?"

She folded her arms, fixing Qobras with a determined look. "I've been hunting for Atlantis my whole life. If I'm going to die because of that, then I want to know exactly *why*. I want to see the whole story. I don't think that's too much to ask."

"Dr. Wilde, it's too dangerous," said Matthews. "For all you know, he'll just kill us anyway."

"I'm offering him a deal in good faith. I'm hoping he'll accept it in the same way. What about it, Mr. Qobras?" she asked. "You said you weren't a cruel man. Are you an honorable one?"

Starkman continued to glower at her, but Qobras was unreadable. He moved closer, his flint-gray eyes looking right into hers. "You realize, of course, that even after we destroy the final temple we cannot allow you to live? Are you still willing to offer your deal to save their lives?"

She swallowed before answering, mouth dry. "Yes."

For a moment, he seemed almost impressed. "You are a very brave woman, Dr. Wilde. And noble. I wouldn't have expected it, considering your . . . heritage."

"What's *that* supposed to mean?"

He stepped back. "We will have time to discuss it later. But I will spare the people on this ship, if you agree to show me how to reach the last temple. Do we have a deal?"

"We do," said Nina.

Qobras nodded. "Very well. Jason! Prepare the lifeboats, put the crew aboard."

"Are you sure that's the right thing to do?" Starkman asked.

"We shall see. Search them first, though—make sure they have no radio transmitters or flares. I want to be certain we have enough time to leave the area before they are picked up." He pointed to the north. "The Portuguese coast is a hundred and forty kilometers in that direction, Captain. I hope your crew can row that far." Matthews shot Qobras a hateful look as Starkman and the other men led the crew away.

"What about the people in Atlantis?" Nina asked. "My friends are still down there."

"And that is where they will stay," Qobras replied.

"What? Wait, we agreed—"

Qobras grabbed her, pulling her close as he hissed into her face: "We agreed to spare the people on this ship, Dr. Wilde. They are not on this ship. If you object to that, then I will order the crew to be shot! Do you understand me?"

"Yes," Nina said, defeated.

"Dr. Wilde," called Matthews, as one of Qobras's men gestured with his gun for him to follow the rest of the crew, "do you have any family I should contact?"

"No, I'm afraid not," she sighed. "Just . . . if you see Eddie, tell him I'll send him a postcard."

Matthews looked puzzled, but didn't have time to say anything else before he was shoved away. Qobras waved a hand towards his own ship. "Now, Dr. Wilde, if you'll step aboard my vessel . . . we can discuss the location of the last Atlantean temple."

vvv

Even three-quarters filled with cold, dark water, the genuine Temple of Poseidon was even more impressive than its replica in South America.

"This is absolutely incredible," said Kari, the danger of the situation overpowered by her awe at the sheer magnificence of the surroundings. Above her, ranks of slender ribs adorned with gold, silver and orichalcum rose to the peak of the curved ceiling. "Look at the roof! The whole thing is lined with ivory, just as Plato described it."

"Incredible's not the word I'd use," said Chase, swimming to her. "It's like being inside something's ribcage. That bloke who did the *Alien* films'd love it in here." He cracked another glow stick and tossed it across the chamber, where it bobbed on the water. Beyond the beams of their flashlights, the chamber was now illuminated with a soft orange glow. The head of Poseidon rose above the water, watching them balefully with blank golden eyes. "Did you find any way out?"

"No. What about you?"

Chase pointed down at the southern end of the chamber. "It's just like the other temple, and I mean *just* like it. I bet if we went all the way down the passage, we'd find the same challenges."

"There's a passage? Can we get out that way?"

He shook his head. "It's at ground level, remember? There's thirty feet of sediment over the exit."

"We might have to try it. Since the roof is intact, that must be how the water got in. We could still get out the same way."

"There's a quicker way out," said Chase. He held up one of the explosive charges.

"No, it's too dangerous," she protested. "If you blow a hole through the ceiling, the whole thing might collapse!"

"I'm not planning on blowing the whole thing up. Look." He swam to a section of wall where the decorative ivory had broken away, exposing bare stone. "We only need to make a hole big enough to fit through— even shifting one of those blocks would be enough."

"Assuming your bomb doesn't bring the whole roof down."

Chase shrugged as best he could inside the suit. "Well, what's life without a bit of risk?" He aimed the flashlight beam at the exposed stones, examining the joins between them. As in Brazil, they had been carved so precisely that there was no mortar holding them together, their own weight supporting the structure. Probing one of the joins with his knife, he found that the tip only penetrated a few millimeters. "We need to find the weakest spot to plant the charges." He pushed away from the wall, turning around to look up at the statue of Poseidon. "So big that he touched the roof with his head . . ."

Kari looked impressed. "Have you been reading Plato?"

"Thought I ought to give it a shot. But, see? If we climb onto old bighead there, we can stick the charges right under the top of the roof. The blocks lower down the walls have the weight of all the other stones on top of them keeping them in place, but at the top there's nothing holding them except gravity."

"And twenty-five atmospheres of water pressure," Kari pointed out. "If you make a hole at the very top, you'll flood the entire temple. You'll destroy it—and probably us too!"

"If we're not out of here in an hour, it's not going to matter either way. We don't have time to clear the tunnel. Come on." He leaned forward, using his thrusters to propel himself across the water to the statue. With deep reluctance, Kari did the same.

⋆

Castille continued his circuit of the temple, coming around the southern end. So far he had seen no sign of any holes, the great stepped curve of the roof as solid as a turtle's shell.

On some impulse, he touched down on the building itself. The stones might be thick, but if he was close enough, radio waves should be able to penetrate.

"Edward?" he said. "Kari? Can anyone hear me?"

He stood in silence, not even breathing so that the hiss of his suit's regulator wouldn't drown out any faint reply. But nothing came.

"Merde." Kicking off, he headed back up the temple's western side.

⋆

The *Evenor*'s lifeboats bobbed in the water as their occupants rowed clear of the survey ship. Nina watched the sight with fearful resignation from the bridge of Qobras's vessel, flanked by a pair of armed guards. The last of his men jumped back aboard, others untying the ropes holding the two ships together.

Starkman entered the bridge. "Giovanni. The explosives are all in place." He handed Qobras a pair of radio detonators. "This one'll set off the charges at the bow, this one the engine room."

"Are the hatches open?" Qobras asked.

"Yeah—everything up to the engineering bulkhead. Blow the bow, and the front two thirds of the ship'll fill up with water. Then once the bow's submerged, blow the other charges, and *pow*! Three thousand tons, going straight down."

Qobras examined the detonators. "A sword of Damocles . . ."

"Very clever," Nina said bitterly. "Pity you couldn't put that kind of ingenuity into something constructive."

"You have no idea how much time and effort I have put into being constructive, Dr. Wilde."

"Well, why don't you enlighten me?"

"Maybe I will. Who knows, you might even come around to my point of view."

"I doubt that," she snorted.

"Unfortunately," Qobras sighed, "so do I." He addressed the captain. "Move us to a safe distance, then turn the ship about to face the *Evenor*. I want to watch this."

\vv

The builders of the statue had obviously never meant for anyone to stand on top of it, Chase thought. Plato hadn't been entirely accurate; Poseidon didn't literally touch the ceiling, although from ground level it would look that way. There was actually a small amount of clearance, into which he was now awkwardly wedged on his back. The gold-plated statue was sculpted with hair and a crown of what he guessed was supposed to be seaweed, none of which made a stable platform for the inflexible shell of his deep suit.

"How are you doing?" Kari asked.

"Nearly there." He had connected both his charges so they would go off simultaneously. The detonator was a simple mechanical timer, designed to be foolproof even in hundreds of feet of water. Once activated, he would have one minute to reach a safe distance. In open ocean, with the help of the suit's thrusters, that wouldn't be a problem.

In the confines of the temple, on the other hand . . .

"I still think this is a bad idea."

"If it doesn't work, you can sack me. Okay, I'm done." The explosives were somewhat precariously stuck to the ceiling, wedged above one of the ivory ribs. The rib would be reduced to splinters within a millisecond of the charge detonating—the question was, how much of the explosive force would be directed upwards at the ceiling?

He had years of demolitions experience, but on this occasion, Chase was trusting to luck. It was all he *could* do.

"Get clear," he told Kari, waving a hand at the far end of the temple. "And get as deep underwater as you can."

"Okay." She rolled and disappeared beneath the rippling surface, the lights on her suit fading like a departing spirit as she descended.

Chase looked back up at the detonator. "All right," he said, psyching himself up. Activating the timer was a two-stage process: a pin had to be turned and removed before the detonator switch could be pressed. After that, a basic but effective clockwork mechanism counted down the sixty seconds. "Here goes . . ."

He twisted the steel pin through a half-turn, then pulled it out. The bomb was now armed. As soon as he pressed the button, there was no going back.

"Okay, Kari," he said, not even sure if the signal from his suit radio would reach her through the water, "get ready. Sixty seconds starts . . . now!"

He pushed the switch and rolled off the statue's head—

And jerked to a halt.

His equipment belt had snagged on the crown!

"Oh shit," he gasped, trying to kick himself free. To no effect. "Oh *shit*!"

The timer ticked down relentlessly.

w

"Five hundred meters, sir," announced the captain.

"Good," said Qobras, looking through the bridge windows. Ahead, the gleaming white *Evenor* was almost directly side-on, the bright yellow bulk of the *Sharkdozer* swaying gently from its crane at the bow. The lifeboats had dispersed, trying to get as far from the doomed ship as they could.

"Please," Nina begged, "you don't have to do this . . ."

Qobras didn't look at her, his eyes fixed on the ship. "I'm afraid I do."

He raised the first radio detonator and pushed the trigger.

w

Castille released the thruster control, drifting to a halt just above the temple roof. He had just heard something in his headphones, a brief crackle that sounded like a truncated obscenity.

"Edward?" he asked, swimming closer to the expanse of stone below. "Edward, is that you? Can you hear me?"

Then he heard something else.

Not in his headphones this time, but transmitted through the sea. A dull, echoing boom.

A sound he recognized all too well. An explosion in the water directly overhead.

There was only one thing it could mean.

vw

Nina had expected a huge fireball to consume the bow of the *Evenor,* but the actual explosion was oddly anticlimactic. A vaporous blast coughed from the open hatches, small pieces of debris and fluttering papers flying out behind it. A white froth surged from beneath the waterline before rapidly dying away.

The full destructive effect, however, instantly became clear.

The ship's bow almost immediately tipped downwards into the water, listing to starboard. Loose items slid across the decks and dropped into the sea, the *Sharkdozer* swinging violently out over the water. On the aft deck, the helicopter lurched, straining against the lines securing it to the pad.

The speed of the sinking amazed Nina. She watched in horrified fascination as the bow dropped into the ocean, gusts of compressed air blowing more debris out of the hatches. At this rate, it would take less than a minute before the foredeck was completely submerged.

vw

Chase struggled to pull his belt from the crown, but, hampered by the shell of the deep suit, he couldn't get a proper grip.

Forty seconds.

"Shit!"

A noise, a dull thud somewhere outside the temple. An explosion!

And then a muffled crackling in his headphones, someone's voice fighting to pierce the static. Kari . . .

No! *Castille!*

"Edward! Can you hear me? Edward!"

If the radio was working without the relay, then he

was close, very close. "Hugo!" Chase yelled. "Get out of here! I've set a bomb! *Get out!*"

"Edward! Say ag—"

Thirty seconds.

"Bomb!" screamed Chase. He fumbled for his knife. The equipment belt was pulled taut around his suit's waist; he hacked desperately at it, trying to drive the point of the blade under the plastic-coated cord.

\/\/\/

Castille's eyes widened. Most of Chase's transmission had been too distorted to make out, but the final word came through almost too clearly.

He kicked hard off the temple roof and propelled himself into open water at full power.

\/\/\/

The *Evenor*'s list became a roll, the deck now tilted at almost forty-five degrees as the tip of the bow dropped beneath the waves. The helicopter broke free of its ties and skidded across the pad to smash against the water. Its tail sank first, air in the cockpit keeping the nose above the surface for a few seconds before the weight of the aircraft dragged it under.

On the foredeck, one of the cables supporting the *Sharkdozer* tore loose, the heavy craft swinging like a pendulum and hitting the water in an enormous burst of spray. Stressed past its limits, the crane sheared away at its base, plunging down the sloping deck to impale the stricken sub. Water surged through the gaping wound, and the *Sharkdozer* sank within seconds.

More debris plummeted from the ship as it capsized. Its stern rose out of the ocean, water streaming from the propellers.

Qobras held up the second detonator and, his face expressionless, pressed the trigger.

\\\\/

Twenty seconds—

"Come on, you *bastard*!"

Chase pushed the knife upwards like a lever, the point digging into the casing of his suit. Something cracked, and the belt snapped.

He dropped the eight feet to the water, landing flat on his back and banging his head against the inside of his helmet. But there was no time to think about the pain, because he had less than fifteen seconds to get clear.

\\\\/

With a final jet of steam and fumes from the fantail, the *Evenor* disappeared into the Atlantic, the last echoing sound from the dying ship like the cry of a wounded animal. A churning whirlpool of bubbles spewed up in its wake, hundreds of pieces of flotsam too light to sink swirling around in the maelstrom.

Its generators failed as water surged through the aft compartments, but its emergency lights were still aglow, battery-powered units all over the ship automatically activating as the main power went off. Trailing a jetstream of air bubbles behind it, the survey ship began its rapid, nose-first descent towards the seabed.

Towards Atlantis.

Qobras turned to his captain. "Take us back to port. Full speed."

"Aye, sir." The captain issued orders to his bridge crew. Ignored in a corner, Nina held a hand to her mouth as she tried to stop herself from sobbing.

She failed.

w

Chase jammed his thrusters to full power, not having time to do anything more than aim away from the statue and dive.

Five seconds, four, three . . .

He glimpsed a faint light below him—Kari!—and twisted towards it—

The explosives detonated.

TWENTY-TWO

The head of the statue of Poseidon, which had with-stood the sinking of Atlantis and stood lonely vigil over the temple for over eleven thousand years, was blasted to pieces. The ivory ceiling disintegrated, razor-edged shards raining into the flooded chamber.

But the stone block *above* the charges also took the full force of the blast.

Under the immense pressure of the water, the block barely rose more than a foot.

But that was enough.

After waiting patiently for hundreds of centuries, the Atlantic finally found a way into its oldest prize. Frigid seawater surged through the gap, the colossal force clawing at the ancient stones. A hole over twenty feet wide ripped open as the ceiling gave way. Thousands of tons of water plunged like a piledriver to smash what was left of the statue of Poseidon into golden rubble.

The impact sent a massive shockwave through the water already in the temple. Statues were snatched from the floor and tossed around like toys.

Chase felt as though he'd been hit by a truck. His flashlight was ripped from his grasp, spinning into the churning vortex. He slammed against a wall. Hard. He couldn't move, pinned like a butterfly to a board by the horrific force.

Then the noise subsided. As did the pressure grinding him against the wall, the whirling currents dying away. A fierce burning pain rose in his left wrist. He dimly remembered his arm smashing against the wall, but only now was his mind actually able to process the sensation.

His suit lights were still working, but they would be useless for some time. Sediment that had lain undisturbed on the temple floor since the flooding had been stirred up by the fury of the deluge, making the water as opaque as milk.

But now that the temple was completely flooded, the influx of water had stopped. Which meant he could get out through the hole in the ceiling . . .

Kari!

There was no way she could have been fully prepared for the unimaginable onslaught of the ocean. She would have been hit just as hard as he had been.

He tried the radio. "Kari! Kari, can you hear me? Are you there? *Kari!*"

No answer.

She might be out of radio range—or injured, even dead.

He dropped towards the floor and swam forwards, wincing at the pain in his left arm. Using the thrusters would have been faster, but he didn't want to risk running into anything before he could see it.

He felt debris beneath his feet, broken statues and stones. It was like the aftermath of a bombing.

A faint light ahead. Distances were deceptive in the silt-laden water; it looked to be forty or fifty feet away, but in the current conditions it was probably more like five.

"Kari!" he called as the lights took on form. It was the spotlights on her suit—*spotlight*, rather, as one of them was dead.

And for all he could tell, so was she, hanging motionless just above the floor.

He pulled her upright. Their helmets clunked together as he tried to see her face through the murk. Her eyes were closed, and he couldn't tell if she was breathing. The deep suit was a closed system, with no telltale release of air bubbles. "*Kari!*"

Her eyelids flickered.

"Oh thank Christ!" Chase gasped. "Kari, come on, wake up. We've got to get out of here."

Her eyes opened, regarding him blearily. "Eddie? What happened?"

"Short version? Bang! Splash! Hole. Are you all right?"

Her face tightened in pain. "My leg hurts . . ."

"This place could still collapse. We need to get out—if we go straight up, we can follow the roof until we get to the hole."

"It worked?"

"Oh yeah. It worked." He took her hand. "Use your thrusters and go up." He reached for his thruster control. "On three. Ready?" Kari nodded, and he counted down to zero—

Kari took off vertically. Chase stayed put.

"Whoa, whoa, stop!" he cried, jumping off the temple floor after her. The whirring of her thrusters cut out.

"What's wrong?"

Chase pushed the control wheel back and forth with his thumb. Nothing happened. "Houston, we have a problem. My thrusters aren't working."

"Is your suit damaged?"

"Well, yeah, kind of. The whole 'not working' thing was my first clue."

She banged a hand on his chest. "I'm serious! These suits are *tough*—if it was hit hard enough for one of the systems to be damaged, it might not be the only one. Is your air supply working?"

"Seems fine, but—" He stopped. "Wait a minute. Either I just pissed myself . . . or I've got a leak." He shifted uncomfortably. There was a cold, clammy sensation at the top of his legs, *inside* the suit. "Shit! Water's coming in."

As if on cue, a tiny air bubble rose up between them, touching the glass of Chase's helmet before disappearing upwards. "Grab onto me, and whatever you do, don't let go," Kari ordered.

Chase took hold of her equipment belt, seeing that most of her gear was missing, ripped away by the torrent. She fired her thrusters, which strained under the extra load as they ascended.

"Slow down," Chase warned as they approached the roof. "You don't want to bang into it."

"And you don't want to drown!" But she eased off, raising her free hand over her head until it touched something solid. "We're here. There's still an air pocket, I can feel it." She rose until the top of her helmet bumped against the ivory ceiling. There was just enough of a space for her to put her eyes above the waterline.

To her surprise, there was light. The glow sticks were still there, bobbing on the surface.

"What can you see?" Chase asked.

"The roof's sagged about ten meters away, that's how there's still air." She turned in the water. "I can see one of the end walls."

"That's the south wall, where we were. We need to go the other way."

"Okay." She dropped back down a few feet, pulling Chase with her, then tilted forward to propel herself along the apex of the roof. The soft orange light of the glow sticks guided her to the sagging section of ceiling.

"Watch out, the stones could be loose," Chase cautioned.

"High explosives might do that, yes." Her probing of the ceiling became more tentative when she realized the explosion had shattered the ivory, leaving sharp talons jutting out.

Unexpectedly, she felt a faint current ahead. The swirling particles suspended in the water thinned out. "Eddie! I think we found it!"

"Great! Be care—"

With a crack like breaking bone, one of the huge stone blocks succumbed to gravity and dropped from its resting place, tearing great chunks of ivory with it. It slammed against the back of Kari's deep suit, knocking her aside.

Chase grabbed her arm and pulled her upright. "Shit! Are you okay?" He checked her suit. The top of the bulbous casing housing the air tanks and rebreather system was flattened, cracked like an eggshell. "Your suit's fucked—can you still breathe?"

Kari drew in a worried breath. "Something's wrong— I'm still getting air, but it's harder to breathe. I think the regulator's damaged!"

Chase gripped her hand to reassure her. "Kari, stay calm. We're almost out of the temple. Once we're out, we can find Hugo and head back to the surface. Fifteen minutes, that's all it'll take. Just conserve your air and breathe slowly. Okay?"

"Okay." She nodded, her face betraying her concern.

They reached the gash in the ceiling. Kari used her thrusters to rise out of the temple, pulling Chase with her. The water rapidly cleared. Chase looked around for lights. He spotted some almost immediately—but they weren't familiar.

"Another submersible," said Kari, looking at the wreckage of the vessel. Even though its crew compartment had imploded, its battery section was still watertight, uselessly feeding power to the spotlights. "Qobras."

"Hugo's here somewhere." Chase swam clear of the hole. "Hugo? Do you copy? We're outside the temple, I repeat, we got out. Can you hear me?"

Silence, then: "Edward!" The voice was faint, shrouded in static, but it was unmistakably the Belgian's. "I can hear you! Where are you?"

"Above the north end of the temple. You?"

"I'm descending from the southwest! Can you see me?" Chase looked up. Sure enough, he saw Castille's suit lights approaching. "Are you okay?"

"Kari's suit's damaged—and mine's screwed as well. I've got a leak and no thrusters. We need to get to the surface, fast."

Castille shone his light over Chase's suit. "There's your leak," he said, pointing at its waist. Chase realized the cause. When he'd used the knife to cut his equipment belt, its sharp tip had pierced the polycarbonate shell. Even as he watched, another tiny air bubble popped out and shot upwards.

"You got anything we can use to patch it?"

Castille shook his head. "Edward, listen, something's happened on the surface. I heard—"

Clank.

"What the hell was that?" Chase asked. The unexpected noise sounded like metal tapping against stone. He turned. Something gleamed faintly, an object lying nearby. He moved closer to examine it. A spanner.

Clong!

Another noise, much louder and sharper. They all whirled to see a long pole standing upright on the stone roof. It keeled slowly over and skittered away down the temple's sloping side.

Castille swam after it, stopping when he realized what it was. "It's a boat-hook," he said. "Why is—"

In his peripheral vision, Chase became aware of other objects falling around them, a metal rain. He looked up—

"Hugo! *Move!*"

Too late.

The *Evenor's* helicopter crashed down tail-first onto Castille like a javelin. The Belgian was hammered down onto the temple roof.

One of the rotor blades stabbed through his deep suit.

"*No!*" Chase roared. He tried to swim towards his friend, but the shockwave as the rest of the helicopter's fuselage smashed against the stones knocked him back.

A dark, swelling cloud obscured Castille's spotlights. Blood.

"*Hugo!*" The wave subsided; he swam again, kicking furiously, ignoring the pain in his arm.

Kari grabbed his suit, using her thrusters to pull him back. "He's *gone!*" she cried. "We've got to get out of here! *Now!*"

Chase rounded on her, full of anger and despair. "I can't leave him behind!"

"You have to! *Look!*" She pointed upwards—

More debris was raining down. Tools, hatch covers, pieces of railing, even a section of the *Evenor's* radar dome.

And something larger, a hulking yellow shape charging at them through the gloom—

Kari blasted away at full power, dragging Chase with

her as the *Sharkdozer* plummeted past and punched straight through the temple roof, barely missing them. A chain trailed behind it, its links rasping hideously over the stones. The crane at the other end crashed down onto the temple, then scythed down the slope right behind Kari and Chase. They both felt its passage through the water as it passed just inches from their feet.

Kari leveled out as she cleared the temple. More debris fell around them, slow-motion explosions erupting as objects smacked into the seabed.

Chase looked up. "Oh, fuck! Go right! *Go!*"

She obeyed, turning her head to look—and her heart jumped in terror.

It was a constellation of falling stars, a pattern of lights racing to engulf her.

The *Evenor*!

Emergency lights still ablaze, monstrous groans of metal echoing through the ocean, the ship was a three-thousand-ton missile dropping straight at them!

Kari jammed her thumb even harder on the thruster control as she pulled herself and Chase out of the path of the plunging vessel—

The *Evenor* hit the seabed like a bomb.

The bow was crushed flat on impact, the force of the water driven back through the ship's interior ripping apart seams and welds as destructively as any explosive. What little air was still trapped inside gushed from the hundreds of new rents in the hull. Rivets, portholes, even doors blew outwards like shrapnel from a grenade.

Caught in the shockwave and almost deafened, Kari and Chase could do nothing except be carried along as pieces of the wrecked ship whirled around them, smacking against their suits.

Another awful screech of tortured metal moaned

through the depths as the *Evenor* slowly but inexorably toppled over, falling sideways and slicing through the temple like a guillotine blade, no amount of architectural precision able to withstand the sheer destructive force of thousands of tons of steel.

The temple roof blew outwards as the *Evenor* displaced the water inside the main chamber. Support gone, the walls collapsed, crushing everything within.

The Temple of Poseidon, the very heart of the citadel of Atlantis, was now truly lost forever.

The noise subsided. Head ringing, Chase was almost startled to realize that he was still alive.

Kari . . .

They had lost their grip, become separated. He turned, trying to catch sight of her. "Kari! Where are you?" There was no sign of her lights in the darkness.

"I'm here," she said weakly through the distortion. "Behind you, about five meters below. I'm coming up."

Chase looked down. Still nothing. "I don't see you!"

"My lights have gone. Hold on." A moment later, an orange glow appeared, the ghostly outline of her suit rising behind the small glow stick in her right hand. "My air system's failing—it's getting harder to breathe."

"Are your thrusters still working?"

"Yes. What about your leak?"

Chase squirmed inside the suit. The coldness had spread. "Shit. I think it's getting worse."

"It can't be a big hole, or you'd be dead already—but it's only going to deteriorate." Kari reached him, holding the glow stick in front of the damaged area.

"Is there anything you can do to plug it?"

"No. But there's something *you* can do."

"What?"

"Put your thumb over it."

"Oh." Chase felt oddly embarrassed for not thinking

of that himself. He looked down at the temple. A few of the *Evenor*'s lights still burned amid the wreckage. "Hugo . . ."

"It's Nina I'm worried about," said Kari. "For all we know, she was in the ship. Qobras doesn't leave witnesses." Even right next to him, the radio interference at a minimum, her voice was still weak.

She fired her thrusters, beginning their ascent. Chase held her belt with one hand, the thumb of the other pressed against the crack in his suit. There was a little digital depth gauge inside his helmet, the number decreasing.

Decreasing too slowly. With his extra weight, Kari's suit could only manage less than half its top speed.

He struggled to work out how long it would take to reach the surface. At least twenty minutes. Probably more like thirty. And with Kari's air supply damaged . . .

"How's your breathing?" he asked.

"It's getting harder. The regulator sounds like it's sticking. I'm not getting a full supply."

"How are you feeling?"

"Light-headed. And . . . and a little drowsy."

The first symptoms of hypoxia, Chase knew. Oxygen starvation. There was no way Kari could stay conscious long enough to get them to the surface. Which meant he would have to work the thruster controls.

Which meant . . . he would have to take his thumb off the hole in his suit. He'd need both hands to hold onto her—the control stick wasn't designed to bear a load. If he put all his weight onto it, it would snap, condemning them both.

"Kari," he said, trying to sound calm as much for his own benefit as for hers, "keep your thumb on that wheel for as long as you can, okay? If you have any trouble, I'll take over. Don't worry. We're going to get to the surface."

"But if you take the control, won't you . . ."

"Don't worry about me. We're going to make it. Okay?"

"Okay . . ." she replied, voice drowsy.

They rose in silence for another few minutes. Chase checked the depth gauge: 650 feet. Still a long way to go.

"Eddie?"

"Yeah."

She sounded on the verge of falling asleep. "I'm sorry about Hugo. I liked him."

"I'm sorry too," he replied, a surge of anger rising inside him. He fought to keep it down. It wouldn't help. Yet. "I don't normally do revenge, it's unprofessional— but Qobras is going to regret it."

"Good. We're so close, he can't stop us . . ."

"So close to what?" No reply. "Kari?"

The thrusters stopped. Kari's left hand dropped limply from the control stick.

"Oh, *bollocks*," he muttered. Six hundred feet. At that depth, his suit was still under almost twenty atmospheres of pressure. If the crack widened, the water coming in wouldn't be a trickle. It would be a *jet*.

But he had no choice.

He swam up, taking hold of Kari's waist with his aching left hand as he closed the right around her thruster control. The cold dampness inside his suit was spreading. He shivered.

No time for that.

He pushed the control to full power. The thrusters whined to life again, the depth gauge ticking down, foot by agonizing foot. He swam, doing whatever he could to increase their rate of ascent. Despite his training and physical conditioning, he was rapidly tiring, the pressure and cold of the ocean sapping his strength.

Five hundred feet. Still nothing above but darkness. The damp chill spread up his body.

At four hundred feet, the first hint of light from the surface reached him, absolute blackness giving way to a strangely beautiful ink-blue glow from above. More fish appeared as they ascended, flitting past the interlopers with cold-eyed disinterest.

He looked at Kari. Her eyes were closed, and she looked almost serene. Chase couldn't even tell if she was still breathing. Either her breaths were so shallow he couldn't make out the tiny movements of her nostrils . . . or she was already dead.

Two hundred feet, and Chase realized he could see the sun, a brighter patch of light. The depth counter flicked down, one foot at a time . . .

The thrusters died.

Chase jabbed his thumb harder on the control, hoping the cold had merely numbed him, making his hand slip. It hadn't. The knurled wheel was pushed as far as it would go.

The deep suits were meant to be used in conjunction with a submersible for descending—and ascending again. They weren't designed to make the journey on their own.

The batteries were dead.

And they were still over a hundred feet below the surface.

"Buggeration and fuckery . . ."

He stared at Kari, then shook her, willing her to wake up and help him. Her eyes remained closed. It was all up to him.

He swam with all his remaining strength, pulling Kari with him. She weighed less than ten stones, but the extra bulk of her deep suit meant the effort was like dragging a burly commando, complete with pack, up a ladder.

Ninety feet. Eighty. Seventy.

Each foot on the depth counter took an eternity to traverse. He wanted nothing more than to stop and rest, regain his breath and let the burning in his muscles die away, but he had to get Kari to the surface.

Forty. Thirty.

Flashes of sunlight glinted mockingly against the waves above. But the counter was still falling. Ten feet, nine, eight . . .

He could feel the swell of the waves, his suit bumping against Kari's. Five, four . . . He was gasping for breath now, his muscles about to give up . . .

Clear!

He broke the surface, blinking at the fat red sun hanging above the horizon. Straining, he pulled Kari up with him. Water streamed down her helmet. Underwater it had been impossible to gauge her true color; now, even in the warm sunlight, her skin looked pale and blue.

The suits were closed with multiple clips and locks, meant to be removed with the help of two people, but that wasn't an option. Chase clawed at the seal around her neck, numbed fingers struggling to unfasten the latches. He wrapped his arm around the helmet, fighting for enough leverage to turn it.

It twisted, the locking pins coming free. He pulled the helmet off and tossed it aside. Kari's head lolled.

"Kari! Come on, wake up!" Chase patted her cheek, trying to hold her upright so water wouldn't slosh over the neck of her suit. She needed the kiss of life, but it would be impossible for him to remove his helmet without letting go of her.

"Kari! Come *on*!"

She took in a sharp breath, then coughed, gasping for air. Her eyelids fluttered. "Eddie?" The word was barely more than a whisper.

"Hey, hey, you're alive!" said Chase, breaking into a huge smile. "We made it! Are you okay?"

"I feel sick . . . and I have a *really* bad headache."

"But you're alive, that's the main thing. Give me a hand, help me get this fucking bucket off my head." She tugged at his helmet latches. "Aw, shit."

"What?"

He gave her a defeated look. "It's not going to matter. We're still a hundred miles out in the Atlantic, and our ship's in pieces all over the bottom. It's a bit too far to swim."

To his surprise, she smiled. "I don't think we'll need to swim."

"Why not?"

"Because I can see Captain Matthews rowing towards us."

He looked around. "Well, fuck me." The lifeboat was a hundred yards away, but Matthews was clearly visible in his white uniform at its prow, waving. "So Qobras left 'em alive . . ."

"That's not his style," said Kari, puzzled but relieved. "Something must have happened; he must— Oh God." She grabbed Chase's arm. "Nina! He must have taken Nina!"

"Why would he do that? He wanted her dead—why would he change his mind now?"

"She must know something," Kari realized. "Something we saw in the temple, some piece of information valuable enough to trade for the crew . . ."

"Well, we can ask 'em in a minute. Come on, get this helmet off."

"Actually, it's probably better if you keep it on until you're in the boat."

Chase frowned at her. "Why?"

"Because I get the feeling your suit radio is the only one we have . . ."

w

Five minutes later, Chase finally took a breath of fresh ocean air.

Kari was right: the *Evenor*'s crew had been set adrift with no radio. Once the lifeboat rejoined its fellows on the fringe of the debris field from the sunken research vessel, one of the engineers set to work on the deep suit's transmitter. It wouldn't have much range, but it didn't need it. The Gulf of Cádiz was, by maritime standards, a busy place. However, as Matthews pointed out, they couldn't use it just yet—there would be no point issuing a distress call if the closest vessel was Qobras's ship.

Chase and Kari used the interim to learn what had happened aboard the *Evenor*. "So Nina voluntarily gave herself up to save you?" Kari asked.

Matthews nodded. "Even though Qobras told her he was still going to kill her. We all owe her our lives."

Kari fell silent, staring pensively towards the sunset. Chase put an arm around her. "Hey, hey. She's still alive, for now. Whatever she knows, she won't have just blurted it right out to him. She'll drag it out for as long as she can. We can still find her."

"How?" Kari asked gloomily. "Even if we trace his ship back to port, he won't be on it. He'll have been picked up by a helicopter or gone ashore in a speedboat long before we can get anyone to intercept it."

"We'll work something out." Chase leaned back,

looking up. The first stars of the night had appeared, twinkling gently in the clear sky.

"Actually," said Matthews, "Dr. Wilde had a message, although I've got no idea what it means. She said to give it to you if I saw you."

Chase sat up again. "What did she say?"

"Not much. Just that . . . she'd send you a postcard."

"A postcard?" Kari's forehead creased, questioning. Her confusion increased as Chase started laughing, a cackle of sheer glee. "What? What does it mean?"

He managed to bring himself under control, a wide grin practically splitting his face in two. "It means," he announced, "that I know exactly where she's going."

TWENTY-THREE

Tibet

The sun had not yet risen over the Himalayan peaks, but Nina could see the predawn glow to the east as the helicopter clattered through the mountains.

She sat under guard in the rear compartment of the aircraft, an armed man on either side. Opposite were Qobras, Starkman and Philby. Her former mentor hadn't once dared to meet her gaze during the flight.

Following them, she knew, was a second helicopter carrying more men and something concealed inside a large crate. She doubted it was anything good.

"Go on," prompted Qobras. "You were saying about the eruption . . ."

"Yeah." The image of the final inscriptions from the temple returned to her mind's eye. "The island was subsiding, and the volcano at the northern end was active—they knew the writing was on the wall. I don't think they realized how fast the end would come when it finally happened."

"Not fast enough," said Qobras. "Some of them escaped."

Nina shook her head. "You really do have some serious issues with the Atlanteans, don't you? Considering that their empire was destroyed eleven thousand years ago, it's a long time to be holding a grudge."

"Their empire was never *completely* destroyed, Dr. Wilde," Qobras said. "It still exists, even today."

"Oh, this would be the mighty and *invisible* Atlantean empire, I guess."

Qobras ignored her sarcasm. "If you mean 'invisible' in the sense that nobody knows it is there, then yes, you're right. The descendants of the Atlanteans are still among us, seeking control over those they believe to be their inferiors. The difference now is that their control is not solely through force of arms, but through force of *wealth*."

"Sounds like we're in conspiracy theory territory now," Nina scoffed. "I suppose you're going to tell me that the Atlanteans are really the Illuminati."

"Hardly. *We* are the Illuminati."

Nina stared in disbelief. "What?"

"Not in the sense that I'm sure you're imagining. Our organization dates back to long before any of the sects that adopted the name from the sixteenth century onwards. And the name, Illuminati, is derived from Latin, whereas our name comes from the ancient Greek. The Brotherhood of Selasphoros—the light-bearers."

"*Ancient* Greek?" Nina turned to Philby for some support against the lunacy, but while he still couldn't look her in the eye, there was nothing in his expression suggesting he doubted Qobras's words. "So you're saying you're the leader of some secret anti-Atlantis organization that dates back two and a half thousand years? *Bullshit!*"

"It dates back much farther than that," said Qobras, unfazed. "I'm sure you remember *Critias*—the mention of the war between the Athenians and the kings of Atlantis?"

"Of course. 'The war that was said to have taken place between those who dwelt outside the Pillars of Heracles, and all who dwelt within them.' But that's the *only* mention, apart from a few lines in *Timaeus*."

Qobras shook his head. "No. There is more."

"*Critias* was never finished."

"*Critias* was *suppressed*," Qobras countered. "By the Brotherhood. The complete text included an account of the war between the two great powers, and how the Athenians and their allies drove the invaders from the Mediterranean. It also described the Athenian counter-attack on Atlantis itself—which ended with the Athenian army caught on the island as it sank."

"That's not consistent with *Timaeus*," Nina objected. "'And in a single day and night of misfortune all your warlike men as a body sank into the earth, and the island of Atlantis in like manner disappeared in the depths of the sea.' Two different events."

"The same event, according to the original text of *Critias*."

"But that—" Nina stopped as the full import of Qobras's words hit her. "You mean the *original* text? As in, transcribed directly from Plato's own words?"

"We have more than you could imagine in our vaults, including the complete text of *Critias*—and the *third* of Plato's dialogues about Atlantis, *Hermocrates*."

"But *Hermocrates* was never written . . ."

"So we convinced the world. The Brotherhood has been working to prevent the rediscovery of Atlantis for thousands of years. Anything that might assist the descendants of the Atlanteans in that task, we have gone to great lengths to keep out of their hands."

"Great lengths including murder," Nina scowled.

"It is not something we are proud of, but sometimes

it has been necessary. Other times . . . it has been justified."

"But *why*?" Nina asked. "This is *insane*! Yes, Atlantis is one of the most famous ancient legends in the world, but in the end it's just an archaeological site, a dead city full of ruins!"

Qobras rose in his seat. "The city might be dead, but what it stands for is very much alive, Dr. Wilde. And it is just as dangerous today as it was in 9500 BC. The discovery of Atlantis would serve to rally all the descendants of the Atlanteans, uniting them as one powerful force for evil."

"Atlantis has already *been* discovered," Nina pointed out. "By me. And everybody from the *Evenor* knows where it is. You think you can keep that quiet?"

"The *site* may have been discovered, but the knowledge it contained has been destroyed. And the Brotherhood has influence in many areas." He glanced at Philby. "We can keep the academic world distracted, certainly."

"So that's why you turned down my proposal, Jonathan?" Nina asked. "You were in this guy's pocket the whole time?"

"I was trying to *protect* you," Philby replied. "I didn't know if your theory would bear any fruit or not. But I couldn't take the risk that it would. I didn't know they would try to kill you right there in Manhattan to suppress it, you have to believe me! I never wanted you to get hurt!"

"I'm *so* grateful for your concern." Philby avoided her eyes, shamefaced.

"As for those others who might take an interest," Qobras continued, "there are ways in which we can divert their attention. But now it may no longer even be necessary. If you are telling the truth about the last outpost of the original Atlanteans, then we can destroy that too. With the last link gone, their descendants will never be able to unite to begin a new war of conquest."

"The Frosts are hardly warmongers," protested Nina. "Unless you count philanthropy as a WMD?"

Qobras let out a harsh laugh. "Philanthropy? Hardly! Everything Kristian Frost has done is in support of his ultimate goal, the restoration of Atlantean rule under his leadership. Spending millions on medical aid is just a means to that end. Do you really think the Frost Foundation's work is about helping the sick?"

"Then what *is* it about?"

"Kristian Frost has been using the Frost Foundation's medical projects as a cover to map out the worldwide distribution of the Atlantean genome, finding the people who share his DNA," said Qobras. "People like *you*. Yes, we know about the DNA test the Frosts carried out on you. We also know that over the last decade, he has devoted an enormous amount of money and resources to finding Atlantis—far more than he has revealed publicly, or, I suspect, to you. You are not the first person with a theory on the location of Atlantis whose expedition he has funded."

"Did you try to kill them too?" Qobras's look was the only answer she needed. "Oh God."

"As I said, we are not proud of the fact, but it had to be done. Yet despite that, because of *you* . . . the Frosts are building to the culmination of their plan."

"And what plan would that be, exactly?"

"We don't know the precise details. None of our operatives have been able to penetrate Frost's organization deeply enough to discover his true objective. But we have learned enough to know that his plan hinges upon not merely the discovery of Atlantis, but the recovery of certain Atlantean artifacts. But the Brotherhood is about to ensure that never happens." He gestured at the window. "We are approaching the Golden Peak."

Looking out, Nina saw the first light of the morning sun as it rose over the rugged silhouette of the Himalayas . . .

And to the west, the pinnacle of the middle of three peaks lit up with a dazzling orange glow, as if the tip of the mountain had burst into flame. Even the streaks of bare rock visible through the pure white snowcap seemed to be on fire, sunlight glinting from slender veins of gold within the cold stone.

"My God," she whispered.

"The Golden Peak," said Qobras. "A local legend, which supposedly hid a great treasure. The Ahnenerbe believed it was connected to Atlantis. As did your parents."

Nina looked sharply at him at the mention of her family, but Qobras had turned away to issue instructions to the pilot. The helicopter descended, sweeping towards the mountain. It landed on a broad snow-covered ledge.

"The Path of the Moon," Qobras announced as he climbed from the helicopter, his feet crunching in the snow. "I never imagined I would see this place again."

Nina pulled her coat tightly around herself as she stepped out after him, her ever-present guards following. "You've been here before?"

"Yes, but I thought there was nothing of value here. It seems I was wrong." He put a hand on Philby's shoulder. "Perhaps you and I should have spent more time here. It would have saved us a lot of trouble."

"*You've* been here as well?" Nina asked Philby. He made a vague, almost fearful sound of confirmation.

"He was here with your parents," said Qobras. Nina gaped at him, shocked.

"Giovanni, don't, *please*," Philby pleaded. "There's no need to . . ."

Qobras gave him a stern look. "I've done many things I am not proud of, but I *will* admit my part in them. You should do the same . . . Jack."

"Jonathan?" Nina strode up to him, no longer caring about her guards. "What does he mean? Did my parents come *here*? What do you know?"

He tried to turn away. "I . . . Nina, I'm sorry, I . . ."

She grabbed him by his coat. *"What do you know, Jonathan?"*

"Come this way, Dr. Wilde," said Qobras, pointing up the slope. Starkman pulled her away from Philby. Despite the cold, the professor was sweating.

The group trudged uphill, the second helicopter announcing its arrival with a biting spray of ice particles as it landed behind them. Qobras led the way, examining the rock face intently as he ascended. At last, he stopped.

"There," he said. Nina looked where he was indicating. At first she saw nothing but snow and barren rock, the strata twisted to the vertical by eons of geological pressure, but upon closer inspection she spotted a patch of darkness against the cold blue-gray of the mountain.

A crack in the rock, an opening . . .

"Kind of a tight squeeze," noted Starkman. At its widest, the crack was less than a foot across.

"There must have been another rock slide. Have the men bring the digging equipment."

Starkman issued the order. Within minutes, another ten men arrived from the second helicopter. They set to work tearing into the pile of loose stones beneath the snow with picks. Before long the opening was clear enough to allow passage, but Qobras ordered his men to keep digging. "We need it wide enough to fit the bomb through."

"*Bomb?*" gasped Nina. "What bomb?"

He shot her an almost impatient look. "This is not an archaeological expedition, Dr. Wilde. We came here to *destroy* the last link to Atlantis. Whatever lies inside this mountain, nobody else will ever see it."

"You're worse than the Taliban," she growled. "They destroyed priceless artifacts out of dogma. You're doing it for a conspiracy theory!"

"A conspiracy that I'm happy to say will end here. Once the last outpost is destroyed, every trace of the ancient Atlanteans will be gone forever."

"So then what? You going to retire to the Bahamas? Or are you just going to keep on killing people you don't like because of their DNA?" Qobras didn't answer, looking back at the widening opening.

After another five minutes of activity, he finally seemed satisfied. "Bring the bomb," he ordered. "We're going inside."

His men headed back to the helicopters as Qobras led the way into the cave, followed by Starkman and Philby. Nina came next, her two guards flanking her. Powerful flashlight beams flitted through the dark space. To Nina, it looked as though a natural cavern had been widened to form a passage leading into the mountain.

"Over here," said Starkman, aiming his light off to one side. Nina gasped in surprise when she saw what he had found.

Bodies.

Five desiccated corpses stared silently back, their skin shriveled and reduced to parchment. The way they were sitting, in a row against one side of the cave, suggested to Nina that they had succumbed to starvation or exposure—but it also appeared that somebody had searched them after their death.

"The fourth expedition of the Ahnenerbe," said Qobras grimly. "Jürgen Krauss and his men. They followed the path from Morocco to Brazil, and finally to Tibet."

"The *fourth* expedition?" asked Nina. "There were only three."

"Only three that were recorded. At least, in known records. There were other documents." His tone became somber. "Your father came into possession of some of them. They were what led him first to Tibet, in search of the Golden Peak . . . and then to here."

"Here?" said Nina, puzzled . . . but also with a growing sense of awful foreboding.

"This way." Qobras directed his flashlight down the passage at the rear of the chamber, nodding at Starkman to bring Nina. Philby hung back, his face filled with fear.

And something else, Nina realized.

Guilt?

She followed Qobras down the passage. His light illuminated what lay at the end of the passage.

It was a tomb, an Atlantean tomb; the aggressive architecture and Glozel inscriptions were unmistakable. That realization, though, became insignificant when Nina saw what else was within the chamber.

More bodies.

But unlike the corpses of the Nazi expedition, these had not died peacefully. They lay against the walls in twisted, frozen poses of agony. She saw pockmarks in the stone behind them: bullet holes, surrounded by faded brown splashes that could only be long-dried blood.

And among the faces of the dead were . . .

Nina raised her hands to her mouth. "No . . ." she

whispered. Qobras looked back at her, then gestured to Starkman, who pulled her forward. She resisted, only for him to drag her.

"*No!*" This time it was a wail, an uncontrolled release of horror and despair.

Time and cold had turned the skin a dry leathery brown, soft tissues long since decayed to leave the eye sockets as empty black holes. But Nina still recognized the faces. They had been in her thoughts every day for the past ten years.

Her parents.

They hadn't died in an avalanche. They had died *here*, gunned down.

Murdered.

Starkman forced her forward, closer to the terrible reality pinned in Qobras's light. She struggled and kicked at him, not wanting to look but unable to avert her gaze. "You did this!" she screamed at Qobras. "*You* killed them! You bastard, you *fucker*! I'll fucking *kill* you!" The two guards moved as if to protect their boss, but he held up a hand for them to stop. They stood back and waited as Nina's screams lost coherence, reduced to angry, anguished sobs.

"I'm sorry," Qobras said in a low voice. "But it had to be done. Kristian Frost could not be allowed to obtain the secrets of the Atlanteans."

"*What* secrets?" Nina cried bitterly. "There's nothing *here*! It's just a tomb!" Her eyes narrowed with hatred. "You killed my parents for *nothing*, you son of a bitch."

"No . . ." Qobras slowly panned his flashlight around the walls. "I thought there was nothing here ten years ago, that the tomb had been plundered. But if the last inscription from the temple in Atlantis itself is true, there *must* be something more to this place." He turned to the two guards. "Search every centimeter of the walls. Look for *anything* that might indicate another opening—a crack, a loose block, a keyhole—anything!" As they moved to obey, Qobras himself started examining the walls around him in minute detail. Starkman kept hold of Nina.

Her sobs of grief slowly died away . . . replaced by a cold, expressionless mask.

Almost expressionless. Only her eyes gave away the fury burning inside her.

The search took only a few minutes before one of the guards called out to Qobras. Everyone hurried to where he stood, carefully tracing a line almost concealed between the columns.

"Doors," said Qobras, sliding a fingertip down the narrow gap. "There doesn't seem to be any way to open them from outside. We'll need to break them open."

One of the guards was sent back to the helicopters to bring the necessary equipment. In the meantime, more of Qobras's men arrived, hauling with them on a fat-tired cart the large crate Nina had seen being loaded onto the second helicopter. A chill of fear ran up her back. Even if the bomb it contained was only half the size of the crate, it would still be larger than a man.

The charges Qobras intended to use on the doors, however, were far smaller. A drill was used to carve out a fist-sized hole in the stone. Once the hole was made, Qobras placed the explosive—a fat disc the size of a silver dollar—into it.

"You're just going to blow it up?" said Nina.

"Yes."

"What about them?" She pointed at the bodies. "You going to blow them to pieces as well? It's not enough that you killed them, now you're going to desecrate them too?"

Starkman made an impatient noise, but Qobras

paused, considering her words. "Jason, get some of the men to take them into the entrance chamber," he said at last.

"It's a waste of time, Giovanni," Starkman said, barely concealing his disapproval. "We should be getting the job done, not letting her delay us. And what difference does it make? They're already dead."

"Dr. Wilde is right. Move them."

Starkman scowled, but followed his orders, summoning a group of men to assist in removing the bodies. Nina couldn't watch, feeling a new burst of almost unbearable anguish as the corpse of one of the Tibetans was lifted up as if he weighed no more than a child. That was all that was left of these people, of her *family*, nothing more than husks. Her throat clenched so tightly with resurgent grief that she could barely breathe. She fought past it, refusing to break down in front of her enemies.

Once the bodies were gone, Qobras returned his attention to the explosive. He attached a timer to it before quickly retreating, ushering everyone else back to the cavern.

"CL-20," explained Starkman to Nina, without being asked. "The most powerful chemical explosive ever made. A piece the size of an Oreo can blow a hole right through six inches of armor plate."

"Am I supposed to be impressed by that?" she replied sourly.

"Maybe not. But you might want to cover your ears."

Nina saw that the others were doing just that, and hurriedly followed suit. A moment later there was an earsplitting bang and a swirling cloud of dust.

Qobras was the first to move, his flashlight beam slicing through the dust like a laser. "Clear all the debris from the doors so we can get the bomb through them," he ordered. "Jason, Jack, Dr. Wilde—come with me." Nina was unsurprised when her two guards came as well.

What had appeared to be a solid wall was now a gaping hole. Huge chunks of the shattered door were scattered over the tomb floor. The other door was still in place, though seriously damaged.

Beyond the doors lay darkness.

Qobras stepped over the debris, leading the way down what turned out to be a smooth slope descending deeper into the heart of the mountain.

The air was cool and, to Nina's surprise, fresh, lacking the almost indefinable stale, ancient mustiness she associated with long-sealed environments. Presumably there was another entrance, or at least some way for air to reach it from outside.

Like the entrance chamber, the long tunnel had been widened out from an existing natural passage. Considering its length, with only basic hand tools it must have taken years to excavate.

And as for whatever lay ahead . . .

"It's opening up," said Qobras. Distance reduced his flashlight beam to a tiny coin. The echo of their footsteps faded, suggesting they were about to emerge into the open.

But that was impossible. They were inside the mountain.

Which meant the space they were about to enter was *huge* . . .

They emerged onto a road, a broad paved lane stretching beyond the range of their lights. Buildings lurked on either side, imposing pillars glinting with gold and orichalcum rising into the darkness.

"Christ, it's huge," said Starkman. He cupped his hands to his mouth and yelled, "Hello!" A very faint echo returned a couple of seconds later.

"We need more light," Qobras said. Starkman nodded and took off his pack, taking out a stubby flare gun. He quickly loaded it and fired it up at an angle. A brilliant red light fizzled to life, drifting on its small parachute . . .

Everyone was stunned by the sight it revealed.

"My God . . ." said Nina.

TWENTY-FOUR

The scene before them was spectacular, an awe-inspiring tableau lost since the dawn of history.

Nina instantly recognized what lay at its center. It was another replica of the Temple of Poseidon—but this time, it was not alone.

Surrounding it were other buildings—smaller, but no less grandiose. The architectural style was familiar, starkly elegant, yet at the same time somehow brutal.

They were palaces, and temples; the citadel of Atlantis as described by Plato, re-created thousands of miles from its inspiration. And unlike their ruined counterparts in Brazil, these had withstood the test of time, shielded from the elements, perfectly preserved.

As her eyes adjusted to the flickering glow of the flare, however, she realized the scene was not complete. Vast as the cave was, it still wasn't large enough to accommodate the entire citadel. Even the Temple of Poseidon itself was incomplete, its far end disappearing into the cave wall. There were indications that the Atlanteans had tried to carve out part of the wall to make room for the structure, but in the end they had, she assumed, simply dug the temple's inner chambers directly out of the mountain.

The flare sputtered and died, dropping the colossal cave back into darkness. The only light came from the group's flashlights.

"It's . . . it's unbelievable," said Philby. "Giovanni, at the very least we have to photograph this. This is an even more important find than Atlantis itself!"

"No," Qobras told him firmly. "Nothing can remain. Nothing! The Atlantean legacy will end *here*." He turned his back on Philby, addressing Starkman. "This road leads straight to the center of the citadel. Call the others and have them bring in the bomb."

"How big is this bomb?" Philby asked nervously.

"It's a thousand-pound fuel-air explosive," Starkman told him. "The explosive core is fifty pounds of CL-20. In terms of destructive force, it's the next best thing to a tactical nuke."

"My God," Philby gasped.

"These are the people you've gotten yourself in bed with," Nina reminded him coldly. "Destroyers and murderers. I hope you're proud of yourself."

"Nina, please," he begged, stepping closer, "I'm so, so sorry! I never wanted to do anything to hurt Henry and Laura—I went on the expedition with them hoping they *wouldn't* find anything!"

"But you still betrayed them. To *him*." She shot a look of cold hate at Qobras. "They died because of *you*, Jonathan. They were *murdered* because of you! You son of a *bitch*!"

Before her guards could react, Nina punched him in the face. The pain that exploded in her knuckles was eclipsed by the pure primal satisfaction she received from the sight of Philby falling on his back, a bead of blood running from one nostril. He stared up at her aghast.

The guards pulled her back as Starkman, looking almost amused, helped Philby to his feet. "Nice punch, Dr. Wilde. Been taking tips from Eddie?"

The word came over the radio that it would take about fifteen minutes for the bomb to be brought down the tunnel. Qobras glanced at his watch, then looked at Philby and Nina. "That's how much time you have to explore this place, Jack. Dr. Wilde, I promised you would have the chance to see the last outpost of the Atlanteans. I am a man of my word."

"Before you kill me, you mean," she said with a bitter smile.

"As I said, I am a man of my word."

"Right. I'm sure that helps you sleep at night."

Starkman fired another flare, and they headed down the road towards the citadel. Nina couldn't help but feel the thrill of discovery as they approached, but at the same time she was painfully aware that every step she took was counting down the seconds to her death.

In the harsh, wavering light of the flare, she realized there was another structure before the Temple of Poseidon, a much smaller building raised up from the cave floor on a steep-sided mound. It was surrounded by a wall about fifteen feet high. A wall of . . .

"Gold," said Starkman, awed. "There must be *tons* of it. How much is gold worth per ounce? Eight hundred dollars? Nine hundred? There's hundreds of millions of dollars there!"

"Be careful," Qobras warned. "That kind of thinking led Yuri to betray us. We're here to destroy all this, not profit from it."

They walked up to the gleaming wall. It completely encircled the little building, with no apparent way in. "It's the Temple of Cleito, Poseidon's wife," Nina said. "Plato said that it was inaccessible."

"Inaccessible, huh?" said Starkman, putting down

his gear and unslinging his grappling gun. "We'll see about that."

"Jason." The single word from Qobras stopped Starkman midmotion.

"Oh, come on," Nina chided. "Aren't you the least bit curious about what's inside? It's the very beginnings of Atlantis, a replica of the spot where it was founded—for all we know, this might contain the *original* contents of the temple, rescued from Atlantis itself. Don't you want to know what you've been fighting all these years? Don't you want to know your enemy?"

Qobras contemplated the golden wall, then nodded to Starkman, who took the grapnel from the gun and unspooled a length of cable. Once he had enough, he stepped back and tossed the grapnel over the top of the wall. He pulled the line; it caught.

"Okay, let's see what's in here," Starkman said, quickly climbing the cable. One of Nina's guards threw another line up and scaled it, though more slowly.

Reaching the top, Starkman swung around, supporting himself on his stomach. "Dr. Wilde, you're next." He gestured to her other guard to hoist her up so he could take her hands.

"You realize I could just push you off and break your neck," she muttered once she reached the top.

"You realize I could just shoot you in both legs and leave you to die in agony when the bomb goes off," Starkman retorted. He lowered Nina down the other side.

Philby was next, awkwardly assisted over the top by Starkman, then her second guard and Qobras followed. Qobras was surprisingly agile and limber for a man of his age, Nina noticed. An analogue of Kristian Frost, a dark mirror-image.

Steps led up the steep mound to the temple's entrance. Again Qobras took the lead; this time, Nina was right behind him, determined to see what was inside.

There was actually surprisingly little to be found. A pair of golden statues awaited them inside the doorway: Poseidon, no longer the giant found inside his own temple, but still larger than life, and facing him Cleito, his wife. Beyond them . . .

"It's a mausoleum," Nina said. A pair of large sarcophagi occupied the rear of the room, the plain, almost crude stonework contrasting sharply with the carefully wrought precious metals lining the walls.

"Yeah, but whose?" Starkman wondered. He directed his flashlight at an inscription chiseled into the end of one of the coffins. "What does this say?"

Nina and Philby began to offer a translation at the same moment, before Philby shrank back. "It says that this is the tomb of Mestor, last king of . . . I guess that means New Atlantis," Nina said. The letters were styled differently from the familiar Glozel alphabet, but in this case it didn't appear to be the result of mutations in the language over time, more from simple sloppiness. She moved to the second coffin. "And this is his queen . . . Calea, it looks like." The letters were equally crude.

"The *last* king?" mused Philby. "What happened to his successors? Even if he had no heirs, there would always be *somebody* in line for the throne . . ."

"Give me your flashlight," Nina ordered Starkman, all but snatching it from his hand as she bent down to read the rest of the inscriptions.

"You're welcome," he said sarcastically. She ignored him, focusing on the ancient letters.

"They were dying out," she realized as she read on. "They thought they could sustain a new empire from here, rule the lands around the Himalayas and use the mountains as a natural fortress. They were wrong."

"What happened?" asked Qobras.

"What happens to *every* empire?" Nina replied. "They overstretched themselves, got lazy, decadent. And let's face it, they didn't pick the breadbasket of the world to settle in. I guess they thought they could just have the peoples they conquered bring what they needed as tribute, but it didn't work out." She almost laughed as she worked through the text. "This place? The last outpost of the great Atlantean empire? They *abandoned* it. The king and queen here were the only reason anybody stayed. As soon as they died, everyone else hightailed it out and sealed the place up behind them. In fact, it wouldn't surprise me if they actually killed the king and queen themselves to speed up the process."

"Where did they go?" asked Starkman.

"I'd guess they went right where your boss here always thought they did—into other societies. Except . . ." this time Nina actually did manage a hollow laugh, "they didn't take over as conquerors. They were assimilated the same way as people are now—as immigrants, *refugees*. They moved in at the *bottom* of their new societies."

"That *can't* be true," Qobras growled.

"That would be an accurate interpretation of the text," confirmed Philby. "The people who wrote this knew their society was dying out, and that the only way to survive was to integrate into the other cultures in the region."

"So much for your conspiracy theory, Qobras," said Nina, not bothering to conceal her contempt. "This Brotherhood of yours, it's been spending thousands of years fighting something that didn't even *exist*."

"It exists!" Qobras asserted. "The Atlanteans would never accept subjugation by people they considered inferiors. It's how they think, it's in their *genes*. They would work their way back up—it would take generations, but they would regain power."

"Where's your proof?" Nina cried, jumping to her feet and jabbing the flashlight at him like a sword. "So Kristian Frost is tracing the Atlantean descendants from their DNA, and wants to find Atlantis itself, the greatest legend in human history—that doesn't mean he's trying to take over the world!"

Qobras wheeled on Nina, dazzling her with his light. "You don't know what Kristian Frost is capable of doing."

"He can't be any worse than you!"

His eyes narrowed. "You have no idea . . ."

Any elaboration was interrupted by Starkman's radio. "They've brought the bomb," he announced after responding to the call.

"Tell them to prepare it for detonation immediately," Qobras snapped. "Let's go." Everyone moved to the temple entrance, but he held out a hand to stop Nina. "Not you."

"What?"

"You're staying here. It seems the appropriate place."

The full horror of Qobras's words squeezed her chest like an ice-cold vice. "Wait, no . . . you're just going to leave me in here? You're going to leave me in here until the *fucking bomb explodes*?"

Starkman put a hand on his holstered pistol. "We could just shoot you in the head if you like."

"You won't have time to feel any pain," said Qobras. "You'll be vaporized instantly."

"Well, that makes me feel *so* much happier! You can't leave me in here!"

"Good-bye, Dr. Wilde." Qobras tossed an unlit glow stick at her feet, then left the temple. The others followed.

Philby glanced back with an expression of pained sorrow as if about to say something, but then walked silently away.

Nina wanted to run after them, to punch and kick them as they tried to scale the wall, tear down the lines and trap them inside with her . . . but she couldn't. Her body refused to cooperate, admitting defeat even as her mind demanded that she fight on. She sagged against the king's sarcophagus, sliding down to the dusty stone floor.

The men scaled the wall, leaving her in darkness.

This was it? This was how she was going to die? Trapped in a tomb with the last rulers of Atlantis?

She drew in a long, trembling breath, then felt for the glow stick, cracking it to unleash a sickly green light. Not knowing what else to do, she turned around and regarded the text carved into the coffin once again.

So this was how the story of Atlantis ended. Not with a crash of waves wiping a great power from the face of the earth, but in mundane ignominy, dying out through decay and corruption like every other fading empire in history.

In some ways, it was a good thing. The legend would remain exactly that, a story of wonder. The greatest mystery of all time.

But it didn't make her feel any better.

Nina heard sounds from over the wall, clankings and clatterings as Qobras's men opened the crate and prepared the bomb. She wondered how long she had left to live. Fifteen minutes? Ten?

Raised voices outside. She lifted her head. Their tone had suddenly changed: confusion mixed with concern.

The glow stick in her hand, Nina quickly descended the steps to stand by the wall, straining to hear the voices outside. Qobras was demanding answers, Starkman talking into his radio.

And getting no reply.

Then Qobras shouted something all too clearly, freezing her breath in her lungs. *"Start the timer!"*

Running footsteps. The sound quickly faded as they hurried up the road towards the tunnel.

"Oh, shit . . ." The urge for survival kicked back in; she ran around the wall, looking for any sign of an exit.

There was none. It was a solid ring of metal, the gold supported by iron, completely enclosing the temple.

The temple . . .

Maybe there was some hidden escape route like the one in the Temple of Poseidon! She raced back up the steps into the mausoleum, a flicker of hope in her heart.

But it was quickly extinguished. The interior walls and floor seemed solid, the only possible place anything could be concealed being inside the coffins—and she quickly found she wasn't strong enough to open the heavy stone lids.

Helpless minutes passed, and the bomb was still ticking down to detonation—

A sudden noise made her jump. Not the bomb, but . . . *gunfire!*

The distant rattle of automatic weapons. Distant—but getting closer.

What was going on? She ran down the steps, listening at the wall. More gunfire echoed through the huge chamber—as did the thud of an explosion. A grenade? Another followed moments later, a scream abruptly cut off by the sharp bang.

Red light flooded the cave above her. Flares. She rushed back to the top of the steps to see over the wall.

A group of people—Qobras and his men, though fewer than before—were running towards her, firing wildly behind them at a larger force that was spreading out between the surrounding buildings. Muzzle flashes licked out from the new arrivals. One of the running men fell.

Other weapons fired, deeper thumps followed by explosions *ahead* of Qobras and his team. Their attackers were using grenade launchers! Debris flew in all directions. Nina ducked.

Qobras had been trying to reach the bomb. But he was now cut off from it, hemmed in by grenadiers who had his range.

The attackers had much greater firepower than the Brotherhood's team. More weapons joined the fray, new notes added to the symphony of destruction. Dazzling bursts of light and piercing bangs came from flash grenades, blinding the defenders. Machine guns opened up, streams of bullets ripping into the ancient palaces and the men hiding behind them. More grenades exploded— followed by a thunderous crash as one of the buildings collapsed. Screams echoed through the cavern.

She heard Starkman's voice over the din. "Cease fire! *Cease fire!*" Gradually the noise of guns died down.

They were surrendering!

Nina heard other men charging towards the temple. "Hey!" she cried, jumping down the steps two at a time. "Hey! I'm in here! Can you hear me? Get me out of here!"

More voices—then with a loud clank, a grapnel hooked over the top of the wall, shaking as somebody climbed up the cable.

A light shone over the top of the wall, a familiar face behind it. Balding, gap-toothed—and right now the most beautiful sight she'd ever seen in her life.

"Ay up, Doc," said Chase, grinning down at her with unconcealed delight. "Did you miss me?"

TWENTY-FIVE

"A re you okay?" Chase asked as he lowered Nina from the golden wall.

"I'm fine. Thanks. And I'm glad you are too—I thought you were dead!"

"Takes more than a sinking ship to kill me." His look of triumph quickly faded.

"What is it?" Nina asked, fearing the worst.

His jaw muscles clenched before he answered. "Hugo didn't make it."

"Oh . . ." She touched his hand. "Oh God, I'm sorry . . ."

"Yeah." He was silent for a moment, then shook his head. "Kari's okay, though. She's on her way down."

"Kari's here?" Nina asked, excited.

"Yeah, I told her to keep back until the shooting stopped."

She surveyed the scene, lit by flashlights and glow sticks. The eight survivors of Qobras's team—including Qobras himself, Starkman and Philby—were kneeling with their hands behind their heads, surrounded by a dozen men in black combat gear and body armor. At least another ten men were patrolling the surrounding area. She didn't recognize any of them. "Who are these guys with you?"

"Frost's security; they work for Schenk at Ravnsfjord. Military backgrounds, most of 'em—not SAS level, but good enough. Everyone I could round up in a hurry. I didn't know how much time we'd have, so I figured the sooner the better."

"You're not kidding." She gestured at the bomb, a malevolent dull green cylinder the size and shape of a water heater. "They'd set that thing to blow up."

"I know. We stopped the timer with about five minutes to go."

"Five minutes?" Nina shuddered at the thought of how close to death she'd been. "I hope you've switched it off."

"It's just on pause. Don't worry," Chase added, seeing Nina's worried look, "nobody's going to muck around with it and accidentally set the bloody thing off."

"How did you find me?"

Chase grinned. "I got your postcard, so to speak. Good job I remembered the name of that village. If I hadn't, we'd have been screwed. Tibet's a big place."

"You found me just from that so quickly?" Nina had thought her clue to Matthews was a longshot, but anything more specific would probably have earned the captain—and maybe herself—an instant death sentence. "I never had a chance to tell anyone the information in the last inscription from Atlantis—how they traveled up the Ganges to the Himalayas, how to find the Golden Peak, any of that."

"You didn't need to. Kari's old man used his pull with the Chinese government to get us into the country, and we came straight to Xulaodang in choppers. Turns out the people there remembered the *last* time some Westerners came looking for one of their local legends. Kari got them to give us the directions and we flew right here. Knew we'd found the right place when we saw Qobras's helicopters. Which are now in about a million smoking bits, by the way." Chase glanced over at the prisoners, frowning. "Pity that bastard wasn't inside one of them. Would have been good payback for Hugo."

"What are you going to do with them?"

"No idea. Leave that up to Frost, I guess . . ."

"*Nina!*"

Nina looked around to see Kari practically sprinting towards her, dressed entirely in white with her blond hair streaming over the top of her fur collar. She skirted the captives and ran to Nina, embracing her. "Oh my God, you're alive, you're okay!"

"Yeah, I'm fine, I'm fine!" Nina replied. "And I'm glad you're okay too! When Qobras sank the *Evenor*, I thought I'd never see you again."

"You almost didn't." Kari gave her a final squeeze, then released her. "I wouldn't have made it without Eddie."

"Not 'Mr. Chase' anymore?" Nina asked, a little mischievously.

Kari smiled, almost coy. "I think the employer-employee relationship changes somewhat after about the sixth time he saves your life."

"Yeah, you can thank me with a threesome later." Chase grinned. Kari jokingly rolled her eyes.

"I see *some* things haven't changed," Nina observed wryly. "But Kari, can you believe this? Can you believe what we've found?"

"What *you've* found," Kari corrected. She gave an order in Norwegian to one of the black-clad commandos; he fired a flare, illuminating the buildings in the unearthly red light. "A re-creation of the citadel of Atlantis, almost intact . . ."

Chase glanced over at the collapsed remains of one of the nearby structures. "Er, yeah. Sorry about that."

Nina patted his arm. "Considering the circumstances, I forgive you."

"And another replica of the Temple of Poseidon as well," said Kari. "It's incredible."

"Not as incredible as what's in there," Nina told her, indicating the much smaller temple inside the wall of gold.

"Is that the Temple of Cleito?" asked Kari.

Nina nodded. "Only it's being used as a mausoleum. And guess who's in it? The last king and queen of Atlantis!"

Sheer delight momentarily overcame Kari's ability to speak. "Are you sure?" she finally gasped. "The actual bodies?"

"Well, I didn't *look*, but that's what it said on the sarcophagi—"

"Show me," said a new voice, deep and full of authority. Nina looked around and was taken aback to see Kristian Frost, dressed in white cold-weather gear, striding towards her. He glanced at Qobras and the other prisoners before marching past, flanked by a muscular man whom Nina belatedly recognized as Josef Schenk, and a tall, square-jawed young guy with a blond military-style buzz cut.

"Father," said Kari, her attitude immediately changing to one of respectful deference. Nina raised an eyebrow. Apparently here, Kristian Frost was 100 percent in charge.

Frost pointed at the Temple of Cleito. "Is it in there?"

"Yes," said Nina, "but there's no way in, you'll need to climb over—"

Frost snapped his fingers. The blond man put down his backpack, quickly unzipping it and taking out an electric circular saw. He walked to the wall, sliding his fingertips over it as if feeling for flaws, then donned a pair of safety goggles and started the saw. It made a piercing squeal as the blade sliced through the gold.

"Well, that'll work too," Nina said, shocked, "but what about preserving the site? We should be trying to keep the place as intact as possible."

"For now, my main concern is getting what I came here for," said Frost. "How long will it take to cut through?"

"Just a minute or two," the blond man told him.

"Enough time to take care of other business, then." Frost pulled off his gloves, slowly slapping them against his palm as he turned around. "Giovanni. We finally meet."

"You'll excuse me if I don't shake your hand," Qobras snarled.

Frost walked to him, the circle of guards around the kneeling prisoners opening up to let him through. "What are we going to do with you? This would have been so much simpler if you'd been shot during the battle, but now . . ."

"Do what you will. You can't hope to defeat the Brotherhood. Whatever you do, they will be there to fight against you."

Frost laughed. "No. They won't. Not after I take what's in that temple." He looked at the mausoleum for a moment. "You know, I'm almost tempted to let you go. Just so that you can fully realize how completely you and your organization have failed. Everything you've fought for, *killed* for . . . All for nothing."

Qobras's lips curled into a sneer. "You think that killing me will end the Brotherhood?"

"You really have no idea what's going to happen, do

you?" said Frost, laughing again. "I suppose I was more worried about your agents than I needed to be."

"Just do whatever you're going to do to me," Qobras growled.

"I'm not going to do anything," Frost said. "I think Dr. Wilde should have that privilege."

"What?" Nina asked, confused.

Frost walked to her, his voice falling to a velvety burr. "Dr. Wilde . . . *Nina*. This man murdered your parents. He has to pay for what he's done. Justice must be served."

"The only criminal here is you, Frost!" Qobras shouted. One of the guards kicked him hard in the chest, leaving him gasping.

"Well, yes, but . . ." Nina looked at Qobras. "Shouldn't he be put on trial for everything he's done?"

"By whom? This man is above the law. He's murdered with impunity for decades all around the world." Frost unzipped his jacket and reached inside it. "The only justice he deserves is the same kind that he believes he delivers." He pulled out a pistol, and pressed it into Nina's palm. "For all the crimes he has committed, for everything he's done to hurt *you* . . . you know what you have to do."

Nina stared at the gun in disbelief, then looked up at Frost. There was no sign on his face that he was anything other than deadly serious.

"Hang on a minute," said Chase, concerned. "I want this bastard dead as much as you do, but a summary execution? That's not justice, that's *murder*. And you can't ask Nina to become a murderer!"

"Please stay out of this, Mr. Chase," Frost said, almost dismissively. "This is a decision that only Dr. Wilde can make."

"Kari!" Chase looked at her for support. She seemed torn, glancing between Frost, Nina, Chase . . .

"It's . . . my father knows best," she said eventually, not sounding entirely sure of her words.

Frost put his hands on Nina's arms as he dropped his voice almost to a whisper. "It's up to you, Nina. You know what he's done, you know that he has to pay." One hand closed softly around the gun, squeezing her fingers on the grip. "He killed your parents, Nina. He *murdered* them, right here inside this mountain. You should take from him what he took from you. Do it."

Nina's eyes filled with tears. Lips clenched tight, jaw trembling, she looked past Frost at the kneeling figure of Qobras.

"Far . . ." Kari began, but a single look from Frost silenced her. He released Nina and moved back.

Nina took a step forward, every muscle and tendon taut. The gun felt cold and heavy in her hand. Qobras watched her, the expression on his face one not of fear or anger, but cold contempt.

The burning pain in her heart transmuted, taking on form. *Hate.*

"Nina!" Chase called behind her, but she barely heard him.

She raised the gun, pointing it first at Qobras's chest, then, more decisively, at his face. Starkman tensed, but remained still, his one eye watching warily.

Qobras stared silently back up at her. The man who had tried to kill her and her friends. Who *had* killed her friends, Castille and the crew of the *Nereid*.

Who had killed her parents, her *family*, the people she loved . . .

Tears blurred her vision. She blinked them away, feeling them turn cold as they ran down her cheeks. Qobras swam back into sharp focus, still regarding her icily.

Her finger tightened on the trigger. The pistol's

hammer drew back slowly, only the tiniest amount of extra pressure needed to fire . . .

Then it stopped.

Eyes brimming with tears once more, Nina stepped back, lowering the weapon.

"I don't know who you think I am," she whispered, "but you're *wrong*. My DNA doesn't control who I am or what I do. I wanted you to know that." She carefully eased her grip on the trigger, the hammer returning to its original position, then walked back to Frost. "I can't kill him. I *won't*."

To her surprise, Frost's tone was light. "Well of course you can't!" he exclaimed, taking the pistol back. "I didn't think you could. But just in case you surprised me . . . it's not even loaded."

"What do you . . ." Nina gaped. "You were *testing* me?"

"I'm sorry. But I wanted to be sure of the kind of person you really are."

Kari hurried over to Nina, standing almost defensively between her and Frost. "You had no right to do that to her! How could you not trust my judgment?"

"I'm sorry," he repeated. "As I said, I wanted to be sure."

The screech of the saw ceased abruptly. A moment later came a heavy bang as the section cut out of the wall fell to the ground.

"Watch them," Frost ordered his men of the prisoners, before crossing to the wall and peering through the new gap. He took a flashlight from the blond man, then clambered through the narrow hole and looked back at Kari and Nina. "Come on."

Sharing a look, the two women slipped through after him. Chase followed without being asked, which Nina noticed earned him a somewhat irritated frown from

Frost. Schenk then entered, the blond man moving in front of the hole as if guarding it.

Frost hurried up the steps into the temple. By the time Nina caught up, he was already examining the lid of the king's sarcophagus, probing for gaps. "Help me with this," he ordered. Schenk pushed past her, wielding a crowbar. Chase joined them to heave at the top of the sarcophagus.

The three men strained, Schenk pulling down on the crowbar with all his weight. The lid shifted slightly.

"Come on, you bugger!" Chase groaned. "One, two, *three!*"

They all strained again—and this time the lid lifted enough for them to slide it aside. Another push and the interior of the coffin was exposed; a third, and the stone slab crashed to the floor of the temple and broke in two. Nina winced at the destruction.

Frost picked up his flashlight and leaned eagerly over the side of the sarcophagus. "My God, look at it!"

Nina and Kari joined him. Nina felt an involuntary flash of fear at the sight, a literal face of death staring up at her like a refugee from a nightmare. The body inside the sarcophagus, sealed in the stone container for thousands of years, was blackened and shriveled, the remains of the long-rotted lips twisted back into a malevolent sneer around jutting teeth.

"Hello, mummy," Chase whispered, grinning. Nina jabbed him with her elbow.

Frost examined the corpse more closely. "The last king of the Atlanteans . . . still intact." He took a small pouch from his coat and removed a needlelike probe from it, poking carefully at the wizened skin. "Open the other one, quickly," he told Schenk and Chase.

"What's the rush?" asked Chase. "It's not like they're going anywhere."

"Just do it," Frost snapped. He switched the probe to his other hand, taking a scalpel from the pouch and bending down over the dead king's face like a surgeon about to operate.

"What are you doing?" Nina asked, concerned. "This isn't anything like standard practice."

"I need to get a DNA sample," said Frost, as if that explained everything. The faint scrape of the scalpel cutting through the mummified flesh was drowned out by the crunch of stone against stone as Chase and Schenk lifted the lid of the other sarcophagus.

"But really, we should . . ." Nina cringed again as the second lid slammed to the ground. She went to look inside while Frost was still engrossed with the first corpse, teasing a piece of the king's curled lips into a plastic container.

Queen Calea was in much the same state as her husband, only the tattered remains of the clothing providing any immediate indication that the body was that of a woman. "It's Camilla Parker-Bowles!" Chase exclaimed jovially as he peered into the sarcophagus.

"Will you shut up?" Nina demanded.

"Kari," said Frost, not looking up from his "operation," "I think it might be safer if you took Nina back to the helicopter."

Kari looked puzzled. "Safer? I'm sure Josef's men can keep Qobras's people under control."

"I want to be sure. Go on, Kari."

"But there's still so much to do. We haven't even started to explore the other temples yet," Nina objected.

"Once the site is secured, we can return to it at any time. This was a rescue mission, not an archaeological survey—we don't have any of the necessary equipment."

"Except for your surgical kit, apparently . . ."

Frost fixed her with a stern look. "I'm not prepared to argue about this. Kari, you told me her safety was your first concern. You can make sure she stays safe by taking her back to the helicopter. Go."

Kari seemed about to object, but then gave in. "Yes, Far," she said. "Come on, Nina."

"What about Qobras?" Nina asked dubiously.

"We'll turn him and his men over to the Chinese authorities," said Frost, snapping his sample container closed and moving to the second sarcophagus. "He committed murder on their territory, they can handle him."

"Might be hard to prove after all this time," said Chase. "And I thought you said he was above the law."

"I have some influence with the Chinese." Frost looked up at Kari and Nina. "Please, go to the helicopter. I'll take care of things here."

"Okay . . ." said Kari with a little reluctance, taking Nina's hand. Considerably more reluctantly, Nina allowed herself to be led out of the temple. Chase waved at her. She returned the gesture.

"He's right," said Kari. "It's safer, at least until we can secure the site."

"You don't sound convinced," Nina observed.

"I'm . . . disappointed," she admitted. "I wanted to explore this place as much as you do. But . . ." She looked at the black-clad guards around the prisoners. "Father's right, it's not safe."

She told two of Frost's men to escort her and Nina back to the helicopter, and they began the trek out of the vast cavern.

vw

"Got it," said Frost, closing a second plastic container. He carefully placed it next to its twin in the pouch, then slipped it back inside his coat. "That's it. Everything I came for."

"I thought you came here to rescue Nina?" Chase said pointedly. Frost ignored him, leaving the temple. Schenk went with him. Chase made a face, then jogged down the steps after them.

He clambered through the hole and took in the scene. Nina and Kari had gone, but Qobras and his surviving companions were still on their knees surrounded by guards. Frost and Schenk were talking quietly.

He decided to check the bomb again. Its timer was paused at just over five minutes to detonation. "Shouldn't we disarm this thing?" he called to Frost.

"It will be fine for the moment, Mr. Chase," Frost replied, before resuming his muted conversation.

Chase shrugged, then walked over to the prisoners. He stood before the kneeling Starkman, who still had his hands behind his head. "So, Jason. Now that we can actually have a proper chat, you mind telling me why you betrayed your mates and joined up with this twat?" He jabbed a thumb at Qobras.

"Because he's the good guy, Eddie," said Starkman, his eye glittering in the flashlight's beam.

"Murdering innocent people, blowing stuff up, sinking ships—yeah, he sounds like a right Samaritan to me."

"It's for the greater good, believe me. You know me—"

"I *used* to know you," Chase interrupted. "I *thought* I knew you. Now? I don't have a fucking clue what's going through your head."

"You should still know that I wouldn't take on a job if I didn't believe in what I was doing. *That* never changed in all the years I knew you. It still hasn't."

"So you believe in what you're doing," Chase was forced to concede. The Texan had always been consistent in that much, at least. "Doesn't make it right."

"There are things I haven't been proud of, sure. But the alternative's worse. Which is letting your buddy Frost there get what he wants."

"I already *have* what I want, Mr. Starkman," Frost cut in.

"And *why* do you want it?" Qobras demanded, still defiant. "You've found the last outpost of Atlantis—and a sample of pure Atlantean DNA. But for what purpose?"

Frost gazed down at him, a half-smile on his lips. "I'm almost tempted to let you go to your grave without ever knowing the truth. But . . ." The smile vanished, his expression turning to stone. "We're going to remake the world as it should be. With a ruling elite of pure-blooded Atlanteans—and the worthless trash of humanity removed."

Qobras's disbelief slowly turned to horror. "My God . . . you're even more insane than I thought. You never wanted a pure DNA sample so you could identify the rest of your kind—you wanted it so you could *immunize* yourselves! That lab of yours—you're using it to create a bioweapon!"

"Wait, what?" said Chase, looking anxiously between the two men. "A *bioweapon*? Is this true?"

"That doesn't concern you, Mr. Chase," Frost replied, not taking his eyes off Qobras. "But now, Giovanni, now that you know the truth, now that you know the Brotherhood has *failed* . . . it is over."

He pulled out his pistol and fired.

He had lied to Nina. It was loaded.

The crack of the shot echoed off the surrounding buildings as the back of Qobras's skull blew open, splattering the men behind him with gore. Philby screamed, trying to scramble away until one of the guards kicked him back.

"Jesus!" Chase gasped, appalled.

"Get him up," Frost told one of his men, indicating Philby. The professor shrieked in terror as he was hauled to his feet. "Shut up," Frost snapped. "We're taking you with us. Move him away from the others."

Philby was pulled aside as the other guards, responding to a nod from Schenk, raised their MP-7s to a firing position.

"Wait, wait, stop!" Chase protested, stepping between Starkman and the nearest guard. "What the hell are you doing? You can't just execute them!"

"Actually, Mr. Chase," said Frost, "I can. In fact, now that I have what I came for . . ." his expression turned more stony than ever, "I'm terminating your employment." He barked an order in Norwegian . . . and Chase found the guards' guns pointing at *him*.

"What the fuck is this, *boss*?" he asked, warily raising his hands. Schenk took his Wildey and pushed him back into the circle of prisoners.

"This is the end," said Frost. He looked at Schenk. "Restart the timer."

"There's only five minutes left," Schenk replied. "Will that be enough time to get clear?"

"It will if we run."

"Wait," said Chase, "after everything you've been through to find this place . . . you're just going to blow it up?"

Frost shrugged. "I no longer need it. These DNA samples are worth more than any amount of ancient treasure. Start the timer," he ordered Schenk again. The German nodded and moved to obey.

"I told you," Starkman muttered to Chase.

"So you're just going to leave us in here with the bomb?" Chase asked.

Frost sniffed dismissively. "No, I'm going to kill you so you can't stop the countdown. Ready!"

Each of the guns found a target. Chase saw at least two aimed at him.

Shit!

He needed a plan, *fast*.

But he had no gun, nobody to back him up.

Unless—

He stepped back as if cringing away from the guns, bumping into the kneeling Starkman. "Jason? Going to need a *flash* of inspiration here . . ."

Starkman shifted position behind him, raised hands nudging against Chase's side.

His little finger reached out, and pulled.

Frost took in a breath, about to issue the order to fire—

Starkman flicked one of the flash grenades from Chase's belt, the pin still hanging from his finger. They clapped their hands over their ears as the dark metal cylinder arced to the floor behind them—

The clank as the grenade hit stone drew the attention of all Frost's men, eyes involuntarily darting to it—

The dazzling flash of igniting aluminum powder and potassium perchlorate was followed a millisecond later by a deafening bang as the grenade exploded, hitting the senses of anyone looking at it like a blow to the head. Even though the blast was only a fraction of the explosive force of a lethal grenade, it was still strong enough to knock the two nearest guards off their feet.

"*Go!*" yelled Chase, opening his eyes.

Years of training and experience told him everything he needed to know in a split second. The men circling the prisoners, including Frost, had been caught off guard by the grenade and were briefly blinded and disoriented. But the rest of Frost's men, farther away, were less affected. And they were already reacting.

He drove a fist into the face of the nearest guard, feeling his nose flatten under the crunching impact. Behind him, Starkman sprang to his feet to deliver a powerhouse blow to the throat of another man.

Chase snatched the MP-7 from the guard he'd just hit and swung it around. A swath of fire spat from the compact weapon's barrel. The unique 4.6-millimeter ammo of the MP-7 was specifically designed to penetrate body armor—at point-blank range, it ripped straight through everyone it hit.

He caught four of Frost's men with the burst. They fell, jets of blood spurting from the holes punched through their armor. The more distant men dived for cover, unable to shoot back without endangering their comrades.

Another crackle of gunfire erupted behind him as Starkman opened up at the guards on the other side of the circle. Three men dropped, the cordon broken.

Chase saw that a couple of the prisoners had managed to protect their ears and were lashing out at their captors. The others were as dazed as Frost's men.

There was nothing he could do for them. Individual survival was all that counted right now.

He spun to see Frost reeling, clutching his head. If he took out Frost, his plan would stop right here . . .

The young blond man, Rucker, sprung from seemingly nowhere and tackled Frost to the ground as Chase brought up his gun. He fired anyway, but the MP-7 clicked empty after just two shots. Holes exploded in Rucker's back. The bullets hadn't reached Frost.

And with their boss flat on the ground, the other men could open fire—

Beyond the mausoleum, Chase saw the Temple of

Poseidon. The third one he'd seen—and the first two had been identical inside.

He smashed an elbow into the face of one of the remaining guards and sprinted away. "Get to the temple!" he shouted.

No time to see who was following him, and no time to care either. Off to one side, near the golden wall, Schenk crouched by the bomb. But there was nothing Chase could do to stop him from restarting the timer—the guards were firing!

Bullets sizzling past him, he ran like hell for the Temple of Poseidon.

TWENTY-SIX

Chase sprinted around the wall circling the mausoleum, using it as cover—however temporary. It would take only seconds for Frost's men to flank it and cut him down.

Running footsteps sounded behind him. Starkman, two more of his men following farther back.

The light from the flashlight clipped to his chest danced crazily over the temple wall. The entrance should be dead ahead . . .

Dull impacts of metal on metal as bullets struck the golden wall. Someone screamed, and one of the sets of sprinting footsteps became thumps as a body tumbled to the ground.

He didn't look back. The entrance was ahead, a square of absolute darkness in the wall. Starkman was almost alongside him. The bastard always had been a good runner—

Frost's voice carried over the noise of the guns, yelling orders. "Kill them! *Kill them all!*"

Another frantic chatter of MP-7 fire, followed by screams. *They were slaughtering the prisoners!*

The black square expanded, jittering torchlight revealing the perspective lines of the tunnel inside the temple.

A bullet whipped past so close that he felt its heat, but he was in!

"Those *motherfuckers*!" Starkman gasped right behind him. "They killed my men!"

"Like you wouldn't have done the same to them!" Chase spat back. The first corner was just ahead—

Orange light lit the tunnel, a lethal strobing as their pursuers reached the entrance and fired wildly into it. The trailing member of Starkman's team took the full force of the bullets, his shadow thrashing wildly on the wall in front of Chase.

The corner—

Chase dived around it, Starkman following a step behind as more bullets smacked against the wall. Splinters of stone flew in all directions. Shielding his eyes from the stinging debris, Chase pulled a hand grenade from his webbing and yanked out the pin, the metal spoon pinging free.

He silently counted to three, then tossed the grenade around the corner at the approaching footsteps.

Boom!

Shrapnel filled the air like a swarm of enraged bees as Chase threw himself flat on the ground, dragging Starkman with him. The thunder of the explosion died away. The running footsteps had ceased.

Starkman sat up, recovering his MP-7. "Thanks."

"Don't thank me yet," Chase growled. "I haven't decided if I'm going to let you live."

"I've got the gun," Starkman pointed out.

"And *I'm* the only one who knows how to get out of this temple. Come on!" Chase stood, pulling Starkman to his feet. "We've got five minutes before this entire place gets blown to buggery!"

"The bomb's set!" said Schenk. "I disabled the controls— there's no way to stop it!"

"If you want to stay alive, start running!" Frost yelled to Philby as he ran for the cavern entrance. With a gasp of fright, Philby raced after him.

vw

Down the tunnel, around the corners . . . and into the chamber containing the Challenge of Strength. The wooden handles above the stone bench had long since crumbled to dust, but . . .

"Shit," snapped Chase, seeing that the barbed vertical bars, though gnarled with corrosion, still obstructed the passageway just as they had in Brazil. "I thought they'd have rusted away by now!"

"What are they?" asked Starkman.

"A pain in the arse!" He took his last grenade and moved to the wall by the narrow passage. "Hang on!"

The grenade clacked along the stone floor, exploding halfway down the passage. The blast ripped the corroded metal bars to pieces and filled the air with a blizzard of scabbed metal flakes.

Chase looked along the passage. Only a few of the bars were still intact. "Okay! Follow me down there, on three, as fast as you can!"

"What happens if I don't?"

"You go splat! One, two, *three*!"

Chase rushed down the passage, weaving between the stubs of the poles. A misstep could drive one of the rusty spears deep into his leg—although tetanus was the least of the threats to his life right now. "Get ready for the—"

Clunk!

The stone slab under his foot moved.

At least part of the ancient mechanism was still intact. With a rasping groan the ceiling blocks started to descend, dust raining through the gaps between them.

"What the fuck is this?" Starkman shrieked.

"Booby trap! We've got to get to the end before we get squashed!"

He ducked to avoid the stalactite-like remains of a pole, unclipping the light from his body armor. With no one on the bench to slow its progress, the ceiling was descending far quicker than in Brazil. But he could move faster.

The end of the passage was only feet away, but the last two bars were still intact, the gap between them narrow enough for the barbs to snag him.

He kicked, driving the heel of his boot against the nearest pole. It split in two, the top half plunging from its hole in the ceiling and slashing his leg.

But there wasn't time for pain—the ceiling was still descending.

He cleared the last pole, sweeping the flashlight beam around as he tried to find the lever or switch or whatever the hell he was supposed to pull—

"Chase!" Starkman cried behind him. "Help!"

Chase looked back. Starkman, taller than him, had been forced into a crouch as the stones dropped—and his empty holster had snagged on one of the broken poles.

But if Chase went back to pull him free, the ceiling would crush them both within seconds.

"Eddie!"

Chase ignored him, hurriedly searching the wall—

There! A dark recess in the stone.

He thrust his fist into the square opening, fingers outstretched.

Nothing but dry, broken splinters.

The ceiling pushed down, forcing him to his knees. In a few more seconds, the last block would reach the hole in the wall and crush his arm, and then the rest of him . . .

The mechanism had to be made of something stronger than wood, or it would have decayed—

Chase forced his arm deeper into the hole, fingers clawing.

Wooden fragments, cold stone . . . *metal*!

The stub of some lever, part of a switch—it didn't matter. He clamped his hand around it as tightly as he could, and pulled—

It moved!

It was only the slightest shift, but it was enough. Something inside the wall tripped with a hollow clunk—and the ceiling stopped.

Dust cascading all around him, Chase withdrew his hand from the hole to find that his palm was bleeding. The metal stub's edges were as sharp as the rusted poles.

He turned the flashlight, looking for the spot where the exit had been in the Brazilian temple. A new crack appeared between two of the blocks. He shoved a foot against the stone. It moved.

"Little help?" said a quiet voice.

Starkman was hunched in an extremely uncomfortable position, twisted around the broken spike. The ceiling was less than three feet above the floor. Whatever machinery had retracted the stone blocks in Brazil was obviously out of action here.

Chase extended his uninjured hand to Starkman, then leaned back and pulled. For a few seconds it seemed as though Starkman was trapped—then the pole gave way with a grinding snap, pitching the American onto his front.

"Thanks," he said, crawling forward. Chase kicked the hinged block aside.

"There's still two more of these to go," he warned, crawling through the hole and standing up in the next passage.

Starkman followed quickly. "How long have we got?"

"Three and a half minutes! Come on!"

"Is that long enough?" Starkman asked, running after him.

"It'll have to be."

The passage followed the same route that he remembered from Brazil. So far, so good—there was still a chance of survival.

A small one, but . . .

The echo of their footsteps changed, the tunnel opening out ahead. The Challenge of Skill.

Chase swept his light around the chamber. No caimans or piranhas here—in fact, there was no water at all, the stone pool completely dry. All that remained in the bottom of the nine-foot-deep channel was a scabrous, discolored residue of algae.

He looked to his right. The exit was there, but the bridge wasn't. Not intact, anyway. It had rotted away and collapsed, its remains scattered across the pool like a broken skeleton.

"We've got to get over there," he said, pointing at the exit and jumping down into the channel.

"How long?"

"Two and a bit minutes!"

They ran to the remnants of the bridge. Chase looked at the top of the wall. He might be able to jump and grab the edge, but it would be tough to keep his grip while climbing up.

"Give me a leg up!" Starkman said.

"Or you could give *me* a leg up," Chase countered.

"You don't trust me?"

"Fuck, no!"

"Fair enough, but you know the way out and I don't!"

"Good point," said Chase, bending down and clasping his hands together for Starkman to use as a foothold. The American scaled the wall and disappeared over the top.

For a horrible moment Chase thought he wasn't coming back, then Starkman stretched his arms down the wall. Another few seconds, and Chase had pulled himself up.

"Thought I was gonna disappear, huh?" Starkman said as he stood.

"Wouldn't be the first time, would it?" Chase looked at his watch. Two minutes. "Shit! Run!"

They sprinted down the tunnel. Next stop, the Challenge of Mind, but at least he knew how to find the back door.

He rushed into the chamber and got his bearings. "There's a secret switch in the wall," he began, hurrying to the corner—

To find nothing but blank stone.

No hole. No switch.

No back door.

"Shit!" He darted the flashlight beam along the base of the wall, hunting for another little nook, some sign that the builders of this temple had varied the design.

Nothing!

"What is it?" Starkman demanded.

"It's not here! There's no fucking back door!" He looked back at the stone door blocking the exit, at the symbols carved into the wall above it.

The trough of lead balls was there, as was the metal

scale, and the spiked grid suspended from the ceiling, ready to plunge and impale anyone beneath it if the wrong answer was given.

The answer . . .

Chase frowned, desperately trying to recall the memory. Nina had *told* him the answer after figuring out how the numbers worked. What was it, what *was* it?

Forty-two—

No, that was the fucking *Hitchhiker's Guide*!

Forty!

"We need to put forty of those balls in there!" he said, pointing to the scale as he scooped up a handful of the heavy pellets. "Two lots of ten each! Fast!"

Starkman obeyed. "What if we fuck up the count?"

"We die!" Chase counted ten of the pellets and dropped them into the cup before grabbing another handful.

Starkman did the same as Chase counted off another ten. Twenty, thirty . . .

Forty!

He grabbed the lever, paused for a fraction of a second to hope that Nina's math had been correct, then pulled it—

Clink.

The stone door moved slightly as the catch was released.

"I *love* brainy women!" Chase whooped. "Give me a hand!" They forced the door open.

Starkman was right behind him as they entered the last passage. "Now just *run like fuck*!" Chase yelled.

He couldn't even spare a moment to check his watch, but he knew they were almost down to their last thirty seconds.

Into the main chamber of the temple, gold and orichalcum glittering all around them. But none of it mattered except the huge statue of Poseidon at the far end, and the flight of stairs behind it.

He hoped that removing the hidden switch in the last challenge was the only change the architects had made.

"Up here!" he gasped, taking the steps three at a time. The muscles in his legs burned, sweat stinging the deep cut in his calf, but he couldn't stop now. "Back of the room, there should be a shaft!"

"*Should* be?" panted Starkman.

"If it's not, sue me!" They reached the top of the stairs, the riches of the altar room shining around them, but the only thing of value to Chase was the shaft—

w

The bomb exploded.

The fuel-air explosion swept through the cavern with earth-shattering force. Temples fell, palaces were smashed as the shockwave expanded. And behind it came a swelling fireball, a fury that seared and melted everything it touched.

Even the ancient walls of the Temple of Poscidon were unable to withstand the full force of modern weaponry. Blocks weighing tons were pulverized in the blink of an eye.

The cavern itself succumbed to the devastation just as quickly. A million tons of stone plunged downwards as the ceiling collapsed, obliterating the citadel.

w

Chase could hear the shockwave approaching like an express train, a wind rushing through the altar room ahead of the blast itself.

The "priest hole" was just feet away—

He dived into it. There was no time to worry if it was

blocked. Because if it was, he would be dead either way in a few seconds.

Unlike the vertical shaft in Atlantis, this one was slanted, a steep slope of at least sixty degrees. Starkman was right behind him as he slid down it.

The wind rose to a gale . . .

w

The helicopter pilots had received a garbled radio message to prepare their aircraft for a rapid takeoff. Now, Nina and Kari watched in horror as Frost—and only about half his men—charged out of the cave and raced through the snow towards the choppers.

"Oh my God!" Kari cried as Frost and Schenk jumped into the cabin. Outside, two of his men practically threw Philby into the second helicopter. "What happened?"

"Go! *Go!*" Frost yelled at the pilot. "Qobras got loose, started the timer again! Couldn't stop it!"

"Where's Eddie?" Nina shouted.

"He's dead! They shot him!"

Her breath stuck in her throat. "What? *No!*" Kari looked shocked.

"Faster! The bomb's going to—"

A colossal jet of smoke and dust and rubble erupted from the cave entrance with an unbelievably deep thump like the pounding of a mile-wide drum. Nina felt the detonation in her chest cavity.

The pilot threw the ascending helicopter sharply sideways to get out of the path of the avalanche charging towards it. An avalanche not of snow, but of stones, loose rocks knocked free by the explosive pulse, sweeping others away as they cascaded down the cliff.

The second helicopter followed suit. Flying stones pounded its hull like hail as the avalanche smashed down, causing a huge chunk of rock to shear away from the side of the mountain, the ledge disintegrating in an enormous cloud of dust.

The Path of the Moon was gone forever, the road to the last outpost of Atlantis swept away.

Nina pressed her hands against the helicopter's window as she watched the destruction below. Other rock slides tumbled down the mountain, the Golden Peak of Tibetan legend shaken to its core.

And everything within . . . lost.

"Eddie . . ." she whispered. Losing him once had been bad enough. Twice was almost too much to bear. Her eyes filled with tears.

w

Chase screamed as the blast wave ripped past, dust and grit and fragmented stone scouring his exposed skin. The noise was unimaginable, a roaring thunder shaking every bone, every organ in his body as he was swept helplessly down the shaft.

Light in the tunnel, a rising brightness . . .

Not daylight ahead, but fire behind, the burning fuel-air mix superheating as the collapsing cave compressed it and drove it after them.

And all he could do was skid down the slope towards the darkness ahead, while the glow from behind went from red to orange to yellow as the fire rushed after him—

A rectangle of daylight suddenly burst open before him, the snow covering the exit blown away. Chase had no time to reflect on his luck. Instead he acted entirely on reflex as he shot out of the end of the shaft onto a snow-covered pile of scree, throwing himself sideways to avoid the tongue of flame.

Snow flashed to steam as a fireball erupted from the

shaft behind him. He hit the ground hard, the layer of snow doing little to cushion the impact as he slammed against the rock beneath.

But there wasn't even time to feel the pain, because a hissing rattle from above warned him that a wave of loose stones was careening down the mountainside—

He rolled and flattened himself against the rock face, praying that the vestigial overhang was large enough to deflect the falling stones over him rather than crushing him flat.

Rocks ranging in size from a clenched fist to a man's torso blew apart like grenades above him. Chase shielded his head as the rest of him was pounded by flying fragments. He yelled, barely hearing his own voice over the noise of colliding stones.

Eventually the tumult died down. Painfully Chase forced himself onto his knees, chunks of debris clattering off him, and took in his surroundings.

The slight lip on the rock face *had* saved him—less than a foot away was a boulder, split cleanly in two by the impact, which would have crushed his skull like a watermelon had it landed on him. Beyond that was a random mass of broken dark stone. Through the dust, the snowy peaks of the Himalayas stretched into the distance.

Looking down, he saw he was on a ledge overlooking a wide valley. The slope seemed shallow enough to descend without climbing gear.

Which was lucky, because the sum total of his equipment now amounted to whatever he had in his pockets. He'd even lost his flashlight.

An odd, out-of-place smell reached him: steam. Misty swirls where the fire had evaporated the snow coiled past, carried on the breeze. He looked around, and saw Starkman partly buried under lumps of stone.

He ran to him. "Jason! Come on, stay with me," he said as he threw the larger pieces aside. "Can you hear me?"

"Eddie?" Starkman's voice was dazed. "Is that you?"

"Yeah, it's me. Are you hurt? Can you move?"

"I dunno, let me . . . ow, shit!"

"What?" Chase asked. "What is it?" If Starkman were seriously injured, there was practically nothing he could do to get him off the mountain.

"I landed on my keys . . ."

Chase stared at him, then started to laugh. "Oh, you bastard, you funny fucker," he finally spluttered. Starkman joined in, wheezing. "Come on, get your lazy American arse off the ground."

Starkman pushed himself upright. His eyepatch had been torn off, exposing a sunken eye socket behind the discolored, closed lid. "Son of a bitch," he groaned. "That hurts . . ."

Chase looked up at the mountain. Smoke and dust drifted from its flanks. "Well, your boss got what he wanted," he sighed. "The place's been blown to buggery—nobody'll ever get anything out of there again."

"Yeah, but your boss got what *he* wanted too," Starkman reminded him.

"He stopped being my boss the second he tried to kill me," Chase said coldly. "Think I'll have to have words with the bastard about that."

"You never did take betrayal very well, did you?" said Starkman pointedly.

Chase regarded him silently for a long moment. "Not really."

"Still not the forgiving type?"

"No. But," he added, "there's some things I can *forget* a bit more easily than others. Temporarily."

Starkman's good eye watched him warily. "I never touched her, Eddie. Whatever she may have told you, I never screwed around with your wife. I'd never do that to a friend."

"You know, Jason," said Chase, holding out his hand, "I actually believe you."

"You offering a truce, Eddie?"

"For now." Starkman took his hand; Chase pulled him up. "I think we both want the same thing—to get that bastard Frost for what he's done. And I've got to rescue Nina."

"You stopped being paid to protect her at the same time Frost stopped being your boss."

"Money stopped being the reason I was protecting her a while ago," Chase told him, getting a raised eyebrow in response.

They both looked around at a new noise. Early morning light glinting from their windows, Frost's helicopters rounded the mountain, rotor noise booming down the valley as they sped into the distance. Chase stared after them, then turned back to Starkman, holding out his hand again. "Even with Qobras dead, do you still have access to the Brotherhood's resources?"

"Some of them," replied Starkman. "What do you have in mind?"

"I fancy a trip to Norway. You interested?"

"Definitely." They shook hands. "Fight to the end, Eddie?"

"Fight to the end."

Starkman looked around. "Just one slight problem— we're stuck in the Himalayas with no transport and no equipment."

Chase managed a half-smile. "Good thing I looked at a map before coming here." He pointed down the valley. "If you're up for a yomp, there's a village that way. We should be able to reach it by tonight." The half-smile became a full one. "I know a girl there . . ."

TWENTY-SEVEN
Norway

The stark beauty of Ravnsfjord stretched out below her as the Gulfstream descended, but Nina barely noticed it.

Her mind was elsewhere, thinking back over the events of the past days. Despite all Kari's efforts to help, she still felt a sadness, an underlying core of loss. The resurgent grief she'd felt on seeing the bodies of her parents, Chase's death . . . and the destruction of Atlantis itself, every last trace of the civilization finally wiped out by Qobras. All buried, irretrievable, the search that had defined her existence brought to an abrupt end.

In a way, her life as she had known it was over. Everything in her world had changed.

"Are you all right?" Kari asked.

"Hmm? Yes, I'm fine. Why?"

"You looked a little . . . distant."

"Did I?" Nina considered it. "I suppose I did. I was just thinking."

"About what?"

"About how I found what I'd been looking for all these years, I found Atlantis . . . but now it's gone. Everything's different. And I don't . . . I don't know what I'm going to do now."

Kari smiled. "What you're going to do, Dr. Nina Wilde, is take your place with us. You're one of us, and we always look after our own."

"I haven't really thanked you for that. For everything you've done."

"You don't need to thank me. And you haven't lost Atlantis."

"How so?"

"Because now we can build a *new* Atlantis. We don't have to look to the past anymore, because we'll be creating the future."

Nina cocked an eyebrow. "Just out of interest, when are you going to tell me exactly *how* you're going to be creating this future? I still don't see how a sample of eleven-thousand-year-old DNA can change the world."

"It will, trust me." Kari leaned closer. "I think you're ready."

"Ready for what?"

"It's time I showed you what we're going to do. How we're going to remake the world."

The plane made its final turn, dropping towards the long runway.

w

Chase gave Starkman a dubious look. "If you had this operation planned all along, why didn't you just bloody *do* it and save everyone a lot of trouble?"

"We didn't know for sure what Frost was doing. And Giovanni didn't want to risk an attack unless it became absolutely necessary," Starkman explained. "It would have exposed the Brotherhood—there would have been no way to keep the organization secret anymore."

"I think the time for sneaking about's over." Chase rose from his seat and walked across the aircraft's hold to peer out of a porthole. The plane, a twin-prop C-123

Provider cargo aircraft, had crossed the Norwegian coast a few minutes earlier, and was now cruising north over the snow-streaked landscape.

They would soon be making a steep descent, however.

Chase looked back at the other passengers in the hold. Twelve of Qobras's—now Starkman's—men, all members of the Brotherhood, assembled following the four days it took the two survivors of the Golden Peak to return to Europe.

He just hoped twelve men was enough.

ᴡᴡ

"Far," said Kari, entering Frost's office above the biolab with Nina at her side. Frost was at his desk, the vista of Ravnsfjord spread out behind him through the windows. "I think it's time. Nina's ready."

Frost's expression suggested to Nina that he wasn't himself sure, but he said nothing.

"What is it you want to tell me?" she asked. "What's the big secret? Kari's been very mysterious about it."

"The big secret, Dr. Wilde . . ." Frost began. Kari gave him a look. "I mean, *Nina*. If that's all right with you?"

"Fine by me," Nina said with a grin.

Frost smiled back, then stood up. "The big secret, as you say, is that . . . well, today we are going to change the world. Forever."

"That's quite a big challenge."

"Indeed it is. But it's a challenge I have been working on all my life—and thanks to you, it can now be accomplished. Your discovery of Atlantis made it possible."

"But everything was destroyed," said Nina. "Maybe we can recover some relics from under the sediment at Atlantis itself, but all the intact structures we found, all the artifacts they contained . . . they're gone."

"That doesn't matter," Frost said.

"It doesn't? But . . ."

"The DNA samples I recovered from the bodies of the last king and queen are worth more than any amount of gold or orichalcum. *They* are what will change the world. *Save* the world, even."

"How?" Nina asked. "Are you using them to create some sort of vaccine or something?"

"Something," replied Frost, smiling again, this time with an air of mystery. "Come with me and I'll show you." He rounded his desk, and was about to join Nina and Kari when his intercom beeped. Clearly irritated at the interruption, he pushed a button to answer the call. "What is it?"

"Sir," said Schenk's voice from the speaker, "the control tower just informed me that a plane has requested permission for an emergency landing. They have engine trouble, and can't make it to Bergen."

"Where are they now?"

"About ten minutes out, coming from the south."

Frost's lips tightened. "Very well, give them permission to land. But . . . watch them."

"Yes, sir." Schenk closed the line.

"Sorry about that," said Frost, joining Nina and Kari.

"No problem," Nina told him. "I mean, if you're going to save the entire world, you might as well start with just one plane, right?"

"Indeed." Frost smiled. "Come, follow me. I'll show you how."

w

"They've given us emergency landing permission," Starkman told Chase over the noise of the engines. "Ten minutes."

"Any problems?" asked Chase.

"Norwegian ATC keeps wanting to know why they don't have our flight plan. The pilot's stalling them, but I think they're getting suspicious."

"So long as they don't get suspicious enough to send fighters after us, it won't matter." Chase turned to the other men in the cabin. "All right! Ten minutes, lads! Better get ready to jump!"

w

Frost led the two women into the containment area, passing through another airlock and proceeding deeper into the underground facility.

"In here," he said. The door at the end of the corridor was solid steel with no view of the room beyond, unlike the transparent aluminum entrances to the other labs. The logo of a trident was painted on the metal. He pushed his thumb against a biometric reader beside it. The heavy door slid open. "Please, you first."

Nina wasn't sure what she was looking at as she entered. A few pieces of scientific equipment she vaguely recognized, but most of the gleaming hardware was a mystery. The banks of supercomputers at the rear of the large lab were among those that were easy to identify, towering blue cabinets hooked up to liquid cooling systems. In one corner of the lab was an isolation chamber; it had windows, but they were blacked out.

"This," began Frost with an air of theatricality, "is where my life's ambition has finally been fulfilled. Everything else in my business empire merely supports what has been done in this room. For thirty years I have been using the resources of the Frost Foundation to search the entire world, to identify the genetic lineage of every group of people on the planet."

"Looking for the Atlantean gene?" Nina asked.

"Precisely. Only about one percent of the world's

population carries what I would consider to be a 'pure' form of the genome—we are members of that one percent."

"One percent of the world . . . that's, what, sixty-five million people?"

"Equivalent to the population of the United Kingdom, yes. But they are spread out all across the planet, in every ethnic group. Then there are those who have an *impure* form of the genetic markers—either from dilution over time due to interbreeding with those who do not possess it, or from natural mutation. These people make up around fifteen percent of the population."

"Nine hundred and seventy-five million," Nina said immediately.

Frost smiled. "You're definitely one of us. One of the traits of the Atlantean genome is an innate skill with logical systems like mathematics."

"Considering what you've found out," added Kari, "we now think it's almost certain that the descendants of the ancient Atlanteans were entirely responsible for the development of the numerical and linguistic systems all around the world."

"Even after the sinking of Atlantis itself, the Atlantean survivors were still the driving force in human civilization," said Frost. "They were the leaders, the inventors, the discoverers. They devised the systems that allowed humanity to thrive and expand—language, agriculture, medicine. But ironically . . ." his expression darkened, "in doing so, they sowed the seeds of their own subjugation. Before they brought civilization to the world, the survival of the human race was entirely in the hands of natural selection. Those who were weak perished. But by reducing the threat from external forces of nature, the Atlanteans made it possible for the weak to *thrive*."

"I don't know if I'd put it quite like that . . ." Nina began.

"I would," Frost insisted. "And the process has accelerated out of control over the last fifty years. Within four years, the world's population is predicted to reach seven billion. Seven *billion* people. That is an unsustainable figure. And eighty-four percent of them do *not* possess the Atlantean genome. That means more than four-fifths of the entire population of the world is useless."

Nina was startled by the bluntness of his words. "What do you mean, useless?"

"I mean exactly that. All those billions provide nothing of value to humanity. They don't innovate, or create, or even *think*. They just *exist*, breeding and consuming."

"How can you *say* that?" Nina protested. "That's—that's just . . ."

"Nina," said Frost, leaning closer, "just look at your own country. You can't have failed to see it. America is dominated by the indolent, the stupid, the wilfully ignorant masses who do nothing but *consume*. Democracy does nothing but perpetuate the system, because it allows the masses to take the path of least resistance and continue to avoid work, avoid *thought*, and achieve nothing. And those who should be leading them out of that state have become corrupted by greed, wanting to do nothing more than exploit them—for *money*!" He sounded almost disgusted by the word. "That is not the role of a leader! The Atlanteans knew that for society to advance, the people had to be *led*, not left to indulge their gluttony."

"But the Atlanteans fell into the same trap," Nina reminded him. "Remember *Critias*? 'They appeared glorious and blessed at the very time when they were full of avarice and unrighteous power.' And the gods destroyed them for it."

"A mistake that will not be repeated."

"It'll *always* be repeated! Atlantean or not, everybody's still *human*. 'The human nature got the upper hand,' as Plato put it."

"We will learn from the past."

"How?" Nina demanded. "You're going to do—what? Change the world with a DNA sample from an eleven-thousand-year-old corpse?"

"That is *exactly* what we're going to do!" said Frost. He gestured at the supercomputers. "Until now, these machines have been working on simulations, coming up with a million, a *billion* variations of the same thing. But without a sample of pure, untainted Atlantean DNA to use as a base, there was no way to know which was the right one. Even *our* DNA has been changed by time to some degree, and we are the closest there is in the modern world to pure-blooded Atlanteans. But now . . ." He looked at the black-windowed chamber. "Now, I know exactly what those changes are. And I have been able to take them into account."

"Into account for *what*?" asked Nina.

"For a way to restore the world to how it used to be—how it should always have been. A world where the Atlanteans retake their place as the rightful rulers of humanity, to lead them to new heights without being held back by the useless, unproductive masses." He walked across the lab, Kari following. Nina went with them almost against her will, unable to take in what Frost was saying. Had he gone mad? He sounded nearly as crazy as Qobras!

"This," said Frost, indicating a glass-sided cabinet with thick rubber seals, "is what the discovery of the true Atlantean DNA has finally let me create. It was one of the variants the computers had simulated—but until now there was no way to know if it was the right one."

Nina peered into the cabinet. Inside was a line of glass and steel cylinders filled with a colorless liquid.

She was certain it wasn't water.

"What are they?" she asked uneasily.

"That," Frost told her, "is what I call *Trident*. Poseidon's most powerful weapon. Each of those cylinders holds in suspension a genetically engineered virus."

Nina jumped back from the glass. "*What?*"

"It's perfectly safe," Kari assured her. "At least to us."

"What do you mean, to us?"

"We are immune," said Frost, "or rather, the virus is harmless to us. It's been engineered so that it cannot attack the unique genetic sequence contained in Atlantean DNA, even if the sequence has been mutated. But to anyone who does not possess that DNA sequence . . . it is one hundred percent lethal."

Nina felt as though the air was being drawn out of the room. "Oh my God," she gasped. "Are you *insane*? No, don't answer that—you *are* insane!"

"No, Nina, please listen," implored Kari. "I know this is hard for you to accept, but deep down, if you look past all your social programming, you *know* we're right. The world is a mess, and it's getting worse—the only way to stop it from passing the point of no return is for us to restore the rule of the Atlantean elite."

"Thinking that mass murder is a bad thing is *not* social programming!" Nina spat. "Are you seriously telling me you're planning to wipe out eighty-four percent of the human race? That's almost five and a half *billion* people!"

"It's necessary," said Frost. "If we don't do it, then humanity will be choked by its own waste. The worthless will outnumber us by hundreds to one, and consume every available resource until they are all gone. This way, those fit to rule will be able to rebuild the world as it should always have been. The Frost Foundation will unite the survivors worldwide."

Nina slowly backed away. "With you in charge, huh? You are out of your fucking mind. You're talking about *people*, not *waste*! When were you planning to start your little apocalypse?"

Frost gave her a grim smile. "I'm not *planning* anything, Dr. Wilde. I am already *doing* it."

The airless sensation returned. "What?"

"There's a plane on the runway across the fjord, an Airbus A380 freighter. It will take off within fifteen minutes, flying first to Paris, then on to Washington. While it is in flight, it will disperse the Trident virus into the air over Europe, then into the North Atlantic jetstream, and finally over the eastern seaboard of the United States. Our projections show that within a month, the virus will have been carried to every populated part of the planet. Everybody who does not carry the Atlantean genome will be infected."

"And then what?" Nina whispered.

"And then . . ." Frost went over to the chamber, operating a control panel. The black windows depolarized, turning transparent. "This happens."

Barely daring to look, Nina slowly stepped forward. The interior of the chamber came into view. An antiseptic white cell, bare except for a stainless-steel toilet bowl and a low bunk, on which lay . . .

She clapped her hands over her mouth in horror. "Jonathan . . ."

Philby stared sightlessly up at the ceiling, the whites of his eyes stained a bloody red by ruptured blood vessels. His skin was clammy, a deathly gray, chest barely moving with each labored breath.

"He was infected yesterday," Frost said in a chillingly matter-of-fact tone. "The Trident virus attacks the autonomic nervous system, shutting down the organs. If it runs its course as the simulations predicted, he'll be dead within six hours."

"Oh my God . . ." Nina turned away, sickened. "You can't let him die like that. Please, you made your point—give him the antidote, the vaccine, whatever he needs."

"There *is* no vaccine," Frost said. "That would defeat its purpose. Once the virus is released, it will do what it was created to do. The only cure is death."

"Nina," said Kari softly, "he got exactly what he deserved. He betrayed us—he betrayed *you*. He sold out your parents to Qobras. And he was going to do the same thing to you. He wasn't your friend—the only reason he looked out for you was out of guilt."

"Nobody deserves that," Nina replied. Kari reached up to put a hand on her shoulder, but she shrugged it off angrily. "Don't touch me."

"Nina . . ."

She whirled to face them, filled with a sudden rage. "Did you think I'd go along with this . . . this *genocide*? My God! This is insane! This would be the biggest act of . . . of *evil* in human history! What kind of person do you think I am?"

"You're one of us," Kari insisted.

"No! I'm *nothing* like you! I'm not going to be a part of this!"

"That's unfortunate," Frost stated coldly. "Because this is a situation where either you are with us . . . or you are opposed to us."

"You're goddamn *right* I'm opposed to you!"

"Then you'll die." Frost reached into his jacket.

Time dropped into slow motion as Nina watched him pull out a sleek silver gun. The glinting barrel came around, the black hole of its muzzle pointing at her chest. She wanted to turn and run, but shock and disbelief conspired to stop her, paralyzing her legs. She saw the tendons in the back of his hand tighten, finger about to pull the trigger—

"Far! *No!*"

Kari shoved Frost's arm just as he fired. The bullet whipped past Nina, hitting the wall behind her. She tried to scream, but only a choked gasp emerged.

Frost's expression was one of barely contained fury as Kari desperately pleaded with him in Norwegian. Then his anger subsided. Slightly. "My daughter just saved your life, Dr. Wilde," he said. "For now."

"Nina, please," Kari said, talking quickly, "I know you're overwhelmed by all this, but *please* listen to me. I know you, I know that you're one of us, that you think like we do. Don't you see? You can have anything, *everything* if you join us. Please, just think about it rationally."

"Rationally?" Nina gasped. "You're planning to exterminate most of the human race, and you're asking me to be *rational* about it?"

"This is useless," said Frost. "I knew she would respond this way when she refused to kill Qobras. She's been too indoctrinated by her society. She'll never come around."

"She *will*," Kari insisted, a hint of desperation entering her voice. "I know she will!"

"Very well," he said at last. "She has until the first release of the virus. If she still refuses to change her mind . . . then *you* will kill her."

Kari gasped. "No, Far, I can't . . ."

"Yes." Frost's face was stern. "You *will*. Do you understand me, Kari?"

She bowed her head. "Yes, Far."

"Good. Then take her to the plane."

Kari looked up in confusion. "The plane?"

"The pilot can give you a countdown to the first release of the virus. I assume you want to allow her every possible second to make the right choice?" Kari nodded. "Then you'll both know exactly how long she has. If she refuses to change her mind, kill her and dispose of the body over the sea."

Still keeping his gun trained on Nina, he went to a telephone and punched in a number. "Security, this is Frost. Have two men come to the Trident lab and accompany my daughter and Dr. Wilde to the airfield. Dr. Wilde is under arrest—I want her handcuffed. If she attempts to escape, kill her." He glanced over at Kari. "Even if my daughter tells you not to. You have your orders." He replaced the receiver.

"Am I supposed to be grateful to you for that?" Nina snarled.

"Be grateful to Kari. Be *very* grateful. She's the only reason you're still alive."

The door slid open, two uniformed guards entering, hands on their guns. Nina offered no resistance beyond a hate-filled glare as her wrists were fastened behind her back.

"Get off in Paris and use one of the company jets to come home," Frost told Kari as they left. "Dr. Wilde?"

"What?" she snapped.

"I hope you have enough sense to be on that return flight with Kari."

Nina said nothing as the door clanged shut behind her.

w

Chase looked out of the cockpit window. Ravnsfjord lay ahead.

He hurried to the hold. "One last thing!" he said to Starkman as he hooked his parachute release line onto the ceiling rail. "Some of these people are civvies. Just 'cause they work for Frost doesn't automatically make them targets—only shoot at anyone who's shooting at you!"

"Always were a do-gooder, weren't you, Eddie?" Starkman replied.

"I just don't like killing anyone who doesn't deserve it."

"What if we run into the company lawyers?"

"That's tempting . . . but still no! Okay, everyone hook up!"

Chase pushed the button to lower the Provider's rear ramp. The plane was descending rapidly. Freezing wind blasted in with the near-deafening rasp of the plane's engines. The office buildings passed below; coming up fast was the Frosts' house, overlooking everything from the top of the crag, and beyond it the biolab.

The plane roared barely a hundred feet over the house, then the ground dropped away. The minimum altitude at which the parachutes would work was 250 feet, and the terrain between the house and the biolab was just far enough below . . .

"Jump!"

Chase threw himself out. The parachute exploded from its pack as the release line ripped free. At such a low altitude, if the chute didn't deploy perfectly he would smash into the ground before having a chance to do anything about it.

Grass and snow and rock rushed towards him, a car heading towards the bridge over the fjord—

Sudden deceleration hit him, the chute snapping open and yanking the harness tight around his chest.

He braced himself—

Whump!

It was a bruising landing, the parachute barely having enough time to slow him to a survivable speed. He ignored the shock of impact, shrugging off the parachute as he checked his surroundings. The other parachutists were dropping around him, hitting the ground hard. Chase hoped Starkman's men knew what they were doing. Anyone who was hurt in the landing was screwed—they didn't have the time or the manpower to carry wounded with them.

Having dropped its passengers, the C-123 made a sharp turn, pulling up to gain altitude as it rose over the fjord.

A line of smoke lanced out from the edge of the fjord, the trail of a Stinger antiaircraft missile as it homed in . . .

And *exploded*!

One wing blown off in a burning cloud of fuel, the Provider corkscrewed helplessly into the steep-sided valley, plowing into the rocky wall and bursting apart in a thunderous fireball.

"Holy shit!" Starkman yelled.

"Looks like we're walking home!" Chase shouted back. Now free of his parachute, he readied his weapon, a Heckler and Koch UMP-45 submachine gun. "Okay! Let's melt the Frost!"

TWENTY-EIGHT

Nina watched in horror from the Mercedes as the plane plunged into the side of the fjord and exploded. "Jesus!"

"Qobras's people—it has to be!" Kari shouted. "They're making a last stand!"

"Well, hoo-ray for them!" Nina twisted to look out of the rear window. The last of the parachutists were now on the ground. "I hope they blow the place to hell, and your father with it!"

Slap!

Nina reeled. Kari had *hit* her! The hot sting across her cheek wasn't so much painful as humiliating, but somehow that actually made it worse.

Kari issued orders as the Mercedes approached the bridge. "Call the security center and warn them that we have fourteen intruders heading for the biolab! And you," she added, turning to the driver, "get us to the plane, now!"

ᴡᴡ

"*Melt the Frost*?" Starkman said in disbelief as the team ran towards the biolab. "How long have you been waiting to say *that*?"

"Since Tibet," Chase admitted. He assessed the tactical situation. The open ground provided little cover—for Frost's men as well as for Starkman's. The buildings would give their opponents some protection, but it would be easy to outflank them.

The Stinger had been fired from the security building at the northwestern corner of the facility. If Frost's men had any other heavy weapons, that was where they would be.

"Jason! Six men, cover!" He made a chopping gesture towards the security block. Starkman nodded and passed on the order.

The team of six split off from the main group. Chase quickly advanced on the lab's entrance. The biolab didn't have many exits—aside from the main doors and the security entrance, the only other ways in or out were through fire escapes and the ramp leading to the underground garage. Which meant that the closest place any of Frost's forces could emerge was . . .

The dark glass doors of the main entrance flew open, uniformed guards rushing out. *Armed* guards, equipped with MP-7s. Armor-piercing rounds, like the ones Chase himself had used in Tibet.

"Hit 'em!" he shouted, diving to the ground and bringing up his UMP. Starkman and the other six men did the same. The front wall of the biolab erupted with fountains of dust as they raked the building with .45-caliber fire. The doors burst into black shards, blood spraying among the glass as the guards fell.

More MP-7 fire crackled off to Chase's left as another group of guards ran from the security block. They were better prepared than their late colleagues, and also had more cover, ducking behind the walls on either side of the steps.

Starkman's second team was about thirty yards distant from them, out in the open with the road still to cross. They had split into two groups of three, one group diving to the ground to give the other covering fire as they raced for the nearest building.

The security forces fired back, trying to catch the running men before they reached cover. One of the guards put his head too far above the wall and had a chunk of his skull blown away by a .45 round, gore sluicing through the air as he fell backwards.

But the others kept firing.

One of the running men fell, bloody wounds blossoming across his chest. His companions didn't even break their stride until they reached the building and flung themselves into cover.

The guards turned their fire on the men lying on the ground. Clods flew up into the air as bullets thudded into the earth. Chase saw a line of spraying dirt advancing on one man like a snake at its prey, but there was no way he could warn him.

Red blood spouted into the air among the churned-up soil.

The guards redirected their fire, trying to pin down the other men on the ground—

A pair of grenades arced through the air, tossed with precision by the team in the cover of the building. They exploded at head height over the steps and showered the guards with lethal shrapnel. Every window within thirty feet shattered under the double blast.

"Main doors!" yelled Chase, sprinting towards the entrance. Starkman and the others followed, spreading out to provide cover.

Chase reached the wrecked doors, flattening himself against one side and glancing into the building's interior. The horseshoe-shaped reception desk was unmanned, the guards staffing it now dead at his feet.

Starkman took up position on the other side of the doors. Chase moved into the lobby, backed up by another of the American's men. Beyond the desk was the entrance to the glass-roofed central corridor; to one side, stairs led up and down.

A door opened, and Chase snapped up his gun. A young blond woman emerged, freezing in fear as she saw him.

"Hi," said Chase, waving for Starkman to hold fire. "You speak English?"

The woman nodded, wide-eyed.

"Okay. Get out of the building. There's going to be a fire. Well, more of an explosion, actually, but . . ." He spotted a fire alarm on the wall nearby. "Anyone else in there?"

She nodded again, too frightened to speak.

"Okay, tell them to get out . . . and run like hell!" He smashed the glass covering the alarm with the stock of his UMP. Bells rang. Chase winced at the noise—it would make it harder to hear any approaching guards—but the faster the civilians were out of the building, the better.

Because in five minutes, there wasn't going to *be* a building.

He moved past the door—keeping his weapon aimed at the people running out, in case any of them were armed—and kicked open the next one. A security station. Empty.

But he knew there were more guards elsewhere in the building . . .

Starkman and the rest of his men clattered into the lobby as the civilians fled. "Set charges in there!" Chase shouted over the clamor of the fire bells, pointing at the door from which Frost's employees had come. "Make sure all the civvies get out first!"

"This is gonna get messy!" Starkman complained. People from the floor above were hurrying down the stairs. "If there's any guards mixed in with the staff—"

"Then *aim*! You Yanks do remember how to do that, don't you?" Chase shot Starkman a sarcastic smile before taking cover behind the desk, watching the stairs and the central corridor as the biolab employees rushed through the lobby. Scientists, technicians . . .

And *guards*! Shoving through the crowd, MP-7s coming up—

Chase hoped the civvies had the sense to keep their heads down. He fired a three-round burst, deliberately aiming high, before ducking. People screamed. MP-7 fire echoed through the lobby, the expensive marble top of the reception desk splintering as armor-piercing rounds ripped into it.

More gunfire, the deeper thudding of UMPs as Starkman and his men fired back. More screams, and the firing stopped. Chase peered over the desk, and was relieved to see that only the guards had been hit.

"You were right!" Starkman called. "That whole aiming thing really *does* work!"

Chase grinned, then gestured to the people on the stairs, directing them towards the doors. "Everybody out! Jason, get your guys to plant some more charges on the support columns in the garage—we can drop this whole place into the ground!"

"What about you?" asked Starkman.

Chase nodded at the central corridor. "Frost'll have the virus in the containment area—we need to collapse the hillside and make sure it stays in there!"

"Sounds good to me. I'll cover you. Aristides, Lime, with me—the rest of you set your charges in the basement, then get out!"

Chase checked the corridor. More people were running up it, trying to escape the building. "Come on!"

He ran into the corridor, Starkman and the others following. The men and women coming the other way reacted with predictable fear to the sight of four armed men in body armor charging towards them, and desperately tried to get out of their way, cowering by the walls.

"Get out of the building!" Chase roared. "Go!"

"We got company!" Starkman yelled, pointing down the corridor. Chase saw two uniformed men crouching behind the security post at the far end, taking aim—

He threw himself sideways as a spray of bullets flew down the corridor, cutting down one worker who had been trapped in the middle of the passage, paralyzed by his own fear and indecision.

"Shit!" Chase spat. The civilians were still scurrying helplessly across the corridor, blocking his aim, and the guards weren't bothered about casualties among the workers.

A bloody wound burst open in the shoulder of a woman a few yards from him, bright red spots staining her face as she fell.

No choice.

He raised his UMP and fired a burst at the security station, trying not to hit any of the panicking civilians. The guards ducked as bullets cracked around them.

"Cover fire!" shouted Chase. A man tried to run past him; he grabbed him and pointed at the injured woman. "Get her out of here!" Terrified, the man nodded, then dragged the woman along the corridor.

Chase fired another burst to keep the guards occupied, then rushed down the corridor, staying to one side to give Starkman a clear angle. He jumped over a man cringing in a doorway, the heavy doors of the first airlock not far ahead.

The gunfire behind him went from three guns to two, then one as the others reloaded. Frost's men would take that as an opportunity to pop up and start shooting back. Right on cue, one of the men sprang up from behind the counter, MP-7 at the ready—

Only to fly backwards against the wall in a spray of blood as Chase emptied his magazine into him.

Chase dived, the spent magazine ejected even before he hit the polished floor.

The second guard jumped up.

At least three seconds to reload . . .

The guard saw him and brought around his MP-7—

His head snapped back, a single shot from Starkman's UMP catching him in the forehead.

Chase looked back to see the other men jogging towards him. He reloaded his gun, then got up. "Nice shot."

"Yes, very nice," said another voice.

Chase whirled.

Frost!

He fired at the figure on the other side of the doors at the same moment as Starkman, their UMPs now on full auto and unleashing a savage burst of firepower at the glass.

Tink. Tink.

The flattened bullets fell harmlessly to the floor at the base of the door. The transparent aluminum armor wasn't even scuffed.

"Son of a bitch!" Starkman muttered.

Frost stepped forward. His voice emerged from a speaker below the thumbprint reader. "Mr. Chase. I have to admit, I'm surprised to see you."

"You owed me some back pay," said Chase, looking for a way to open the door. Maybe there was an override at the security station . . .

"Don't bother," said Frost. "This section of the lab is completely sealed. There's no way you can get in."

"Maybe we can't get in, but I'm gonna make goddamn sure you don't get *out*," Starkman told him. He opened one of the packs attached to his belt and took out the contents. "CL-20. Two *pounds* of it. We're gonna bring the place down on you just like you tried to do to us in Tibet."

Frost merely smirked. "I wish you luck." He turned his back on them and started to walk away.

"Frost!" Chase shouted. "Where's Nina?"

Frost paused, glancing back at him. "Dr. Wilde is with my daughter. Kari persuaded me to keep her alive—she hopes to convince her to see reason and join us before the virus is released."

"And when'll that be?"

"In however many minutes it takes their plane to reach thirty thousand feet." Chase and Starkman exchanged shocked looks. "Yes, it's already happening. You're too late, Mr. Starkman. Qobras failed to stop me, and so have you. You might want to reflect on that . . . before you die. Which no matter what happens will be sometime in the next twenty-four hours." He smirked again. "Good-bye, gentlemen." With that, he walked away. The second set of doors slammed decisively behind him.

Starkman angrily fired another burst at the door, which remained unscathed. "Mother*fucker*!"

"If there's one thing I hate," said Chase, "it's a smug bastard."

"You think he was lying? About the virus, I mean?"

"If the plane hasn't taken off yet, we still have a chance. If it has, we're fucked, and so's the rest of the world. Either way . . ." He took out his own CL-20. "We do what we came here to do—and blow this place to fuck."

w

The Mercedes stopped beneath the massive wing of the Airbus A380. The huge cargo plane was waiting on the runway apron outside its hangar, engines idling. Kari pushed Nina up the boarding steps, the two guards following.

The A380 had three decks; on an airliner model the middle floor they entered would have been the lower of the two passenger levels, but all three decks of the cavernous freighter version were designed for cargo containers. They entered the crew room. A door at the rear opened into the hold. Nina glanced through it. The windowless deck was about a third full.

Somewhere among the containers, she knew, was the virus, waiting to be released . . .

A steep flight of stairs led up to the top deck. Kari directed her up it. Nina expected to see another huge cargo space, but was slightly surprised to emerge in a luxurious cabin.

"My father installed a private office," Kari explained. She unfastened Nina's handcuffs. "Please, sit."

Nina reluctantly did so, looking around. Portholes lined each side of the cabin, and a door in the rear wall presumably opened into the upper hold. An L-shaped desk had a computer monitor and a pair of telephones built into it.

Kari sat facing her on a leather sofa. The two guards hadn't come up the stairs with them, staying in the lounge below. Nina wondered if she might be able to overpower Kari and flee the aircraft before it took off . . . but dismissed the idea even as it took form. She had no chance of beating Kari in a fight.

"I don't know what you think you're going to accomplish," Nina said. "If you think I'm going to happily go along with what you're doing . . ."

"I don't expect you to come around with a click of the fingers. I know the whole thing is hard for you to accept. But you *have* to accept it—it's going to happen."

"You are deluded! No, you're *insane*! Do you seriously think I want anything to do with you, ever again?"

Kari looked wounded. "Please don't be like that, Nina! Don't you understand? You're one of us. You're a true Atlantean, the very best of humanity! You *deserve* to be one of the rulers of the world!" She rose and came across the cabin. For a moment Nina thought she was going to hit her again, but instead she knelt down before her. "I don't *want* to kill you, I don't! Just say that you've changed your mind—you don't even have to be telling the truth! Once everything changes, then I know you'll come around, that you'll realize we were right. But you *have* to say it if you want to stay alive."

"You'd still kill me even though I'm one of the best of the best?" sneered Nina.

"I can't disobey my father. I won't." Kari tried to reach for Nina's hands, but she pulled them away. "Just one word, that's all I ask. Lie! Please, I don't care!"

"Not a chance," Nina told her.

The low noise of the engines rose in pitch. The lights flickered, then the A380 shook itself from its torpor, starting to move.

"The first batch of the virus will be released about fifteen minutes after takeoff," said Kari, going back to the sofa. "That's how long you have to change your mind. Nina, *please*. Don't make me kill you."

Nina turned away to stare through the starboard portholes at the landscape across the fjord, feeling lost.

w

Chase could hear intermittent gunfire from outside as he, Starkman and his companions ran for the exit. His gun was in his hands, but he wouldn't have time to aim it at anybody when he emerged. All that mattered now was getting as far from the biolab as possible.

They sprinted into the open. Chase saw the last of the civilians running away across open ground, a pair of white Jeep Grand Cherokees parked to block the road two hundred feet away. Taking cover behind them were a number of uniformed guards, a couple of bodies lying on the ground nearby. They were shooting at the two other surviving members of Starkman's team.

And across the fjord, he saw an aircraft slowly moving towards the runway, a gleaming A380 freighter.

The virus was on board—maybe there was still a chance to stop Frost's plan.

Nina was on board as well.

He didn't have time to think about it. The guards behind the Jeeps had seen them, and were shooting at the men running from the biolab. Chase fired back one-handed, knowing that the chances of hitting them while running were almost zero—but he only needed to keep them off-balance long enough to get clear of the building.

Lime crashed to the ground as a bullet ripped into his hip. Every ounce of Chase's training told him to go back and drag him to safety, but in this case there *was* no safety.

The CL-20 would detonate any second *now*—

w

One moment, Nina was looking numbly at the distant biolab buildings. The next, she jumped in her seat as the complex disintegrated, multiple explosions pulverizing it and sending tons of debris spinning hundreds of feet into the air. A torus of dust swept outwards like the shockwave of a nuclear bomb. "Jesus!"

Kari leapt up and ran to the portholes. "Oh my God!"

"That's one hell of a last stand," Nina said triumphantly. Qobras's men had succeeded!

Then it hit her. *It didn't make any difference.*

The virus was already out of the lab, on the plane. In fifteen minutes, it would be released. The Brotherhood had destroyed the wrong target!

w

Ears ringing, Chase staggered upright. He raised a hand to shield his eyes from the hailstone-sized pieces of debris still dropping from the sky and looked around.

Nobody was shooting at him anymore. Both Jeeps had been caught sidelong by the blast and flipped over, crushing the men behind them.

The biolab had been almost completely obliterated. What few sections remained were smashed beyond recognition, walls jagged and tilting like broken teeth. Bent and twisted steel girders protruded from the rubble.

Chase squinted through the drifting cloud of shattered concrete, trying to see how much damage had been caused to the underground containment area. Its entrance was blocked by debris.

But that wouldn't take long to clear—and to his dismay, he saw that the exposed part of Frost's office farther up the hill was more or less intact. While the facade was cratered and cracked, it was still all in one piece—and even the windows had survived the blast, apparently made from the same transparent armor as the airlock doors.

That meant Frost and the virus had also survived.

The virus . . .

"Shit!" He looked across the fjord. The A380 was still trundling towards the eastern end of the runway. Once there, it would turn and accelerate down the long concrete strip, taking off and heading along the coast to release its deadly cargo.

Starkman groaned nearby. Aristides was several yards behind him, eyes wide in death. Chase rushed over and grabbed the American, hauling him up. "Come on! The virus is on the plane—we can still stop it!"

Starkman wiped dirt off his face. "It's heading for takeoff, Eddie." He indicated the bridge spanning the fjord. "We'll never get there in time."

Chase jerked a thumb in the direction of the house. "I know where to find a very fast car . . ."

w

The monitor on the desk came to life, casting a glow onto Kari's worried face. "Ms. Frost," said a woman's voice, "I have your father on videolink."

"Oh, thank God!" Kari exclaimed. "I thought you were dead!"

Frost's voice emerged from the cabin speakers. "I'm fine. The containment area survived almost totally intact."

"Was it Qobras's people? I saw men parachuting into the grounds."

"It was Starkman—and Edward Chase."

Kari looked stunned. "What? But you said Qobras had—"

"Eddie!" Nina jumped up and ran to the desk. "You mean he's alive? What happened, is he okay?"

"You might want to remind Dr. Wilde that she isn't

helping her case by sounding so pleased about that," Frost said, voice acidic. "Chase was working with Starkman against us."

Kari frowned at the screen. "You *lied* to me! If you knew he wasn't dead—"

"None of this matters," Frost cut in. "All that does matter is that they've *failed*. We still have the virus cultures in the containment area, and Schenk is moving our security teams to make sure they can't get across the bridge to attack your plane. I thought Chase and Starkman were already dead—they soon will be for sure."

WW

"Nice wheels," said Starkman, impressed. He and Chase stood in the garage beneath the house, before Kari's collection of cars and motorcycles. "What's the fastest one? Lamborghini? McLaren?"

Chase shot open the cabinet containing the keys to the vehicles. "No, we need a convertible—the Ferrari." He pointed at the bright scarlet F430 Spider, noticing that Kari's racing bike was no longer in its neighboring parking spot, then hunted for the right key. It was easy to find—the black and yellow prancing horse logo was instantly recognizable from his schoolboy fantasies.

"A convertible? Why?"

"Because I'm going to need to shoot from it. There'll be more guards on the way—they're not just going to let us drive straight across the bridge!" He tossed the keys to Starkman. "Come on! You're driving!"

"What the hell are you planning?" Starkman demanded as Chase jumped into the Ferrari's passenger seat.

"I don't know, I'm making this up as I go!"

"Always the wise-ass, weren't you?" Starkman

climbed into the driver's seat and put the key in the ignition. The Ferrari's engine crackled to life with an almost animalistic growl. "You think you can bring down the plane with just a UMP?"

"I don't *want* to bring it down—Nina's still aboard! Okay, go!"

The Ferrari peeled out of its bay with a shriek of tires as Starkman overrevved the engine. "Whoa! Little touchy!" He eased off and turned for the main door, which started opening automatically as they approached. "You're going to try to *save* her? What're you gonna do, jump onto the plane while it's taking off?"

"If I have to!" Chase looked at the gear on Starkman's back. "Give me your grappling gun."

"You're out of your fucking mind!" Starkman objected. But he handed the device to Chase anyway.

The door rose high enough for the low-slung Ferrari to fit beneath. Starkman stomped on the accelerator, the engine howling. The car blasted forward like a bullet. "Holy *shit*!"

"I always wanted one of these!" Chase checked the load on his machine gun, then looked ahead. The driveway from the house zigzagged down the hill to join up with the road leading to the bridge—where another pair of Grand Cherokees had been positioned into a roadblock. Beyond them, halfway across the bridge itself, was a silver BMW X5.

Starkman pointed; more of Frost's security forces crouched behind the Jeeps. "Hate to tell you this, but Ferraris aren't bulletproof!"

"Nor are Jeeps! You ready?" The F430 swooped into the last curve.

"As I'll ever be!" Starkman hefted his UMP in his left hand, holding the steering wheel with his right. The

Ferrari straightened, the makeshift roadblock directly ahead—

"Fire!"

Chase opened fire as the Ferrari accelerated, sweeping his shots across the right-hand Jeep at window height. Starkman extended his arm from the side of the car and blasted away at the other SUV, spent bullet casings clinking off the windscreen.

The Jeeps shuddered under the onslaught, glass exploding and metal panels cratering as shots ripped through them. Chase saw a man fall. He didn't expect to take out all the guards—he just needed to keep them down until the Ferrari could blast past.

"Get on the pavement!" he yelled.

"What?"

"The sidewalk, *sidewalk*!" The SUVs had blocked the two-lane roadway, but there was a pavement for pedestrians on the right.

"We won't fit!"

"Yes we will!" Not that they had a choice—in a collision between a lightweight Italian sports car and a two-ton American SUV, there was no doubt which would come out worse.

Starkman swerved the Ferrari to the right, both men still firing at the Jeeps. Chase's gun clicked empty. Bullets clonked into the side of the F430 as the security men shot back.

"Shit!" cried Starkman. "We're not gonna fit!"

"Just *go*!" screamed Chase, bracing himself as the F430 hit the curb. The front spoiler splintered on impact—then the low-profile wheels slammed against the unforgiving concrete with a bang that pounded up his spine like a hammer blow.

Chase's side of the car screeched against the bridge's railing while the front wing on Starkman's side clipped the rear of the Jeep and crumpled back like tinfoil. Both wing mirrors were sheared off, spraying the two men with glass.

"Duck!" Chase shouted as Starkman swung the Ferrari back onto the road. More bullets struck the car as they hunched down in their seats, one clanking against the hooped rollbar just inches behind Chase's head.

Starkman accelerated again. Chase was shoved back in his seat as the Ferrari blasted away from the Jeeps. He let out an involuntary whoop of excitement at the sensation. "Bloody hell!"

"Good choice of car!" Starkman called over the rush of the wind. "Okay, so—"

The windscreen shattered.

Starkman spasmed as blood sprayed from a wound in his chest, a ragged hole blown right through his body armor. The engine note dropped abruptly as his foot slipped from the accelerator. The Ferrari coasted, slowing fast.

"Jesus!" Chase cried. He grabbed the steering wheel, trying to keep the F430 from hitting the parked BMW ahead.

Standing beside it, a gleaming gun in his hands, was someone Chase recognized instantly.

Schenk.

He recognized the gun, too. Frost's chief of security had just shot Starkman with a Wildey.

His Wildey.

Chase brought up his UMP, remembering too late that he needed to change clips. Schenk aimed the long silver barrel at him—

He released the wheel and flung himself bodily over the top of his door. The distinctive boom of the Wildey reached him as a Magnum round blew a fist-sized hole in the back of his seat. He hit the ground hard and rolled.

Another boom. A chunk of asphalt flew into the air inches from his legs. He rolled again, the awkward shape of the cable gun digging into his back. There was a crunch of metal as the slowing Ferrari banged into the side of the SUV and came to a halt. The engine stalled. Schenk jumped back, taking cover behind his vehicle.

Chase sprang up and ran for the BMW. Schenk saw him and fired again, but Chase dived behind the X5, fumbling for a new magazine.

Shit!

Touch alone told him something was wrong. The open end of the clip was crooked, bent out of shape. He'd crushed it under his own weight when he rolled over the road. It wouldn't fit into the UMP's receiver.

Chase dropped the useless magazine, instead flipping the UMP in his hands and sweeping it at ankle height as Schenk rushed around the side of the X5, the Wildey ready in his hand—

The German's shot went wide as Chase hooked one foot out from under him with the UMP's stock. Schenk grunted as he was knocked off balance, and staggered, arms windmilling.

Chase rugby-tackled him, driving him back until he crashed against the guardrail, trying to force him over.

But Schenk was a solid slab of muscle, too big even for Chase to overpower by brute force. He realized the danger he was in and bent at the knees, dropping his center of gravity below the top of the railing. His arm swung, and the butt of the Wildey smashed down on Chase's neck, felling him with a bolt of pain. Schenk's boot cracked against the side of his skull. Chase dropped onto his side. Head swimming, he looked up.

The Wildey was pointed straight at his face. Beyond it, Schenk came into focus. The German grinned—

Blam!

Chase flinched.

But it wasn't the Wildey that had fired.

It was Starkman's UMP, the last bullet in its magazine gouging a bloody hole in Schenk's right shoulder. The Wildey dropped from the German's hand as he lurched back against the railing.

Chase caught his gun and flipped it around. "I think this is *mine*."

He fired. The bullet hit Schenk in his left eye, the eyeball bursting in a revolting spray as the shot continued through his brain and exploded out of the top of his skull. His head snapped back with the impact and he toppled over the railing, falling hundreds of feet to the icy waters below.

W

Clutching his aching head, Chase staggered to the Ferrari. Starkman was slumped over the door, bubbles of blood dripping from his mouth. For a second Chase thought he was dead, but then his one eye twitched, looking up at him.

"Bet you're glad you didn't kill me now, huh?" Starkman said weakly. He pulled himself upright and flopped back into the seat. "Come on, you got a plane to catch . . ."

Chase opened the door to lift him into the passenger seat, but Starkman shook his head. "Leave me . . . I'm fucked, and company's coming." He looked in the direction they had come. One of the Jeeps from the roadblock was already chasing them, and more vehicles were speeding up the road from the corporate buildings. "I'll stop 'em . . ."

"With what?"

Starkman somehow managed a half-smile and held up a block of CL-20—the timer already running.

"Just make sure you're off this bridge in twenty seconds," he wheezed, with his last ounce of strength forcing himself out of the Ferrari to lie on the road at Chase's feet. "Fight to the end, Eddie . . ."

"Fight to the end," Chase repeated as he jumped into the Ferrari and restarted the engine. He jammed it into reverse and pulled away from the BMW, then clicked into first and poured on the power.

Riding in the passenger seat didn't even remotely compare to the experience of controlling 483 horsepower. The acceleration was so fierce it felt like taking off in a jet. By the time he remembered to change up a gear, he was already doing over sixty miles an hour, the engine wailing like a banshee behind him.

Into third, now doing eighty, snicking the gear lever through the gleaming chrome gate . . .

In the mirror he saw that the Jeep had almost reached Starkman, the other vehicles now pouring onto the bridge.

The other end of the bridge was coming up fast, but he could only guess how much time he had left before the explosive detonated. Just moments.

One hundred miles an hour and accelerating, but still a few seconds from solid ground—

The image in the mirror disappeared in a flash of light. A moment later came a huge crack like a thunderbolt, immediately followed by a lower, more sinister rumble.

The flat plane of the bridge suddenly became a slope—

It was collapsing!

Starkman's bomb had blown out the center of the

sweeping arch, the two halves of the structure plunging into the river below. All Chase could do was keep his right foot jammed to the floor and hope the Ferrari reached the end of the bridge before the whole thing dropped out from under him!

He was now driving *uphill*, speed falling alarmingly as a wave of jagged cracks swept past up the road surface. "Oh shit—"

Everything tilted, and the road disintegrated beneath him—

The Ferrari shot off the end of the collapsing bridge as it tumbled into the fjord, crashing down onto solid ground. The exhaust pipes were torn away as the underbody hit the road, the engine note becoming a raw, ragged rasp.

Chase fought to keep the car under control as it slewed around. He stamped on the brake. The Ferrari juddered as the antilock system kicked in, but it was skidding sideways, tires straining, threatening to burst.

He hauled at the steering wheel. The car spun backwards towards a wall.

Foot off the brake, and *accelerate*—

With a shriek of tortured rubber, the Ferrari came to a stop in a cloud of acrid tire smoke barely a foot from the airfield's perimeter wall. Chase coughed as the swirling mist blew past him. Through the smashed windscreen he saw another cloud, a ghostly line of dust marking where the bridge had been. The security forces pursuing him were gone, having plunged into the river with their boss.

And Starkman.

Chase paused to give his ex-comrade a silent word of thanks.

Then he turned to look down the runway. In the distance, he saw the hulking white shape of the A380 against the dark backdrop of the surrounding hills, about to turn around.

About to take off.

He put the battered Ferrari into gear, then set off with a screech of tires.

TWENTY-NINE

The A380 slowed as it approached the end of the taxiway, preparing for the wide half-turn to point it down the two-kilometer-long runway.

Chase kept his eyes fixed on the aircraft as he accelerated, clicking up through the Ferrari's gears. The blasting wind forced him to squint, eyes streaming, but all he had to do was keep going in a straight line.

He had never been aboard an A380, knew almost nothing about its internal layout beyond it being a double-decker. But that was the passenger version—this one was a freighter, meaning he was even more in the dark. He would have to wing it when he got on board.

He would have to wing it to *get* on board. Trying to block the plane's takeoff with the Ferrari would be like trying to stop a tank with a cardboard box. The enormous aircraft would blow the sports car aside as if it weren't even there.

And he couldn't try to stop the plane by shooting at it—there was too much risk of killing Nina if it caught fire or crashed as a result.

Although if it meant stopping the virus then it might have to be a necessary sacrifice—with himself going the same way . . .

He was doing over 140, barely able to see the speedometer through his watering eyes. The A380 was a white blur ahead as it moved into its turn.

Whatever he was going to do, he had to think of it fast . . .

W

"Ms. Frost!" The pilot's voice echoed over the intercom. "There's a car on the runway!"

Kari went to the port side of the cabin to look down. "What?" she gasped. Nina peered past her. She saw the runway stretching off into the distance as the plane turned—and racing down it, a scarlet Ferrari convertible!

The car charged towards them at incredible speed, its lone occupant taking on form. Even at a distance she recognized the balding head behind the wheel the moment she saw it. "Oh my God! It's *Eddie!*"

Kari reacted with shock, then went to the intercom. "This is Kari Frost. Under *no* circumstances are you to abort the takeoff. Whatever he does, *get this plane into the air.* That is an order." She returned to the window. "What the hell is he doing?"

"Trying to stop *you*," said Nina.

Kari set her jaw, her expression turning hard. "He won't succeed." She moved to the top of the stairs and shouted down to the guards, "Get your guns and open the hatch! Somebody's trying to stop us from taking off—"

Nina realized that Kari's back was to her, and she had only the lightest hold on the handrail.

She didn't even have time to consider the thought rationally. Instead, she acted on pure instinct, rushing at Kari with both arms held out like battering rams and pushing her down the stairs.

Taken completely by surprise, Kari had no chance to stop herself from falling. She screamed as she tumbled down the metal steps, flailing limbs smashing against the hard edges, then hit the floor with a bang, bleeding and dazed.

Nina stared down at her almost in shock at what she'd done before instinct took over again. Fight or flight . . .

Flight!

She ran to the door at the back of the cabin, praying it wasn't locked. It wasn't. Darting through, she found herself inside the upper hold, a vaulted tunnel of bare metal ribs holding a line of cargo containers, rattling against their restraints. Banks of white LEDs mounted along the ceiling provided ghostly illumination.

There was no lock on the door. She hurriedly looked around for some way to secure it.

The nearest container was just a few feet away, held in place by thick straps attached to lugs in the floor. She yanked at what she hoped was the release lever. With a loud clack, the strap came free. She looped it behind a spar in the wall before tying it around the door handle, pulling it tight. It wouldn't stop the door from being opened, but it would make it much harder for anyone to squeeze through the narrow gap.

She stepped back, looking down the hold.

The virus . . .

For the virus to be released in flight, whatever container it was in had to be somehow plumbed to the skin of the Airbus. If she could find the container, there might be some way to sabotage it.

Loud footsteps from the cabin: someone racing up the stairs.

Nina ran down the hold.

W

The A380 was about to complete its turn, and Chase was almost at the end of the runway. He wiped his eyes, trying to get a clear look at the aircraft. Under the fuselage were *five* undercarriage legs, one at the nose and the other four spreading out the plane's weight as widely as possible.

When the undercarriage retracted into the plane's belly, there should be access hatches he could use to enter the fuselage if he got onto one of the landing legs.

Might be access hatches, he reminded himself.

He had to take the chance. It was now or never. The A380's four gaping engines were spinning up.

The Ferrari's tires screeched again as he swerved to one side of the runway. Not to get out of the plane's way, but to make as tight a turn as possible without losing too much speed, preparing to come in *under* the aircraft.

The cable gun was ready on the passenger seat beside him.

He would *literally* only get one shot—if he missed, there was a good chance he would die when the Ferrari was caught in the engine backblast. If he survived that, he would be dead soon after, killed either by Frost's men or by his virus.

Even if he *succeeded*, he was probably dead anyway. But he had to try.

Heat scoured his face as he passed behind the engines on the left wing. The Ferrari threatened to spin out, and he eased off the accelerator slightly—if he made a mistake now, there would be no chance to catch up.

The hatch at the plane's nose opened. Someone leaned out, a gun in his hand—one of Frost's men looking for him.

The overstressed tires strained for grip—

Now directly behind the fuselage, Chase straightened the car, aiming between the two pairs of landing legs in the A380's belly.

The engine noise rose to a scream, and the plane started to accelerate.

For its colossal size, the Airbus was frighteningly quick off the mark. Burning air blasted Chase like a hurricane as the Ferrari darted under the plane's tail. The massive fuselage filled his vision, a giant hammer ready to crush him flat at any moment.

He was between the rear undercarriage legs, still outpacing the aircraft—but not for long.

He grabbed the cable gun.

Now he was level with the front landing legs, foot to the floor to keep up with the racing Airbus. A slight turn of the wheel brought him closer to the left leg, the four giant tires a whirling blur.

One shot.

The wheels were less than a foot from the Ferrari's side.

As the plane pulled away, Chase aimed the cable gun into the undercarriage well.

One chance—

Fire!

The grapnel shot out, the line whipping behind it. It flew into the wheel well and struck the inner wall. If it fell out, it was all over . . .

It held!

The grapnel had pierced the metal bulkhead.

He only needed it to hold for a few seconds. Hitting the switch to retract the cable, he shoved the gun through the center of the steering wheel, looping the line back around on itself. Then he let go of the wheel, forcing himself upright against the hundred-mile-an-hour slipstream, and held the cable as it snapped taut—

The Ferrari swerved, dragged in behind the undercarriage.

He jumped over the door and pulled himself hand over hand up the line. Dust and grit kicked up by the plane's wheels spat into his face. He only needed to traverse a few feet, but the line was already straining.

His feet scraped the runway, almost tearing him loose. Blood oozed between his fingers as the cable cut into his flesh.

The landing leg was just a foot away—one more swing of his arm and he would be able to pull himself onto the undercarriage—

The cable lashed. The Ferrari skidded sideways, dragged behind the plane like a toy. Chase felt the steel line jolt. The grapnel was giving way—

He lunged desperately for the landing leg, blood-soaked fingers closing around the metal just as the cable snapped free.

The Ferrari broke away, spinning out of control behind him. The cable shot past, the grapnel a lethal barb flashing past his face. He instinctively looked around to follow it, in time to see the Airbus plow right over the sports car, flattening it instantly. Mangled debris flew in all directions.

The impact shook even the massive aircraft. Chase struggled to keep hold, kicking in a frantic attempt to find a foothold before he suffered the same fate as the F430.

His boot found solid metal. He pulled himself up. If his guess had been wrong, if there wasn't an access hatch, he would be crushed when the undercarriage retracted into the belly of the plane.

He looked up, seeing nothing but metal walls and skeins of cables and hydraulic lines.

Shit—

As the Airbus left the runway, the shriek of the engines almost deafening, the landing leg began to retract, folding into the confines of the wheel well. Chase twisted desperately as he was pushed towards the ceiling, the metal ribs of the fuselage like blades about to slice him into pieces—

A hatch!

An access panel, barely two feet wide, with a recessed ring-shaped handle at its base. He grabbed the handle.

It didn't move.

Either it was stiff through newness, or it was locked. He bet on the former, twisting it harder, and the hatch popped open. He hurled himself through the narrow gap, landing with a thump as the undercarriage clanked into position behind him. The gap between the leg and the ceiling of the wheel well was barely three inches.

The light level dropped sharply as the outer doors slammed, the engine noise falling to a dull roar. Chase took in his surroundings. He was inside a crawl space, less than four feet high and lit by small but intense LED clusters. More cables lined the walls, leading towards the center of the aircraft.

He closed the hatch and followed them, hunting for a way into the holds.

W

Nina heard someone banging at the door. She moved more quickly down the hold.

What was in the containers, she had no idea—only that none of them were connected to the plane's hull. Holding the securing straps to keep upright as the A380 rose steeply into the sky, she headed for the back of the aircraft.

The banging on the door intensified. She didn't have much time, and there were two more decks still to search . . .

w

Chase opened another hatch, emerging from the crawl space to find himself in the forward lower hold. The A380's bottom deck was split in two by the undercarriage, and he'd chosen to head forward rather than aft with the thought that he might be able to reach the cockpit and threaten the pilots.

If the virus was in the aft hold, he was screwed . . .

The hold was full, no way for him to squeeze around the aluminum containers and barely a foot of clearance between them and the ceiling. He climbed onto the nearest one and crawled forward on his belly as fast as he could.

w

Kari squeezed through the door. She ducked beneath the strap tied to the handle, then surveyed the hold, catching a glimpse of movement at the far end.

She wiped blood off her bottom lip, staring at the crimson stain on her skin for a moment. "Oh Nina, I wish you hadn't done that . . ."

Then she raised a gun and set off after her.

w

There was a door at the front of the hold. Chase opened it, finding a cargo lift just large enough to fit a catering cart, and next to it a ladder leading upwards.

He ascended the ladder. It emerged in a utility room, a cramped space lined with lockers. He glanced at the labels on them—emergency equipment of various kinds—then took out his Wildey and opened the door a crack to peer out.

Nobody was in sight. He was near the front of the plane. The room seemed to be some kind of crew area, a row of seats against the back wall next to an open door through which he could see the main hold. Another door led forward.

That had to be the cockpit.

Chase stepped out of the utility room, the Wildey at the ready. To his left was a flight of stairs leading up to the top deck; he looked up it, but no one was there.

What should he do? He needed to find Nina. But Frost said the virus would be released when the plane reached its cruising altitude, and with the A380 still in a steep climb, that wouldn't take long.

Chase made his decision.

He marched to the cockpit door and flung it open. The copilot glanced around, obviously expecting to see one of the other crew members—then barked a warning in Norwegian to the pilot.

The pilot twisted in his seat, grabbing for something.

Chase saw the gun, and reacted exactly as training and experience had taught him. In the confines of the cockpit, the Wildey sounded like a cannon. The bullet blasted a hole right through the back of the pilot's seat and the man himself to embed itself in one of the monitor screens. Blood splattered over the instruments.

The pilot slumped forward, dead, his hand dropping from the control stick. The plane rolled sharply to one side, throwing Chase against the cockpit wall. He regained his balance, looking up. Instead of trying to keep control, the copilot had gone for a gun of his own—

The Wildey boomed again.

w

The two security men heading down the main hold to cut Nina off heard the first shot—and the A380's lurch instantly confirmed that something was seriously wrong. By the time the noise of the second shot reached them, they were already running back towards the cockpit.

w

Nina shrieked as she was pitched against one of the containers. She grabbed a strap for support and pulled herself back up.

She was certain she'd heard a gunshot just before the plane banked.

A very distinctive gunshot.

"Eddie . . ." she whispered, barely daring to believe the possibility. Had he somehow managed to get on board?

The plane shook again.

If he *was* aboard, then he was causing as much trouble as ever . . .

w

Chase struggled to squeeze between the seats of the two dead men. The A380's ultramodern systems had replaced the traditional heavy yoke of an airliner with a small joystick. Which was less physical for the pilot—but also harder for Chase to reach. "What the hell did you have to do that for, you stupid twat?" he growled rhetorically at the pilot.

He managed to grab the stick and nudged it to one side. To his enormous relief, the plane's tilt began to level out.

Then it struck him—he had no clue what to do next.

He'd jumped out of plenty of planes, but he didn't know how to fly *any* kind of plane, much less a five-hundred-ton behemoth.

"Shit!" He looked desperately at the control panels. The only thing he could identify at a glance was the artificial horizon, which showed the plane still in a climb, and banking more steeply than he liked.

Where the hell was the autopilot?

There! "Autopilot Engage," near the top of the control panel. He jabbed at the prominent switch, tentatively releasing the control stick. A synthetic female voice announced that the autopilot was active, the plane smoothly bringing itself to a level attitude. He searched for the altimeter. The A380 was at just over twelve thousand feet, well short of cruising height.

He hoped that whatever system was being used to release the virus wasn't activated by a timer.

vvv

Kari pulled herself upright as the A380 leveled out. The two booming shots from the direction of the cockpit suggested that both pilots were dead—and that Chase was responsible.

Chase! How the hell had he gotten aboard?

Not that it mattered. He was here, and he posed a threat.

More so than Nina? She weighed the dangers. The virus canisters were inside a container at the very rear of the middle deck, plumbed into pipes that would disperse the deadly solution into the jetstream from the A380's tail. If Nina could get the container open, she might be able to interfere with the release mechanism.

But she had to find the container first, and then break into it.

Chase, on the other hand, was in the cockpit. He was the greater danger.

With one last look after the retreating Nina, Kari turned back.

w

Nina reached the rear of the upper hold. None of the containers showed any signs of being connected to the plane's exterior.

Which meant the virus was on one of the other decks.

She feared she would have to return to the front of the hold and somehow make it past her pursuers, but then spotted a hatch in the rear bulkhead. It opened into a small compartment. She poked her head into the low-ceilinged space. It was an access area, with what looked like large fuseboxes connected to fat skeins of wires on the walls.

And another hatch set into the floor.

She clambered into the cabin and turned the catches on the hatch, pulling it open. Below she saw another metal container, in front of it a pallet onto which was strapped a large, sleek blue-and-silver motorbike. She recognized it as Kari's, the racing bike she was so proud of.

She dropped down into the middle hold.

w

The plane now on autopilot, Chase stepped back from the controls. He hoped that would buy some time. How exactly he would get back down to the ground with both pilots dead was another matter . . .

Running footsteps sounded behind him, and he threw himself against the port wall as shots cracked past him, slamming into the instrument panel. Through

the cockpit door he saw a man duck behind the bulkhead, waiting for his companion to give him cover so he
could whip around and shoot.

Chase fired first. A single Magnum bullet from his
Wildey blew a hole through the bulkhead, and the man
standing behind it. Blood sprayed over the cabin, the
guard slumping face-first to the floor.

One down. But there was still another man outside.

More bullets slammed into the cockpit, splinters of
plastic and fiberboard flying everywhere. The other
guard was using the same trick, shooting *through* the
bulkhead. Chase threw himself flat on the deck as shots
smacked into the cockpit wall and side panels above
him.

He could see the dead man's pistol on the cabin floor,
a SIG-Sauer P226. Presumably the other guard had the
same weapon, which meant he had fifteen bullets in his
clip, thirteen of which had now been fired, fourteen—

Fifteen!

If his count was wrong, it would get him killed.

Chase rolled, arms stretched out in front of him as he
threw himself at the open cockpit door. He saw the second of Frost's guards frantically loading a new clip into
his pistol—

The Wildey boomed. The guard flew off his feet, collapsing at the rear of the compartment.

Chase jumped up and hurried aft, kicking the guns
away from the two men in case they weren't dead. A
moment's experienced examination told him that they
were.

Unless there were other crew members he didn't
know about, that just left Kari aboard.

And Nina.

Nina heard the gunshots and ducked down next to the motorbike in case any of them found their way into the hold.

The last shot was from Chase's Wildey. Which she hoped meant he was the last man standing . . .

"Eddie?" she called. "Eddie!"

w

Chase heard the female voice coming from the hold.

Was it Nina—or Kari? It was hard to tell over the engine noise. He went to the door, seeing nothing but metal containers under the cold lights. "Nina! Is that you?"

A head popped up towards the rear of the hold. Chase recognized the auburn hair instantly. "*Nina!*"

He ran into the hold.

w

Kari heard Chase shout from below as she went back into the executive cabin. She paused, peering down the stairs to make sure he wasn't lurking in ambush, then descended silently.

Gun at the ready, she entered the crew room. No sign of Chase, but her two men were dead on the floor. The cockpit door was open. One look told her that both pilots were also dead.

She could lock herself in the cockpit and regain control of the plane. However, the holes in the bulkhead told her that would be a risky option. Chase could shoot her right through the door.

And if she were locked in the cockpit, that would leave Chase and Nina free to locate and sabotage the virus canisters . . .

She hurried into the cockpit anyway, to check the plane's status. Several panels had been damaged by bullets, but she was able to find the information she most urgently needed. The autopilot was engaged, the A380 at 12,000 feet and 320 knots. The fact that it was off-course and hadn't reached its cruising altitude would already have alerted air traffic control that something was wrong, as would the lack of communication. If the plane failed to respond for more than a few minutes, the air force would be sent to intercept. *Damn it!*

The plane had to be brought back to the ground before the military got involved. If she returned to Ravnsfjord, a private airport, then the events aboard could be covered up, blamed upon human error. A second attempt to release the Trident virus could be made with little delay.

She examined the autopilot controls, which luckily were undamaged. The A380's computers were state of the art, and the runway at Ravnsfjord had been upgraded with the latest navigation aids; in an emergency, the plane could literally fly itself to a safe landing without any human intervention.

Which was fortunate, because there was no longer anybody aboard capable of piloting the enormous aircraft.

Suddenly sweating, Kari activated the emergency landing sequence.

vvv

Chase squeezed past containers until he reached Nina, who was waiting by Kari's racing bike. He hugged her. "Jesus, you're okay!"

"I thought you'd died!" Nina cried.

"Not me, love, I'm indestructible." She kissed him. "Oh, hello! Where did that come from?"

"Just happy to see you!" The smile fell from her face. "Eddie, listen—somewhere on the plane there's—"

"A virus, I know. Any idea where?"

"No, but it must be hooked to the outside of the plane. There's nothing in the upper hold."

"There wasn't anything like that forward of here," said Chase, "and I didn't see anything in the lower hold."

"Then there's not much left to check! Come on!" Nina pulled him with her towards the rear of the hold. "You check the ones on the left side, I'll go right."

There were fewer containers on Chase's side of the plane, and none were out of the ordinary. He reached the huge aft cargo door, stopping to check the controls. Maybe if he opened the door—or even ejected it entirely, as closer inspection revealed a warning notice and instructions about firing its explosive bolts—he could force the plane down . . .

"Eddie!" He looked around, the door already forgotten as he saw Nina waving frantically from the rear of the plane. "Over here, I've found it!"

Chase hurried to the back of the hold. Nina stood by a pair of steel hoses leading from the rearmost container to fittings in the aft bulkhead. "Here!" she said. "Any idea how to stop the virus from being released?"

He shook his head. "Normally when I deal with WMDs, I just blow up the whole fucking building!" There was a padlock on the container's front panel, but a couple of blows with the butt of his Wildey took care of it.

"Oh my God," Nina exclaimed as she looked inside. What Frost had shown her in the biolab had led her to expect small flasks of the virus; the three containers she saw here were more like oil drums. "Now what do we do?"

"Put this out of action," said Chase, pointing at an electric pump at the base of one of the drums. There was a simple control panel beside it. One button would open the valves, and the other would pump the virus through the pipes and out into the open air.

"What if it's booby-trapped?"

"Why would it be? They didn't expect anyone else to be aboard!" He aimed his gun at the panel.

"Whoa, wait!" Nina yelled. "You can't just *shoot* it! What if it causes a short circuit and sets the thing off?"

Chase gave her a look. "I could *dismantle* it, but we're kind of running out of time!" He took aim again—

The A380 banked, throwing them both off balance. "Shit!" said Chase. "What was that?"

Nina looked towards the front of the hold. "Kari. She must be in the cockpit! What's she doing?"

"Turning us around," Chase said grimly. "Taking us back to Ravnsfjord so they can have fifty guys surround us."

"But—but she can't fly this thing!"

"She doesn't have to, the computer'll do it all for her. Here." He took out his Swiss Army knife and handed it to her. "There's a screwdriver and some scissors in it. Take the front panel off, and then cut every wire you can find."

"I'm an archaeologist, not an electrician! What are *you* going to do?"

"Take care of Kari." He hefted the Wildey and pushed past Nina, heading forward.

Nina fumbled with the knife, trying to pry open the stiff blades. All she succeeded in doing was painfully snapping her thumbnail. "Shit!" She tried again, with no more luck. "Eddie, wait!" He didn't hear her. Frustrated, she ran after him.

ᴡᴡ

Chase reached the crew room, looking cautiously inside. The cockpit door was still open. No sign of Kari.

He raised his gun and entered the room. The two bodies still lay where they had fallen.

Where was she?

She hadn't gotten past him in the hold, so she was still in the forward section. That meant she'd gone up the stairs to the upper deck, was hiding in the cockpit, or was in the utility room.

Watching the cockpit door, he advanced on the utility room, paused—then yanked the door open and aimed the Wildey inside.

Empty.

He closed the door and pressed his back against it, ready to whip around the corner and aim up the stairs.

Go!

Nobody there.

He relaxed . . . and Kari swung down from where she'd been hiding directly above, both her feet slamming into his face.

THIRTY

Chase staggered back, eyes watering from the resurgent pain in his broken nose. With the A380 still banking, he had to fight to keep his balance.

Another kick flew at him, Kari pivoting on one foot in a roundhouse move. Her boot heel crashed into his chest like a pickaxe blow. He gasped for breath.

Her foot snapped up again, smashing into his gun hand. Agony shot through him as his little finger broke. The Wildey spun away and hit the rear bulkhead.

He lashed out with his left fist, and Kari's head snapped back as his punch caught her cheek. She yelled, as much in surprise as in pain, and dropped back a step with a poisonous expression.

Chase realized she had a gun tucked into the waistband of her leather jeans. Kari saw his eyes flick down to the gun. As she grabbed it, he plowed into her shoulder-first, smashing her against the door of the utility room and driving the breath from her lungs—

The gun went off.

Searing pain exploded in Chase's left thigh. His leg immediately gave way, pitching him on to his side. He clutched the wound. The bullet had gone right through his thigh, missing the bone, but his clothing was wet with blood.

The A380 leveled off, the autopilot now on course for Ravnsfjord.

Kari gasped for breath. "Damn you, Eddie," she choked out. The smoking gun came up, pointing at his face . . .

And held there.

A second passed, two, Kari's finger tight on the trigger—

"*Kari!*"

Nina stood in the door to the hold, Chase's Wildey held in both hands. Aimed at Kari.

"Drop it," Nina said.

"Nina?" Kari looked at her in surprise, but didn't move the gun away from Chase.

"Kari, put the gun down. Put it down!"

"Nina, there's still time for you to change your mind." Kari's tone became almost pleading. "You can still come with me!"

Nina set her jaw. "I'm not going to let you kill Eddie."

"I can't let him threaten the plan." Kari looked back down at Chase. Eyes narrowed in pain, he clutched his wounded leg, unable to respond. He turned his head towards Nina, willing her to shoot. *Only amateurs talk,* he wanted to tell her, but the words refused to emerge.

"The plan's insane!" Nina snapped. "Your *father's* insane!"

Kari's face twisted with a flash of anger. "Don't say that!"

"You *know* he is, Kari! You *know* what he's doing is wrong! For God's sake, you've been working for years to *save* lives all over the world! Think of all the people you've helped! Doesn't *any* of that mean anything to you?"

"I *have* to do it," said Kari, though her expression was conflicted. "I can't disobey my father."

"You already did!" Nina reminded her. "When you wouldn't let him kill me! And I saw you in here just now: you could have killed Eddie, but you didn't. Because you care about him too! He saved your life!"

"But he's not one of us . . ."

"Kari, there's no 'us' and 'them,'" insisted Nina. "We're all still *people,* human beings. So the world's got some problems—big deal, it always has!"

Kari looked back at her, uncertain. "But we can solve them . . ."

"By killing billions of people? *That's* your idea of solving problems?" Still keeping the heavy gun pointed at Kari, Nina stepped closer. "Kari, I *know* you. You're not Hitler, or Stalin or anybody like that. And you can stop your father from becoming one of them. Just put the gun down."

Kari's gun didn't move. "I . . . I can't."

"I won't let you kill him. Or anyone else."

Now the gun moved, Kari aiming it at Nina. "I don't want to kill you," said Kari. "Please don't make me."

"Nina, *shoot her*," Chase managed to groan.

"I don't want to kill you either, but I will if I have to," Nina said. The huge gun wavered in her shaking hands.

"I'll count to three, Nina. Please drop it." Kari was almost pleading. "One . . ."

"*Shoot her!*" rasped Chase.

"Two . . ."

"Kari, put it down!"

"Three!"

Kari fired.

At such short range, it should have been impossible to miss, but she did, twisting her wrist at the last instant to fire wide. The bullet flew past Nina to smack harmlessly into the rear wall of the cabin.

Nina instinctively flinched.

And fired.

The Wildey kicked in her hands with such force that the recoil almost tore the weapon from her grip.

Kari slammed against the door. A bright rose of blood burst over the metal behind her as the .45-caliber bullet tore through her body. She slid down the door and slumped onto the deck next to Chase.

Nina stared at her in horror. The Wildey dropped to the floor. "Oh my God . . ." she breathed, unable to accept what she'd just done.

"Nina . . ." whispered Kari, a tear trickling down one cheek. Then her eyes closed.

"Oh my God!" Nina repeated. "I didn't mean to . . ."

"She just tried to *kill* us," Chase growled, clutching his injured leg again and trying to sit up. "Come on, I need your help." After a moment of hesitation, unable to take her eyes off Kari, Nina raised him into a sitting position. "Thanks."

She examined his leg, seeing his trousers were soaked with blood. "Jesus! We've got to find some bandages—"

"No time. Get me to the cockpit, I've got to switch off the autopilot."

Nina hauled him upright. A groan escaped Chase's lips as new pain shot through his leg. "And then what?" she demanded.

"We've got to stop the virus from being released, then contact the authorities, warn them what Frost's doing."

"But what about the virus at the biolab?" she asked as she helped him limp towards the cockpit. "By the time you convince anyone that he's trying to kill billions of people, he could already have another plane in the air!"

Chase paused midstep. "The biolab . . ."

"What about it?"

"I blew up the buildings, but the containment area's still intact. We've got to destroy it."

"How?" Chase looked away from her, at the aircraft around them. "Oh no . . ." She remembered the horrors of 9/11 all too vividly. Ground Zero was less than two miles from her apartment.

"Five hundred tons of plane and a full load of jet fuel'll blow that place right open and incinerate everything inside," Chase said grimly.

"But we'll die! Except if— Are there any parachutes aboard?"

He shook his head. "There's no way off. Unless . . ." His expression changed, and he twisted around to look behind him. "Forget the cockpit—help me into the hold, quick!"

W

Frost stood at his office window, surveying the still-smoking ruins of the biolab below. Beyond it lay the fjord, and the broken stubs of the bridge. Chase and his companions had caused a massive amount of damage to his property. He had already had calls from the local authorities demanding to know what was going on.

But none of that mattered. The containment area was intact, and despite somehow managing to board the A380 as it took off, Chase had failed to destroy it.

"Sir, the control tower just informed us that the plane is on its way back to Ravnsfjord on automatic," said a man through his speakerphone.

"Any word from my daughter?"

"Not yet. Sir, air traffic control wants to know what's going on."

"Just tell them there's been a minor malfunction and the Airbus is returning as a precaution." Frost looked across the fjord at the airport. "When will it land?"

"About six minutes."

"Keep me informed." He closed the line, gazing into the distance for the first sign of the massive freighter. The lack of communication was a concern, as was the aircraft's use of its emergency automatic systems—but the fact that the A380 was returning home told him his people were still in control. Chase would have tried to fly it elsewhere and alert the Norwegian authorities.

Once it landed, the situation could be contained.

The plan was still viable.

w

"These three, undo all the straps holding them down," Chase ordered, pointing at the rearmost containers on the port side of the main hold.

"But then they'll come loose when the plane moves," said Nina, confused.

"They'll do more than that. Go on, quick." As Nina pulled the release levers on the securing straps, Chase limped to the controls for the cargo door.

"What are you doing?"

"I'm going to blow the door."

Nina froze. "You're gonna do *what*?"

"We need to get these containers out of the way. See that bike?"

Nina looked back at the motorbike on its pallet. "Yes?" It suddenly struck her what Chase was thinking. "*No!* No way, you're *insane*!"

"It's the only way off! If we just jump out, we'll still

be doing over a hundred miles an hour—there's no way we'd survive the impact!"

"As opposed to what'll happen if we ride a motor-bike out of the back of a flying plane?"

"So it's not a perfect plan! But it's better than being *shot* when we land!"

"I think the blood you've lost came straight from your brain," Nina complained unhappily, but she continued to release the containers from the lugs in the deck.

Chase read the warning sign. "Okay," he yelled when Nina had unfastened the last strap, "get back to the bike and hold tight!" She hurried up the hold as Chase let go of his injured leg to grip a fuselage spar with one hand. With the other, he turned the first of the two red-painted levers that fired the explosive bolts.

Then the second . . .

The cracks as the bolts detonated, severing the heavy hinges of the cargo door, were nothing compared to the ferocious roar of wind and engine noise as the door blew out. A hurricane-force gale screamed into the hold. The A380 was descending, so the aircraft didn't depressurize, but it was still traveling at over three hundred knots.

The plane lurched. The computers were already trying to counteract the unexpected movement, but the first container shifted, moving backwards over the rollers set into the deck with a banshee shriek of metal against metal. It crashed against the container holding the virus, then plunged through the gaping hatch to be whipped away by the slipstream.

Chase watched it fall. They were still over the sea, but it would only be a few minutes before they made landfall.

The A380 swayed again as the autopilot compensated for the shift in its balance caused by the loss of the container. Another metal crate screeched over the rollers, slewing sideways—coming right for him!

He had nowhere to go, no way to dodge the container—

He let go of the spar and flung himself backwards. The blasting wind caught him, snatching him off his feet.

The rear frame of the cargo door bisected his vision like a knife blade. To its left was the narrow gap between the side of the virus container and the hold wall; to the right, open sky and certain death.

He hit the frame, pinned for a moment by the wind . . .

And was blown left.

He grabbed a strap and clung on as the loose container juddered over the rollers and fell through the door. The third container was right behind it like a train carriage, the A380's sudden upwards lurch as it shed more weight sending it hurtling at him. It smashed into the container holding the virus and jolted to a stop less than an inch from Chase's face. Then the wind hammering against its flat front flung it out of the hold into empty space.

The freezing gale hit him again. Eyes forced almost shut, he squinted up the hold. Nina clung to the container next to the bike. Through the door, he could see a dark line on the horizon ahead. The Norwegian coast.

Chase pulled himself around the mangled corner of the virus container. Each step on his wounded leg was like a spike being driven through his flesh. He continued forwards, using the straps on the starboard line of containers to drag himself towards Nina.

Once past the door, the wind lessened slightly. He reached Nina and the Suzuki, yelling over the roar, "Unfasten the bike and start it up!"

"What if there's no gas in it?" she shouted back.

"Then we're fucked! Get it ready—I've got to get back to the cockpit!"

"What for?"

"To switch off the autopilot!" Using the containers for support, Chase hobbled up the hold, emerging in the crew area. The bodies of the two guards had been thrown to the side of the cabin by the plane's maneuvers, and Kari was now lying facedown at the foot of the stairs. He spotted his Wildey and tried to bend down to pick it up, but a fireball of pain in his leg deterred him. *Get it on the way back*, he decided.

He entered the cockpit and checked the autopilot display. As he'd thought, Kari had engaged all the plane's automatic emergency systems. The A380 was following a course back to Ravnsfjord's main runway, using signals from the ground to guide it in for a landing.

Even from several miles away, he could see the runway lights through the cockpit windows. The Airbus was still over the North Sea, but the coastline was only a few miles distant, the airport three miles inland. He checked the other controls. The plane was losing speed, the engines slowing as the computers brought it down in a shallow descent, trying to make the landing as simple as possible.

Chase looked back through the windows. There was the fjord, a dark indentation in the coastline. A line of black smoke marked the location of the biolab . . .

His target.

The central pillar of the windscreen acted as his guide to the A380's course. Right now it was aimed directly at the runway lights. He had to bring the plane around a few degrees to the right . . .

He checked the altimeter. Eight thousand feet and descending. He needed to be lower. A *lot* lower.

Leaning painfully over the dead pilot, Chase took hold of the joystick with one hand as he deactivated the autopilot with the other.

A warning buzzer shrilled, but he ignored it. Instead, he gently tipped the stick to the right, banking the plane. Slowly the runway lights drifted to the left of the pillar. He held the stick in position until the column of smoke was dead ahead, then pushed it upright. The A380 swayed queasily before leveling.

So far, so good. Now for the tricky part . . .

He pushed the stick forward. The nose dipped, the altimeter's countdown suddenly accelerating. He would have to judge everything entirely by eye: too high and the A380 would fly right over his target; too low and it would plow into the rocky side of the fjord . . .

The plane dropped below four thousand feet. The coastline loomed ahead. They were running out of time.

He pushed the stick farther forward, steepening the descent. Another alert sounded. "I know, I *know*," he snarled at the instrument panel. Three thousand feet. He checked the airspeed indicator. Just under a hundred knots.

Too fast, but there was nothing he could do about that now. If he slowed the plane too much, it might stall.

Two thousand feet. The coastline was coming up fast. The plane was still aimed right at the smoking ruins of the biolab. He reached over to the autopilot panel and hammered repeatedly at the "cancel" button, praying he was wiping all the commands Kari had entered. If the plane tried to follow its previous programming and make an emergency landing at Ravnsfjord, it was all over.

One thousand feet. A honking klaxon filled the cockpit, the synthetic female voice speaking beneath it. "Warning. Ground proximity alert. Warning. Ground proximity—"

"I *know!*" Six hundred feet, five hundred . . .

He leveled off. The artificial horizon tipped sluggishly back to the central position. Four hundred, 370 . . .

Three-fifty. Level. The terrain on the southern side of the fjord was roughly three hundred feet above sea level. He looked ahead. If the A380 held its course and altitude, it would pass right over the fjord and fly just above the remains of the biolab to plow into the mountainside behind it.

If he'd guessed the correct altitude. If not . . .

He activated the autopilot, hand hovering over the control stick in case the computers tried to ascend or turn back towards the runway. They didn't. All other instructions deleted, the autopilot held the Airbus on a steady course and speed.

He turned and clamped one hand around his leg, ignoring the pain. He could already feel the telltale sensation of blood loss swirling at the fringes of his consciousness, dizzying weakness circling him like a pack of jackals, waiting to strike. There wasn't much time. Limping, he traversed the stairs from the cockpit into the crew area—

And stopped in horror.

Kari was gone!

A spattered trail of blood led to the door of the hold.

Painfully he snatched up his gun and staggered to the door. "*Nina!*"

∿

The Suzuki was freed of its restraints, supported by its stand. The keys were in a plastic bag taped to the fuel tank; Nina ripped it open and took them out, the documents with them immediately scattered by the blasting wind.

Her experience with motorbikes was limited, but she managed to get the Suzuki running with little trouble. The fuel gauge was flat against "empty," however, all but the last dregs having been drained for transport. She looked around to see if Chase had finished in the cockpit—

And saw Kari leaping at her!

She tackled Nina from the bike. Both women landed heavily. Nina tried to push Kari off her—only to have Kari's elbow smash into the side of her head. Stunned, she looked up.

Kari's hands clamped around her throat. The Norwegian's face was twisted with pain and fury, framed by a windblown mane of blond hair. "Bitch!" she shrieked, teeth speckled with blood. "I gave you everything, and you betrayed me!"

Nina couldn't breathe. She pulled at Kari's hands, but they were like steel, unmovable. Her fingers tightened, thumbs pressing deep into Nina's windpipe. Blackness swirled in, a hissing noise rising in Nina's ears that overpowered even the thunder of the wind.

∿

Farther up the hold, Chase saw Kari on top of Nina, strangling her, but the two women were too close together for him to risk a shot—

∿

Unconsciousness loomed, death close behind it. All Nina could see now was Kari's enraged face above her. She made a last feeble attempt to pull her hands from her neck . . .

Her fingers brushed against something cold and hard.

Something *sharp*.

Her pendant—

With the last of her strength, she gripped the piece of orichalcum and slashed it across the inside of Kari's right wrist.

Kari shrieked. She jerked back, blood spurting from the cut as she released Nina, and looked down in disbelieving shock—

Nina punched her in the face. Kari fell backwards, rolling off Nina to slump dazed on the deck.

"Nice punch!" Chase shouted as he staggered to Nina.

"Thought I'd try things your way," she gasped.

"Get on the bike!" Through the cargo door, he saw the coastline receding into the distance behind them. The plane was now less than two miles from the biolab, and the A380 would cover that distance in under a minute.

He straddled the Suzuki, gasping in pain from his wound. Nina clambered on behind him. The insanity of what they were about to do hit home. There was almost no chance of survival . . .

But even a tiny chance was better than none. She wrapped her arms around him. "*Go!*"

Kari sat up, saw what they were about to do.

Chase twisted the throttle. The rear wheel whirled, the noise of the high-performance engine becoming a buzzing screech as the bike shot from the pallet and raced down the hold towards the open door.

Kari grabbed at Nina, but it was too late.

By the time the Suzuki reached the cargo door, it was already doing seventy miles per hour, and still accelerating.

Chase turned the handlebars, and the bike flew out into open space.

Riding out from the back of the plane had canceled out some of their forward airspeed—but not enough. And they were over solid ground, falling fast!

He'd mistimed it, and now they were *dead*.

"Close your eyes!" he yelled, as the clifftop on the northern side of Ravnsfjord shot past just beneath them.

They were falling into the fjord!

Chase looked down. Water rushed towards them at terrifying speed—

"*Jump!*"

vw

Kari staggered back to the cockpit, blood running from her wounds. If she could reactivate the autopilot, the computers could still bring the A380 back to an emergency landing.

But as she entered, she realized she was too late.

Her home flashed past to the right. Coming up below were the ruins of the biolab, and directly ahead were the mountainside and the expansive windows of her father's office—

She screamed.

vw

Frost was paralyzed with shock by the sight of the airliner as it flew over the fjord, charging right at him. Now movement returned, the primal urge to flee overpowering all other thought, but there was nowhere to go, and no time . . .

vw

Chase kicked with his good leg, throwing himself clear of the tumbling bike. Nina did the same. Together they plunged towards the water—

vw

The Airbus plowed into the mountainside at over a hundred miles per hour.

Five hundred tons of metal and composites and jet fuel was more force than even the reinforced containment area could withstand. The four massive engines ripped free on impact, tearing through the walls of concrete and steel like bombs. Behind them, fuel ignited as the wings disintegrated. A wave of liquid fire swept through the complex and incinerated everything it touched.

The inferno reached every corner of the containment area. The lab in which the virus had been developed and stored was blown open, searing flames consuming everything within and finally ending the tortured life of Jonathan Philby. Then the mountain itself collapsed, reclaiming the space carved out of it and sealing the virus beneath millions of tons of rock forever.

vw

Chase knew that falling onto it from a height, water becomes as hard as concrete.

Unless something breaks the surface first.

The heavy motorbike hit the water, kicking up a huge plume of spray. A fraction of a second later, he and Nina plunged in after it.

Broken surface or not, it felt like he'd just thrown himself from a building. Agony speared through him as his wounded leg buckled. And the water was *cold*, almost freezing.

More pain as he hit something else. Not water, something solid.

The bike—

It had landed on its side, water resistance slowing its descent. And now he'd smashed down right on top of it!

More pain, so intense that he almost blacked out.

Almost. Through his agony he just about managed to keep focus on his goal—staying alive. He was under the water. He had to swim, break the surface, breathe.

More pain from his injured leg, now completely useless—and his other leg was caught on the bike.

His clothes were snagged on part of the machinery. He kicked, trying to tear himself free. No good. He couldn't get enough leverage. The bike was sinking, an anchor dragging him to the bottom of the fjord.

Panic rose despite his training. He thrashed frantically, ignoring the pain, but still couldn't break loose.

He was going to drown!

After everything he'd been through, everything he'd survived, *this* was it—

Someone grabbed him.

Nina!

Chase felt her hands on his leg, tugging at the material of his jeans. It ripped. The bike plunged into the cold darkness below as Nina swam with all her strength, hauling him upwards.

He breached the surface and drew in a long, anguished breath of cold air. "Oh God!" he gasped. "I thought I was dead there!"

"Just returning a favor," said Nina. She supported him from beneath as she swam for the nearest bank of the fjord. "Jesus, I can't believe we made it!"

"Are you okay?"

"I hurt like hell all over, but I don't think I've broken anything. What happened to the plane?"

Chase tried to raise a hand to point, but was too weak. Instead, he tipped his head down the fjord to the east. A thick, oily column of black smoke roiled into the sky. "Hard landing."

"The virus?"

"Fried. Along with everything else."

Nina looked sadly at the dark cloud. "Kari . . ."

They reached the rocky shore, Nina dragging Chase from the water. "Oh my God," she exclaimed when she saw his leg. She pressed her hand against the wound, trying to stop the bleeding. "We've got to get you to a doctor."

"Right," said Chase, through gritted teeth. "There's a clinic at the top of this cliff, in the company headquarters. Too bad it belongs to the bloke we just blew up. I don't think they'll be happy to see us—"

Almost as if in reply, a rock beside Chase suddenly shattered. The crack of a rifle shot echoed around the fjord.

"No kidding!" Nina yelped. She looked for the shooter. On the opposite bank, she saw several men silhouetted against the sky, pointing down at them.

Another bullet smacked into the ground close by, chipped fragments of rock spitting into their faces. "Get into cover!" Chase ordered.

"I'm not leaving you!" Nina protested. She bent down to drag him with her.

"Nina, don't!"

"*I'm not leaving you!*" she repeated, holding him under his arms and pulling him over the rocks.

Something shot past her, whipping up her hair. Another stone burst apart right behind her. "They've got us," Chase groaned. They looked up at the figures on the cliff top, catching a glint of light reflected from a telescopic sight.

Nina crouched, squeezing Chase more tightly and pressing her cheek against his face. "Eddie . . ."

Gunfire—but not from the rifles across the fjord.

Machine-gun fire, somewhere above. Dust and dirt kicked up from the top of the far cliff. One of the men fell over the edge, screaming all the way down until he smacked sickeningly onto a rocky outcrop.

"What the *fuck*?" Chase said in wonder.

The answer came a second later as three helicopters in the colors of the Norwegian army swept over the top of the cliff, gunners visible in their cabins. Two of the choppers continued across the fjord, moving to circle the gunmen, while the third dropped towards the water, turning to face Nina and Chase.

"Where did they come from?" Nina gasped.

"Somebody must have called the fire brigade. The Norwegians probably wanted to know why so much of Kristian Frost's property was getting blown to buggery." A voice boomed from a loudspeaker aboard the helicopter. "You speak Norwegian?" Chase asked.

"Not a word."

"Me neither." Chase painfully raised his hands as high as he could. "You'd better put your hands up too. You don't want to have gone through all this only to get shot by some trigger-happy Norseman."

"Not really." She lifted one hand, keeping the other in place to support him. Her cheek was still against his. "Oh, and Eddie?"

"What?"

She kissed him. "Thank you for saving my life. Again."

He returned the kiss. "Thank *you* for saving mine.

Even if . . ." he grinned his gap-toothed grin, "we're not exactly level in the whole lifesaving stakes."

Nina smiled. "Tchah. That's bloody gratitude for you."

They kissed again as the helicopter moved into a hover, men rappelling down.

New York City

Nina opened her apartment door and walked wearily inside. Everything was as she'd left it, weeks earlier.

She dropped a stack of mail onto the kitchen counter and filled the kettle. Her coffee would have to be black. She couldn't even imagine what state the contents of her fridge would be in after so long. Maybe it would be safer just to throw the whole thing out without daring to open it and buy a new one.

The kettle on the stove, she slumped onto her couch and looked around. The apartment was at once intimately familiar and almost strange, a forgotten memory brought back to life.

She could barely come to terms with the sheer normality of being home again. After everything she had experienced, she was now back in New York, back home, as if nothing had happened.

Except that wasn't true. She had discovered Atlantis—and then lost it again. She had rewritten human history, but had nothing to show for it.

She reached up and touched her pendant, correcting herself. She had nothing to show for it . . . except the knowledge and satisfaction that human history would continue. Frost's insane plans had been stopped, all his research into the virus destroyed. She turned her head to look out of the window at the lights of Manhattan. She wondered if the millions, *billions* of people whom he had planned to condemn to death would ever know how close they had come to extermination.

Probably not. Once first the Norwegian government, then its NATO allies, became involved, it had been made very clear to her that the true purpose of the Frost Foundation should remain a closely guarded secret.

Nina stretched out on the couch until the kettle boiled, then padded into the kitchen. She took out a mug, then rummaged through the cupboards for the coffee jar. Where had she left it?

Something plopped onto the counter next to the mug, making her jump. She whirled around.

Chase stood at the door, clad in his more-battered-than-ever leather jacket. He still looked battered himself, but handsome, in his own way. He grinned.

"Give those a try," he said, gesturing at the tea bags he'd just tossed onto the counter. "Better for you than coffee."

"Eddie!" cried Nina, caught between delight and surprise. She glanced at the apartment door. All its locks were intact. "How did you get in?"

"Got my ways and means," he said, beaming even more widely. "Come here, Doc . . . *Nina*," he quickly corrected himself on her joking glare. They embraced, then kissed.

"What are you doing here?" Nina finally asked. "I thought you were going back to England."

"I did. But I've been offered a new job. Actually, it's sort of why I'm here."

Nina raised an eyebrow. "Oh yeah? So you didn't

come here just because you wanted to be with me?" she asked, mock-chiding.

"No, but it's a bloody good bonus! Kidding," he added, hugging her again. "I really did come here to see you. Thing is, my new job . . . whether I'm going to take it or not kind of depends on you."

"What do you mean?"

"Well, now that the top brass knows Atlantis really existed, they thought maybe there's other ancient myths that might actually be real as well. So they want to find them—and protect them, make sure nobody like Frost tries to get their hands on them. So the United Nations is going to set up a sort of international archaeological preservation agency to look for them. And the person they want to be in charge of it . . . is you."

"Me?" Nina exclaimed. "Why me?"

"Because you're the one person in the world who knows most about Atlantis. You know what to look for. So," he said, holding his arms wide, "you up for it?"

"What's *your* part in all this?"

"Me? Well, hopefully I get to look after this really hot American babe who once saved my life . . ."

"Be her bodyguard, huh?" smiled Nina.

"Actually, I was hoping to do more with her body than just *guard* it!"

"I think that could be arranged . . ."

Chase's grin almost split his skull in half. "So, you going to take the job?"

Nina smiled, then took his hand and led him towards her bedroom. "Let's sleep on it. Atlantis waited for eleven thousand years—it can wait one more day."

ABOUT THE AUTHOR

ANDY MCDERMOTT is a former journalist and movie critic who now writes novels full-time following the international success of his debut thriller, *The Hunt for Atlantis*, which has been sold around the world in more than twenty languages to date. He lives in Bournemouth, England. Visit Andy McDermott's website at www.andy-mcdermott.com.

An ancient warrior. An incredible treasure. A lethal enemy.

READ ON FOR A SNEAK PEEK
AT ANDY McDERMOTT'S NEW
ADRENALINE-FUELED RIDE

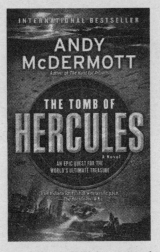

For archaeologist Nina Wilde, it's the opportunity of a lifetime—to prove that a tomb containing the remains of legendary warrior Hercules may actually exist. But as Nina and her ex–SAS bodyguard Eddie Chase begin their search, it's clear that others want to find the tomb—and the unimaginable riches contained within—and will do anything to get there first.

On sale November 2009

And the adventures continue in
THE SECRET OF EXCALIBUR and
THE COVENANT OF GENESIS
—look for them starting in April 2010!

PROLOGUE
The Gulf of Cádiz

One hundred miles off the southern coast of Portugal was hidden one of the greatest secrets in human history.

For now, it would remain hidden, guarded by another secret of much more recent origin.

Officially, the giant six-legged floating platform was listed as SBX-2, a sea-based X-band radar station. Nicknamed the Taj Mahal for the huge white radar dome dominating its upper deck, the high-tech U.S. Navy behemoth swept the skies to the east for thousands of miles, its stated purpose to monitor North Africa and the Middle East for ballistic missile launches. In function and application, it was what it claimed to be.

But that was not the real reason for its presence. The truth lay eight hundred feet below.

Fifteen months earlier, the citadel at the heart of the lost civilization of Atlantis—long believed to be nothing more than a legend—had been discovered directly beneath where the SBX was now anchored. Though the only visible structure, the huge Temple of Poseidon, had been destroyed, radar surveys had revealed many more buried beneath the silt covering the seafloor. Since the discovery of Atlantis had ultimately turned out to be part of a conspiracy to exterminate three-quarters of humanity with a biological weapon, the Western governments that stepped in after the plot was foiled decided that not only the circumstances of the ancient city's discovery, but also the mere fact of its existence, should remain a secret. At least, until a more benign story of its finding could be concocted—and any danger of someone repeating the genocidal plan eliminated.

So while the SBX stood vigil over the skies, beneath it scientists and archaeologists explored the site in secrecy under the auspices of the International Heritage Agency, a United Nations organization established a year earlier with the mandate of locating and securing ancient sites such as Atlantis. The central leg on the starboard side of the giant radar platform had been converted into a submersible pen, a section of the pontoon at its base now open to the sea. Shielded by concrete walls six feet thick, the IHA scientists were normally able to conduct their explorations with no interference from the outside world.

But not tonight.

"Jesus," muttered Bill Raynes, the IHA's expedition director, clutching a handrail as the rig swayed again. The SBX was so massive and securely anchored that normally even an Atlantic storm did little more than gently rock it.

This was clearly a much bigger storm than usual.

One of the bright yellow two-man submersibles swung on its chains as it was winched out of the water. Raynes watched it anxiously. Its twin was already secured over the dock, but if conditions got much worse there was a danger that the loose sub could become an uncontrollable pendulum.

"Get a line on the damn thing!" he ordered. Two of his men hurried to obey, staggering around the edge of the moon pool as the floor lurched beneath them. They waited for the sub to swing back towards them, then snagged one of the chains with a boat hook, damping its motion. The dangerous swaying reduced, the winch operator raised the submersible fully into position above the dock, where more chains were quickly attached to secure it.

"Okay! Good work, guys," Raynes called, letting out a relieved breath. Both subs were now safely in place, which meant the day's operations were concluded. On most evenings, that would have been the cue for him to go up to the main deck and enjoy a cigar.

Not tonight, though. He wasn't going to set one foot outdoors if he didn't have to. He felt a brief stab of pity for the Marines stationed aboard the platform, who had guard duty no matter what the conditions. Poor bastards.

The unexpected weather aside, it had been a good day. The high-resolution sonar mapping of the citadel was ahead of schedule, and the excavation of the first site had already produced results, an exciting haul of Atlantean artifacts valuable in both historical and monetary terms. He may not have *discovered* Atlantis, but Raynes had already decided that he was damn well going to be the person famous for *exploring* it.

The actual discoverer of Atlantis was Dr. Nina Wilde, fifteen years Raynes's junior and—on paper at least—his IHA superior. He wondered if the red-haired New Yorker had any idea that by accepting a senior post in the IHA she'd effectively ended her archaeological career before even turning thirty. Probably not, he decided. While she was certainly cute to look at, Nina also came across to Raynes as naive. It seemed to him that she'd been given the position of director of operations as a way to keep her—and her bodyguard-turned-boyfriend, Eddie Chase, whom Raynes regarded as little more than a sarcastic English thug—quiet and out of trouble while more experienced hands got on with the real work.

He made his way to the elevator cage running up the inside of the support leg, glancing at the dark void overhead. The SBX's main deck, the size of two football fields, was twelve stories above sea level. Carrying the case of artifacts, Raynes slammed the gate closed and pushed the button to ascend.

Water sprayed up into the dock below as waves slapped noisily against the sides of the pool. He had never seen conditions inside the sub pen so bad before. Normally, the ocean surface inside the moon pool did little more than ripple. If it was this bad inside, he didn't even want to think about what it would be like outside.

Spray blasted almost horizontally over the surface of the Atlantic, waves pounding explosively against the forward leg on the rig's port side. The metal staircase that rose from the submerged pontoon to a ladder stretching up the towering structure rattled and moaned under the onslaught. It was not a place where anyone in his right mind would choose to be.

But someone *was* there.

The man was a giant, six feet eight inches tall, with every hard-packed muscle in his athlete's body picked out by his skintight black wet suit. He emerged from the water and made his way up the stairs, hands clamping around the railings with the force of a vise, even the thunderous impact of the waves barely throwing him off his stride.

Once clear of the churning ocean, he paused to remove the scuba regulator from his mouth, revealing perfect white teeth—one inset with a diamond—surrounded by ebony skin, then began his climb up the ladder. Considering the distance and the conditions, most men would have been lucky to make it in under five minutes, and exhausted by the time they reached the top.

The intruder made it in two, and was breathing no more heavily than if he'd climbed a single flight of stairs.

Just below the top of the ladder, he stopped and carefully raised his head above the edge of the deck. The blocky gray superstructure of the SBX was three floors high, catwalks running along each level at the platform's bow. Sickly yellow lights made a feeble attempt to illuminate them. Rain spattered on the man's diving mask, obscuring his view. He frowned and pulled it from his face, revealing calculating black eyes before he flipped down another pair of goggles from the top of his head.

The weak yellow lights disappeared, replaced by shimmering blobs of video-game-vivid red and orange. Almost everything else was either blue or black. Thermographic vision, the world represented by the heat it gave off. The metal walls of the rig, lashed by freezing rain, were visible only as shades of blue.

But there was something else that stood out against the electronic darkness, even in the storm. A glowing shape in green and yellow and white moved closer, gradually taking on human form through the false-color fuzz.

One of the platform's U.S. Marine guards, on patrol.

The intruder silently lowered himself so that he was poised just below the edge of the deck, barely moving even as the storm pummeled him.

The Marine came closer, boots clanking on the metal as he reached the end of the catwalk. One hand holding the railing, the other on his gun, he peered down the ladder—

Fast and fluid as a snake, the intruder's hand snapped up and seized him by his gun arm. Before the startled Marine could react, the giant almost effortlessly yanked him over the edge of the platform and flung him to his death in the spume over a hundred feet below.

The killer flipped up his thermographic goggles and looked along the catwalk to see his next target only a few meters away. An electrical junction box, protruding from the metal wall. He hurried to it.

The rat's nest of wires and cables inside seemed impenetrably complicated, but the man already knew exactly where to find the main feed for the rig's security cameras. He tugged one particular skein of wires clear of the others, then sliced a combat knife straight through them. A few sparks popped, but the blade was insulated. He returned the knife to its sheath and reached down to click the key of the radio on his belt.

Go.

In the submersible dock, a man's head broke the surface of the sloshing water. Eyes glinting behind his mask, he turned in a full circle to survey the surroundings. Two of the rig's crew were on the dock, backs to the moon pool as they secured their equipment.

He sank back under the dark water and took a gun of unusual design from his belt. Then he resurfaced, raising the weapon out of the water. Trickles of seawater ran out of the drainage holes along its barrel as he took aim. Another man emerged next to him, doing the same.

Two flat thuds, so close together that they could almost have been the same sound, echoed around the concrete chamber. The guns were gas powered, compressed nitrogen blasting the darts they fired across the dock to slam into the backs of the two crewmen. They gasped in pain, hands clutching behind them . . . then collapsed to the floor, unable to move. The dart guns were designed to fire tranquilizers. But these were loaded with something else.

Something deadly.

The men in the water swam for a ladder leading out of the moon pool. Other divers appeared, following them onto the deck. Seven men in all. They quickly shed their scuba gear and crossed the dock to the elevator.

The two crewmen lay nearby, frozen, helpless. Only their eyes, bulging in fear and pain, could move. Paralysis of the voluntary muscles had occurred almost immediately.

Paralysis of the *involuntary* muscles, specifically the heart, would soon follow.

One of the intruders bent down to pull out the darts, which he tossed into the moon pool. They sank out of sight. His companions dragged the paralyzed crewmen to the rim of the pool and unceremoniously dumped them into the sea.

The team entered the elevator cage and closed it. A security camera looked on uselessly with its dead eye. With a rattle, the elevator started its ascent.

The black-clad giant cautiously raised his eyes just above the level of the rain-lashed top deck. The flat metal expanse was dominated by the giant radar dome. It was illuminated from within, a colossal lantern glowing through the wind-whipped deluge. Everything else on the deck was indistinct, lost in the storm.

He lowered his goggles again. The view sprang to gaudy life. At the stern, beyond the dome, was a swirling red haze—exhaust from the platform's power plant, and heat pumped out by the banks of container-size air-conditioning units cooling the electronics of the enormous radar array.

But other shapes stood out brightly. Two more Marines flared in his thermal sights as distant amorphous blobs, shambling through the cutting rain towards each other. They were following a set path, meeting up to confirm that all was well before turning back along their patrol routes.

They would never make it.

The intruder raised a weapon. Unlike the dart guns used by his team in the submersible dock, this was a rifle, a telescopic sight mounted above the grip.

Flipping the goggles back up, he brought the sight to his right eye. Without the thermographic enhancement the Marines were little more than gray silhouettes, flapping rain capes outlined in yellow by a nearby light. He fixed the crosshairs on his target, the closer of the two men, waited for them to meet, to stop—

The indistinct figure in the scope spasmed, then fell to the deck. The other man reacted in surprise, dropping to his knees to help him.

Saw the dart protruding from his back. Looked up—

The assassin had already reloaded. He barely needed the sights, the rifle almost an extension of his body as he fired again. He didn't need to see an impact to know that he had hit.

He ran to the second downed Marine, ignoring the man's desperate, twitching eyes as he checked where his shot had landed. The dart had caught the man square in the chest, an inch below his heart. The sniper made a noise of annoyance. He'd been aiming for the heart itself. Sloppy.

But only his pride was affected. The result was what mattered here. He tugged the dart out of the man's flesh and threw it across the deck, then did the same for the first victim. The darts would be swept away into the sea, lost. And nobody would pay any attention to the tiny puncture wounds when there would be a far more obvious cause of death.

The radio on his belt clicked, twice. A signal. The second team was in position.

Right on time.

The deck was clear. He returned the signal, clicking the key three times.

Take the platform.

The seven men had already shot the pair of surprised Marines in the cabin at the top of the support leg, immobilizing them with darts as soon as the elevator emerged. Then they waited for the signal from their leader. As soon as it came they split up into three groups—one of three men, two of two—and headed into the superstructure.

The group of three quickly made their way towards the platform's stern and the power plant section. While the SBX resembled a stationary oil rig, it was actually a vessel in its own right, able to move under its own power. It carried a crew of around forty, not counting the platoon of Marines and the IHA contingent. With the radar station itself being highly automated, most of the crew actually performed the same tasks as sailors on a warship: running and maintaining the vessel.

Which meant the majority of the crew were concentrated in one area.

Dart guns raised, the trio advanced through the gray corridors, one man checking at each junction before signaling the other two to move on. They went up a steep flight of stairs to B Deck, listening for any sounds of activity around them.

A door opened ahead. A bearded petty officer carrying a toolbox stepped out, froze in surprise as he saw the three men—

A dart stabbed into his throat, instantly delivering its toxic payload. The sailor let out a choking gasp, his killer already rushing forward to catch him and his toolbox before they crashed noisily onto the deck.

The other two men checked the label on the door—an engineering storeroom—and flung it open, guns up as they checked that it was empty.

It took only a few seconds for the paralyzed sailor to be dumped inside the storeroom and the hatch closed again. The men moved on, ascending more stairs to arrive at their target.

A hatch was set into one of the bulkheads, the low thrum of machinery audible behind it. Warning signs told the intruders what they would find within.

The primary ventilation shaft for the aft section.

The SBX's superstructure was essentially a sealed metal box. There were only three windows on the entire vessel, in the bridge at the bow, and even those didn't open. The only way to get air inside the rig was to pump it through the vents beneath the giant intakes on the upper deck.

The assault team forced open the hatch, exposing an access panel into the shaft. A huge fan whirled behind it. The three men donned insectile respirator masks before taking a cylinder that one carried on his back and manhandling it through the access panel. A twist of a valve and the cylinder began to pump cyanogen chloride gas into the vent. Colorless, odorless—and deadly within seconds.

They jogged back to the stairs and slid down the steep banisters to B Deck, heading forward. They ignored the strangled, agonized gasps from dying men and women in the rooms they passed.

One of the two-man teams stealthily made its way to the platform's accommodation section. The SBX's small crew worked on a two-shift system: twelve hours on, twelve hours off. Right now, those on the second shift would probably be asleep.

Including half of the Marines.

The long room serving as the Marines' barracks had two doors, one at each end. One of the men waited by the first door until his comrade reached the other entrance. Then he took a small cylinder of cyanogen chloride from his harness and opened the door.

Most of the twelve Marines inside were asleep, though one man looked up at him. A moment of hesitation, replaced by trained response as he saw the black breath mask—

"Marines!" he yelled, before a dart fired from the open door at the far end of the room thudded into his back. Other men jumped upright in their bunks, startled into life by the shout of alarm.

Then they slumped back down as the two gas cylinders rolled through the room, spewing invisible death.

The second team of two headed for the front of the rig and the command section on A Deck. This area was always guarded, four Marines stationed at the entrance.

Poison gas was not an option in this part of the rig; there was one man who needed to be kept alive at all costs, and gas was too indiscriminate and unpredictable a killer. The dart guns were also unusable, too slow to reload and carrying the risk that a dart might embed itself uselessly in a target's equipment. At this critical stage of the operation, instant kills had to be guaranteed.

So the two men simply walked around the corner and shot each of the Marines in the head with silenced pistols before any of them had a chance to respond.

The corpses would have to be removed when the attackers left the rig—a body with a bullet wound would give everything away. But that had been planned for.

One of the men clicked his radio. *In position.*

A single click came from the huge man's radio. He nodded to himself, then cautiously looked around the edge of the rain-streaked window.

There was only one person on watch in the bridge, a young female lieutenant. Since the SBX was stationary and the Command Information Center behind the bridge acted as the vessel's nerve center, there was no need for anyone else. He could see more people through the glass doors to CIC, including the platform's commander.

It was time.

Lieutenant Phoebe Bremmerman looked up from her console at the bridge windows. There had been a noise, something other than rain pounding against the glass.

And there was something on the glass itself, a dark gray object the size of a large coin.

She stood, about to call out to her commander in CIC—

The window exploded.

Fragments of glass sprayed into the bridge, the muffled rumble of the storm outside instantly rising to a howl. The lieutenant screamed as a chunk of the broken window slashed her cheek.

A huge black man in a wet suit leaped through the window, a pistol aimed at her. Simultaneously, more wet-suited men burst into CIC, weapons raised. One of the radar operators jumped up, only to fall back over his chair, a dart protruding from his neck.

The giant grabbed Bremmerman and dragged her into CIC, the noise of the storm dropping as the bridge door thumped shut.

"Commander Hamilton," he said to the SBX's commander, shoving the woman to join the other occupants of the room in a group surrounded by four armed men. "Sorry for the intrusion." He smiled, the diamond glinting in his flawless teeth. His Nigerian accent was smooth and sonorous. "My name is Joe Komosa, and I'm here for one thing only." The smile reappeared, but with menace behind it. "Where is Dr. Bill Raynes?"

The remaining crew of the platform were taken to the large lab on B Deck assigned to the IHA team and forced to kneel in the center of the room.

None of the Marines had survived the assault. The navy crew had also suffered severe losses; aside from Hamilton himself, there were now only ten alive, including the five others from the CIC. Of the ten members of the IHA contingent, three were missing.

The attackers had been joined by another three men, who had brought in the other survivors at gunpoint. Whoever they were, Hamilton realized, they were utterly ruthless; another sailor had protested when he'd been shoved into the lab—not even fighting back, just shouting—and been shot in the chest at point-blank range, dying on the deck right before Hamilton's eyes.

And there had been nothing he could do.

Komosa pulled off the headpiece of his wet suit, revealing a gleaming shaven head with a row of piercings, silver studs, running back from each temple. Then he pulled down the zip to expose his bare chest, which was marked by lines of more glittering piercings. Pausing for a moment to admire his reflection in a glass partition, he slowly strode back and forth before the prisoners without a word, arousing nervous glances, then rounded on Raynes with his dazzling smile.

"Dr. Raynes," he said, "as I told Commander Hamilton, I have come here for one thing only. Do you know what this is?" He held up a small white object he had taken from a waterproof pouch.

Raynes peered uncertainly at it as if being asked a trick question. "It's . . . a USB flash drive?"

"It is indeed a flash drive." Komosa went to one particular computer in the corner of the lab—Raynes's own workstation. "And I would like you to fill it for me."

Raynes swallowed, voice dry. "With—with what?"

"With certain files held on the IHA's secure server in New York. Specifically, those concerning the lost works of Plato held in the archives of the Brotherhood of Selasphoros."

For a moment, confusion almost overcame fear on Raynes's face. "Wait, you did all this to access our server? Why?"

"That's my concern. Your only concern right now is to do what I tell you."

"And if I refuse?"

Komosa's arm snapped up. Without taking his eyes off Raynes, he fired a dart into the heart of one of the other IHA scientists. The man clutched weakly at his chest before collapsing.

Raynes flinched, eyes wide with fear. "Okay, the server, okay! I'll-I'll—whatever you want."

"Thank you." Komosa nodded, and one of his men led Raynes to the computer.

"Don't do it, Doctor," Hamilton warned. "You know we can't let anyone else reach Atlantis."

"Atlantis!" said Komosa with a dismissive laugh. "I don't care about Atlantis!"

"I don't believe you. Dr. Raynes, under no circumstances whatsoever are you to give this man access to that computer."

Komosa sighed. "You *will* give me access, Doctor." He crossed to the prisoners, taking Bremmerman by the arm and pulling her to her feet. She gave Hamilton a fearful look, unsure what to do.

"Leave her alone," Hamilton barked.

Komosa moved behind the lieutenant, towering over her as he slipped one thick arm around her waist and the hand of the other to her neck. "Dr. Raynes." He turned away from Hamilton, moving Bremmerman with him as he faced the scientist. "I'm sure you noticed this young lady around the rig before. She *is* very pretty." He lowered his head, stroking her hair with one side of his chin. Despite her fear, she slammed an elbow into his stomach.

He barely flinched. The diamond smile widened. "And very spirited." His thumb moved slowly up her neck, stopping an inch below her chin—

And *pressed*.

Something inside her throat collapsed with a sickening wet crunch. The young woman's eyes bulged, her mouth opening in a desperate attempt to draw a breath that could never reach her lungs. Komosa released her. She reached up to her face, fingers twitching. A drop of blood ran from the corner of her mouth as she convulsed.

"And very dead," said Komosa, voice like stone.

"You bastard!" roared Hamilton. He tried to charge at Komosa, but one of the other wet-suited men viciously clubbed him down with the butt of his gun. The commander dropped to the floor. Bremmerman fell too—but, unlike Hamilton, she didn't get back up.

Komosa turned back to Raynes. "I will kill one of your shipmates every minute until you give me what I want. Their lives are entirely in your hands. Are you computer files really so valuable that you're willing to let your friends die to protect them?" He aimed his gun at the head of one of the IHA scientists. "Fifty-eight seconds."

Sweat beaded on Raynes's face. "B-but even if I wanted to, there's no way I could now! The security system, it—"

"I know about the security system, Doctor. Forty-nine seconds."

Frantic, Raynes sat down at the computer and began working, his hand so slick with frightened perspiration that it slipped off the mouse. A password box popped up. He typed a string of characters and stabbed at the return key. The box vanished, replaced by an alert: THUMBPRINT VALIDATION REQUIRED. With a worried glance back at Komosa, he pressed his thumb against a black square set into the top right corner of the keyboard. A red light pulsed. The alert disappeared, replaced by another.

VOICEPRINT VALIDATION REQUIRED.

"Seventeen seconds to spare," said Komosa, lowering the gun. "Well done."

"I can't get you any further. I can't!" Raynes pleaded. "The voiceprint ID, it's got a—"

"It has a stress analyzer, I know." The giant moved over to the desk, his free hand reaching for something on his belt. "It denies access even to authorized users if they seem to be under duress. But don't worry—in a moment, you'll be perfectly relaxed."

And with that, he jabbed a syringe into Raynes's arm and pushed the plunger.

Raynes stared at the syringe in horror, opening his mouth to cry out . . . before a tremor ran through his entire body. He sagged, bones turning to jelly. What had tarted as a cry emerged as a long, almost orgasmic sigh.

Komosa leaned closer. "Now, Doctor, I know you can

hear me, and I know you're still lucid. There were seventeen seconds left on the clock. That is how long you have to enter the final code before I shoot your friend. Do you understand?" Raynes nodded, the muscles in his face slack. "Your time starts now." Komosa aimed the gun back at the other scientist, taking Raynes by his shirt collar and lifting him closer to the computer.

Raynes cleared his throat, then spoke, voice low and dreamlike. "In this island of Atlantis there was a great and wonderful empire." A small microphone icon flickered, acknowledging that the computer had heard.

Nothing happened. The man Komosa was aiming at whimpered. Then—

The screen lit up with a directory window. The satellite data link had been established. A few of the prisoners let out relieved sighs.

"Thank you, Doctor," said Komosa, plugging the drive into a port on the computer. "I'll take it from here."

That was the signal.

The flat hissing thuds of dart guns filled the lab. Those people who weren't hit by the first volley started to shout—only to fall silent within seconds as the guns were reloaded and a second round fired. Outside the main group, Hamilton jumped up with a roar of fury.

Komosa fired. The dart slammed deep into Hamilton's right eye socket, unleashing a welter of blood. The commander instantly fell to the swaying deck, dead even before the toxins took effect.

Turning back to the computer as if nothing had happened, Komosa copied files to the drive before accessing a different directory. Even through the influence of the powerful muscle relaxant, Raynes managed a look of surprise when he saw the directory name.

Komosa caught his expression. He grinned. "Yes, IHA personnel records. Don't worry, we're not going to kill them." The grin hardened as he selected two particular files and copied them to the drive. "Yet."

The files transferred, Komosa pulled the drive from the computer and returned it to its pouch. He straightened, turning to his men. "Disperse the bodies throughout the command section—it needs to look as if they were on duty when the rig capsized. I'll go to the bridge and flood the starboard pontoon—once the pumps start, we'll have five minutes to get back to the sub." They acknowledged and hurried out, dragging the paralyzed navy personnel after them.

Komosa tugged the zip of his wet suit back up to his neck and followed his men out of the lab, stepping over the slumped, helpless civilians.

All Raynes could do was stare at the computer screen as he waited to die. The names of the last two files Komosa had copied were still highlighted. He knew both of them.

CHASE, EDWARD J.

WILDE, NINA P.